GENERATION
Dead

GENERATION

Dead

DANIEL WATERS

HYPERION · NEW YORK

Printed in the United States of America
First Edition
10 9 8 7 6 5 4 3 2
ISBN 978-1-4231-0921-1
Library of Congress Cataloging-in-Publication Data on file.
This book is set in 12-point Griffo Classico.

Designed by Elizabeth H. Clark

Reinforced binding

Visit www.hyperionteens.com

For Kim, a love story

CHAPTER ONE

*P*HOEBE AND HER FRIENDS held their breath as the dead girl in the plaid skirt walked past their table in the lunchroom. Her motion kicked up a cool trailing breeze that seemed to settle on the skin and catch in their hair. As they watched her go by, Phoebe could almost tell what everyone was thinking. Everyone, that is, except for the dead girl.

Across from her, Margi shook her head, her silver teardrop earrings dancing among the bright pink spikes of her hair. "Even I don't wear skirts that short," she said before sipping her milk.

"Thank God for that," Adam said from two seats away.

Phoebe risked a glance back at the girl and her long, bluish-white legs. Fluorescent lights were kind to the dead, making them look like they had been carved from veinless blocks of pure white marble. The girl went to the farthest table and sat down alone, and without any food, the way the dead always did during lunch.

Sometimes Phoebe used to joke that she possessed psychic powers. Not useful ones like being able to tell when small children have fallen into wells or anything; more like being able to foresee what her mother was making for dinner or how many bangles Margi was going to wear on her arms that day. She thought her "powers," if that's what they were, were more tel*pathetic* than telepathic.

Phoebe knew as soon as she saw her that the dead girl in the short skirt would get Margi rolling on a whole host of zombie-related topics, none of which she really wanted to discuss.

"I heard that Tommy Williams's eye fell out in homeroom," Margi said, on cue. "I heard that he sneezed or something, and there it went, *splat*, on his desk."

Phoebe swallowed and placed her egg salad sandwich back atop the wax paper wrapping it came in.

"Zombies don't sneeze," Adam said around a mouthful of meatball sub. "Zombies don't breathe, so they can't sneeze."

The girls lowered their heads and looked around to see who was in earshot of Adam's booming voice. *Zombie* was a word you just didn't say in public anymore, even if you were the center on the football team.

Air hissed through Margi's teeth. "You aren't supposed to call them zombies, Adam."

He shrugged his massive shoulders. "Zombies, dead heads, corpsicles. What's the difference? They don't care. They don't have feelings to hurt."

Phoebe wondered if Tommy Williams and the girl in the plaid skirt really didn't have any feelings. The scientists weren't clear on that point yet.

She tried to imagine how she would feel losing an eye, especially losing an eye in public. And in homeroom, no less.

"You could be expelled for saying things like that, Adam," Margi was saying. "You know you're supposed to call them *living impaired.*"

Adam snorted, his mouth full of milk. Ten years ago a milk snort would have been the height of biological grotesquerie at Oakvale High. Today it seemed kind of lame next to losing an eye in homeroom.

"Living impaired," Adam commented after recovering. "I think you two are living impaired. They're just dead."

He stood up, his huge body casting a long shadow over their uneaten lunches, and brought his empty tray to the conveyor system that took all of the dishes and garbage away. Phoebe just looked at her beautiful egg salad sandwich and wished that she had any desire left to eat it.

Phoebe's locker popped open on her third try. She figured that her inability to remember the three-digit combination did not bode well for her impending algebra class, which was always right after lunch. Her stomach rumbled, and she tried to tell herself that the spikes of hunger would give her mind an alert sharpness, like a lynx in winter between successful hunts.

Yeah right, she thought.

Tommy Williams was in her algebra class.

The door to her locker shook with a metallic vibrating sound. Inside were pictures of bands like the Creeps, the Killdeaths, Seraphim Shade, the Rosedales, Slipknot, and the Misfits; bands that dressed like the living dead before there were any dead actually living. There was a picture of her, Margi, and Colette in happier times, all gothed up in black fabrics, eyeliner, and boots outside the Cineplex in Winford, ready to be first in line for the premier of some vitally important horror movie she couldn't even remember. Phoebe, the tallest, was in the middle, her long black hair hiding one side of her naturally pale face, and her visible eye closed as she laughed at whatever vulgar comment Margi had just made. Colette had done her eyes like an Egyptian princess, with a single thick line of make-up at each corner. Colette and Margi were also laughing.

There was also a picture of her dog, Gargoyle. Gar was a Welsh terrier and not half as frightening as his name would suggest.

A mirror was on the door opposite the shelf where Phoebe's algebra book lay. On her mouth was a streak of smeared violet lipstick. Her long hair, normally jet-black, shiny, spiky, and tousled, now just looked dull, flat, and messy.

She thought she looked scared.

The lipstick smear was the only flaw that seemed fixable, so she rubbed it away before walking toward Mrs. Rodriguez's class down at the end of the hallway. She arrived there the same time as Tommy Williams, whose eyes, she was relieved to see, were still fixed within their sockets. He gazed at her with the blank stare of the living impaired.

Phoebe felt like cold feathers were dancing along her spine. The stare was bottomless. It made her think that she could fall forever into his eyes, or that he could see through to the very heart of her. Could he see her wondering if his eye had popped out in homeroom?

Tommy motioned for her to precede him into the room.

She held her breath as he lifted his arm, realizing it only because another one of her essential life functions had ceased, namely her heartbeat. She smiled at him. It was a reflex; courtesy was not very common in the halls of Oakvale High. She stepped into the room, and as she did, she was almost certain that Tommy was trying to smile back at her. Wasn't there a faint upturn of the lips at one corner of his mouth, or the briefest flash of light in the flat undead eyes?

She took her seat, breathing again, heart beating again. Not only beating but beating *fast*.

She didn't know much about Tommy Williams. She knew that he'd come to Oakvale High last May, just a few weeks before school had let out. Oakvale was starting to get a reputation for having a good living impaired program, good enough that families with living impaired kids were moving to Oakvale from the surrounding area. Phoebe's father had pointed out an article in the *Winford Bulletin* that said Oakvale High's living impaired population had doubled in a year. There were at least seven in her class of about a hundred and twenty.

Algebra was not a subject that Phoebe struggled with; she usually completed the next day's assignment while Mrs.

Rodriguez started to probe for answers among her slower, struggling classmates. Algebra was a class that she could drift in and out of in the way music from a car passing will drift into an open bedroom window.

She wondered how Tommy Williams had died.

She looked at the back of his head, at his gray-blond hair, and her thoughts drifted, again, to the topic of death. They started with the mundane—Do living impaired people need to get haircuts? (The answer: Yes. Both hair and fingernails can grow during living impairment.) And proceeded to the philosophically complex—What is it like to be dead? What is it like to be living impaired?

These questions had preoccupied Phoebe when she was a young girl, long before the world had heard of the living impaired. She looked out the window and tried to think of the time before dead teens began to pick themselves off of mortuary slabs and sick beds. It hadn't been all that long ago; she was fourteen when she saw the first footage of a zombie—of a *living impaired* person—sitting stiffly between his parents on some CNN talk show. Her parents always made her leave the room when the Dallas Jones video came on. That video was the Zapruder film of their generation, as it showed Dallas, the original zombie, die and come back to "life."

A dog trailing a broken leash ran across the field opposite the classroom window, and Phoebe wondered why living impairment seemed to be a phenomenon exclusive to teenagers. American teenagers, specifically. Dogs didn't come back. Neither did monkeys or goldfish, or old people, or small children. Apparently, neither did teenagers in Uzbekistan, Burkina Faso, Sweden, or Papua New Guinea, for some reason. But kids from Oklahoma, Rockaway Beach, The Big Apple, Arkansas, or The Big Easy all bore at least a chance of winding up living impaired, as long as they croaked during the delicate teen years. The newest Frankenstein Formula theory was that a certain mixture of teenage hormones and fast food preservatives set up the proper conditions for living impairment. The medical community was still testing the theory, having begrudgingly let go of fluorocarbons and brain patterns rewired by a lifetime of first-person shooter games.

Outside, the dog lifted a matted hind leg on a bike rack where a number of bicycles were chained. Do the dead go to the bathroom? They didn't eat or drink, so the answer would seem to be no.

Mrs. Rodriguez then did a strange thing, strange enough to interrupt Phoebe's train of thought. She called on Tommy for the answer to a problem even though his pale hand wasn't raised.

Tommy looked up from his papers. There was a pause that sucked the air out of the classroom; there was always a pause like that when the dead were called on.

The dead could think, and they could communicate. They could reason, and once in a blue moon, one might even initiate a conversation. But they did so very, very *slowly* . . . a question, even one as simple as the one from Mrs. Rodriguez, could take a living impaired person ten minutes to process, and another five to respond.

Phoebe covertly tried to gauge the reaction of her classmates. Some were suddenly absorbed in their textbooks, doing anything to avoid the reality—or unreality—that the dead kid represented. Others, like Pete Martinsburg, who was taking Algebra One for the second time and who was normally only interested in football and girls, were rapt with attention. Pete was looking at Tommy with the same expression of manic glee that he wore when he'd tripped Norm Lathrop and sent him sprawling into a bank of big rubber garbage cans in the lunchroom last week.

"One hundred and seventy-four," Tommy said, his voice halting and without inflection. No one hearing his voice could tell if Tommy thought his answer was wrong or right, so most of the class looked at Mrs. Rodriguez for her reaction.

She looked pleased. "That is correct, Thomas."

Phoebe noted that she always called the living impaired kids by their formal first names. It wasn't something she did with the "normal" kids. Pete Martinsburg was just "Pete" when she called his name, which was often, and usually to reprimand him. Phoebe was secretly thrilled to see the leer smacked off of Pete's face.

Mrs. Rodriguez went on with the class like it was no big deal to call on a dead kid. For the most part, the rest of the class reacted the same way.

But Phoebe noticed that Tommy did not go back to looking at his papers. His head remained high for the remainder of the class.

* * *

8

Margi was waiting for her at the door after algebra.

"How did you get here so quickly?" Phoebe asked. Margi took her arm and pulled her aside.

"Sshh. I've mastered the art of bilocation; I'm really heading off to our English class right now."

Phoebe laughed. "Me too. Let's go."

"Hold on," Margi said. "I want to see that living impaired kid for a minute."

"Whoever told you about the eye thing was yanking your chain. He still has both," Phoebe whispered, and then Tommy walked out of the classroom, the last one to leave.

"I've got something even bigger. I heard he signed up for football tryouts. He's supposed to start practice tomorrow."

Phoebe looked at her friend, wondering just how it was that Margi always knew what was going on with the dead kids.

"Don't look at me like that, Pheebes. I overheard Coach Konrathy arguing with Principal Kim. He wasn't going to let the dead kid try out, but Kim is making him."

"Really?"

"Really. Can you imagine that? Playing with a living-dead kid? Having to shower with one of them? Brrrr."

Did the dead have to shower? They weren't rotting corpses like in all the movies, and they didn't sweat, either. Phoebe didn't think they smelled like anything; at least they didn't smell like anything dead.

"He looks like he could play," Phoebe said, watching him make his patient way down the hall.

"What do you mean?"

"Well, he's built for it."

"*Phoebe,*" Margi said, making a face. "*Ick.*"

"He is. He's really, you know, sort of handsome."

"Yeah, if he wasn't, like, *dead,*" Margi said. "Double ick. Come on, we have to get to class."

"What about bilocation?"

"I can't do it when someone is asking me a bunch of questions. Let's go."

Phoebe made one stop after the final bell before she went out to the bus. Adam was methodically stacking books in his locker, lifting half the stack with one big hand.

"Hey," she said, "I hear that a corpsicle is going out for your precious football team."

"Yeah?" he said, not looking up from his task. "Whatever. As long as he can play."

Phoebe smiled. She thought it was cute the way Adam tried to be all gruff around her. She wondered if he even knew he was doing it.

"Listen," she said, "would you be able to give me a lift home tomorrow? I want to stay and get some work done in the library."

"Sure, as long as you can wait until practice is over," he said, pushing his locker closed. "And as long as the STD doesn't take away my driving privileges."

STD was Adam's term of endearment for his stepdad, who he got along with about as well as he did with Winford Academy's defensive line.

"Great," she said. "See you. I've got to catch my bus."

Adam nodded. If he really did have an opinion one way or another about playing football with the living impaired he didn't show it. Adam had matured a lot over the summer. Maybe it was the karate.

"Is Daffy coming?"

Phoebe laughed. Adam was more mature around everyone other than Daffy, his nickname for Margi. "I don't think so."

"Okay. See you."

"Later." She watched him walk away. She'd known Adam since she'd moved next door to him years ago, but he was different now—in the way he walked, in the way he talked, in the way his face had slimmed down to reveal a strong, angular jawline. His upper half, always big, had broadened out into a wide V from his narrow waist. Phoebe smiled to herself. If it *was* the karate, it was a good thing.

She almost missed her bus home. Colette was already sitting alone and staring ahead out the windshield. Phoebe saw her, and the familiar pang of sadness and shame flared inside her chest.

Phoebe had grown up with Colette Beauvoir, at least until Colette stopped growing when she drowned in Oxoboxo Lake the previous summer. Colette would be fifteen forever, and yet she was not the same fifteen she used to be. Phoebe had tried to talk to her—once—but the experience had been so disturbing that she'd never tried again. That was months ago. Margi was even worse; she would get up from her seat and leave if Colette entered the room. As gabby as Margi was, she couldn't even bear to discuss what happened to Colette.

The dead always sat alone. The school dismissed them five minutes early so that they would have time to shuffle out to the buses. Every school day since Colette died, Phoebe would pass her sitting there all alone and wonder if she remembered the fun they used to have listening to Colette's brother's old Cure and Dead Kennedys records in the basement.

"Colette." It was the first word Phoebe had said to her since the one failed conversation. The memory of her tears still felt fresh in Phoebe's mind.

Colette turned, and Phoebe liked to think that it was the sound of her name and not just sound that caused her to turn. She regarded Phoebe with a fixed blank stare. Phoebe considered sliding into the seat next to the dead girl. Her mouth opened to say—what? How sorry she was? How much she missed her?

She lost her nerve and moved toward the back of the bus, where Margi was, whatever words she'd hoped to say caught in her throat. Colette's head turned back slowly, like a door on a rusty hinge.

Margi was engrossed in her iPod, or at least she was pretending to be. Colette was like a dark spot on the sun to Margi; she never spoke about her or even acknowledged that she existed.

"Did you hear that the bass player for Grave Mistake died?" she said. "Heart attack after overdosing on heroin."

"Oh?" Phoebe said, wiping her eye. "You think he'll come back?"

Margi shook her head. "I think he's too old, like twenty-two or twenty-three."

"That's unfortunate," Phoebe said. "I guess we'll know in a couple days."

Tommy Williams was the last one on the bus. There were plenty of open seats.

Tommy stopped at Colette's seat. He looked at her, and then he sat down beside her.

That's weird, Phoebe thought. She was going to say so to Margi, but Margi was intent on her iPod and trying furiously not to notice anything about their dead friend.

CHAPTER TWO

*P*ETE MARTINSBURG ENJOYED the subtle hush that settled in the locker room when he and TC Stavis walked in. He liked the way Denny McKenzie, their pretty boy senior quarterback, stepped aside to let Pete pass when he approached. He liked the way the newer kids cut their eyes from him when he looked their way.

As the reigning Alpha, he knew that there was no better place to reassert that position than in the locker room before football practice.

"Lame Man," Pete said, making a big show of clapping his hand on Adam's back as Adam sat lacing up his cleats. Adam was the biggest kid on the team, with a few inches and a lot more muscle mass than even Stavis, so a display of force with him was a good way of showing everyone what the social hierarchy of the team was. "What's the good word?"

He felt the larger boy's shoulders tense as Adam

shrugged. "Same old same old, Pete. How about you?"

"Same here, horny as hell," Pete said. "You gonna set me up with that freaky chick you hang out with, or what? Morticia Scarypants?"

"No."

Pete laughed. "One night with me and she'll be wearing bright colors again."

"You wouldn't get along."

"Oh, so you're actually admitting you're friends, now?"

Adam didn't reply, and Pete enjoyed the flush that came to the big guy's ears and neck. It was all about finding the weak spots.

"Who's Morticia Scarypants?" Stavis asked. "Are you talking about the new art teacher?"

"No, you moron. Phoebe something, one of those goth chicks. Our boy Lame Man likes them pale and scary."

Stavis frowned, which Pete knew meant he was concentrating. "Is she the skinny one with the long black hair, kind of like a Chinese girl's, or the short one with the knockers and too much jewelry?"

"The first one," Pete said, enjoying that the conversation was making Adam look like he'd just bitten into a jalapeño sandwich. "Why? You interested?"

"Sure I'm interested. I got a thing for boots, and she wears those heeled ones all the time. And dresses. Hell, throw in the short one, too. A twofer."

The look Adam gave Stavis would have silenced anyone else in the room, but Stavis was too dumb and too big to notice or care.

Pete socked Adam in the shoulder. "Easy, big man," he said.

"You guys are pretty funny," Adam said. "A riot."

Pete smiled. "Don't you think that the whole gothic thing doesn't really make a lot of sense today? I mean, why would you walk around pretending you're dead when you could actually be dead and walk around?"

"It's more than that," Adam said.

"Yeah? Like what?"

"I don't know. Music. The look, whatever."

"The look, huh?" Pete said. "The look sucks. She ought to get some color in her cheeks and start wearing normal chick clothes. She looks like a freakin' worm burger, you know? One of those zombies."

"Then I guess you shouldn't waste your time on her," Adam said.

"Just the opposite, man. I want to convert her before it's too late. Besides," he said, smiling down at Adam, "you know and I know she's a virgin."

Pete laughed and sat down beside him, and from the corner of his vision saw that runt Thornton Harrowwood looking over at them. The kid hadn't played freshman or sophomore year.

"Can I help you?" Pete said to him, sounding anything but helpful. The kid gave a frightened shake of his shaggy head and looked away. Pete chuckled to himself and turned back to Adam.

"You work out this summer, Lame Man?" Pete knew that

something had changed over the summer with him and Lame Man, but he had no idea what it was. He, Lame Man, and TC had been the three amigos, the Pain Crew, all through high school, and now they'd barely had a whole conversation since they'd started football practice again.

"Little bit. I took a karate class."

"It shows, it shows. Looks like you dropped a few pounds and got a little more cut."

Adam nodded. "Thanks. You want to sleep with me?"

Pete laughed and peeled off his own tight shirt. He'd worked on his body over the summer as well, and the results showed in the definition across his chest and abdomen, and the lines were deepened by the rich tan he'd cultivated. He made the tight muscles along his arms ripple in case any of the wannabees were looking.

"I would, but I'm still sore from the summer."

He folded his shirt and then folded it a second time when the first fold didn't look right.

"Don't you want to hear what I did?"

"Sure," Adam said, sighing. "What did you do this summer? Go visit your dad again?"

"Yeah. I was in Cali all summer, nailing college girls at the beach."

"Sounds great," Adam said, yawning.

"Yeah, it was," Pete said, trying to ignore his disinterest. "It was like an endless supply, man. Drinking, partying, and sex, sex, sex. Talk about an endless summer."

"Wow."

Adam didn't see his frown, because apparently his sneakers were more interesting than Pete's stories. That hacked Pete off, because this time the stories were true. Partially true, at least. College girls had been populous and friendly to him this summer. But Pete left one key detail out of his oft-told tales; most of the college-age girls he'd hung around were friends of his Dad's newest girlfriend, Cammy—herself a college-age girl. Whatever. Adam's silence was beginning to frustrate him. It took him three tries to fold his T-shirt the way he wanted it.

"Is it just me," Pete said to the room, "or is this stinking hellhole overrun with dead kids this year?"

"Not just you," Stavis said. "There's like fifteen of them this year. I counted."

"Good for you," Pete said, punching Stavis in the meaty part of his shoulder. "Keep up the good work and maybe you'll pass math this year."

TC's grin was a lopsided slash on his round, doughy face.

"There are more dead kids this year," Adam said, without looking up from his laces. "There was an article in the newspaper that said this was a good school for the living impaired. Some of them are bussed over from Winford."

"Just what we need," Pete said, "a bunch of corpsicles shuffling around. Maybe this place really is hell."

"Hell on earth," TC said, shoving his sneakers and pants into his locker. The kid was hopeless, Pete thought. An overweight slob whose flesh hung from his barrel-shaped frame.

"Dead kids are getting up all over the country," a sophomore running back named Harris Morgan added.

Not all of them, Pete thought, giving him a sidelong look. Julie never came back.

Harris caught his look and panicked. Harris had been sniffing around Pete and TC since they'd started practicing in late August, and Pete figured he was looking to join the Pain Crew. He decided to favor the kid with a snicker and a quick nod of the head. With Lame Man acting like a wuss, it wouldn't hurt to round out the ranks.

"Did you see that one dead chick?" TC said, his wide belly hanging over the front and sides of his briefs. "The one in the skirt?"

"Yeah, I saw her," Pete replied. "And I think I could bring her back to life, if you catch my meaning." TC and Harris barked out forced laughter. "If the dead didn't disgust me so much."

His audience, on cue, fell silent.

"Hey, Adam," Pete said, leaning in close so that only Adam could hear, "did you hear who's trying to join the team this year?"

"Thorny? The kid you just terrified?"

"Naw," Pete said. He saw that he was going to have to work on Adam a bit this year. Adam just wasn't picking up on the backfield signals like he used to. "Somebody else."

Adam looked at him, waiting. That was something, too. Adam used to be a nervous sort of kid, awkward and gawky, uncomfortable in his own skin, and now he had a self-confidence and poise uncommon in most guys his age. Pete thought that Adam was becoming more like him. He gave Adam his best conspiratorial smile, hoping to rekindle the early days, back when Adam gave him unwavering loyalty instead of grief.

"Somebody dead."

"Oh," Adam said. He flexed his ankle and decided he didn't like how the lace on his left cleat was tied.

"Oh?" Pete said. "Oh?" He looked over at Stavis and made the universal "I'm dealing with a moron" face. Stavis grinned and shook his head. "That all you've got to say?"

"What am I supposed to say, Pete?"

Pete frowned, because there it was again, that *attitude*.

"You don't care that a dead kid is joining the team?"

"I don't have feelings about it either way."

Pete had a temper, but he was good at riding it, turning it into something useful. He wanted to smack the kid, giant or no. Time was, Pete could have slapped him around and Adam would have taken it. But back then Adam didn't have that muscle tone, and Pete wasn't sure this was the right time to test how solid Adam had become.

"Well, Coach has feelings about it. Big time. I heard him arguing with the Kimchi over it." *Kimchi* was his name for Ms. Kim, the much beloved principal of Oakvale High.

"Really?"

"Yeah. He tried just about everything. Not fair to the other kids, practice season already started, blah blah blah. She wasn't having it."

"Well then," Adam said, getting up, "I guess he plays."

Pete rose with him. "Well, I guess we get some say in that."

Adam waited him out again.

Pete flexed his hand. "Coach wants us to take this dead kid off the board."

"He say that?"

"Not in so many words," Pete said, "but his meaning was pretty clear."

Adam nodded. "I'm going to play," he said. "I'm not going in for any assassinations."

"Oh?" Pete said, a wide smile on his face. "Not like last year?"

Adam stared back at him, a look of fury burning through his passive mask.

Pete showed his teeth. "Not like with Gino Manetti?"

Adam didn't reply. He gave each lace a final tug and seemed satisfied with the results.

"I don't think we can hang out this year, Pete," he said.

"Just like that, huh?"

"Just like that."

"Did I say something? Are you pissed because I was talking about Scarypants?"

"It isn't so much the things you say, Pete," Adam told him, "it has more to do with what you are."

Pete looked at him and felt the rage constrict his hands into fists.

"What I am," he repeated. "You want to explain that?"

Adam picked his helmet off the bench and shouldered past Pete.

Pete called Adam an asshole under his breath, but he

said it loud enough for just about everyone to hear.

Gino Manetti had been an all-star running back for the Winford Academy Warriors. In a game in which Manetti had already scored three touchdowns on the Badgers, Adam put an end to his season—and his career—with a late and illegal hit to the knee.

Coach Konrathy had ordered the hit.

Not in so many words, Pete thought, shucking his jeans off. But the meaning was clear. He and Stavis had put the hurt on kids before at Konrathy's request; they didn't call themselves the Pain Crew for nothing. But neither had taken somebody out in such a permanent way before.

Pete thought about that kid from Tech he'd knocked unconscious late last season. He'd laughed out loud when he read about the game in the paper the next day and found out the kid had a broken clavicle. The news had him pumped up for days.

Not Adam, though. Adam was never the same person again after hitting that Manetti kid.

"Get back in there, Layman," Coach said, pushing Adam back into the locker room. Pete noticed that if Adam hadn't allowed himself to be moved, Konrathy wouldn't have been able to budge him. Adam had changed.

"I've got an announcement I have to make, and I want the whole team to hear it," Coach said.

"This about the dead kid, Coach?" Stavis said.

"Yes, it's about the dead kid," Coach said, his tone laden with a level of sarcasm he reserved for only the most boneheaded of players. "But you are never, ever to call him a dead kid if he's within earshot, understand? We are required to refer to them as the *living impaired*, okay? Not dead kid. Not *zombie*, or *worm buffet*, or *accursed hellspawn*, either. Living impaired. Repeat after me. *Living impaired.*"

Pete watched the other boys in the locker room repeat the term.

"I want you to know that the decision to include this kid—" He took off his Badgers ball cap and ran his hand through his thick, close-cropped hair. "—this *living impaired* kid—has nothing to do with me. I have been ordered to let him on the team. So there it is. He'll be at practice tomorrow. Now hurry up and get your asses on the field."

Pete watched him turn on heel and start back up the stairs.

He didn't want any dirty dead kid in the locker room with him. He didn't want dead kids around him anywhere—not in school, not in his classes, and not on his football field. He wanted all the dead kids in their graves, where they belonged.

Like Julie.

Maybe if Julie had come back, he thought. Maybe if she'd come back he'd feel differently, and he'd learn to stand them despite their blank staring eyes and their slow, croaking voices. But she didn't come back anywhere except in his dreams. And now, ever since the dead began to rise, when she returned even to that secret place, she came back changed. She wasn't the girl he'd held hands with at the lake, she wasn't the first girl he'd kissed on the edge of the pine woods. She wasn't his first and only love.

She was a monster. She was a monster much like the one that was about to put on pads and a helmet and take the field with him.

CHAPTER THREE

T HE STD PUSHED THE PHONE into Adam's chest with the hand that wasn't holding the beer.

"It's some girl," he said.

Adam breathed through his nose, catching the phone before it fell to the floor. There were oil stains on his new T-shirt from where the STD's knuckles pressed against him. Adam watched him walk back into the living room, where Adam's mom sat with one of his stepbrothers, watching sitcoms on Fox. The breathing helped.

"Hello."

"Hi, Adam," Phoebe said, "how was practice?"

Adam kept focusing on his breathing when he heard the STD tell his mom to get him some chips. The chips in the kitchen he'd just left with his second beer. God bless America.

"Adam?"

"Hey, Pheeble," he said, "sorry. I was just having a domestic moment with the STD."

"Oh, I'm sorry."

"Me too. What's up? Practice was grueling. Just got home. I was getting sweaty and sore on a muddy field playing for a man who might have been separated at birth from the STD himself. What are you up to?" His mother walked past him, smiled and patted his shoulder.

"Just listening to music, doing some homework. You know."

"Let me guess: the song playing right now has one of the three following words in its title: sorrowful, rain, or death."

Phoebe laughed, and the sound of her laughter relaxed him enough to stop using Master Griffin's breathing technique. Pete, Gino Manetti, the STD's constant harassment. Her laugh blew it all out the door.

"'The Empty Chambers of My Heart,' by Endless Sorrow, actually."

"I was close," he said.

"Death is always one of your three words, I've noticed."

"I've been right most often with it." Adam liked a lot of the music that Pheeble and Daffy listened to, the faster, more guitar-driven stuff, anyhow. The really heavy goth stuff didn't do much for him other than get him thinking about things he didn't want to think about.

"That's probably true," she said. "Hey, did Tommy Williams practice today?"

"Williams? That's the dead kid, right?"

"Yes, Adam. That's the dead kid."

"Oh. No. Coach says he's starting tomorrow. He isn't too pleased with the idea."

"Margi said she heard him arguing with Principal Kim about it."

"I've heard that too," Adam said. His stepbrother John's car roared into the driveway. "From Pete."

"Ah, yes. Pete. He's a big fan of the idea, I'm sure?"

"Why do you say that?"

"Maybe because I've watched your buddy Pete bully and mock just about everyone outside of you and his little band of cronies ever since he moved here."

"Pete has issues," Adam said. "I don't think we'll be hanging out much this year."

He heard her sigh through the phone, or at least he thought he did. Phoebe seemed awfully interested in this dead kid all of a sudden. Johnny walked in and punched him on the shoulder his mother had just patted. Adam caught him with a slap to the back of the head as he went to join the rest of the not-Laymans watching television.

"Really? Why not?"

"Pete and I are on divergent paths."

"I'm so glad you took karate, Adam." He could hear the smile in her voice.

"Really? Why is that?"

"You're different. Not different, really. But more of who you've always been. I can't explain it."

He thought she'd explained it just right, but didn't say so. "That's good, right?"

"I think it's great. Maybe now you'll actually be able to acknowledge me in the hallways if you're with one of your little cheerleader snips."

"Don't count on it," he said. "My cheerleader snips have got pretty high standards."

"Except in men," she said, and they laughed. "So, can you drive me tomorrow?"

"Yeah," he said, dropping the volume of his voice. "The STD is letting me use the truck."

"The beat-up brown thing? That's pretty big of him. What happened?"

"Mom's been working on him. I think she pointed out that it was a little unfair for us to have six vehicles and I was the only one who didn't get to drive one."

"Yeah, your yard looks like a used car lot. Or a 'well-used' car lot, as my dad says."

He heard the amused lilt in her voice and he closed his eyes so he could imagine her expression, one green eye peeking out at him beneath a swath of jet-black hair.

"He must be pretty ticked. We're like a bad cliché." He could picture Mr. Kendall arriving home from work and frowning as he looked over from his front steps at this weeks' crop of rehab vehicles littering the driveway and yard.

"He's okay, really. If we ever get ready to move, he'll probably ask the STD to clean things up until the house is sold."

"Don't ever move, Phoebe," he said. "You might be the only sane person I know."

She laughed. "Then you're in more trouble than I thought. Seven fifteen?"

"It's a date," he said, and hung up. A date. The idea of Phoebe moving left him with a weird feeling, a feeling that had nothing to do with Phoebe being the only sane person in his personal cosmos.

"Layman!" his older and frailer stepbrother, Jimmy, called from the other room. "Get off the flippin' phone! I'm waiting for a call."

"Okay," Adam said, and started his breathing again before heading down the hall to his room.

"About time," Jimmy said, shoulder checking him on his way to the phone. It was pathetic, Adam thought. Jimmy was half his size, but Adam had to pretend that he was intimidated by him to keep the peace in Casa de STD.

Adam lay on his bed and opened *Wuthering Heights*, the first major punishment of the school year, one that he was supposed to have endured over the summer. He closed it again after two paragraphs. There were a lot of things bugging him about his home life and the first week of school, and it took a few moments to identify which one was bothering him at the moment, but then he had it.

Phoebe cared as much about football as he did about the Brontë sisters. What was it about that dead kid?

"Is that a new dress?" Adam asked, observing Phoebe with a scrutiny only a childhood friend could get away with. He forced himself to say something, because if he didn't, he knew he'd be sitting there slack-jawed, his eyes goggling at her. The dress went down to her ankles, but somehow accented her gentle curves despite all the fabric. She had on her calf-high boots and a light gray vest, and her jewelry was all silver or silver-colored. He thought she looked like a gothic cowgirl.

Phoebe might dress a little weird, and sometimes she went overboard on the makeup, but there was no disguising how beautiful she was. She had wide hazel-green eyes that were mirthful no matter how funerary her clothing appeared, and her long dark hair softened her somewhat angular features and framed them in a way that made her face look heart-shaped from a distance.

He realized he might be blushing.

Her glance was quizzical, and he hoped she hadn't sensed the growing shift in how he felt about her. There was a hollow feeling in his stomach even though he'd filled it with eggs and sausage not a half hour earlier. The hollow feeling grew when he realized that the new dress probably had more to do with Tommy Williams than it did with him.

"It most certainly is," she said, brushing strands of her long black hair away from her eyes. It was one of his favorite mannerisms. "Thanks for noticing."

"And black, a completely different look for you," he said, taking refuge in the light banter that was as natural as sleep to them.

"Har-har. See, karate has made you more observant, too."

"All part of my never-ending quest to be more of the person I always was."

"Excellent. I applaud your dedication," she said, and he felt her light touch on his arm. "And how was your date with Emily last night?"

"Emily?"

"Brontë. *Wuthering Heights?*"

"Oh yeah, her. We've kind of hit a rough patch, me and Em."

"Too bad. I always thought that she could help you . . . you know . . . become the person you always were."

"That's just it," he said, mock-punching the dashboard. "She keeps trying to change me!"

They had a good laugh over that, and Phoebe, catching her breath, leaned her head against his shoulder. A clean hint of scent, some island flower that Adam could not identify, wafted from her jet-black hair, and the laughter died in Adam's throat.

"So," he said, "you're hanging out after school today?"

"Yeah. I thought I'd get some stuff done in the library."

"Library closes at four. Practice can go pretty late some days, especially when Coach is hacked off. And I think he'll be hacked off today."

"Why do you think he'll be hacked off?"

"Dead kid walking."

"About that," she said. "How does the rest of the team feel?"

"Oh, they're thrilled. Who doesn't want to hit the showers with a corpse?"

"Adam," she said, and there might have been a warning in her voice.

"I think Williams will have a difficult time," he said, being careful. "Many people are still terrified of the living impaired."

Phoebe nodded, hugging herself even though he had the heater on in the truck.

He stepped out on the ice; why not? "You seem interested in Williams," he said, pretending to glance in the rearview mirror. "In his situation, I mean."

She nodded. "I am. Some of the living impaired kids that moved into town this year are pretty interesting, you know? Like that girl we saw yesterday in the cafeteria."

"Yeah, she sure is."

"Pervert," she replied. "But really, dressing like she does, him trying to play football—I think it must take a certain bravery on their part, you know?"

"That's what interests you? Their bravery?"

"Well," she said, "the whole idea of the living impaired interests me. There's so many questions, so much mystery about the whole thing."

"Like with Colette," he said, and as soon as he said it he wished he'd stuck with the Williams angle.

"Like with Colette," Phoebe whispered, putting her head back on his shoulder. He hoped that she didn't notice how slow he was driving.

CHAPTER FOUR

*P*HOEBE WAITED IN THE
foyer for Margi after arriving
with Adam at school. At least
that's what she told herself she was doing, even as she peered
over the top of her history textbook, watching Colette and then
Tommy get off the bus. Colette moved with a dragging, side to
side motion, her eyes fixed on a single point on some unseen
horizon. She had trouble with the steps of the bus and then the
steps leading up to the door, and Phoebe knew from previous
observations that the motion required to open doors was very
complex for her.

Tommy exited after her but reached the school first. He
moved more like a student who had stayed up too late the night
before, drinking soda and eating pizza, than he did a "typical"
living impaired person. There was a pause between the motion
of gripping the door handle and the motion of opening it, but
the motions themselves weren't all that awkward. He held the

door open for Colette and a pair of living girls, who sidestepped him in favor of another entrance rather than allow themselves to be victimized by Tommy's courtesy.

She watched Tommy enter the building. He was wearing a slate-blue polo shirt and jeans and white high-top sneakers. He seemed to stand straighter than the other boys she saw milling around, but that might just have been a side effect of the odd way he walked.

His shirt matched the color of his eyes, she thought.

Margi was the second to last person off the bus, having wedged herself in the backseat with her iPod and a dark, cloudy look on her face beneath her pink bangs. Phoebe waved, hoping to cheer her. No such luck.

"Hi, Margi," she said. Maybe excessive perkiness could win the day.

"Don't you 'hi' me," she said. "You, the traitor who abandons me to ride the doomsday bus. I wish that Lame Man had failed his driver's test. I'm going to fail my spelling quiz today."

"Oh my. You need to relax, girl."

"Relax, nothing."

"Doomsday bus? Come on."

Margi held up one bangle-covered arm. "Colette is really freaking me out."

"I know. Did they sit together again today?"

"I didn't notice."

"Yeah, you did."

Margi pinched her eyes and stuck out her tongue at her.

"They sat together. He stepped back so she could get off the bus before him."

"Quite the gentleman, I've noticed."

"You would."

"Of course I would. We have the poet's eye, you and me."

"Please. I don't want to see any of it."

"Margi," Phoebe said, catching Margi's wrists as they waved around in front of her, "we'll need to talk to her sometime. It will be good. For all of us."

She thought that some of the color left Margi's already pallid cheeks. "Not yet," she said. Phoebe barely heard her over the boisterous entrance of another busload of students.

"We're going to be late," Margi said, and shook free of Phoebe's grip before giving her a weak smile. "Come on."

Phoebe got her bag from off the floor and followed her to their lockers, and then to homeroom.

Just eye contact, Pete thought as he leaned back in his chair, stretching and flexing his arms. That's all I need.

"Am I boring you, Mr. Martinsburg?" Ms. Rodriguez asked. No one other than Stavis and that blond bimbette Holly, who had dated Lame Man for a while, dared laugh.

"I'm not bored, Ms. Rodriguez," he said. "I'm just a little sore from yesterday's practice. I'm sorry I distracted you."

Ms. Rodriguez shook her head and went back to the board to discuss some thrilling quadratic equation or whatever.

I bet you were distracted too, you old bag, he thought.

It isn't every day you get to check out guns like mine.

He turned quickly toward the windows, where Lame Man's freaky chick sat, and there he had it: contact. He gave her the look that always worked with Cammy's empty-headed friends, and if Morticia Scarypants didn't just melt away, he knew at least that her heart would trip a couple beats faster.

She looked away, just as quickly.

Got you, he thought, making a mental note to follow up on her later. He took a full inventory of her, half hoping that she would glance back and see the look of open appreciation on his face. She was one of the only girls in the class wearing a dress, and her sleek black hair really was striking. It fell past her shoulders, and she was pretty good at using it to keep her pale face in shadow most of the time. Pretty green eyes, but not fake contact-lens green. Her hair reflected the light falling through the windows.

Ms. Rodriguez called on the dead kid a few minutes later—the dead kid who would soon be putting on a nice new practice uniform and some spanking-new pads and helmet. New gear, old dead kid. Pete wanted to puke. He tapped his desk with his pencil and didn't stop until the dead kid answered—correctly, as luck would have it. That would make two questions more than Pete had been able to answer, and the school year wasn't even a month old yet.

He thought that Scarypants was looking over at him again, which was great, just great. It would really frost Lame Man if he were to tag her, even if the big dummy was too emotionally stunted to realize his true feelings for her. Pete thought maybe he'd tell Adam he'd quit with her if Adam would wise up and get his head back in the game. Maybe.

Pete lingered when the bell rang, figuring that if Scarypants engaged in a little more eye contact he'd go ahead and make his play right there between classes. He saw her stand up, and he liked the way her skirt cut in at her waist—she had a nice little figure under all of those layers.

She was taking her time as well, but it wasn't Pete Martinsburg, slayer of college girls, that she was waiting around for. It was the dead kid.

Huh, Pete thought.

She just won't shut up, Adam thought as he nodded his head to every third or fourth point that Holly Pelletier was making, and yet she wasn't really saying anything.

Holly must have noticed the insincerity of attention, because she moved close enough for him to smell the strawberry scent of her gum. Or maybe it was her lip gloss that he was smelling, or her hair spray. Adam realized that there was a time when the smell, and Holly's proximity to him, would have activated certain chemicals and drives in his body, but now all he could think was how artificial the scent was. He knew that if he were to bend down and kiss Holly, as he'd done many times before, it wouldn't be strawberry he would taste but some chemical version of strawberry. And for the first time, the idea of kissing Holly was not exciting; it was faintly nauseating.

What the hell is happening to me? he thought.

Holly never made full eye contact with him during her

hallway monologues; she was too interested in who was walk-ing by. Adam was having trouble maintaining focus as well because he'd seen Phoebe lingering by the bulletin board in front of the office down the hall, waiting to talk to him before he headed into practice. He almost missed the sudden wave of disgust that clouded Holly's traditionally pretty face. Adam turned and saw what she was sneering at: the pretty dead girl, she of the risqué hemlines.

"Ugh," Holly said. "I feel so bad for you, having to practice with that dead kid. Imagine if *that* went out for our squad?" She pointed at "that," not caring who heard her.

"Imagine," Adam said, watching the girl pass. She didn't move like a dead girl, that was for sure. Adam realized that her clothes had distracted him from another difference—she had a slight, barely perceptible smile on her lips. A bemused smile, one not so different from the one he often caught on Phoebe's face. Most of the other zombies he'd seen wore blank expres-sions, as if their facial muscles had hardened into place like old caulk.

Holly watched the girl pass, her fake strawberry lips curling. "It's so gross. Imagine having to touch her? I feel *so* bad for you. I hope the zombie gets cut from the team. There shouldn't be a dead Badger on the field. That would be *so* wrong. Can you imagine?"

I can *so* imagine, Adam thought. He watched Phoebe turn from the bulletin board when the dead girl approached, and he saw Phoebe smile at her before turning back and pretending to read whatever was posted there for the eleventh time.

Phoebe was holding some books against a cocked hip, her opposite shoulder dragged down by a black canvas bag stuffed with still more books. "Get it? A dead Badger?" Holly was saying.

"Hey, Holly. You'll have to excuse me. I need to go talk to Phoebe."

Holly's sapphire-blue eyes narrowed with such speed that Adam thought she would pop out a contact. "Phoebe? Who's Phoebe?"

"She is," Adam said, nodding over to where Phoebe stood, leaning precariously against the weight of her enormous satchel, while at the same time rubbing at the back of her calf with the toe of her black boot. "She's my best friend."

"Her?" Holly said. "That goth over there?"

"Yep," Adam replied. "I'll see you later."

People moved out of his way when he cut across the hall to join Phoebe. He wasn't into pushing kids around like Pete and Stavis were, but he'd spent the past two years hanging around them, and he'd never lifted a finger to curtail their actions, either. That was something else that needed to change, he thought.

"Hey, Pheeble," he called, a weird lightness spreading through his chest.

"Hello, Adam," Phoebe said, looking startled. Adam lifted the heavy bag of books off her shoulder.

Phoebe peeked out around him. "Uh, I think you might have ticked off Whatsername. She looks ready to rip the letter off your jacket."

"Yeah, I just dropped a bomb on her."

"Really?" Phoebe said as they started to walk toward the library. "Did you propose marriage?" She giggled, and Adam felt the lightness move out to his extremities. "Or was it something more earthy?"

"Ha-ha. And what makes you think it would be me doing the proposing?"

"Good point."

He heard his own voice slip out of banter mode, and for once he didn't care if Phoebe picked up on it. "I told Holly that we were friends. You and me."

Phoebe stopped. "Really?"

He looked at her. "Really."

She lowered her gaze, but when she looked back up at him her eyes were filled with mirth. "Won't they revoke your charter membership in the cool kids club?"

They started walking again. "Let 'em. The truth has set me free."

She bumped into him, trying to throw him off balance, but it was like a butterfly trying to unsettle an oak tree.

"I wish you'd taken karate a few years earlier, Adam," she said.

"Shut up, Pheeble. Or I'll chop you."

"Kii-ya!" she said, beating him to it.

He walked her to the library, and then headed off to go practice with the living and the dead.

CHAPTER FIVE

*T*OMMY WILLIAMS WAS THE last one to finish the warm-up lap around Oakvale Field. When he was a freshman, Adam had arrived back at the starting point consistently in the back of the pack, but Coach Konrathy didn't care, because Adam was about as wide as any two students and about as strong as any three. Six-foot-five freshmen were rare enough, but a six-foot-five freshman with muscles was like some exotic animal where Oakvale athletics was concerned.

But now there was an even more exotic specimen on the field. Namely, a dead kid.

Never before had a zombie tried out for any sport in the district. Tommy trotted—and what a weird trot, like someone was yanking his ankle from behind with each step he took—over to the loose cluster of players near Coach Konrathy. Many of the players were covered in sweat beneath their pads and trying to control their breathing, but the dead kid wasn't even winded.

He doesn't breathe, Adam remembered. Adam was sweating freely but his breathing was pretty good. Trying to keep in shape in the off-season with lifting and karate was paying dividends. He knew he'd never be the fastest guy on the field, but there was no reason he needed to be the most out of shape. Karate gave him some techniques that were going to keep him on the field longer, and it also gave him some tricks he couldn't wait to spring on those bastards from Winford. The season couldn't start soon enough, as far as he was concerned. Normally he loved the practice and the discipline of it, but the recent tension with Pete took some of the luster away—and that was before the dead kid joined. Adam tried to avoid getting caught up in the philosophical aspects of the new addition to the team, but it was undeniable that the presence of Tommy Williams cast a hush over what was usually a pretty boisterous event.

Adam liked to be the first one into the locker room, but not today. He found it was eerie to walk into the locker room and see the kid sitting there on the bench, all suited up, his eyes glossy and staring from within the shadow of his helmet.

Focus, Master Griffin whispered in his mind. Adam thought the interior voice was starting to sound more and more like Yoda now that he had cut back his trips to the dojo to once every couple weeks rather than twice a week like he had over the summer. Master Griffin would have to wait his turn behind Coach Konrathy and Emily Brontë.

And Phoebe.

Adam started some post-running stretching exercises, feeling his muscles lengthen and contract. This was Konrathy's first late practice—he liked to do a few a season to get the team used to playing under the lights—and Adam was pleased with the way his body was responding to the shifts.

Coach Konrathy frowned at Tommy as he joined the other players. He took his cap off and put his hand through his thinning hair, and Adam knew that some punishment was coming their way.

"We're going to start out with some tackling drills," Konrathy said. Adam thought he could hear him wheezing; he looked like he needed a shave and his eyes were glassy. "All the rooks line up. We're going to see how you take a hit."

Adam watched Tommy Williams take his place at the end of the rookie line. There were about twelve kids trying out for the team this year; mostly freshmen. Oakvale didn't have enough players to field both a JV and a varsity team, so pretty much all of the new kids would at least get a uniform to wear on the bench. Every year, though, there were a few who washed out, didn't make it through the practices, or decided they didn't enjoy peeling themselves off the ground with a headache and a bloody nose.

Adam watched Konrathy looking over his tacklers. Adam's instincts at the line caused him to read meaning in everything: eye contact, nonverbal cues, the inflection of the quarterback's voice as he called the signals. He watched a look pass between the coach and Pete Martinsburg.

"Look alive, Williams!" Coach shouted, drawing a dark laugh from some of his veteran players. Adam saw Pete watching Coach like a guard dog waiting for the attack sign. Pete smiled before putting his helmet back on, and then Adam saw why. Coach's left hand was held flat at his waist with thumb down.

Adam wasn't grinning at all. He was thinking of the last time he saw Coach make that sign, when he'd ended Gino Manetti's career by hitting him in the knee. He could still hear the tendons pop as he drilled into the side of Manetti's leg with his shoulder, and he could still hear the other boy's shrill cry of pain as he went down. It wasn't until Adam saw Manetti months later at the mall that he realized what he'd done. Manetti, his once-proud shoulders slumped as he gimped along with the old folks, had a cane, and there was a pretty girl, his girlfriend probably, loping along with him, alternately trying to encourage him to pick up the pace or slow it down. Watching them—the look of pained resignation on his face, and the look of total loyalty and sympathy on hers—Adam thought that it was one of the saddest things he'd ever seen. He knew as soon as he'd made the hit that Manetti would never walk right again. He damn sure would never *play* again.

A week later Adam had signed up for lessons at Master Griffin's dojo. He had read a little about karate and thought it would help him with control. He also hoped it would help him with his guilt.

"You aren't still mad at me, are you, man?" Pete said, slapping

Adam on the shoulder pads and snapping him out of his reverie.

"I'm not mad at you, Pete," he said, although he wanted to hit back. He wanted to blame Pete for his part in making him the ass he'd been for the past two years, but really he just wanted to punch himself.

"You saw it. Coach wants us to take out the dead kid," Martinsburg said. The lines were beginning the drill.

Adam looked back at him.

Pete gripped his shoulder. "Time to pick a team, Adam."

Adam shook off Pete's hand and held his ground without replying. Stavis and Pete weren't shy about using their fists— neither was Adam, for that matter—but he hoped it wouldn't come to that. He hoped Pete would allow Adam to outgrow him gracefully.

Right, he thought. That's how it will happen.

"You take first crack, Lame Man," Martinsburg said. "Case of beer to whoever puts him out."

First crack, Adam thought. There were a lot of things that living impaired people couldn't do—normal things like breathe and bleed.

He didn't think they could heal either.

The hollow resonant sound of Phoebe's heels on the metal bleachers echoed in the cool air of dusk, drawing looks her way from the few spectators sitting in small clusters and watching the action on the field below. Most of the watchers were parents, girlfriends, or kids from the marching band waiting for rides. Phoebe was used to getting stared at. Her all-black wardrobe, an even mix of vintage and trendy clothing, practically guaranteed she would get odd looks from her classmates. Knee boots with heels, long black skirts, dyed hair, and a flowing shawl ensured a raised eyebrow here and there. She didn't mind. She found that her look repelled people she didn't want to talk to and attracted those she did. The goth look wasn't nearly as popular as it once was, probably due to the appearance of the living impaired, but to Phoebe that just gave the style a subtle hint of irony, a private joke to be shared by a special few.

She stood for a moment, scanning the low ridge that rose up behind the bleachers. Koster Field, so named for a scholar athlete who had set track and field records for the state back in the early eighties, was surrounded on three sides by the Oxoboxo woods. A short perimeter of grass ran about twenty feet from the waist-high chain-link fence to the edges of the forest, making the tree shade that reached into the field late in the day appear to be a wall of spectators.

Phoebe sat down by herself. The bench was cold beneath the thin material of her skirt. She took her iPod out of her backpack and slipped the padded earphones over her ears. She also took a thick rectangular notebook and a silver pen out of her bag and set them on the bench next to her.

At least my ears will be warm, she thought, punching up the new album by the Creeps and drawing her shawl tighter around her shoulders. There were a few girls wearing letter jackets over their cheerleader outfits at the end of her bench, whispering and pointing at the field. Phoebe could fit all of what she knew about football onto the first four lines of her notebook. The only thing she could make out from the action on the field was that some of the boys were running and some of the other boys were trying to knock them down.

Adam was always easy to spot. He was the biggest one on the field just like he was the biggest wherever he was. She looked around for Tommy Williams, but all the boys moved strangely in their padding and helmets.

Then she saw him, his movements stiff, but not because of his padding. He was taking his place in the line of boys about to be knocked over.

Killian Killgore of the Creeps was singing in her ears about being lost on the moors and chased by a banshee. Phoebe tapped on her notebook with her silver pen, the remaining lines of her poem floating somewhere in the air between her and the field, waiting for her to catch them and write them down.

Phoebe set her notebook on her lap and opened it. The first page was blank. She looked up at the sky and then wrote two words. Then she looked at what was happening on the field.

Adam hit Williams cleanly from the side and tried to brush the football out of his grasp. The hit was easy to make, because Williams was pretty slow and didn't try to fake at all. He went down, but Adam thought that if he hadn't jumped into the tackle, Williams might have kept his feet. Tackling the dead kid was like tackling a brick wall.

Dead weight, he thought. Ha-ha.

The ball popped loose and bounced end over end ten yards downfield. If it was the start of the season and Williams was already on the team, he'd offer his hand and lift him to his feet, but in preseason, Adam was supposed to spit next to his head and call him a wuss.

Williams stared up at him with flat, expressionless eyes that reflected the moonlight above. Adam walked away without saying anything. It was creepy, tackling a zombie.

"Layman!" Coach yelled, "did you play with dolls all summer? What kind of hit was that?"

A clean one, he thought, looking back at his old pals Pete and TC. The Pain Crew. It had been funny when they were freshmen and realizing that they were tougher than about ninety-nine percent of the student population; not so funny now that they were juniors and toughness might not be the number-one criteria for success in life.

TC was still grinning, like he was thrilled that he might still win the case of beer, but Pete was wearing that "what happened to you, man?" look that seemed to be on his face a lot when he looked at Adam these days. Pete whispered something to TC, who nodded and took his position at the line.

Adam watched TC hit the dead kid square in the back. With his helmet.

The sound of the impact echoed across the field. Phoebe could hear the hit up in the stands even with loud horror punk playing in her ears.

"Good hit, Stavis!" Coach yelled.

Layman's jaw opened as far as his chinstrap would allow. Good hit? That was spearing, and it would be enough to get you disqualified from a game, if not the whole season. That sort of hit could hurt or paralyze someone.

It could even kill someone.

TC jogged over to pal Martinsburg, and they slammed each other's shoulder pads.

"I think he's dead, Jim," Martinsburg said, loud enough for most of the team to hear. He was laughing.

Adam walked toward Williams, who wasn't even twitching. He thought that the force of the hit might have shut him off like a radio being dropped on the concrete, but the dead kid pushed himself up from the turf with the knuckles of his hands, brought a knee up under him, and rose to his feet.

Adam couldn't help but smile when the dead kid flipped the ball to Coach Konrathy. A hit like that and he'd held on to the ball. That kind of focus deserved respect.

The attack continued for the rest of the drills. TC and Martinsburg always seemed to line up against the dead kid even though there were more tacklers than runners. Adam watched Pete hit Williams in the knees on his next turn, followed by TC wrapping his apelike arms around Williams for a neck tackle. Every hit was a dirty hit, but the only disappointment that Coach Konrathy showed was when Williams would pick himself off of the turf after each punishing slam.

The drills stopped when the pattern changed. Martinsburg was about to lay in a shot at knee level when Williams's hand came out and hit the tackler on the helmet. The stiff arm sent

Martinsburg face-first into the field while Williams lumbered away untouched. Adam noticed that some of the rookies—who themselves had been taking a beating in the drill—were trying to suppress sly smiles.

"Stay away from the face mask, Williams!" Coach yelled.

Adam shook his head. Williams hadn't come anywhere near the face mask.

Later in the practice Konrathy set up a scrimmage drill. By this time most of the players and rookies were spent and wheezing, all except the dead kid. Adam wondered if it was possible for the living impaired to get physically tired.

The drill was simple. The defensive line was to try and get through to sack Denny, and the offensive line was supposed to stop them. Coach put Williams on the defensive line right across from Adam.

Williams, dead or not, was not one of the bigger guys on the field. Five foot ten maybe, and built more like a wide receiver than a lineman. Layman thought that this was cheap, the same way all those hits from the Pain Crew were cheap. Karate class had taught Adam much about honor, and this didn't seem honorable at all.

But it was also dishonorable not to execute one's duty. Cheap or not, he'd have to hit Tommy Williams just like he would hit any other enemy lineman. He'd hit him cleanly, yes, but no less hard.

No one gets through, Adam thought as he spun the ball on the turf and took his stance. No one.

He snapped the ball to Denny and propelled himself

forward, getting all of his leg muscles into the launch. Williams was slower but he was coming up to meet the charge.

And he did. Adam was peripherally aware of the game; he noticed things at the edges of his vision, like Gary Greene on his right slipping and missing his block. He noticed that no one was helping Williams against him, something that other teams always did to keep Adam from ripping a hole open in their line.

He also noticed that he only moved Williams back about a foot.

The play ended. Greene's slip let one of the rookies through, and the rookie pressured Denny enough to throw an incomplete pass near the sideline. Adam unlocked from Williams, who turned without a sound and went back to his place on the line.

Holy crow, Adam thought. Williams had gone up against him unassisted, and Adam had barely budged him.

He looked around at his teammates to see if any of them noticed the amazing feat that Williams had just accomplished, but for the most part they were all bone tired and shuffling back to their places on the line. Adam knew that very few of them showed any real promise beyond high school—Mackenzie and Martinsburg were probably the best players besides him—and few had the sort of "field radar" that would allow them to notice the important details of the game.

Adam looked over at Coach, whose chubby face was pink with anger, his eyes narrowed to slits. He was shaking his head in disgust.

But it was what Adam saw beyond the coach, out at the

edge of the woods, that really caught his attention.

There were a few people standing among the trees, watching them practice: three or four of them just standing like statues, watching. Adam might not have noticed them at all if it hadn't been for the big one, a black guy in a T-shirt as gray as the bark of the large oak he stood beside. Adam couldn't see the others well, but he knew from the way that they stood without moving that they were dead.

Out to watch their boy, he thought, but none of them looked familiar. The black guy had to be as big as he was, and there was no way that Adam would have missed him in the halls.

"Layman!" Coach yelled, taking off his cap and slapping it against his thigh for effect, "are you here to play, or what?"

Adam went back to the line. No one else seemed to have noticed the zombies. The living impaired people, he corrected himself. They were creepy, sure, but he couldn't let their presence distract him from the task at hand. He squared up on the line and looked at Williams. Williams looked back at him with unnerving calm.

He believed in knowing his opponents. On the next snap Adam hit him with equal force and again moved him back maybe six inches. There was no way that Williams was going to get through or around him, but Tommy didn't get knocked over like just about everyone else Adam played against, either.

The play ended with a completion. Coach called Adam a little girl and told him to put some effort into it.

Third time's the charm, Adam thought, and this time when

he hit Williams he shifted his hips in the way he'd learned from Master Griffin. Williams flipped to the side like a gum wrapper caught in a breeze. Denny darted through the Layman-size hole and ran down the field.

Williams was flat on his back. Adam saw light—either that of the harvest moon above or from the stadium lights—reflected in his flat eyes.

He offered Williams his hand, and the dead boy took it.

CHAPTER SIX

THE LINES PHOEBE WROTE glowed with a blue electricity on the white page. She read the words a second time and the energy flowed back up through her fingertips. The feeling was something she rarely experienced when writing, despite the pages and pages of notebooks she'd filled. But when it came, the sensation was like the spark of life to her.

She really thought Tommy would not be able to get up from the first bad hit he took. The successive tackles were no less brutal, but up he rose, no worse for wear, that she could see. His resilience seemed to infuriate the tacklers, who pounded and slammed into him with renewed vigor. When he had stopped Pete Martinsburg with an outstretched hand, she had almost started clapping.

She read her poem a third time.

Harvest moon
Above
The dead boy on the field
Trying to show us
What it means
To be
Alive

If the cheerleaders saw her smiling to herself and thought she was a bizarro, so be it. It was worth it.

Practice ended with a final whistle from Coach Konrathy. She watched as Adam passed by the bleachers. He saw her sitting in the stands and gave her the most imperceptible of waves. She waved back at him like he was a Hollywood celebrity, hoping she'd embarrass him. But if he really had told Whatsername that she was his best friend, there wasn't much else she could do to tweak him.

Phoebe looked for Tommy and saw him standing at the far edge of the players as they moved in a loose knot toward the locker room. Slower than most, he trailed farther and farther until he was a good five paces behind even Thorny Harrowwood, who was limping along after spending the previous hour being pounded into the turf like a tent spike.

Then Tommy stopped, turned, and began walking in the opposite direction, toward the parking lot.

Or, Phoebe thought, toward the woods beyond the parking lot.

Sudden impulse, perhaps the electric spark pumping

through her blood, brought her to her feet after tearing the sheet of poetry out of her notebook and folding it into a small fringed square. Her book, pen, and iPod went into her bag, and then she was moving.

The sounds of her heels were like gunshots on the bleachers as she ran down to follow Tommy across the field.

"Get in here, Layman!" Coach Konrathy yelled, waving him over to his office door. Adam sighed, thinking that it would have been nice to have gotten more of his gear off than his helmet.

He gave Martinsburg a cold look as he passed, but Pete stared back without flinching.

Konrathy slammed the door. "What have you been doing all summer? Playing with paper dolls?"

Layman breathed deeply. Last year, he probably would have thrown his helmet at the wall if Coach yelled at him that way. There was a locker door that was bent and twisted like a pretzel, wedged so tightly in its frame that it no longer opened. Coach Konrathy had taken Adam out of a game last year for missing a block that led to Denny Mackenzie getting sacked for the first time in the season, so Adam had taken his frustrations out on his locker.

But this was the new-and-improved Adam Layman, he of the zenlike calm. The new-and-improved Adam thought before he struck.

"No, Coach," he said evenly, his pulse and breathing under control. "I was taking karate classes and working out."

Coach Konrathy threw his hands up in exaggerated disbelief. "Karate? Karate? I thought karate was supposed to make you tougher, not make you into a total wussy."

Adam felt his breathing quicken, but he concentrated and reeled it back in. No, Coach, he thought, karate has nothing to do with making you tougher, it has everything to do with bringing more control, clarity, and focus into your life.

Focus. When he was ready he answered his coach with a question.

"Is there something wrong with the way I practiced today?"

Coach leaned over the desk so that he was inches away from Adam, close enough that Adam could smell the breath strips that he popped by the dozens during practice.

"You tell me, Layman," he said. "You think there's a problem with your play when you can't even push back a dead kid?"

"I pushed . . ."

"You didn't do squat! You're practically a foot taller than he is, and you couldn't do anything but knock him off balance! And you helped him up! What the hell were you thinking? We don't help rookies up until they make the team, you know that!"

Adam summoned Master Griffin's calm but insistent voice in his head. *Focus, Adam. Focus.*

"He's hard to move when his feet are planted," he said as evenly as he could. "I think he'd be good on the offensive line."

Konrathy drew back like Adam had spit in his eye.

"You do, do you? How about instead of him joining you on the line, you join him on the list of kids I cut from the team?

The last thing I need on this team is an attitude problem."

Master Griffin had taught Adam all about *chi*—the life force that centers all beings—in their studies. Focusing on the chi was good for the breathing. It was good for the heartbeat. It was also good to keep Adam from reaching out and squeezing Coach Konrathy by his fat red neck. Despite all this goodness, he couldn't keep his face from flushing.

"I know your grades, Layman," Konrathy said, getting in Adam's face again. "And I know your stepfather. Without football you've got no hope of getting into or paying for college."

He let his words sink in for a moment, and they sunk deep, plunging through the protective calm that Adam was trying to maintain.

"You'd better straighten up and bring your 'A' game to next practice, Layman," Konrathy said. "Now get out of my office."

There were things that Adam wanted to say and do, but he didn't. Coach was right. Without football he wouldn't be going anywhere; he'd end up staying in Oakvale all his life, working at his stepfather's garage, lifting tires and handing wrenches to his stepbrothers. Oakvale might have an "all-inclusive" approach to their team sports, meaning that they didn't cut kids from the team—but Adam could not take the risk. Excessive bench time would ruin his chances of a pro career.

Stavis snickered as he walked by to his locker. Stavis was another guy destined to be an Oakvale lifer, and if Adam didn't make it to college he'd be stuck here changing oil and replacing brakes for knuckleheads like him for the rest of his life.

He thought he'd rather be dead than live in a future like

that. Dead without returning. Not like the Williams kid. *Permanently* dead.

His old locker, the one he'd smashed last year, was next to his new locker. He wanted it that way so that he would have a constant reminder of who he'd been and who he was trying to be. He breathed in stages, and his fists unclenched without him being aware of it.

I didn't think the living impaired were supposed to be able to move so fast, Phoebe thought as she walked through the muddy field. Her boots, as shiny and slick as they looked, weren't helping, either.

There was an economy of purpose to Tommy's movements, like he was walking the straightest line possible from his last position on the field toward his destination. His path would take him directly into the woods that surrounded Oxoboxo Lake. Phoebe's grip on local topography wasn't great, but she knew that somewhere on the other side of those woods was her house. Tommy's as well, somewhere a little farther along their bus route.

Tommy moved between two parked cars and reached the short band of grass before the tree line just as Phoebe made it to the track at the edge of the football field. She closed the distance somewhat, but she wasn't going to catch up to him before he entered the woods, as she had hoped.

The only hesitation in Tommy's purposeful stride was when he removed his helmet before stepping into the trees. The light of the harvest moon shone on his silvery blond hair in the moment before the darkness swallowed him.

Phoebe's breath preceded her, puffs of vapor like spirits dancing in the light of the moon. It wasn't until she was in the woods and the moonlight had disappeared that she paused long enough to think about what she was doing.

The cover of Oxoboxo woods was nearly total; the canopy of leaves above was like an impenetrable shield against the moonlight.

What on earth am I doing? she thought. Even before dead kids began coming back to life, the Oxoboxo woods was a place of mystery and strangeness, a place where ghosts stories were set and told, stories that had preceded the town and the Europeans who eventually settled there.

But she knew what she was doing, deep down. Tommy Williams was in her head, his white, angular face, the ghost of a smile on his lips, and a pale light in his slate-blue eyes. She knew he would stay there until she summoned the courage to talk to him. And then . . . ?

Phoebe looked over her shoulder, back at the pale parking lot lights visible through the trees. Adam would be looking for her soon, right after he showered and changed. He wouldn't want to be standing around his stepdad's truck, wondering where the heck she was. And if he was too late, the STD would probably flip out like he usually did and ground Adam for the next month of weekends, and it would be her fault.

She looked into the dark shapes of the woods ahead. She could see the vague, grayish outlines of trees now that her eyes had adjusted to the lack of light. She counted fifteen steps and then stopped. The woods were so thick even here at the perimeter that they seemed to swallow sound as well as light. She was aware that there weren't birds or insects making any noise, and how strange that was.

She sighed and stood there a moment, imagining each breath as a piece of her soul, and then imagining each soul fragment rising toward the impervious roof of leaves and seeking a way out to the sky beyond. There was no way she could tell which way Tommy had gone through the forest.

What on earth am I doing? she thought again. A cold wave of fear shuddered through her. She decided that pursuing Tommy through the Oxoboxo woods was a bad idea. She turned around.

And the dead boy reached for her, his pale eyes glowing in the darkness.

Thornton was the only kid left in the locker room while Adam laced up his sneakers. He was standing in front of his locker with a towel around his waist, admiring a huge red bruise that ran the length of his rib cage.

"Wow," the younger boy said, wincing, "I really took a beating today."

"You got up, though," Adam said. "That's the important thing."

"Yeah, I guess I did," Thornton replied, grinning from ear to flapping ear. The poor kid looked like the guy from *Mad* magazine, but without the missing tooth. Adam smiled to himself, thinking that the season was still young. Thornton walked off to the showers whistling, and Adam thought the kid wouldn't have been any happier if he'd thrown a hundred dollar bill at him.

With great power, he thought. The Spiderman clause. Grandmaster Griffin had spent the whole summer drilling that into him, teaching him that being a foot taller and twice as strong as everyone else were not rights, they carried certain responsibilities. He taught Adam that he possessed gifts that could be of great benefit to society or, if abused, could cause great harm to all, including himself.

He was still thinking about that when TC, Pete, and Harris Morgan stopped him in the parking lot.

"Hey, Lurch," Pete said, "where's your zombie friend?"

"I'm not in the mood," he said, waiting for Pete to get out of his way.

"Whose team are you on, big guy?" Pete said, stepping closer instead of aside. "The living or the dead?"

"I play for the Badgers, Martinsburg, same as you. Get out of my way." He looked over his shoulder where his truck was parked but he didn't see Phoebe, which was good. He didn't want her to see this.

And deep down, he knew he didn't want them to see her, either.

"That zombie is coming off the team, one way or another, Layman," Pete said.

Adam was trying to decide if he could take all three of them. TC was the biggest, but Harris and Pete weren't small, and Harris at least was faster than he was. He figured if it came to a head, he should probably try and drop Pete as quickly as he could, because then the other two might lose the heart for it. In fact, Morgan didn't look much like he had the heart for it anyway. Adam was willing his body to stay loose when Pete, either sensing where the situation was heading or having made his point, moved out of his way.

Adam moved past him, his eyes not leaving the senior's sneering face as he walked by. He threw his duffel into the bed of the truck from ten feet away.

"Pick a team!" Martinsburg called after him.

Adam got into the cab of the truck and slammed the door. The engine came alive on the third cough of the ignition, and he turned the radio up. He hoped his three teammates would be gone by the time Phoebe showed up.

Phoebe gasped as the dead boy's hand reached out to touch her hair and let the black strands run through his fingers. She was motionless when he brought his hand away and held it in front of her face. He held it close enough so that she could see the leaf he had removed.

Now the only sound was of her breathing. Tommy dropped the leaf, and she watched it hover momentarily before it disappeared in the dark.

"I . . . I was following you," she said, instantly regretting speaking. Her whisper reached her ears like a fire alarm in the silent woods. He was living impaired, not a moron. Of course she was following him, why else would he pull the stealth act and sneak up on her? She wondered if his eyes—eyes the color of rain clouds in the dull fluorescent glow of the classroom, but reflective, like those of a cat—could register the heat she felt radiating from her cheeks.

"I wanted to talk to you," she told him. "I wanted to tell you that I thought you were brave for doing this. For playing football, I mean."

Tommy didn't say anything, which heightened her embarrassment. He was tall, his shoulders broad. He held his helmet at his side by its face mask. What kind of idiot was she to chase after a living impaired kid anyhow?

Maybe all her common sense had flown away along with her breathing. She was aware, as if from a great distance, of reaching into her pocket and withdrawing the square of notebook paper.

"I also wanted to give you this."

She held the square out to him and watched him regard it with his glowing eyes, his face without expression. There was a moment of agony as he looked at the square without moving, and all Phoebe could think about was the time in seventh grade when Kevin Allieri refused her invitation to a couples' skate at a party in the Winford Rec Center.

But then Tommy reached out and took her poem. She inhaled him when they touched; the smell was like a morning breeze drifting across Oxoboxo Lake.

They stood there without speaking for a minute, each passing second a moment of awkwardness that she felt as acutely as the boys on the field felt their tackles and hits.

"Well," she said, her ears ringing as she was unable to bear the silence any longer, "I've got to go get my ride. Good night."

He didn't say anything—anything at all. Her eyes were downcast as she turned and started walking toward where she thought the parking lot was. But standing in the forest with Tommy, giving him her poem, it was so surreal, so bizarre that she wouldn't be surprised in the least if the Oxoboxo woods, lake and all, went spinning off the surface of the earth and into the stratosphere. Whatever electrical magic she'd had was now engulfed by a cold inky wave of embarrassment and fear. She was about to collide with a tree when she thought she heard her name.

She turned. All she could see of Tommy was a pale shimmering outline and his eyes, two pale disks of moonlight, about fifteen feet away.

"I think," he said, his voice soft and flat, more like the memory of sound than sound itself, "you are brave, too."

The tiny moons disappeared and she was alone. There was darkness all around her, but it no longer flowed within her. She was smiling when she joined Adam in the warm cab of his stepfather's truck.

CHAPTER SEVEN

 $\mathcal{T}$ HE WEEKEND MOVED ALONG with a tired languor, as though time itself had become living impaired. Phoebe spent long hours sitting on her bed listening to music with her notebook and pen on her lap, writing nothing and talking to no one. Friday night had been confusing in so many ways, but part of her wanted to hold on to that confusion a little longer and analyze it.

Margi called Saturday night, but in typical fashion, the hour of conversation was focused mainly on Margi. Her history report, the show she was watching, the shoes she was planning to wear on Monday, her thoughts on the new Zombicide downloads. Phoebe didn't mind; having a Margi-centric conversation was always entertaining, and it allowed her to not talk about what was on her mind—*Tommy*. . . .

She almost gave herself away when Margi asked her if she

was able to accomplish much at the library—she'd forgotten her cover story completely.

"Oh, sure," she said, but really she had just drawn some cartoons in her notebook and flipped through a book she found on the Spanish Inquisition.

"That was convincing," Margi said. "You know, I wish I'd let you talk me into staying, because I'm really having the hardest time doing this history report. Of course, Mr. Adam Lame Man probably wouldn't have driven me home. I swear, Phoebe, he has been crushing on you since the third grade."

"I didn't move here until the fourth grade."

"Well, he probably crushed on you in a past life. Do you ever see him roll his eyes when I tag along?"

"That's ridiculous, Margi."

"Yeah, I know. I'm way hotter than you," she said, and then laughed.

Phoebe had long known about Margi's fascination with Adam, who was the first friend Phoebe made when she moved to Oakvale. They'd hit it off because Adam hadn't known any other girls who liked comic books, and she was a better swimmer and Frisbee player than he was. He didn't acquire his size, or "inflate," as Phoebe liked to tease him, until middle school. Then his taste in athletics started to lean toward contact sports—sports that she had no interest in, despite having a decent outside jump shot.

Adam was a year older but had stayed back in the second grade, so now they were both juniors. High school took them down different paths—Adam was one of the popular ones,

Phoebe drifted on the edges. Neither made a big deal of their friendship at school because the incongruity of it confused their individual circles of friends.

That incongruity, as much as the length of their friendship, was what made it so special. Phoebe still felt that there was no one she would rather play Frisbee or go swimming with in the Oxoboxo.

It was special enough that Phoebe knew neither of them would ruin it with more complicated feelings. She thought Margi was the one who was crushing, but for some reason would never admit it.

"You *are* hotter than me, Margi."

"Right. Is there anything you tell the truth about? You've got the height, the good skin, the cheekbones. What have I got?"

"The wardrobe? And the . . ."

"Don't say it."

"Well, you do. I think they get more attention than my great cheekbones."

More banter, and then they hung up when Margi's father yelled at her to get off the phone. Phoebe went back to scratching in her notebook.

Adam instant messaged her on Sunday night when she was surfing around looking for the latest news on the living impaired. He asked her if she wanted a ride to school on Monday, which was weird because he never asked that. She typed back *Sure* and punctuated it with a goofy emoticon that was the Weird Sisters' trademark, a round, horned smiley with eyelashes, a tail, and tongue wagging moronically out of the side of its open mouth.

Cool, was his return message, unadorned. *Seven?*

Yup.

We should play Frisbee sometime. Then he signed off.

That, she thought, was really weird. The only time they tossed the disk now was when one of them needed someone to talk to. There were things Phoebe couldn't talk to Margi about, and there were things Adam was reluctant to share with any of his friends on the football team. They were an odd pair—but odd pairs were what kept life interesting.

That sentiment instantly brought Tommy to mind. When she switched off the light she imagined his faintly glowing eyes in the darkness of her room, and this time she had no fear at all.

Adam arrived at her house at seven sharp, the STD's pickup coughing in the driveway while he walked into the kitchen and helped himself to a banana. Phoebe, the last one out, wrote a note for her mother telling her not to hold dinner and then locked the door behind her. "Thanks, Adam. How'd you get the truck?"

"The STD's got Mom's car today," he said. "He brought her into work so he could change the oil. We've got time to get a coffee, if you want."

"I'm okay, but you can get one."

He shrugged. "I like the streaks of red. You do it yourself?"

Phoebe reflexively touched the spiked tips of her hair and thought of falling leaves. "Of course. Thanks."

"Yer welcome."

He backed the truck out of her driveway and took a left, which meant he was going the long way, around the lake.

"Soooo . . ." she said, "what's up?"

She now realized how quiet he'd been since Friday. A fair question that night would have been, "Hey, Phoebe, what the heck were you doing in the woods?" But he'd never asked it. He hadn't noticed, and Adam noticed most things around him. She realized she'd been so preoccupied that she hadn't even realized how preoccupied he'd been.

He shrugged again. "Later. I just want to drive around a little."

"Sure, Adam. Driving's good. Smell that clean lake air."

He laughed, and she knew him well enough not to pry it out of him. He would talk to her when he was ready.

The Oxoboxo woods looked different by daylight, and from the outside. She always thought the trees there were set more closely than in other forests, as if they were huddling together to keep secrets from the world outside their sylvan borders. She and her friends had spent a great deal of their young lives in the woods and the lake. The Oxoboxo was a place where one never felt a hundred percent safe, and that was what made being there so exciting.

Exciting, at least, until Colette died there.

"So you never told me how practice was," Phoebe said, turning to look out the windshield. "How was it playing with the corpsicle?"

She'd intended it to be a diversion, but she saw by his shocked look that her words struck close to whatever it was that was eating at him.

"Oh," she said.

"I thought that wasn't PC. Isn't that what you and Daffy were telling me the other day at lunch?"

"I'm *kidding*!" He was fronting and it was obvious, but if he wanted some time before he told her what was bothering him, that was fine.

His shoulders twitched again like they did whenever he was nervous. "You know, the dead kid wasn't so bad."

"Really?" she said, secretly thrilled.

"Really. He's strong as hell. I mean speedwise, he's slow. But he picks stuff up fast. By the end of practice he'd figured out a way to counter me throwing him. It was pretty cool, really."

"Wow, who would have thought?"

"Not me." And that was all he said about Tommy.

He rolled the car into the student parking lot moments later, and then they were out of the truck and making the long trek to school.

"Hey, I've got practice again tonight," he said. "You need to go to the library or anything?"

She smiled at him. "You want to do some midnight Frisbee?"

"Yeah," he said. "I might just need to do that."

Everything was normal on Monday. The living went quickly from class to class, chatting about weekend dates or the hundred subtle liaisons that occurred in the time that elapsed between the morning bell and lunchtime, while the dead moved in straight lines and shared their thoughts with no one, not even each other. Phoebe roamed and looked for Tommy Williams, catching glimpses of him from a calculated distance. He might have the advantage in the Oxoboxo woods with his stealth and his moonlight eyes, but among the living, she held the upper hand. Here in the fluorescent halls she could watch him at all times without him being aware of it.

But that did not mean the dead were incapable of surprises, as Margi proved by dropping the biggest one of all in the hallway after final bell. She was packed and ready to go to the bus before Phoebe even made it to her locker—that's how big it was.

"Sorry, Margi," Phoebe said, "no bus today. I'm hitting the library again."

"You're kidding," Margi said. "I have *got* to talk to you."

"What's up?"

"What's up with *you*?" was her reply, with more than a hint of accusation in her voice.

"Is this twenty questions, Margi? I don't know what I'm supposed to say now, and I don't want to make you miss your bus."

Margi looked at Phoebe, a mixture of impatience and sympathy on her smooth, round-cheeked face.

"Pheebes," she said, "you're my best friend and I love you. You know that. But something is up."

"Right, we've established that. So what, pray tell, is up?"

"Let me ask you: have you ever seen a living impaired kid draw on his notebook?"

Phoebe sighed. Leave it to Margi to bring the melodrama. "I don't think so, no."

"Do they ever contribute to the *Oakvale Review*?"

"No."

"Or take art or music classes?"

"No."

"Pick up digital photography or gardening on a kooky whim? Or basically do anything creative at all?"

"No, not to my vast knowledge."

"Not even decorate their lockers?"

"Margi! Get to the point!"

She did, and drove it home. "Tommy Williams has a poem hanging up in his locker," she said, "and it sure looks like it was written in your handwriting."

The precise moment that Phoebe's mouth opened in response to Margi's statement, the trunk to Pete Martinsburg's car popped up with a click from his key. The car was barely a month old, a birthday gift from dear old long-distance dad.

Pete wasn't stupid enough to think his dad's gift was anything other than an expression of spite for Pete's mom. It was all about getting vengeance on the ex-wife.

But hey, free car.

He led Adam and TC over to the car. It took some convincing to get Lame Man out of the locker room, and even now the big stiff was making a show of how boring this all was to him.

Pete knew how this was going to go, but he felt the need to give Adam one final test of faith before changing his strategy.

He went to the trunk and withdrew his football gear. Beneath the long black duffel bag was a trio of scuffed and scratched baseball bats. Pete took the aluminum one out of the trunk and, gripping it tightly with one hand, snapped it around with his wrist a couple times. His smile was cold and wide.

"Smacked fourteen homers with this baby my last year in the PAL league. I hit .313 that year."

Stavis nodded with appreciation, but Pete could tell that Adam was a hairsbreadth away from making some wiseass comment, and his grip on the bat tightened until his knuckles were white.

"We're going to teach zombie boy another sport after practice," he said, sneering. He dropped the bat back into the trunk, where it landed with a hollow thud, a sound not unlike the one that particular bat would make against a human skull, Adam thought.

Then the trunk slammed down with such force that the thought disappeared.

"Pete," Adam said. He didn't look so smug any longer, which strengthened Pete's resolve to carry the plan through.

"Yes, Lame Man?" he replied. "You have something you would like to contribute?"

"You aren't really suggesting that we go after this kid, are you?"

Pete laughed. "Why not? There's no law against it."

"C'mon, Pete. That's just stupid."

"Stupid? I'll tell you something that's stupid. Your little girl

Morticia Scarypants having the hots for a corpsicle, that's stupid."

"Leave her out of this. I'm talking—"

"You're flapping your jaw, but you aren't talking. Your chick, the one you've had a thing for, for what, your whole life? She's writing poetry to dead guys. She's coming to practice to watch a dead guy. A *dead guy*, Adam. How sick is that?"

"Shut up, Pete." Adam turned a bright crimson shade, and Pete smiled.

"And you're just going to let it happen. You aren't even going to try and get her playing on the right team, are you?"

Stavis, who was still smart enough to catch the signs, moved to Adam's left.

"What happened, Adam?" Pete said, dropping his voice to a low whisper. "What about you is so repulsive that the girl you've been pining after for years turns to a zombie for her lovin'?"

Adam took a step forward, his own hands balled into fists, but that was as far as it went. Pete wished he had taken a swing, because then they could throw a few punches, bloody each other up, and at the end of it they'd be friends again. They'd be the Pain Crew.

"You can walk away, Adam," he said to Adam's back, "but I'm not done. I'm not going to let that charming pale young flower lie down with a corpse. Not while I live and breathe."

Adam continued his walk back toward the school.

Pete said he wasn't done, and he meant it. The rumor making a loop around the school like a brush fire was so absurd that Pete couldn't even get his mind around it. A living, breathing, blossoming sixteen-year-old girl having a thing for a dead kid? It was just plain unnatural. Why not go just go and lie down with a farm animal? At least an animal is *alive*. He decided that he'd better take matters into his own hands.

Pete saw her in the library. He was already late for practice, but what the hell. What was coach going to do, fire him? And lose two interceptions a game? No way.

Besides, getting into this girl's skirt would be well worth the extra wind sprints.

"Hey," he said, sitting across from her.

She looked up and removed a shell-like headphone from one ear. Someone was screaming in pain through the speaker, the volume audible halfway across the library. He liked the way her dark eyeliner made her eyes look even more like a cat's. Slinky. And the best part was that this girl had no idea how slinky she was. She didn't have any friends in Pete's normal datepool, the cheerleaders and other gum-snapping types, the Toris and the Hollys and the Cammys who would have hooked up with him even if he were the ugliest guy on the football team.

He gave her a smile calculated for her to feel it in her toes. Hanging out with the college girls this summer had opened up some new worlds to him, femalewise. This girl was dark, she was serious, and she was bookish. He figured that less experienced guys wouldn't look at her twice, but to Pete, all of those factors were just part of the sweet secret that girls like this held, a sweet secret just waiting to be told to the whole world.

"Hey," he repeated.

"Hey," she said, a hint of question in her voice. He liked that. And she was shy; her pale white skin was turning pink at her throat. He made a point of watching the color spread.

"I saw you at practice yesterday," he said. If there was one thing that girls liked, it was to be noticed.

"You did?"

"Yeah, I did. I'd look up and there you were, watching us."

"I was waiting," she said, "for Adam."

Pete smiled inwardly to himself. Morticia was so far out of her league.

"Layman? He's not your boyfriend, is he?"

She laughed and shook her head, the pink glow hitting her cheeks. Her skin was the skin of angels, he thought, soft and white. He almost reached out to stroke her cheek, but he figured she'd spook. Soon.

"That's good," he said, "because Adam's a good friend of mine, and I'd hate to have him mad at me."

She stopped laughing. "Why would he be mad at you?"

Now it was his turn to laugh, which he did as he leaned back in the creaky library chair, spreading his arms so she could catch the definition of his arms.

"For asking you out."

She looked back down at her history book. Pete leaned forward. Willowy girls liked big guys, and he was a big guy; he made the shadow of his shoulders fall across her like a blanket.

"Because even if he was your boyfriend, I still would have asked you."

She looked like she was having trouble catching her breath.

It made him think of other ways he could make her breathless.

"I need to study," she said, her voice just above a whisper.

You do, he thought. "So is that a yes?" he said, his hand drifting to her arm. She was wearing a light sweater, and he rubbed the black fabric bunched at her elbow with his thumb and forefinger. "I can drive you home if you like. I'll tell Layman we've made some plans. You've probably seen my car around."

"No." Her voice was so soft he almost didn't hear it.

"No, you haven't seen my car? It's the . . ."

"No," she said. "No, I don't want to go out with you."

"What?"

"No," she said again. "Please stop. People are looking at us."

"I don't understand." He really didn't.

"I don't want to go out with you, Pete. Thank you, but no."

"Why not?" he said.

"I just don't want to. Please let go of my sweater."

He did, and leaned back, the chair groaning against his weight. First Layman cops a big attitude, and now this. Pete had been hiding his rage ever since his father packed him off to the airport without even dropping a dime to wish him a good flight, and now it threatened to erupt from his whole being.

"'I don't want to' isn't much of a reason, is it?" he said, his face close to hers.

"It's the best reason," she said, and he was surprised at how poorly he'd misjudged her. "Can this conversation be over, please?"

Pete forced his hands to relax and pushed himself slowly back from the table.

"Hey, I'm sorry," he said. "I thought I was picking up on something that I guess maybe I wasn't. I know I'm a little head-strong, probably because most of the girls I go out with like that. I'm sorry if I offended you."

She softened, but only a little. "It's okay," she told him. "I'm sorry I didn't give you a more graceful answer. Really, I'm flattered."

He gave a nod that he hoped made him appear wounded and crestfallen—as though he really cared what Scarypants thought of him. "Well, I didn't give you much of a chance, did I? Headstrong, that's me."

She smiled. He held out his hand.

"Friends?" he said.

She looked at his hand, and then up at his face, and smiled. "Friends," she said, and held out her hand for him to take.

He was planning on walking away. But something about the feel of her cool, slim hand in his changed everything. She had long, slender fingers, and he blinked and thought for a moment, just one moment, that he was holding Julie's hand. He hadn't had a relationship with anyone like that since Julie died. Julie who died and would not, could not, come back. The rage welled in his mind.

Still gripping her hand, he leaned in close and whispered into her ear. "Layman is tagging you, isn't he?"

She looked up at him then, her eyes more like a cat's than ever. The color returned to her face and she tried to pull her hand back, but he was too strong.

"Least, I hope the Lame Man is tagging you. Because if I find out that you are passing me over for some dead meat, I might get pretty upset. I might get pretty damn upset that the girl I had pegged for a closet nympho is really a closet necrophiliac, you know what I'm saying? And people, dead or otherwise, could get hurt."

She didn't look away even though he was squeezing her hand hard enough to bring tears to her eyes. After a time he blew her a kiss and stood up, giving her hand a gentle stroke as he let go.

CHAPTER EIGHT

*T*HE HITS KEEP ON COMING, Adam thought, watching Stavis rock Williams with a blindside chop block. It would have knocked the wind out of a living kid. Williams was pushed off his feet, and Stavis used his momentum to drill him into the ground.

Williams made no sound. But then, Williams never made a sound.

The play, a halfback draw, was over before Stavis's hit. And it was nowhere near Williams.

Adam was experiencing a tightness in his chest that had nothing to do with his physical conditioning, but with the mental conditioning he'd worked on over the summer with Master Griffin.

He closed his eyes and could see Master Griffin as he met him on the first day of class; his shaved head smooth and glossy in the bright light of the dojo, the merest hint of a smile beneath his thick black mustache.

"We are all gifted with power," he'd said to his students. Adam watched the lithe, catlike way that Master Griffin walked around the practice mat, almost like he was gliding along on the balls of his feet.

"All of us," he'd said, looking at each of them in turn. "It is what we do with that power that is important."

Then he told Adam to try to tackle him. Master Griffin was shorter and more compact than Adam, and much lighter. Adam came at him with a wary confidence. Tackling people was what he did. He moved in low, going for the legs.

Suddenly he was airborne, but it was a short flight. Griffin brought him onto the mat and somehow cushioned his fall. Then instead of letting him go, Griffin maintained a tight grip on Adam's arm with one hand, while his free hand was cocked back and ready for a flat-palm strike. Adam looked at the rigid line of that palm and knew with certainty that Griffin could break his nose or smash his face in with one quick thrust. But he just tapped Adam twice on the chest before hauling Adam to his feet.

"Adam has power," Master Griffin had said to the class. "I have power. Each of you do. What will we do with that power?"

That had been the only physical contact of the first session, Master Griffin tossing his biggest, most athletic student like he'd toss his dirty socks into the laundry hamper. He'd spent the rest of the session teaching them forms and talking about personal responsibility.

"Layman," Coach Konrathy yelled. "wake up and get your ass on the line."

Adam complied and "put his ass" on the offensive line. As he did he could almost hear Master Griffin's calm voice in his head, asking him just how much of his ass he was willing to put on the line for his beliefs.

The dead kid got up the way he always did—slowly— but did not seem injured by Stavis's illegal hit. Adam tried to get into his head. What, if anything, was going on in there? Why was Williams even out here? Did he have something to prove? Was it love of the game? Did he even realize that there were teammates of his working hard to take him out of the game—permanently? There just didn't seem to be any point in offering himself up to the punishment he was experiencing.

And—the thought creeped in like rain through cracks in the ceiling—did Phoebe really have a thing for him? Why would she find him the least bit attractive? How on earth could a dead kid interest her in that way? There had to be some crossing of wires, somewhere.

Back in the locker room, the sudden silence told him that Williams was passing through. Williams didn't shower, at least he never showered with the rest of the team in the gang showers down the hall. He didn't sweat, and one could just as easily wash the mud and turf off one's face at home as in the showers.

Adam shucked off his shoulder pads and covertly watched the reactions of his teammates as the dead kid walked by. The open hostility of the remaining Pain Crew was pretty easy to register: Martinsburg was whispering something to his head thug, Stavis, and to Harris Morgan, who looked to be first on the recruiting list now that Adam had dissolved his membership.

Most of the team turned away, like the presence of the dead kid was an embarrassing secret that no one wanted to acknowledge. Denny Mackenzie, whose neck had been saved today by Williams when he blocked a charging Martinsburg coming in for the sack on Mackenzie's blind side, was pretending to be fully engrossed in something that Gary Greene was saying. Williams opened his locker, withdrew his backpack, and headed for the stairs.

Tommy Williams was a player on the Oakvale Badgers, but no one seemed very pleased about it. Konrathy was leaning in the doorway of his office, watching Williams make a deliberate path toward the exit.

Thornton Harrowwood had the locker closest to the door. He was sitting on the wooden bench with a damp towel wrapped around his skinny waist and was stuffing his filthy uniform into a large green duffel that was nearly as big as he was. He looked up at Williams as he passed and held up his hand like it was no big deal, and Williams slapped it gently without breaking his ponderous stride. Like it was no big deal.

Adam smiled, but then Konrathy called Thornton into his office. Adam became so engrossed in trying to figure out what was being discussed behind the closed door that he almost didn't see his former pals in the Pain Crew skip the showers and follow Williams out the door.

"He's talking to that spooky bitch," TC said as they crossed the lot toward the woods.

"Doesn't change a damn thing," Martinsburg said. He was twirling the aluminum bat, his wrist making swift circles. "Harris, she's your responsibility. If she tries to run or interfere, stop her."

"Aww, man. I ain't hitting no girl."

"I ask you to hit her? Just stop her." Martinsburg pointed the bat at Harris Morgan's chest. Pete outweighed the fit running back by a good forty pounds and Harris took a half step back, but it was Pete's expression more than the bat that did it.

"Stop her," Harris said. "Got it."

"If you plan on punking out like Layman, you'd better tell me now."

Harris shook his head.

Martinsburg looked again at their quarry, who had turned and entered the woods with Little Miss Scarypants.

"Now, what do you suppose they're up to in the woods?" he said, sending a long stream of spit through his teeth and onto the asphalt. "She gonna help him get his pads off?"

The dead kid had knocked the wind out of him at practice today. Pete had been just a few steps away from leveling the quarterback with his shoulder when the dead kid came from *his* blind side and sent him down, driving all of the wind from his lungs.

There was one moment when the zombie stood over him while he lay flat on his back, his closed lungs struggling to draw in air. The dead kid looked down, and Pete felt a moment of breathless panic as he saw the cold gray glare of his eyes under the shade of his helmet.

Now you know what it feels like to be dead. He could hear the zombie's voice in his head, and he thought he detected the slightest tic of a muscle by his mouth.

How do you like it?

Williams left him there on the turf. Pete's breath was slow in returning, and through it all he couldn't get the image out of his mind of the zombie laughing at him. He was frightened by that image, but fear only served to make him angrier. No one, dead or alive, was going to laugh at Pete Martinsburg and get away with it.

"We'll just come up the path," he said, "and when we get close we'll spread out in the woods. I'll kick it off. Unless they smell Stavis here."

"What?" Stavis said, looking down at his grubby and fragrant uniform.

"You could have at least showered," Pete said. "You reek." Harris laughed, nodding in agreement.

There were a few kids and their parents milling about the parking lot, but no one really seemed to notice them. Pete nodded to his two henchmen.

"Okay," he said, "it's on."

They followed him into the woods.

* * *

Phoebe wasn't sure how she was going to broach the subject of her poetry with Tommy, but he saved her the trouble once they stepped into the woods.

"I have your poem . . . in my locker," he said. "I realized . . . that this . . . could be a problem for you."

Phoebe shook her head and tried to think how she should respond. Funny how the clarity of his speech, which flowed more quickly that the average living impaired person's, was giving her speech troubles.

"No," she said, "I was surprised, I guess."

"Your friend," he said, "with the pink hair."

Phoebe laughed. "Margi."

"I did not think of the . . . consequences," he said, somehow getting all those syllables out in one word. "Everyone . . . knows. I am sorry."

She shook her head and took a step closer to him. He didn't smell like someone who had been at football practice for the past couple hours. He didn't smell like a dead person, for that matter, either. The crisp scent of pine and autumn leaves was all she could smell. His skin was so smooth and white; he looked like a sculpture come to life, someone's idealized version of a young man, without blemishes or flaws.

"Don't be," she said, touching his arm, which felt like smooth stone beneath her fingers. "I wanted you to have it."

He gave a slight nod, his bottomless stare fixed on her. His gaze was disconcerting, to say the least. His eyes did not track when they were talking, and when he blinked, which wasn't often, she could count to three before his eyelids touched. He raised his hand as though to touch her cheek, and she thought of how gentle he'd been when he'd removed the leaf caught in her hair.

He surprised her by turning away, the movement sudden and swift.

"This is . . . difficult," he said, "for both . . . of us. Friendship . . . always is. Much less . . ."

She didn't get to hear what else he had to say, because at that moment two figures moving low ran at Tommy. One swung a baseball bat and hit Tommy in the chest, knocking him off his feet and onto a rotting log. His helmet bounced twice and landed near Phoebe, who shrieked as a third figure came from behind her and leveled a bat at her throat.

"Shhh," Harris Morgan said. Then he smiled.

"So you like sports, do you, zombie?" Martinsburg said. The bat he was holding out at his side came down with a sickening crack. Phoebe couldn't see where the blow landed, her line of sight obscured by Harris and the log that Tommy had fallen over.

"Stop it!" she yelled.

"Shut her up," Martinsburg said over his shoulder as he prepared himself for another swing. Harris looked back at Pete, unsure how to translate that particular directive, and Phoebe used the moment to jump on him, swinging her fists.

She punched him once, and they stumbled, but she ended up on her back, the limbs of the trees high above spinning in a kaleidoscope of fall colors. She was dimly aware of Harris rising from her, cursing and licking his lower lip.

Then she heard the sound of Martinsburg's bat whistling again.

It wasn't easy to rise to a sitting position, but she did. Martinsburg, grinning, was motioning for Stavis to take a turn. She tried to stand, but Harris poked her in the chest with the end of his bat and told her to sit down, swearing. She was gratified to see a thin line of blood where her knuckle had cut his lip.

She saw Stavis hefting the bat with both hands over his head.

"You have no idea how big a mistake you have made."

The deep, even voice belonged to Adam. Phoebe turned to see him looming on the path from where Martinsburg and his cronies had launched their attack. He was speaking to Harris, but he turned to look at the other two as well.

"Stay out of this, Layman," Martinsburg said. Stavis lowered his bat and regarded the new threat. Phoebe noticed that he was actually wider and heavier than Adam, although not quite as tall or as fast, but Phoebe guessed it didn't really matter when Stavis was holding a baseball bat.

"No," Adam said, and took two steps, closing the distance between them.

"I told you to pick a team, Lame Man," Martinsburg said.

"Guess I did," Adam replied, still moving right at Pete.

"Be a shame if one of your knees got busted out," Martinsburg said, but there was a shrill quality to his words, an absence of confidence that hadn't been there before Adam had appeared. "Like your gimp buddy, Manetti."

"A shame," Adam repeated. He was about five feet away from Pete when Harris dropped his bat and dove at him.

Phoebe called a warning as she scrambled for the bat, and Adam's left foot lashed out and caught Harris square in the solar plexus, knocking him flat on his back. But Stavis didn't have the qualms that Harris Morgan did about striking a fellow Badger, apparently, because just as Phoebe turned, he stepped in and gave a short thrust to Adam's stomach, and Adam went down on all fours. Stavis made a move like he was going to hit him again, and Phoebe screamed, throwing the bat Morgan had dropped, which Stavis deflected awkwardly, stumbling backward.

She stood up and faced the two, and saw that behind Martinsburg, Tommy had risen to one knee. Martinsburg caught her reaction and turned back toward Tommy.

"You just stay put," he said, "or I'm going to walk over there and beat your girlfriend bloody." He looked back at her and spat. "I might do it anyway."

Phoebe watched as Tommy looked up at his attacker and did one of those three-second blinks. Then he set his leg down and kneeled on the soft soil of the forest floor.

"Yeah, that's right, dead boy," Martinsburg said, twirling the bat, "she might not come back."

There was such hatred in his voice that Phoebe could almost feel it. Stavis stood between her and Martinsburg; Adam was retching into the soil. Harris was groaning, but she heard him starting to get up.

Tommy was staring up at Pete. Pete walked toward him and readied his bat.

The first figure that appeared out of the woods was nearly Adam's size. To Phoebe's buzzing mind it was as though he had materialized out of the darkness of the forest. A second figure and then a third—the girl with platinum hair who liked short skirts, and a pale boy with a shock of faded red hair—appeared from behind trees and clusters of brush, until there were six figures in a loose ring around them.

Harris, still separated from his bat and rubbing his chest as though to erase the print of Adam's sneaker, made another colorful comment as a seventh figure appeared behind him on the path. The eerie silence with which these new players had appeared sent a chill through Phoebe, one that was amplified as yet another figure walked past to stand between her and Stavis.

"Colette?" Phoebe whispered.

Martinsburg and his cronies milled around, not sure how they should react to this new development. There were eight kids total, standing in a loose ring around them, motionless as tombstones.

The giant one, his movements awkward, helped Tommy to his feet. He regarded Pete with an expressionless stare that still managed to convey a threat that was unmistakable.

He straightened up, and Phoebe saw that he was even taller than Adam. He loomed over Stavis and Pete the way the gray trees loomed over them all, the newly risen moon throwing its shadow over them like a shroud.

"You . . . might . . . not," he said, his halting voice filled with quiet force, "make . . . it . . . back."

The ring of dead kids began to close. The giant spoke, and

each of them took one step forward, tightening the circle like a noose. Harris was the first to run, but Martinsburg and Stavis were close behind.

Phoebe, her eyes wide, thought she caught the hint of a smile on Tommy's lips. But the moment passed, and she ran over to Adam, who was still trying to shake off the effects of the hit to the gut.

"Are you okay?" she said, crouching next to him. Her skirt was ripped and there were twigs and leaves all over her. She was going to have a great time explaining this to her parents.

Adam groaned and spit. "P . . . peachy."

The dead kids had begun to disperse, silently shambling back into the forest in the directions they had come from. One of them, the young-looking boy with the red hair, made an odd high bleating sound, and Phoebe realized he was trying to laugh. Short Skirt Girl smiled at her and said "Bye!" in an amused, perky fashion before skipping away down a pine needle–strewn path.

Phoebe scanned for Colette and saw her just as she turned and melted into the forest. Soon all but the giant and Tommy were gone.

"This is Mal." Tommy motioned. "He is . . . large."

"Hello, Mal," Phoebe said, and Mal began lifting his arm. "Tommy, are you hurt? My God, they were hitting you with baseball bats!" Mal finished lifting his arm, and three of his fingers twitched. Phoebe realized he was waving.

Tommy's head swiveled from side to side. "The blows did not hurt . . . as much . . . as the . . . idea . . . of the blows."

"Tommy," she said. Adam coughed.

"Take care . . . of your friend. And"—Tommy paused, but something made Phoebe think it wasn't the half-speed of undeath that was holding him up, but finding the right words—"*thank* him . . . for me."

She watched Tommy walk into the forest, Mal following him like an enormous shadow.

CHAPTER NINE

*P*HOEBE LOOKED OUT THE grimy window of Adam's truck, scanning the woods and thinking about those kids and where they might have come from. Her sleep last night had been restless, and having Adam drive her to school today just made the events of last night seem even more surreal.

Last night Adam hadn't said two words on the entire drive home, and this morning it was she who didn't want to speak.

"Do you understand what happened last night?" Adam asked. "What was that? I don't even know who half of those kids were."

"Colette," she said. Her heartbeat felt like she'd tripled up the caffeine dose in her morning brew. "Colette was there."

Adam was silent for a moment. "Yeah. Colette. And that girl from the lunchroom, I recognized her. But who was that big black kid, and the one that was smiling? Where did they all come from?"

"I have no idea."

"You know, some of them were watching the practice the other night," he said. "They don't go to our school, do they?"

"Some of them do," she replied. "Not Mal, though."

"Colette didn't say anything to you, did she?"

"No. No, she didn't."

Adam nodded as though he understood the significance of that.

"That was weird, is all I can say. It's like they live out there or something. Or whatever you call it."

Phoebe hugged herself. "Not to mention that you were hit with a bat. A *baseball bat*, Adam."

"Yeah," Adam replied. "Yeah, that was a first. Clocked the wind right out of me."

Phoebe looked over at him, and he was actually grinning, like it had been some kind of adventure.

"Adam, has football left you that desensitized to violence? How can you be so flip about what happened?"

"I've gotten into fights before," he said, shrugging. "Never with bats, though."

"Is that all you have to say?" she said. "We watched Tommy get *beaten*. With *clubs*. I think they were trying to kill him."

"He's already dead, so . . ."

"Adam!" she said, her voice loud enough to make him flinch. "You know what I mean!"

"Okay," he said. "Okay, I'm sorry. I guess I wasn't thinking of it like that."

"They could have hurt us too, if Tommy's friends hadn't come."

"I don't think they would have done that, Pheeble. I think . . ."

"So it's okay to beat a living impaired person?"

"That isn't what I mean. I . . ."

"Let's just drop it, okay?" she said, turning toward the passenger window.

"I'm sorry," he said after a moment. "I guess I just wasn't thinking about being threatened. The whole thing was just so weird."

She didn't answer and continued to stare out the window. She thought it was weird, too, and with each passing mile she expected a living impaired person to appear suddenly out of the woods.

"Say," he said, "what were you doing out there, anyhow?"

Phoebe squeezed her eyes shut. "Let's not talk right now, okay, Adam? Can we talk about this later?"

"Sure, Pheeble," he said. His touch was light and brief on her shoulder. "Sure."

Phoebe didn't know why she felt like crying. She opened her eyes and saw dead kids, dozens of them, lumbering through the woods toward the road. She blinked once and they were gone. She looked back at Adam, as solid and sure as an oak tree. He was trying to rescue me, she thought, and the guilty realization cooled her anger.

"I wish I'd gotten some sleep last night." That's all I need, she thought. My mind's playing tricks on me.

"I slept pretty well, surprisingly," he said. "That violent lifestyle I have, always punching guys, living or dead. Gives me inner peace, you know?"

"You're a jerk, Adam," she said, but when her eyes met his, she burst out into a nervous laugh.

She wanted to catch a quick nap in the warm, safe confines of Adam's truck, but when she opened her eyes again, Oakvale High loomed ahead, ready to admit the students coming off the few buses parked in the looping drive. Adam found a space in the student lot, and they started toward the school.

They approached just as Tommy Williams was getting off the bus. He was wearing new jeans, new high-top sneakers, and a navy blue polo shirt.

"He doesn't look like a guy who took a beating last night," Adam whispered.

"No," Phoebe agreed. She thought he looked good. Flawless.

Tommy saw them and tried to smile. Then he waved, and suddenly Phoebe did not feel so tired anymore.

Margi, who didn't have any of Adam's social grace or understanding, began badgering Phoebe the moment she saw her.

"What's wrong, Pheeb? Ohmigod, you look terrible."

"Thanks, Margi. I can always count on you to help build my flagging self-esteem." Phoebe laughed.

"No, really," she said, her bangle-covered arm looping around Phoebe's shoulder. "What's wrong? Did something happen?"

"Yeah, something happened," Phoebe said, almost instantly regretting her words.

"What? What is it?"

"Nothing." Phoebe tried to play it off. "I'm just kidding." Her locker popped on the first try, and Phoebe wondered if her luck was changing.

"Phoebe, talk to me. Did you have a fight with your parents? With Adam? Did he ask you out?"

Phoebe, having been interrogated by Margi dozens of times, knew that eventually she would build up to "the dead kid."

"Colette," Phoebe said. "I saw Colette last night."

Phoebe's strategy worked; she found the only topic on which she could get Margi to shut up completely, and she didn't even have to lie to do it. Margi's eyes narrowed under the fringe of pink spikes dangling from her forehead.

"We need to talk to her, Margi."

Margi sucked at the corner of her lip, the same corner she'd pierced last summer.

"You couldn't have saved her," Phoebe said. "It isn't your fault she died. It's nobody's fault."

Margi looked away, fellow students passing on either side of them in a rush to get to class.

"We didn't handle it right," Phoebe said.

"I know," Margi said finally, "I know."

"But we have another chance. We can . . ."

"I know," Margi said, her voice rising. "I know, I know, I know! I just can't do it now!"

She turned on her heels and jingled down the hall at a rapid clip.

Phoebe watched her go, wondering just why she'd felt the need to alienate all of her good friends in a single morning. "Wait up, Margi!" she called, hurrying to catch up.

"Not another word," Margi said.

"My lips are sealed," Phoebe responded, following her into the classroom.

Moments later Principal Kim's reassuring voice came on the PA after the morning announcements to let everyone know that there would be a schoolwide assembly immediately after homeroom, and that students were to proceed in an orderly fashion to the auditorium.

Margi, never one to enjoy silence, reached over and gripped Phoebe's forearm. She had pink smiley skulls painted over the black background of her fingernails.

"Yes! No history today!"

Phoebe returned her smile. Margi was always quick to bounce back from a tiff, which was a great equalizer for someone as excitable as she was. The bell rang, and they started to proceed toward the auditorium. The halls were already filled with students. Phoebe saw the pumpkin-like head of TC Stavis bobbing above a sea of students. The auditorium was twice the size it needed to be for the average enrollment at Oakvale High; she and Margi were herded into a pair of seats toward the middle of the cavernous half bowl.

"Slide all the way down," Mr. Allen said in his monotone. "Fill every open seat."

Phoebe noticed that there were some open seats around the few dead kids who were scattered around the auditorium.

"Is this about the fund-raiser?" Margi said. "I hope it isn't the fund-raiser. If it is, I hope it isn't the candles. Who wants to buy a candle anyway? For fifteen dollars?"

Phoebe didn't think this was about candles. She watched Principal Kim, looking bright and energetic in a peach suit, lead two people onto the stage—the first a young woman in a pale blue suit. Her shiny blond hair was pulled back in an unassuming ponytail, and she wore glasses with dark frames and wide lenses. She was simply stunning.

She stopped at the edge of the stage to help her companion, a frail old man who held her arm while being assisted on the other side by Mr. Hill, the gym teacher. Phoebe was terrible at guessing anyone's age over twenty, but she had him pegged as being in his eighties. He turned briefly to the crowd while making slow progress up the short stairway, and Phoebe thought there was something familiar in the beaked nose and shock of sculpted white hair.

"Who's the codger?" Margi asked.

Phoebe, not quite able to place his face, shook her head.

Principal Kim quelled the crowd and made introductions.

"Today we are joined by two people who have dedicated their lives to promoting and educating people on the topic of diversity. Prior to the events of recent years, the term 'diversity' had been most typically used to describe a diversity of culture, religion, ethnicity, or sexual orientation. Today the term may also be applied to diverse states of being. Alish Hunter and his daughter Angela have created the Hunter Foundation for the Advancement and Understanding of Differently Biotic Persons, and are here today to discuss an exciting new opportunity that you will have here at Oakvale High. Please join me in welcoming Angela Hunter to the podium."

The applause was halfhearted, but rose in volume when the hormonal males in the audience realized how gorgeous Angela Hunter was. With her intentionally bookish look, Phoebe thought she looked like a youthful teacher in an eighties hair-metal video, the one who would rip off the trappings of schoolmarmery as soon as the guitar solo kicked in, to reveal a hot-pink bikini and stunning tanned body beneath. Ms. Hunter smiled with pursed lips, almost a smirk, which made Phoebe think that she had calculated the crowd's reaction exactly.

"Thank you, Principal Kim," she said. "And thank you, students of Oakvale High, for your attention and the opportunity to speak to you today about differently biotic people. The people that we at the Hunter Foundation refer to as *differently biotic* are those people that most of you would refer to as *living impaired*. They are the people that some of you, and many outside the walls of this school, would refer to as *zombies, corpsicles, dead heads*, the *undead, worm food, shamblers*, the *living dead*, the *Children of Romero*, and a whole host of other pejorative names designed to hurt and marginalize."

"Wow," Margi whispered. Whatever hormonal restlessness Ms. Hunter had inspired in the auditorium was silenced by the quick, no-nonsense manner in which she had lobbed a mental hand grenade into the room. Virtually every student, Phoebe noted, was as silent as—well, as silent as a differently biotic person.

"We at the Hunter Foundation feel that even the term *living impaired*, although created I'm sure with the best of intentions, is in fact pejorative, as it implies that people who are no longer alive but still with us are broken and or defective. In much the same way that the term *handicapped* was widely recognized as being insulting to differently abled persons, so too is living impaired an insult to those who live differently biotic lives.

"At the Hunter Foundation, we do not believe that the dialogue regarding the understanding and promotion of differently biotic persons begins and ends with its terms and definitions, however. It is one thing to create the appropriate language of discourse; it is another to actually move the culture to a point of acceptance, and we believe that the correct way to do that is through the application of science, both with traditionally hard science and the social sciences."

"Whaaaaat?" Margi said. Phoebe shushed her.

"We believe that differently biotic persons are, in fact, alive—and yet no one knows how they are alive. Part of what we do at the Hunter Foundation is aimed at discovering what makes a differently biotic person tick, for lack of a better term, from a biological perspective. But another part of what we do is discovering what makes them tick from a psychological perspective. Being differently biotic puts these people in a very small cultural group. They are a true minority—and the minority status is one that is sure to have deep psychological implications."

Head shrinkers for the undead set, Phoebe thought.

"Another function of our foundation—and the one in which you can help us the most—is to take the results of our studies and tests and bring them to society at large. Our goal is the complete integration of differently biotic persons into society. We dream of a world where a differently biotic person can walk down a crowded city street without fear. We understand that for our dream to become a reality, everyone else on that crowded city street must be able to walk without fear of the differently biotic person, as well. To that end, we are asking for volunteers among you to participate in our learning lab. Your school is unique among Connecticut schools in that you have the highest ratio per capita of differently biotic persons among you; therefore you have both the responsibility and the privilege of helping teach the rest of the country and the world about what DB people have to offer, and vice versa.

"What we are offering is a chance to learn about yourselves and those who are different from you. The Hunter Foundation, while economically solid, is not an organization that many members of the status quo want to participate in. The topic of DB rights is still politically incendiary. We understand that for someone to join us requires a certain degree of bravery and emotional fortitude. But for those of you who are interested in making a positive social statement, at the risk of attacking the norms of society, working with us can be a deeply rewarding experience.

"We have some friends in the political realm, and we have been able to get our Differently Biotic Work Study program accreditation. For those of you who sign up, you will be given three AP credits, providing you give your full and best effort to the program."

She waited a moment for that to sink in. Phoebe wondered if AP credits were enough of a carrot to interest anyone. Many of the students in the audience were clearly put off by the whole topic, and she looked around to see if any of the *differently biotic* students had any feelings about the proposed course.

"There are two components of the work study. First, you will have to work. We have a variety of positions that we need to staff: clerical, maintenance, and security. You will be paid for your time. The second component is that you must participate in a weekly DB focus group, where traditionally biotic students will meet in a moderated discussion with DB students. The goal at all times will be acceptance; we understand the road to acceptance can only be taken through mutual understanding."

She paused, basking in the stillness of the room. "Are there any questions?"

Very few hands went up. Angela pointed at one toward the front.

"What do you mean by 'differently biotic'? Are you saying that dead kids are alive?"

Phoebe couldn't see the girl who had asked the question, but she could see Ms. Hunter's wry grin.

"No," she said, "I am saying they are differently biotic—that they are alive in a different way than, say, you and a mushroom are alive." Phoebe smiled; the smarter kids in the school laughed.

"In truth, we do not understand the biology of a DB person. It is one of the fields that our foundation is endeavoring to explore."

"Why do only teenagers come back as zomb—as differently bionic?"

"*Biotic*. We don't know yet; nor do we know why the phenomenon seems to happen only to American children. But surely there is a clue there; a popular theory is that there is something that triggers the process in the series of immunizations that American children undergo."

Ms. Hunter nodded to a girl on the aisle near the front of the room.

"My dad says that it isn't natural, people coming back from the dead. He says that there's stuff in the Bible that talks about the dead coming up out of their graves, and that it means the world will end soon."

Ms. Hunter frowned, but Phoebe thought her expression was one of concentration rather than disgust.

"With all due respect to your father's beliefs," she replied evenly, "we have found nothing in our extensive studies that suggests the phenomena of the differently biotic is a sign of the Apocalypse. Of course, we could be wrong, but we prefer to look at the phenomenon as a scientific puzzle to be answered rather than a metaphysical conundrum."

There was a thin pale arm among the few that were raised, and when Ms. Hunter smiled and pointed, the question was slow in coming. Phoebe could hear Margi's sharp intake of breath next to her.

Colette.

"Can . . . dead . . . kids . . . join . . . too?"

Phoebe thought she could write all of Colette's post-demise speech on a single Post-it note.

Angela's response was effusive. "Absolutely. As I said, Oakvale High has the distinction of being the first school in the state to commit to creating a DB studies program. I think the experience will be more rewarding for everyone if we get a strong DB enrollment."

She focused on Colette as she spoke, as though the warmth of her smile could bring some color back to her pale dead skin.

"I believe we have time for one more question . . . Yes, in the blue sweatshirt."

"How much do you pay?"

Ms. Hunter laughed. "You could probably make more at the mall. But the educational work study is certain to look better on your college application than a part-time gig at Cinnabon."

Principal Kim rejoined Angela at the podium. She waited for the polite laughter to end, then she said, "Thank you all for giving us the chance to talk to you today. I am hoping to see a good number of you at the foundation."

Principal Kim began clapping and allowed the students to clap for a few listless minutes before talking about how the application process would work, what the qualifications were, and how many would be accepted.

"Applications can be picked up at the front of the stage from myself or Ms. Hunter, or, if you prefer, in the office. The applications are due on Friday."

"Well, that was still better than history," Margi said. "Too bad it didn't cut into English. Phoebe . . . where are you going?"

Phoebe looked back but remained silent as she joined the few differently biotic kids walking against the tide of students eager to make their way out of the auditorium. She saw Tommy, Colette, that boy Evan who was in the woods last night, and a few others. Adam was waiting at the end of an aisle.

"Are you going to sign up?" she asked him.

"Yep. You?"

"Uh-huh."

There weren't many takers, but that fact didn't seem to drain any of the warmth from Angela Hunter's smile as she handed Phoebe an application, which looked to be three grayish sheets stapled together.

"Could I have two?" she asked. "I'm hoping I can convince my friend to join with me."

"Have a whole stack," Ms. Hunter said, peeling off copies. "I don't think I'll need them all."

Phoebe passed Colette on her way back, and Colette seemed to see her for the first time since her death.

Phoebe thought she was trying to smile.

Pete Martinsburg wasn't smiling. He had sat through the entire assembly staring up at the hot blonde.

He hadn't slept well since the debacle in the forest. When he did sleep, his dreams were of Julie, but not the Julie of puppy love, ice-cream cones, and being thirteen. This was dead Julie, returned to the world. He dreamed of Julie holding hands, but it wasn't his hand she was holding, it was Tommy Williams.

She might not come back, this nightmare-Tommy told him. But in the dream it was Pete who moved at half speed; nightmare-Tommy was quick in getting to his car, the one Pete had driven around all summer. The one Pete had never sat in with his father.

Now you know what it is like . . . he heard the cold, hollow voice in his head say as the zombie brought the car to life . . . *to be dead.*

The car lurched into hyperdrive, accelerating as it approached a brick wall that had grown from the asphalt. The car struck the wall as a yellow blur that blossomed into an explosive flame, and Pete awoke with the sound of Julie's screams and the dead boy's laughter ringing in his head.

But of course Julie, the real Julie and not the ashen, flat-eyed Julie who walked his dreams, had not been able to scream. Good old Dad had broken the news ever so gently in his classic style, over the phone with a continent separating him from his son. He'd called at Christmastime. It was right after Pete had tried to tell him what a football hero he'd been that season, how many tackles he'd made, how many interceptions he'd caught for the Badgers.

"Oh hey, Pete," his dad had said. Pete could remember the conversation in exact detail, the way he could recall all of the conversations he'd had with his father since he'd left them. "Hey, you remember that girl Julie you played with over the summer?"

Played with, as though they would be playing hide-and-seek.

"Marissa's daughter? Remember Marissa, that woman I used to date?"

Pete remembered, with growing dread. No news was the only good news Dad was capable of providing.

"Well, her daughter, Julie, died about two weeks after you went back home to your mother. Helluva thing. She had a massive asthma attack. They said it was triggered by a spider bite or something."

Helluva thing.

He watched Angela Hunter laughing with Layman and Scarypants, and the pen he'd been tapping on the back of the chair in front of him snapped in his hand, spilling a long blue bubble of ink onto his skin.

He smeared the ink bubble onto the seat cushion next to him. Dad was utterly clueless about how Pete had felt toward Julie. Just like he was clueless that Pete would never feel that way about anyone ever again.

The sad tale of Dallas Jones, the original zombie, had hit the media a few weeks after his dad broke the news of Julie's death to him. At first, Pete had secretly clung to the hope that Julie might come back, but when she didn't, that hadn't surprised him either. People hung around the edges of his life, but they never really "came back."

His hand was blue from the base of his little finger all the way down to his wrist. People had begun to leave the auditorium, but not Morticia Scarypants; she was still hanging around where the hot blonde stood trying to pass out sign-up sheets. There was something about Phoebe that reminded him of Julie.

Why Scarypants gave him this feeling, he wasn't sure. Julie had been the furthest thing from a goth and she hadn't been the dress-and-boots-wearing type, either. But there was something— an expression, a smile. Something.

He watched Phoebe for a little while, and then he left to go wash his hands in the big lavatory outside the auditorium. He ran the water as hot as he could stand it and squirted six shots of the thin pink hand soap into his palms and worked up a lather. The restroom door swung open, and he heard someone shuffle in. Frowning, he looked up and saw the blue-gray face of Tommy Williams in the spotted mirror.

"Didn't think you'd have much use for this room," Pete said, smiling and shaking his hands over the sink. "Seeing as how the parts don't really work anymore. They don't, do they?"

He watched Williams clench and unclench his hands.

"Leave . . . me alone," the dead boy said, his strange voice echoing over plumbing and tile. "Leave . . . Phoebe . . . alone."

Pete thought about walking over and drying his hands on the dead boy's shirt, but the idea of coming that close to his body without the benefit of football pads and tape was nauseating to him.

"You should be the one leaving her alone," he said. "Freak."

Tommy took another step toward Pete, and Pete had a moment of panic because he really didn't know what he would do if the zombie reached for him or took a swing at him. There wasn't anyone in the school he was afraid to fight with, from Adam on down—anyone living, that is. He'd tried a half-dozen different ways to hurt him in practice, but the zombie had shaken him off like droplets of sweat off his skin.

"I know . . . what you are . . . thinking," Tommy said, the left side of his mouth lifting in a sick approximation of a smile. "You are thinking . . . what do I . . . do . . . if he . . . hits me? What do I . . . do . . . if he puts his . . . hands . . . on me?"

"You can't get inside my head," Pete said, but he saw Tommy raise his hand and cover the light switch with it. Pete looked over his shoulder at the door. He didn't want to be in the dark with the zombie; not in this bathroom, not anywhere, ever.

"I'm already in your . . . head," Tommy said, his voice a dry whisper. Pete felt the exhalation of air touch his cheek, and he shuddered. "Do your worst at practice. It . . . only makes me . . . stronger. But do not . . . threaten . . . my friends."

Pete was about to reply, but he couldn't find the words, and then the lights went out. He threw a punch in the dark, hit nothing but air, and threw another one with the same result, then covered up, expecting a rain of blows that never came. A moment later the lavatory door swung open and the room was illuminated with light from the noisy hallway outside.

Pete felt along the wall and got the lights on a moment before Norm Lathrop entered. Norm hesitated upon seeing Pete, probably debating whether or not he should just run out the door before Pete had a chance to terrorize him.

"You're in my way," Pete said. He took a paper towel out of the dispenser and wiped his forehead.

"I'm sorry," Norm said, almost jumping on the way to the urinals.

I've got to do something about the freakin' zombies, Pete thought, and punched open the bathroom door.

CHAPTER TEN

"So," PHOEBE SAID, SQUEEZING over next to the dirty bus window. There weren't all that many students taking the bus home, but she and Margi usually shared one of the double seats.

"So what?"

"So what do you think?"

Margi was practicing being "obtuse." "About what?"

"About the assembly, brainiac."

"Oh. I don't know." She took her iPod out of her satchel and started to scroll through the long list of bands.

Phoebe sighed. "I'm going to join," she said, "if I can get in."

"I figured you would," Margi said. She selected a song off of M.T. Graves's solo album *All the Graves Are Empty Except Mine* and pushed the volume until they could both hear it, a thin tinny wail, above the chugging of the bus. "You'll get in."

"You figured I would?" Phoebe rocked into Margi's shoulder, applying gentle pressure. "You and me against the world, right, Margi?"

"Yeah. I know why you've been hanging out after school, Pheebes. I know it doesn't have to do with getting your history project done."

"Oh," Phoebe said. "I did get the project done, though."

Margi leaned gently back into her, like she appreciated Phoebe not coming up with some stupid cover story that would have embarrassed them both. Margi's stare normally had a hard edge, but now her eyes were soft and scared.

"What is the deal with you and him, anyhow?"

Phoebe turned to look out the window; they were already on the wooded roads. She saw no zombies—*differently biotic persons*—swaying in place among the birches and oaks.

"I don't know what the deal is. I don't know that there is any deal. There's a connection, I don't know what. We're communicating, and that's rare for you or me to do with anyone. Living or dead."

Margi nodded. "That's our choice, pretty much."

"Pretty much."

They were quiet for a few moments, which was uncharacteristic for Margi.

"Will you join with me?"

Margi shrugged.

"C'mon, Gee," Phoebe said. "Weird Sisters, right?"

Margi leaned her head against Phoebe's shoulder. "Minus one," she whispered.

"Gee . . ."

"No, I know, I know. Maybe it could be a good thing. Like I'll learn how to talk to her or something."

"Colette?" Phoebe asked.

"Yeah, Colette."

"Maybe. Maybe you would. That would be good, right?"

"Sure. But it's still weird, you know? Something is happening. Something is up. Why aren't there any dead kids on the bus today? Colette, or your pal, or the other one? They don't drive."

Phoebe looked around her. The dead kids never missed their ride home. Margi was right. It was weird.

"I didn't even notice."

Margi shifted against her shoulder, like she was nodding. She also rubbed her eye. "I'm not totally brain dead, you know. I see things too."

"I know you do, Gee."

"You'll tell me if you and—Tommy—are more than friends?"

"I'll tell you," Phoebe said. "I don't even know if we are that yet."

Margi sniffed. "Pheebes and Gee against the world, right?"

"That's right," Phoebe said, putting her arm around Margi's shoulder and hugging her.

The old bus groaned to a halt at Phoebe's driveway, and Rae, the driver, said "Good night, ladies," same as she did every time they disembarked. Rae didn't discriminate—she said her farewells to living and dead students alike.

Gargoyle met them at the door, his rump swaying back and

forth with doggy glee when Margi stooped to pick him up and let him lick her face.

"Careful," Phoebe said. "Foundation is poisonous to puppies."

"Shut the hell up and get us some snacks. I'm taking my little pretty boy outside."

Phoebe turned the stereo on and filled the house with The Empire Hideous. She took a pot of coffee out of the refrigerator and poured some into tall glasses in which she added too much cream and too much sugar and too much ice, which was how they liked their coffee. There was a bag of potato chips and a box of crackers and some hummus spread.

Margi came back with Gargoyle and began singing along with Myke Hideous, her husky voice blending well with his doleful intonations. Phoebe smiled, filled with affection for her.

"Today's beverage?" Margi asked, setting Gar down and watching him pad over to the couch and hop on.

"Crème brûlée," Phoebe said, holding out the tray for Margi, who selected one of the glasses.

"Mmmmm," she said. "Tastes sweet."

"That would be all the sugar I added."

"Yes. Good choice. So what are we doing, other than getting caffeinated?"

Phoebe brought the tray over to the coffee table and sat next to Gar, who rolled over for a tummy rub.

"I TiVo'd something last week. I thought we could watch it."

"Uh-oh. My spidey senses tell me this is a setup."

"Wow, Margi, I'm really impressed. First bilocation, and

now precognition. Your telepathetic powers are working in overdrive today."

"It's that psychic bond we share," she said. "Because if there is one thing you are not, it's predictable. Goo-goo eyes at a dead kid, even I couldn't have foretold that."

Phoebe tossed a throw pillow at Margi. "The show was on CNN. It's called *The Young Undead in America.*"

"I sense a theme here," Margi said, flopping ungracefully next to her, with Gar in between. "I don't suppose that we could just listen to Empire Hideous and call it a life?"

"Nope. We're going to be socially conscious today. Topical. I hear differently biotic persons are all the rage these days."

"Hmm. Me too."

Phoebe worked the TiVo remote with one hand while using the stereo remote to kill the music with the other.

"You're good at that," Margi said. "You should have been a guy."

"Too cute," Phoebe said. "And I like smelling nice."

There was an opening montage narrated by someone who'd mastered the art of the grim monotone. Then there was a brief clip of the Dallas Jones video with some explanation of the start of the living impaired phenomena, crosscut with some sound bites from Reverend Nathan Mathers, who seemed to think that the dead coming back to life was a sure sign of the Apocalypse. The montage ended with the narrator suggesting that, as with any other new trend in American society, someone would be on hand trying to profit from the phenomenon. The montage ended by showing a well-dressed man with a toothy smile signing copies of a book called *The Dead Have No Life: What Parents Need to Know About Their Undead Youth.*

Phoebe rubbed her temples. "Telepathetic powers, activate," she said, and then attempted to replicate the narrator's delivery: "One thing is clear: the living impaired phenomenon has changed the very fabric of American society."

"One thing is certain," the narrator replied, "the presence of the living impaired has irrevocably altered the American way of life—no pun intended."

Margi laughed. "You totally watched this before."

"I totally did not," Phoebe said. "If you watched the news occasionally you'd be able to do it, too. And you'd be better at doing the voice."

"Deadpan. No pun intended."

"You're dead right. No pun intended."

"He has a better vocabulary than you do. Irrevocably."

"Someone has to. Inevitably."

They sipped coffee as the Dallas Jones video began to run.

"Ugh, I hate this," Margi said as the now-familiar grainy black-and-white image began to click forward. Dallas Jones walked into the convenience store and withdrew a gun from the pocket of his puffy black bomber jacket and pointed it at the clerk. There was no sound, but it was clear he was shouting at her.

Dallas turned his head to look toward the street, and in the moment he turned back, there was a smoky blur as the shotgun blast caught him high in the chest and blew him back a good five feet into a rack of snacks and a pyramid of soda cans.

"No matter how many times I see that," Margi said, "I will never get used to it."

Phoebe nodded. The image of Dallas Jones being killed was more disturbing to her than what would come later—even though it was what came later that had "irrevocably altered the American way of life."

The shooter—the store owner—came around the counter, clutching the hand of the clerk, who was also his wife. Ahmad Qurati would receive a lifetime of criticism for the risk involved in shooting a robber when the man had a gun pointed at his wife's head. He would also be criticized for not checking Jones to see if the shot had killed him; the video showed him exiting out the door Jones had come in and then locking it behind him—another move that seemed to make little sense. The police department had also come under fire for not arriving until two hours and seven minutes after Jones was shot, even though the dispatch records clearly showed that Qurati did not call 911 until one hour and fifty-three minutes after the locking of the front door.

CNN time lapsed the remaining footage, up until minute 109. Jones was mostly hidden from view by the chip rack, one askew leg clearly visible, as was part of an arm and a dark puddle that spread perceptibly in the first few moments of the time lapse.

At minute 109 the footage reverted to real time, and Dallas Jones's leg twitched. The chip rack fell away, not like it had been lifted and thrown, but like it had been shrugged off. The arm lifted from the floor as Jones apparently—it was hard to tell because most of his body was off camera—pushed himself upright.

"Oh God," Margi said.

A minute later Jones lumbered into frame, the tread of his high-tops never leaving the floor as he shuffled forward. The camera was focused on his broad back, and his jacket was torn and leaking dark down feathers where the shot had ripped through him. He walked forward until he bumped against the glass doorway. He made no attempt to open it, and after another moment he turned and shuffled back the way he had come, toward the camera.

The narrator began talking over the video, giving the sad biography of Dallas Jones, teen hoodlum. Phoebe felt her skin grow tingly with anticipation for the moment that had launched a hundred doctoral theses, and when it came, CNN held it and then panned in, which made the image twice as grainy, but also twice as effective.

Phoebe always wondered why Dallas Jones looked up at the camera at the end of his second aimless lap around the store. The image grew until his eyes filled the television screen, so that individual pixels stood out.

"Dallas Jones was the first," the narrator said, and the image of Dallas's eyes was replaced by some equally grainy home video footage of other dead people moving around, and then some on-location reporters sending back stories about a dozen different undead.

"They didn't show the part where the cops come in," Margi said. Phoebe had studied the full video; after Qurati fumbled with his keys for a minute, two cops came in and tackled Jones. When the EMTs arrived a moment later, one of the cops was covered with blood, none of it his own.

"Repent," Reverend Nathan Mathers was saying. He was screaming, spit flying from his lips. "Repent, for surely the end is nigh. The graves give up their dead and the coming of the Lord is most certainly upon us!"

"I feel bad for whoever is in the first pew," Phoebe said. Next to her, Margi pulled Gar closer.

"I hate when they show this stuff," she said.

The next image was even more hateful. The video jerked around as though the camera were strapped to a hyperactive child, but the image it conveyed was easily understandable, and horrific. Two men with jerricans were pouring gasoline on a sluggish living impaired girl whose arms were bound behind her to a metal basketball pole set into concrete, like you'd see in a school yard. The girl went up in a sudden rush of yellow flame, and her twitching seemed to grow more animated, but that might have been a trick of the flames dancing around her. Mathers was still giving his speech in the background.

"Oh God," Margi repeated, and they were quiet for the remainder of the program, even when Skip Slydell, the young author, began talking about how parents should raise their differently biotic youth and help integrate them into a society that still does not have any legislation that prevents burning them at the stake.

CHAPTER ELEVEN

*T*HERE WERE THIRTEEN NAMES on the list of students accepted into the Hunter Foundation. Phoebe Kendall was the third name on the list, right below Tommy Williams and Karen DeSonne. Colette was next, as was Margi and then Adam.

Phoebe felt a bounce in her step as she turned from the list, but it nearly carried her into the arms of Pete Martinsburg. He pushed her back against the wall.

"You should watch where you're going, Scarypants," he said, looming over her. She had an armload of books, and his hands were free, the left one balled into a fist. "You should watch what you're doing, too."

She could feel her cheeks flush with rage and embarrassment. And more than a little fear, too. This was a person who had no compunction against taking a baseball bat to another student, after all. Margi would already be dragging her hot-pink nails across his face and hissing like a wet cat, but Phoebe was afraid of getting hurt, and she could see in his face that he was not above hurting her.

"That's the most color I've seen on your face in a long time. You scared, dead girl?" he asked, smiling. "You should be."

Phoebe felt like she was shrinking beneath the weight of his stare. She was wearing her knee-high boots, which would have been great if she could have lifted them groin high, but the skirt she had on was tight all the way to her ankles, and barely allowed for a short stride, much less a swift kick.

A clear memory of the sound of Martinsburg's bat as it cut through the air to strike Tommy's flesh rippled through her mind. She noticed that his fists were clenched.

Martinsburg ripped the roster off the wall, tearing a corner where the masking tape held. He folded the list twice and put it in his shirt pocket.

"Everyone on this list," he said, "is going to regret ever hearing about this class."

He walked down the hall, and Phoebe watched him go, tears of frustration and shame gathering at the corners of her eyes. She could go in the office and tell someone what just happened. She could find Adam, and he would probably want to have a chat with Martinsburg. But in the end, all she did was wipe her eyes and wonder what Martinsburg was going to do when he saw Adam Layman's name on the bottom of the list.

Margi found Phoebe in the hall. The flush in Phoebe's

cheeks must have subsided since Margi was back to her usual chattering self, relating a brief tale of an atrocity committed by Mr. McKenna in Spanish that morning, something about his failure to announce a pop quiz.

"Isn't that why they're called pop quizzes?" Phoebe asked. "Because they're surprises?"

"Still, it isn't fair. Speaking of surprises, when are they going to post the list for the work study? I mean, not like I want to do it or anything, but I am your best friend, and I guess it will look good on a college application. And they can't be grading very hard. Can they? I mean, the grading is just a formality with these things, right? I don't want to take it if I'm going to get a bad grade."

"They posted the list. It got ripped down."

"Really? Who would do that? Some moron who couldn't get in? I better not say that; what if I didn't get in? Do you know who got in?"

"You got in. Me too."

"Yay," Margi said with false enthusiasm, clapping so that her hundred bangles clinked together in a soft tinny rhythm. "Who else? Anyone as cool as us? As if that were possible."

"Tommy, Adam," Phoebe said, smiling when Margi made a face. "Colette. Thornton Harrowwood is taking it, for some reason. I saw that living impaired—that differently biotic—girl on the list: Karen with the unpronounceable last name. They only accepted thirteen people."

"Once again, the elite," Margi said, touching Phoebe softly

on the shoulder that Martinsburg had just shoved. "Of course, only thirteen people applied."

The thirteen became twelve before the first bus ride from Oakvale High to the Hunter Foundation, which was a short drive through the woods near the Winford line.

"I heard that her parents refused to sign the permission slip to let her come," Margi said about the last-minute deletion.

"Is this precognition again?" Phoebe said. "Or telepathy?"

Margi shook her head. "It's called divination if you can reveal something that already happened. But no, it is really because I overheard one of the school secretaries telling Ms. Kim."

"Well, that was progressive of her parents."

"These are progressive times, Pheebes my dear."

In homeroom they discovered that they would be missing their seventh period class—which for Margi was a study hall, so she was none too pleased to be attending an orientation. The feeling that Phoebe carried around with her was similar to the one she'd had in the days and hours leading up to the seventh grade talent show. Sometimes the butterflies were there just to make you queasy; sometimes the butterflies were there to let you know that something good was on its way.

The dead kids were waiting when she walked down to the library for orientation. She saw them through the streaky windows in a loose ring of chairs in the study area. Principal Kim was waiting at the door with a clipboard.

"Hello, Phoebe," she said, handing Phoebe the clipboard. "Please sign on the line next to your name."

Phoebe did. The dead kids had signed in already. Not known for their fine motor skills, their "signatures" were mostly block printing that looked as though they'd slashed the letters across the page with the pen. Tommy's name was the only one that was within the lines provided, and the letters were even and uniform in height.

"Hey, Pheeble," Adam said, taking the clipboard out of her hand, startling her. The old Adam was known more for his lumbering than for his stealth, but it gave him no end of amusement to sneak up on her.

"Mr. Layman," Principal Kim said, "please . . ."

"Sign on the line that is dotted, yes, ma'am," he said, scrawling out a name that wasn't much neater than the marks left by the living impaired kids.

"Why don't you two have a seat?"

Phoebe watched Adam as he scanned ahead into the room. If he was apprehensive, he was doing a good job of not showing it, but she did note the slight shrug of his shoulders as he motioned for Phoebe to follow him into the room.

Tommy was sitting in one of the creaky wooden library chairs, his shoulders back and his head straight. Phoebe thought of the last time she'd been in a ring of living impaired kids and recognized a few of them: Colette sat on a cushioned futon next to the girl with streaky white-blond hair who Phoebe'd seen out in the forest.

"Hi, Tommy," Phoebe said. "Hi, Colette." She waved at the

other kids, making brief eye contact with each. The girl with the white-blond hair returned her wave with barely a pause.

"Hello, Phoebe," Tommy said. "Adam."

"Hey, Tommy. Hello, everyone." Adam took the last of the lime-green lounge chairs, leaving Phoebe one of the wooden ones. Her chair squeaked when she sat on it. He laughed, and she made a face at him.

Margi entered the silent lobby like a small black-and-pink twister, her skirt flapping, her spangles jingling. "Ohmigawd, that was the longest history class ever. I think I actually became a historical figure in the time it took for that class to end."

She pulled up short, as though it had just dawned on her where she was and who she was there with. Her greeting of "Hullo, everyone" was mumbled, and she looked relieved when Thornton Harrowwood entered and demanded high fives, first from Adam and then from Tommy. There was a tense moment when Tommy regarded Thorny's raised hand as though he was wondering what it was for, but then he gave a light slap.

Thornton had been the last to arrive, which meant another person had dropped out. Principal Kim led Angela Hunter and her father, Alish, into the room. Ms. Hunter wore a pale blue skirt that ended at her knees, and Phoebe thought her legs could probably cause even a dead kid's heart to race. Tommy was watching her cross the room. The chair did not even creak when she sat on it.

"Well," Principal Kim said, "I must say that I'm quite surprised and pleased to see two football players in this program.

I'm glad to see you boys taking an interest in something other than football. And I have already spoken with Coach Konrathy, so he knows that you will be missing one practice a week."

Adam nodded, and Thornton puffed up as though he had been named running back of the year. Phoebe noticed that Adam hadn't looked up from the spot on the carpet he'd been staring at since he sat down. She looked down. Moss green, slightly variegated with some dark green strands. There was a stain that might have been coffee near the leg of the futon where the two dead girls sat, but Adam didn't seem to be staring at that.

"Three."

She looked up. Everyone looked at Tommy, including the principal.

"There are . . . three . . . football players here."

The principal smiled. "Three. Of course. Thank you for reminding me, Tommy. First, let me thank you all for signing up to participate in what we expect will be a very exciting program for the Oakvale school system. The Hunters are here today to discuss the program in a little more detail with you, as well as to set expectations—yours and those of the school and the foundation."

"Thank you, Principal Kim. And again, thank you for joining our program! I look forward to working with all of you!"

Angela's smile, like her legs, could bring the dead to life. Margi was squirming on the seat next to Phoebe.

Alish spoke next, and his voice was one suited for libraries:

dry, raspy, and soft. He smiled, but there was none of his daughter's restorative power there.

"Yes," he said, and Phoebe thought she could hear an extra "s" in the word, as though the word had been hissed. "Thank you all for choosing to work with my foundation. I am Alish Hunter. I fully expect that the work you do here will change your lives, if not the lives of all persons, differently biotic or not. I know it will change mine."

More smiles from the Hunters.

"I have your files, but I would like to hear from you. I gather some of you are friends, but it will be in the interest of the foundation if we could all become friends. So please, let us all introduce ourselves. And when we do so, let us each give a little of ourselves by saying our names and also something that we like to spend time doing. I'll start. My name is Alish Hunter, and I enjoy wearing a lab coat and conducting experiments like a mad scientist."

There was some polite laughter, mostly from Thornton and Angela, who went next. Contrary to what Phoebe expected, Angela's hobby was running, and not lounging around on Misquamicut Beach in a string bikini.

Thornton liked football. The dead girl with streaky white-blond hair was named Karen DeSonne (de-sewn, Phoebe noted), and she liked to paint. There was almost no pause at all between her words. Adam liked karate. Colette took a full minute and a half to let the group know that her name was Colette Beauvoir and that she liked walking in the woods. Margi liked music. Kevin Zumbrowski was nearly as slow as

Colette, and he liked chess, which Phoebe figured probably worked out just fine for him. Phoebe said that she liked to write, as did Tommy Williams.

"Wonderful," Alish Hunter said. "See that? We've already found some things in common."

Evan Talbot, who could not have been much older than fourteen when he died, confessed to being a science fiction fan, especially *Star Wars*. He was wearing a Darth Vader T-shirt and had a shock of wiry orange hair that stood up from his head like a wick. He was pretty quick, too, much quicker than Sylvia Stelman, who agonized in telling the group that she liked her two cats, Ariel and Flounder. Tayshawn Wade told everyone that he liked to watch movies.

"What sort of movies?" Angela asked brightly.

"Action," Tayshawn replied, giving the word an extra syllable, "and . . . horror."

Alish laughed like it was the funniest thing he ever heard. Phoebe expected clouds of dust to billow out of his mouth from somewhere deep in his lungs.

"Well," he said after a moment, "we are about out of time. Angel has a folder for each of you with more information. There is homework inside, as well as another permission slip that says your parents will allow you to be transported from the school to the foundation and back again. There is also a confidentiality agreement for each of you to sign with your parents. There are some other forms that you should be familiar with. Please read everything and have your parents read everything. Provided that Principal Kim receives all of the necessary documents by the end of this week, we will see all of you next Tuesday at the foundation. You will be leaving after lunch, so please remember to schedule time for yourselves to make up any assignments you might miss. Thank you, and see you next week."

Principal Kim stood and walked the pair to the door after telling the students they were dismissed.

Margi sighed beside Phoebe.

"What a lizard," she said.

"Aw," Thornton said, flipping through his sheaf of paperwork, "we've got to write an essay on why we wanted to do the work study."

A thin pink sheet escaped from his folder. Phoebe watched Adam pluck it out of the air with liquid grace and hand it back to Thornton just as Thornton dropped his pen.

"Be interesting to hear what some people write on that one," Adam said, looking at Phoebe.

Karen was the first to rise. She lifted a slate-gray backpack that had a small pink stuffed dog hanging from the zipper. The dog's tongue, equally pink, drooped from the line of stitching that was its mouth. The eyes were closed, making the dog look as if it were sleeping or hanging from a rope. One corner of Karen's mouth twitched up.

"Don't worry," she said. "Only one . . . page. I think you'll survive."

Phoebe watched Karen walk away. Her blond hair looked almost soft under the bright library lights, and she moved without the hitch that was present in the gait of most of the differently biotic.

There might have even been a calculated sway in her khaki-clad hips.

"She's the one who wears short skirts," Margi whispered.

Phoebe nodded. She saw Tayshawn helping Colette off the futon. "We should talk to Colette."

Margi grabbed her forearm, her hands freezing cold. "We should. And we will. But not now. I really want to get out of here," she said, tugging her toward the door.

Phoebe turned long enough to wave at Tommy. Tommy waved back.

CHAPTER TWELVE

HE FIRST GAME OF THE season was against the Norwich Fisher Cats, which was one of the major rivalries for the Oakvale Badgers. Phoebe had read that this was the first year in many that the game was being played in Oakvale. For a long time the game had been played in Norwich as their homecoming game in accordance with the long-standing tradition of giving the Fisher Cats a team they could demolish for that spirit-building event. But now, with Adam on the team, the Badger's were actually competitive.

Phoebe's dad had agreed to drive her and Margi to the game, and Phoebe noticed as he pulled on his threadbare Fordham sweatshirt and an old ball cap, that he might have been a little too eager to volunteer. She knew how much he liked to spend time with her, and he liked spending time with her and Margi even more—mainly because he loved to try and embarrass them. "Bring some color to those pale, pale cheeks" was how he liked to describe it.

"So Margi," he said, "are you as excited as Phoebe is about this Undead Studies thing?"

"Dad!" Phoebe said. "Study for the Advancement of Differently Biotic Persons. Didn't you read the paperwork?"

He looked back at her in the rearview. "I feel like all I've been reading lately is paperwork."

"I'm with you, Mr. Kendall," Margi said. "Too much paper."

"The newspaper called it the Undead Studies Program," he said. Phoebe wished that he would just watch the road.

"Don't believe everything you read," she said.

Her father laughed, and despite the lines around his eyes, he looked younger than his forty years.

He managed to look away from her just in time to notice the stop sign up ahead. "Good advice for everyone, I think."

Margi giggled, and Phoebe hit her with an elbow and a dirty look. "I think it will be interesting, Mr. Kendall. One of the de . . . differently biotic boys likes horror movies."

"Really?" he said. "Nice to have something in common."

"Sure." Phoebe wondered why everyone thought that commonality was the lynchpin to the whole "why can't we all just get along" deal.

She could sense the next question on his lips. She knew he was about to ask about Colette, but then they turned the corner and there was the school. There was a crowd of maybe twenty people near the front steps, some with poster board signs. A few police cars were parked in the loop where the buses would wait on school days.

"Those don't look like football fans," her dad said.

Phoebe read some of the signs: SPORTS ARE FOR THE LIVING; DEAD = DAMNED; LIFE, LIBERTY, AND THE PURSUIT OF HAPPYNESS; and in bold red letters, BURY YOUR DEAD.

"Nice," Margi said. "Look, they spelled happiness wrong."

"Maybe this isn't such a good idea, kids."

"No, Dad," Phoebe said, "we can't let people like this win."

"Win what?"

"Could you please just drop us off in the student lot? We'll walk up."

"I don't know."

"Dad, we'll be fine. It's just a couple of nuts with signs." She knew what was going on in her dad's head. Visions of bombs under bleachers, handguns in belts, vials of acid tucked away in overstuffed purses.

"Phoebe—"

"Dad," she repeated, "we'll be fine."

"Maybe I'll see the game with you after all," he said. "I've always wanted to hear Armstrong speak."

"Right." At least she'd get to see the game.

There were protestors inside the game as well. Many of them wore latex monster masks, even though Halloween was still a few weeks away.

"Are they actually chanting 'Out of life, out of the game'?" Margi asked.

"I'm afraid so," Phoebe said, selecting seats in the heart of the Oakvale boosters section. She and Margi would normally be huddled together in a corner, away from everyone, each wearing earbuds jacked into the same iPod; but the people who normally seemed insane to them now seemed safe and comforting compared to people who actually *were* insane.

"I could think of some better cheers," her dad said.

"Please don't."

Phoebe had seen only one game last year just so that she could tell Adam she'd seen him play. Adam's role seemed to be to keep the opposing team from tackling Denny Mackenzie, the quarterback, and from what Phoebe could tell, he was very good at it. Denny had gone untackled for the game she'd watched, except for a few plays where he'd run downfield from his blockers. With a routine nonchalance, Adam had blocked or knocked down the one or two people who had run into him.

A young girl in a star-spangled dress, her hair done up in a loose mound of blond curls, skipped out to sing the national anthem, the crowd joining in with a sort of restrained mania. Some of the voices were belting out the words, as they held special significance for the day's events.

The announcer asked everyone to please welcome the Honorable Steven Armstrong, state representative. A trim-looking man in khaki pants and a navy blue windbreaker walked to the microphone where little Kayla Archambault had just finished singing about the land of the free and the home of the brave. The applause became listless and interspersed with booing as soon as the little girl was out of sight.

"A man of the people," her father said. "Excellent."

"Look at all the guys in shades," Margi said, pointing to a row of stern-looking characters on the edge of the field. "Are they part of Armstrong's staff?"

"The Men in Black. I guess they're ready for trouble. Maybe they think the undead belong at Roswell."

"Dad," Phoebe said. Her father was a longtime conspiracy buff who liked to make people think he believed in flying saucers but didn't believe that man ever walked on the moon.

"Thank you," Armstrong said, flashing a wide smile. "And thank you to the students and faculty of Oakvale High for inviting me on what is sure to be a historic event. One cannot help but think of the American athletes of the past who overcame obstacles of injustice and hate to go on to greatness. I am thinking of people like Jesse Owens. Greg Louganis. Billie Jean King. These people were willing to suffer through adversity and discrimination to participate in the sports that they loved, and in doing so, left a legacy that is an inspiration to all who would walk—or run—in their footsteps."

Phoebe was marveling at how quickly Armstrong had silenced the crowd, and then someone shouted "necrophiliac" over the silence. Armstrong continued speaking as though he hadn't heard.

"So I ask you, when you watch Thomas Williams take the field today, I ask you not to think of him as a living impaired young man, because clearly he does not consider himself to be impaired in any way. I ask those of you who would shame our country by singing our national anthem with a mask covering

your face not to think of him as a zombie or a freak or any of
the other hate-filled terms you would seek to tag this brave
young man with. I ask that you forget also, for the moment, that
he is differently biotic—I ask only that you consider him an
athlete, and in that, he is no different than the other young men
set to play today. Thank you."

"He's good," Mr. Kendall said, joining the girls in clapping.

Despite the fine oratory, Tommy didn't play the entire
first half. Adam did his job well and gave Denny time to pass
on most plays, although Denny was sacked for a loss on a play
where Adam blocked right and Denny ran left. Pete
Martinsburg had one interception and seemed to take a special
delight in shoving opposing players into the sidelines.
Thornton Harrowwood was allowed to carry the ball on a play
and was crushed after a three-yard gain.

"Ow," Margi said. "I hope he gets up."

He did, and strutted as though he'd just carried the ball
seventy yards for a touchdown.

"You have to admire his pluck," Phoebe said.

"Yes. He is a plucky young man."

Her dad looked at them, squinting. "What are you two
talking about?"

At halftime the score was ten all. Harris Morgan scored on
a thirteen-yard pass in the corner of the end zone, and the
Badgers tied it up with a field goal just as time expired.

Armstrong came back onto the field after a short but
loud performance by the Badger Band. "Wow, what a game," he
said. "Let's hear it for these athletes." Most people, even the

protestors, were more intent on getting a hot dog or a soda than they were on recognizing gridiron accomplishments, and again, the reception Armstong was given was lukewarm at best. "I'd like to talk briefly about the Hunter Foundation for the Advancement of Differently Biotic Persons. As you are well aware, the foundation is committed to the study—physiological, psychological, and perhaps most important, sociological— of differently biotic persons. The goal of the foundation is, through scientific study, to help create a world where all people, regardless of their biology, can live and learn together. I encourage you to show your support for differently biotic children everywhere through a donation of time or money to the foundation, with offices located right here in Oakvale. Thank you."

Phoebe saw a policeman talking to a guy in a Frankenstein mask in the bleachers across the field. The conversation didn't look pleasant.

"I'm amazed that the coach hasn't put the Williams boy into the game," Phoebe's father said.

The Williams boy. At least he hadn't said "the dead kid." Phoebe thought. "I don't think Coach Konrathy is very excited about putting him in."

"Everyone else is."

"That's the problem," Phoebe replied.

"I think he needs to put the kid in at this point," he said. "You've got half the crowd ready to throw a fit if he goes in, the other half ready to riot if he doesn't. You can feel the tension rising."

Frankenstein must have lost the discussion, because he was preceding the policeman down the bleacher steps. Every few steps he'd stop and turn as though tossing insults over his shoulder.

"If I'm Konrathy," her dad said, "I'm putting him in at the start of the half."

But he wasn't Konrathy, and Konrathy let Williams ride the bench throughout the quarter. Oakvale scored again on a quarterback draw after another nice reception from Harris Morgan. Norwich led a gritty march downfield and into the red zone, but Pete Martinsburg picked off a screen pass and ran it back ten yards before being tripped up. It was the play that served to break the spirit and chances of the opposing team, but Phoebe could not bring herself to cheer.

"That was a nice play," her dad said, nudging her.

"Pete Martinsburg is evil, Mr. Kendall," Margi said.

"Ahh," he replied, and stopped clapping.

Phoebe shot Margi a look so that she wouldn't begin explaining just how evil Pete Martinsburg had been.

Margi returned her look, and stuck out her tongue.

The Badgers kept the ball on the ground, and three plays later they had a first down on a six-yard carry by Thornton Harrowwood. Again he was leveled, and again he sprang up as if he hadn't been touched.

"That little guy is pretty tough," Mr. Kendall said, stifling a yawn. The volume of the crowd tapered off and then rose again as Tommy Williams fastened the strap on his helmet and trotted onto the field.

"He finally put him in! And these knuckleheads are booing. That just isn't right." Her dad clapped louder, and Phoebe and Margi joined him. Someone hit Margi in the back of the head with a french fry, and another sailed past Phoebe's face as she turned around.

Her dad stood up and scanned the upper rows, but whoever it was hid the remainder of their deep-fried missiles.

"Coward," he called, and sat down.

"Not worth it, Dad," Phoebe said.

"It never is," he said. "Looks like Williams is on the line next to Adam. This ought to be interesting."

Mackenzie took the snap and dropped back five steps. Adam and Tommy gave him plenty of time, and he completed an out to Harris Morgan, who let himself get pushed out of bounds. The second play went much the same way, but this time with a curl up the middle of the field so as to keep the clock running. The Badgers were past midfield with a first down, so they ran the next two plays and got short yardage. The next play was third and one, and they ran a draw where Denny pitched the ball to Harris, who swept around to the left behind Adam and Tommy. The hole they left him was big enough to drive a moving van through, and Harris sprinted, juking the one tackler who had a chance, and ran forty yards into the end zone without anyone getting close to him.

The Badger fans cheered, but the Badger players were met with a barrage of fruit as they trotted back to the bench. A flurry of a dozen or so tomatoes sailed from the lower levels of the bleachers, most of them hitting Adam, who stepped in front of Tommy the moment the throwing began. Someone tagged Konrathy in the head with an apple.

The stocky cop who had escorted Frankenstein out earlier headed over to that section of the bleachers, waving to a policeman on the other side of the stadium. There was a lot of shouting and pointing and some shoving, but by the time the cops got there, all the evidence was out on the field and it didn't look like the witnesses were planning to go on record.

"That was pleasant," her father said, shaking his head.

The Badgers won, 24–10. Tommy Williams did not take the field again.

"You understand why I am uncomfortable about this," her dad said.

"I'll be careful, Daddy."

"You know it has nothing to do with my trust in you. But some of these idiots in the stands . . ."

"I know, Daddy. I'll be careful."

"Careful doesn't help if some knucklehead has a gun, or a grenade."

"I know," she said, wondering how many people actually had a stockpile of grenades lying around the garage for day-to-day use.

He looked at her and at Margi, who was lingering by the fence, pretending not to be listening to their conversation.

"We didn't come here so Margi could watch Adam, did we?"

Phoebe smiled. "We didn't come here so Margi could *not* watch Adam, either."

"Phoebe, who . . ."

"I'll be back in fifteen minute," she said. "Promise."

He raised his hands in resignation. She skipped away to drag Margi over to the exit where the players, freshly showered, would be emerging from the school. She looked back at her father, but he was already squinting at the people they passed as though scanning for signs of impending mayhem and destruction.

"My dad never would have let me go," Margi said. "You think he knows you've got the hots for a zombie?"

"Margi!"

"Well, does he? He's pretty sharp about you. He pays attention. I think I could set my head on fire in the living room and my dad would ask my mom what we were having for supper."

"I have a very cool father," Phoebe said, "and I do not have the hots for Tommy. I'm just . . . interested, that's all."

"Whatever."

"Dad thinks that we came here so you could drool over Adam. A very plausible cover story, by the way, and one that he swallowed completely. He's sharp, like you say."

Margi made a disgusted noise and slapped Phoebe's arm, and then chased her to the back door of the school.

"Uh-oh," Margi said as they rounded the corner. The protest had moved to the exit, as had the Channel Three mobile news van. The stocky cop was escorting Adam through the crowd. The reporter from the mobile news van walked alongside, shouting questions.

"What was it like playing with a living impaired kid? Were you surprised at the crowd's reaction today?"

Adam was about as big as the cop. He glared at the protestors, but allowed the cop to lead him through without stopping. Thornton Harrowwood was next, and his appearance on the arm of a young female state trooper drew attention away from Adam.

"Do you have any comment about today's game?" the reporter asked. "What do you think of all the controversy surrounding your teammate?"

"I carried for nineteen yards!" Thornton said, smiling into the camera.

Adam thanked the cop and joined Phoebe and Margi.

"Hey," he said.

"You smell like spaghetti sauce," Margi told him.

"Har-har," he replied. "I don't think I'm going to wash my uniform. Maybe opposing teams will think it is the blood of my enemies."

"Where's Tommy?" Phoebe asked. "How is he doing?"

"He didn't say much," he said, and then raised his hands after catching something in Phoebe's expression. "I'm not trying to be funny. He didn't cry or anything. But he was clearing out his locker."

"Sooo . . . what? What does that mean?"

"I don't know, Phoebe. I asked him if he was okay, and he said he was. That was about it. They're sneaking him out of one of the other exits so he can avoid all this," he said, waving his hands at the cluster of restless protestors awaiting Tommy's exit. Stavis and Martinsburg pushed through alongside the stocky cop, but the protestors didn't have anything to say to the other players. Even the Channel Three guy was getting bored. They overheard him ask the cop if they took the dead kid out another way.

"Yeah," the cop said, smiling. "He's long gone."

"I have to get out of here," Adam said. "The STD said I've got to rake up the leaves. Need a ride?"

"No thanks. My dad brought us."

"Okay," he said. "Oh yeah, I almost forgot—Tommy Ballgame asked me to give you this."

He held out a piece of notebook paper folded into an uneven square.

She opened the note and read it to herself, shielding it from Margi's prying eyes.

"He wants to know if I want to go out some night next week." She looked first at Adam for his reaction, but whatever it was, he kept it to himself.

"Ick," Margi said. Phoebe hit her. "Ouch. *Out*, like as in a date?"

"I don't know."

"That's just weird."

"Shut up, Margi."

"What else does he say?" she said, trying to scan the paper.

"None of your business," Phoebe replied, snatching it away.

"You gals have fun," Adam said. "I'm off to rake leaves."

Phoebe watched him leave, wishing that she could tell what Adam thought about her and Tommy, while at the same time whispering a death threat to Margi should she breathe a word of the note to her father.

Pete Martinsburg watched the dead kid escape out the back door and head out toward the woods, avoiding both the reporters and the food-throwing brainiacs from the stands. Pete debated running after him, but there were a pair of cops making sure he made it without being bothered, so Pete just watched him slip away, undetected by any of the other people who had something to say about a worm buffet playing on a high school football team.

Before the dead kid left, though, he'd made a point of standing next to Pete's locker, blocking Pete from getting to his things. He stood there with his twisted half grin on his face, as though saying to Pete, "What you can do, I can do. Watch out." It was a subtle point and one made for Pete alone.

Pete did something he'd done only once before when faced with a confrontation: nothing.

The zombie was in his head, stomping around with cleats. Pete could only see one way to get him out of there.

After watching the zombie enter the woods, Pete walked back to the locker room, his jersey in hand. Someone had tagged him with an egg just before the game ended. He'd been standing on the sidelines, waiting for the offense to score again, so he could get in and put the hurt on someone, when he'd felt it splat against the small of his back. The dead kid hadn't even been close to him when the egg hit.

He got his locker open and threw the jersey into it, where it stuck to the back wall before sliding down and leaving a viscous trail.

"Yeah, bay-beee!" Stavis yelled, his pale lumpy body nearly plowing into Pete as he stood staring at the yolk trail. "The Badgers win again!"

Idiot, Pete thought. Stavis was holding a blue towel that he'd managed—just—to wrap around his wide waist. He punched Pete in the shoulder, and it took Pete conscious effort not to drive his fist into his grinning moon face.

"Pete, did you see that sack I made?" Stavis said, withdrawing a stick of deodorant from his locker. "Blindside hit, wham! Coughed up the ball and everything."

Pete counted to three so that he could choke back his initial response.

"I missed it," he said. "I was downfield covering that tall kid. Belton, I think his name was."

"Yeah, you shut him down today, man," Stavis replied, chucking Pete's shoulder again with the hand that had been holding the towel while swiping the deodorant onto his pits in a manner that Pete thought insufficient to mask or prevent any odors. "What did he have? One catch the whole game?"

"Two."

"Shut down!" Stavis said, tossing the deodorant back in his locker, where it clanged against the metal walls. He then turned and raised his arms over his head for a double high five.

Pete left him hanging. "Out back," he said. "I want to talk to you. Bring Harris, too."

After they were dressed, he led them outside and back to

the field, taking a seat on the bleachers. Wilson the janitor was going to be pissed, he thought, there was so much food and crap all over the seats and aisles.

As soon as they were seated on the bleacher below, Pete started his speech.

"We're the Pain Crew, right?" he said.

"Hell yeah!" Stavis bellowed, and Harris nodded. This was a promotion for him.

"And the Pain Crew is all about what?"

"Inflicting pain on our enemies," Stavis said, rubbing his thick hands together. "Like we did today."

"That's right, TC," Pete said, smiling. "Like we did today. But we weren't the only ones who inflicted pain, were we?"

TC looked puzzled, so Harris helped him out. "The crowd," he said. "I got hit with a goddam carrot." He shook his head. "Who throws a carrot?"

Pete clapped him on the back. "I got egged, man. Don't feel so bad." He looked at them both in turn. "Yeah, the crowd. But why was the crowd throwing stuff at us?"

"The dead kid," his subjects answered, in unison.

"That's right," Pete said. "The dead kid."

He took the blue paper with the work study students listed out of his shirt pocket. He unfolded the paper and smoothed it on the bleacher between them.

"This paper has the names of a bunch of dead kids, and the living kids that love them. Adam Layman's name is there, as is Scarypants's—Phoebe Kendall."

"Her little friend is in that class, too. Pinky McKnockers," Stavis said. "Thorny is too, I think."

"Yeah," Harris said, nodding. "Coach lets those two and Williams miss practice once a week to go to that thing. And he wouldn't even let me leave early for my grandmother's birthday party."

"Believe me, Morgan, Coach isn't happy about it. Kimchi ordered him to let them go. If he had his way, they wouldn't be going, and the zombie wouldn't even be on the team." He looked at each of them, his fingers tapping on the paper. "Which is why we really need to do something about this."

"You mad 'cause we got punked by those zombies in the woods, huh, Pete?" Stavis said.

Pete wanted to hit him, but he still needed him, so he continued to drum with his fingers on the page.

"Sure, that's part of it. We can't let anybody punk the Pain Crew, ever. But it is more than that. We need to do something because what's going on isn't *right*. Dead . . . *things* walking around, going to school, playing for the Badgers? It isn't *right*. This whole crap about *living impaired* and *differently biotic* is just *crap*. These things aren't even human. I read some stuff that says they're demons or signs of the end of the world or something— and it's probably true."

Stavis, who, Pete knew, had no hope in scoring high on the critical-thinking portion of his SAT, was nodding his head. Harris still looked like he was wondering where Pete was going with this.

"I don't think they're human, and they're certainly not alive.

I'm just waiting for the day they throw down and start shuffling around trying to eat our brains, to be honest with you. But even if that doesn't happen, what's next? Worm burgers making your milk shakes down at the Honeybee? Taking up scholarship money that should be going to kids with a life ahead of them? Just wait until a zombie wants to date your sister, Harris."

"I don't want any zombie sniffing around my sister," Harris said, and Pete knew he'd turned the corner.

"Me neither, pal, and that's why we've got to do something about this list," he said, shaking it in front of their faces before handing it off to Stavis, who pursed his lips and squinted as he read the names. "We've got to do something to . . . discourage them. Whatever they are."

"What do you mean by discourage?" Harris asked.

"I mean we have to take them out of the game," Pete said, "permanently."

"We can't go killing people," Harris said. "That's crazy."

"I'm not talking about killing *people*, man. The actual people on this list—Adam, Julie, and the others—I think they deserve a good beat-down for fraternizing with these monsters, but I'm not talking about killing them." He smiled. "Just the others."

Harris shook his head. "Pete, man . . ."

"Wait up, Harris. I want you to think about it. These aren't *people*. They aren't *citizens*. They don't have any rights at all. Haven't you been hearing all the talk in Washington? What that senator or whatever the hell he is was talking about today before the game, that's all BS, man. They're like mushrooms—

there's no law against killing a mushroom. People destroy these things all the time and nobody cares. It is only a matter of time before these things start to want to get with real girls. And real boys. Then they'll be marrying each other. Can you imagine that?"

"I've got a couple of thirteen-year-old cousins," Stavis said, scratching his stubble-covered head. "I'd kill any zombie that went for them."

"That's why all those zombies crawled out of the forest to attack us," Pete said. "Because that *thing* that they are calling Tommy Williams is trying to get into Julie's pants. And we *cannot* let that happen."

"Who's Julie?" Stavis asked, looking up from his list.

"What?"

"I said, Who's Julie? There isn't any Julie on the list."

Pete felt the heat rise to his cheeks.

"So sue me, idiot," he said. "Phoebe, Julie, Jenny, Katie, Hildegard. Whatever her name is, we have to protect her from them. We have to protect her from *herself*."

Stavis handed back the list and then spread his hands.

Pete held his gaze a moment. "So are you with me on this?"

"Absolutely."

"Harris?"

Harris rubbed his jaw with a nervous hand. "I guess so. Yeah, I guess so."

Pete reached out and clapped them both on the shoulders, the same way he'd slap their pads if they were in a huddle out on the field.

"Good."

His crew leaned in, and he told them his plan.

For the fifth time Phoebe read the note that Adam had given her. Once at the field, once in the car on the ride home, another three times throughout the course of the night, and the last as she sat in front of her computer screen.

There was an e-mail address at the bottom of the note. Phoebe typed a short reply and hit SEND.

CHAPTER THIRTEEN

O N MONDAY A BLUE VAN picked Phoebe and Karen DeSonne up at the school and brought them to the Hunter Foundation so they could do the work part of their work study. They exchanged brief pleasantries and then Karen took a book out of her satchel and read, and Phoebe stared out the window. Phoebe sneezed at one point and Karen coughed a minute later, and Phoebe thought that the dead girl might have been making fun of her, but she wasn't sure. The book Karen was reading was William Faulkner's *As I Lay Dying*.

Phoebe was certain that in getting the clerical job, she'd drawn the dullest detail of the lot. Margi was selected to work in the lab, and it sounded like Adam had a pretty easy gig on the facilities-management crew. The plan was for everyone to switch every six weeks, but after the first day, Phoebe knew she couldn't wait. They spent the entire four hours of their shift opening mail and sorting it into three piles—support, complaint, and junk. Angela stopped by at one point with two thick stacks of paper.

"E-mails," she said. "Please sort them in the same manner. I hope neither of you is easily offended."

Phoebe said that she wasn't, and as she turned, she saw Karen fluttering her eyelids with mock concern, her long lashes twitching with more movement than some of the other zombies seemed capable of. Karen's eyes had a thin corona of crystalline blue at the far edges of her retina but were the color of diamonds close to the pinprick pupils. Phoebe wondered what they had looked like when she was alive.

Most of the mail was hate mail, and it made for interesting reading, at least in the early going, when it seemed that there was some variety in the letters. Phoebe was initially impressed at how creative the writers were.

Dear Necrofiliacs,

What you are doing is sinful and wrong and deep down you know it. Why don't you just die too so you can be with the dead people that you love so much. Dead people are evil and demonaic and should all be burnt up. Jesus is coming and He will be very displeased at the filthy things you are doing. You will burn in Hell.

Sincerely,

A rightious soul

"A rightious soul" wasn't as concerned with spelling as

he/she was with pronouncing judgment, apparently. There were a lot of righteous souls who wrote in with various admonitions, and while Phoebe thought the letters were vaguely creepy, they were nothing compared to the dozen or so that promised threats of a less metaphysical nature.

"Here's a good one," Karen said, walking over from the other cubicle with a piece of yellow notebook paper someone had block printed on. It was a short letter.

You are just like an abortion clinic but worse. You steal the right to death as they steal the right to life and the explosions will reach you, too. This is your last chance.

"Oh my," Phoebe said, looking over at the pile of mail in front of her.

Karen laughed. "Why don't you let me do the snail mail?" she said, scooping the pile off Phoebe's desk. "Who knows what sort of spores or toxins the . . . freaks . . . could send through the U.S. postal service?"

"Thanks, Karen."

"No worries, Phoebe. If I say I smell something funny . . . start running."

Phoebe smiled and hoped she was kidding.

At the end of the shift, she had two communiqués, both e-mails, in the positive column. One from a senator in Illinois who "believes in the work they are doing," and another who had forwarded a PayPal receipt of twenty dollars to an edress of the Hunter Foundation.

*I hope that one day I can send my daughter to you good people.
I thank you for the literature you e-mailed to me and we are
trying our best but it is difficult since my husband moved out.
We are still married and trying to be a family but my youngest
is too scared to live with Melissa right now. Melissa is able to
speak more clearly now but we were worried because when
Jonathan took Emily, Melissa stopped talking all together. Any
advice you have I would appreciate as always. Bless you all.*

Phoebe didn't know who she felt worse for in the shattered
family, the girl who died, her parents, or her little sister. They
were all suffering in their own ways, and Phoebe doubted that
there was an easy answer for it. She wished she could have read
the previous correspondence so she would know what it was
that Angela or Alish wrote that had made such a difference for
the writer of the e-mail.

She was going to show it to Karen, who had not looked up
from her three tidy piles since grabbing the rest of the snail mail,
but then Mr. Davidson, the director of operations, came to let
them know that the van was ready to take them home.

The encounter group that comprised the bulk of their sessions
was led by Angela in a comfortable lounge with a number of
cushioned chairs and sofas arranged in a jagged semicircle.
There were coffee tables, which usually had soft drinks and
bags of potato chips that the living students had taken out
of the adjoining pantry. Sometime during the orientation
Phoebe had mentioned liking coffee and she noticed that they

had added a coffee maker. The cushioned chairs were far more comfortable (and less creaky) than those in the library, and the sofas were long enough to seat two without touching. For the second session Phoebe and Margi plopped next to each other on a sofa.

"Hello," Angela said. "How was everyone's weekend?"

No one answered. The differently biotic kids were silent and still; the living kids, likewise, except for Thornton, who had difficulty remaining motionless.

Angela smiled. "The questions get much harder from here on out."

"I had a great weekend," Thornton said. "We won the game."

She nodded. "That's right. I had forgotten so many of you played."

"Yeah," Thorny added, "Tommy was the star even though he only got in for a few plays."

He meant it as a joke—Thornton didn't have a mean-spirited bone in his body—but the joke fell flat. Phoebe tried to read Tommy's expression but saw nothing there that she recognized. She wished she could tell if he had any feelings whatsoever about their upcoming date—was he nervous, excited, regretful, what?

"Tell you what," Adam said. "Denny would not have gotten sacked in the first half if Tommy had been on the line next to me."

Angela nodded. "No?"

"No. He's better than the kid Coach played instead."

"Why didn't the coach play Tommy more, then, Adam?"

"Come on," Adam said. "Coach was afraid to play the dead kid."

"Differently biotic," she said, still smiling. "A differently biotic kid."

Adam shrugged.

"No," Tommy said, and Angela turned the smile on him.

"No, that wasn't the reason?" she asked.

"No, not . . . differently biotic. Dead . . . is fine."

Angela arched her eyebrows. "You don't mind being called dead?"

"Zombie is fine too," Karen said. "We call each other zombies. With affection. Sort of the way . . . people . . . in cultural and ethnic . . . minorities . . . take back certain. . . pejoratives . . . to use among themselves."

Angela tapped her notebook with her pen. She blinked.

"I see. Is that true for everyone here, or do you see the term *zombie* as a hurtful word?"

Evan gave a slow nod, and Angela called on Tayshawn.

"Depends . . . on who . . . is saying it. And . . . how," he said.

"Living people mean for it to hurt," Thornton said, and when everyone turned toward him he looked like he wished he hadn't spoken. "I mean, sometimes. Not always."

"Do you ever use *zombie* to refer to a living person in a negative way?"

"Don't."

Colette had spoken, and Phoebe thought her voice was nothing like that of the carefree, uncomplicated girl she'd known two years ago. She realized it had taken Colette that long to let everyone know she did not like being called a zombie.

"Why is that, Colette?"

Phoebe shrank into the sofa. What if Colette's answer was that she didn't like being called a zombie because her so-called friends had abandoned her and left her alone in her suffering?

If Colette harbored such thoughts, she kept them to herself.

"People . . . hate . . . us."

Angela nodded, her eyes brimming with compassion. "Thank you, Colette. We appreciate your honesty." She regarded her notepad for a moment. "Which makes this a good time to point out the rules and intent of these sessions. Let me start by saying the goal is to have a greater education and understanding of the rights, thoughts, and concerns of differently biotic persons. We'd like you all to have a better understanding of each other's thoughts and feelings. We want you to leave here able to see through another person's eyes, and for them to be able to see you with greater clarity as well.

"To that end, we need to be able to create an environment of complete openness and honesty. We want you to speak your mind, but please do so respectfully. If you do not understand a person's point of view, please ask them questions. You do not have to raise your hand—we want the tone to be conversational rather than have you feel like you are being lectured to, but we do want to give everyone a chance, so I may interrupt to call on people if the dialogue is dominated by a few."

Phoebe thought that Angela may have glanced at Karen but could not be sure.

"This is the portion of the work study upon which you are graded. The grades you get will be dependent upon the level of your participation. Are there any questions on either the goals or the rules of participation?"

She looked at each person in turn, but no one spoke.

"No? Well, then, I have a question for Colette. Why do you think that people hate you?"

Colette seemed to stare through her, unaffected by her glow.

"Because . . . they . . . have . . . told . . . me."

"Mmmm. Has anyone else been told by someone that they were hated?"

Every hand went up initially, except for Phoebe's. Margi made a face at her.

"What? No one has ever said they hated me."

"Not in so many words," Margi replied.

She spoke for Phoebe alone, but Angela picked up on it.

"What do you mean, Margi?"

Phoebe was taken aback by the intensity of Margi's glare. "People give Pheebes and I a lot of crap because we dress different and act different."

"Hate is a strong word, Margi," Phoebe said. She was surprised at the level of Margi's conviction.

"It's the right one, though," Adam said. "Kids hate at the drop of a hat. People do."

"Who do you think hates you, Adam?" Angela asked.

"I'd prefer not to say."

"Fair enough. That is another rule, by the way. If a question makes you uncomfortable, you don't have to answer it. It won't affect your grade as long as you are participating otherwise."

"The question does not make me uncomfortable. I just don't want to answer it."

"Okay," Angela said, her easy smile remaining on her pretty face.

Adam spread his hands. "Okay."

"Great. Let me change direction here. Who in this room has been told they were loved? By anyone at all."

Most hands were raised except for Colette's and Sylvia Stelman's.

"Sylvia?"

Sylvia closed her eyes. A full minute later one of them opened.

"Not . . . since . . . I . . . died," she said. Her other eye opened.

Angela made a compassionate noise, but it was Karen who spoke up, her white diamond eyes seeming to catch even the pale fluorescent light above.

"I love you, Sylvia." She was seated on the end of the semicircle and she got to her feet and walked over to hug Sylvia. "You too, Colette."

Angela made some marks in her notebook. Colette did not seem to want to let go of Karen.

"Let's take a short break. When we get back, we'll read

some headlines and articles concerning the differently biotic that ran in newspapers and magazines last week."

Phoebe watched Karen hugging Colette. She swallowed twice and turned away, blinking.

CHAPTER FOURTEEN

"*I* CAN'T BELIEVE YOU ARE making me do this."

Phoebe smiled. "I know."

"You owe me big time for this, Phoebe. This is big."

"Big," Phoebe repeated. Raindrops glittered on the windshield, backlit by the light of a passing car.

"So," Adam said, "is this like a date, or something?"

"Or something. I don't know."

"You've got feelings for him?"

"I have *feelings* for everyone, Adam." The more Adam talked, the slower he drove. Phoebe expected they would be crawling to a halt at any moment, the STD's truck rolling off into the grassy shoulder of the road.

"You know he's dead, right?"

She turned toward him in the seat, hot words rushing to her mouth. Adam stopped her by laughing.

"Just checking," he said.

"Watch the road," she said, unable to keep herself from smiling. "I don't know what it is, Adam. He's interesting to me, that's all."

"You can't be attracted to him, can you?" He turned toward her. "Just tell me to shut up if you want to."

"You don't have to shut up."

"Okay. So are you attracted to him? *Attracted* attracted?"

"I don't really know what I'm attracted to. I don't know."

Adam nodded. Phoebe wondered what he thought she was explaining.

"You don't date much," he said.

"I don't date much. Not like you, anyway. How is Whatsername, by the way?"

He shrugged. "She is who she is. I'm just trying to figure out where your head is at."

"Well, where is yours? With Whatsername, I mean."

"Nice segue. I dunno."

Phoebe smiled, leaning her head against the window. "Well, there you are. I dunno, either."

It seemed like a good time to be quiet, so they were.

Some minutes later they rolled up to the gates of the Hunter Foundation at the edge of town. Her new place of employment made Phoebe think of a medieval castle. Instead of a moat, there was a high stone wall and a road that was barred by a retracting metal gate.

Adam leaned out his window and pressed the red intercom button.

"Can I help you?" a flat, male voice answered.

"Adam Layman and Phoebe Kendall," Adam said. "We're here to pick up Tommy Williams."

There was a brief pause before the voice answered.

"Drive to Building One."

They waited for the iron gate to separate, the Hunter logo, a large stylized H and F split down the middle and slowly swung inward.

Adam put the STD's truck into gear. "I think that was Thorny," he said

"Could be. He's working security with you, right?"

He nodded. "Yep. But they call it *facilities maintenance*, probably because we take out the trash in addition to delivering beat-downs to would-be bioist saboteurs."

"How many beat-downs have you delivered?" she said, laughing. "And just what is a bioist?"

"That would be zero beat-downs thus far, but I'm ever hopeful. And a bioist is like a racist but hates dead folk."

"Aha. Do you get guns? I'd love to see Thorny with a gun."

"No guns. He's bad enough with the Nextel. Duke carries a gun, though. And a Taser, if you can believe it."

"A *Taser*? Who's Duke?"

"Davidson. He's a real piece of work, that guy. Even Zumbrowski has more personality and warmth than that guy."

"Adam!"

"Sorry," he said. "I don't censor my thoughts around you."

Adam drove to Building One. Evan Talbot, his shock of faded orange hair wicking up like thin strands of copper wire, was standing underneath the porch awning with Tommy.

"Is Evan coming too?" Adam said. "It'll be kind of cramped."

"I don't know," she said, and stepped out into the rain. "Hi, Tommy. Hey, Evan."

"Hello . . . Phoebe." Tommy took his time saying her name, but she wasn't sure that he needed to. "Can Adam . . . give Evan . . . a lift?"

Adam leaned over and called through the open door. "Hey, guys. I don't think there's room in the cab. I guess somebody can ride in the bed, but I think the rain is starting to pick up. It'll be a pretty wet ride."

Tommy nodded. "I can."

"No way," Evan replied. "I . . . get the . . . back."

He moved to the bumper and started to climb. Phoebe watched him awkwardly make his way into the bed of the truck, his arms and legs angular and stiff. He moved quickly for a dead kid, and she wondered what the difference was—why kids like Colette and Zumbrowski seemed to move at half zombie speed, which was like moving at a quarter of regular speed.

Adam got out of the truck and unlatched the lid of the tool kit that ran the width of the bed. "I think the STD has a painter's tarp back here. You're still going to get wet, but it ought to help."

"Gee," Evan said, "I hope . . . I don't catch a cold."

The right side of his mouth twitched. Zombie humor, Phoebe thought.

Adam spread the tarp out over Evan, who waited until he was finished before drawing it all the way over his head. Adam looked at him, a vague teen-size lump under the tarp, and shook his head.

"That's just creepy," he said.

Phoebe saw that the corner of Tommy's mouth was twitching as well. He looked at her, and she had the sensation that his eyes were illuminated.

"Do you . . . like to dance?" he said.

She laughed. "I guess so."

"Great. We . . . are going to . . . a club. The Haunted House."

Phoebe's eyebrows rose and her lips pursed in concentration. She was hyperaware of her expressions and wondered how they appeared to Tommy, whose facial movements were so minimal. She imagined her face a constantly shifting landscape of twitches and tics. If Tommy noticed her sudden self-consciousness, he did not react.

"We don't really . . . dance," he said. "We just sort of . . . jerk."

The thin line of his mouth turned up at the corner. Phoebe laughed.

"Holy crow," Adam said. "This really is a haunted house."

They pulled into the driveway of a home clear on the other side of the Oxoboxo, an old white colonial, faded and blank-looking in the pale light of dusk, with waist-high gray grass that rippled in the light breeze. There was a wide porch that ran the length of the front of the building, the roof of which had collapsed on one side. She saw a huge barn set back a little farther from the road that slouched at a forty-five-degree angle. On the main house, shutters hung askew from the few windows where they hadn't rotted off completely. Most of the windows themselves were broken, leaving glass teeth that shone in the headlights of the STD's truck.

The windows were rolled up, but they could hear music, loud and fast, blasting from the house. There was dim light somewhere deep inside the house, just a few flickers, as though it were lit entirely by two or three candles.

"Is that Grave Mistake?" Phoebe asked.

"A house . . . favorite," Tommy said. "Please come in."

Said the spider to the fly, she thought. Tommy got out of the truck, as did Adam. Phoebe's left side was warm from being wedged in between them; the right side, which had been against Tommy, felt no such additional warmth. She shivered when she left the truck, but it might have been the cool rain hitting the back of her neck.

They followed Tommy up the creaking porch steps. The music was at a near-punishing level now, as Grave Mistake segued into a metal group Phoebe did not recognize, the double bass drum threatening to send the rest of the roof into collapse. She could feel the vibrations through her boots. The air smelled of old wood and, subtly, of decay. Rotten wood or maybe vegetation smells kicked up by the rain from the surrounding woods.

"Is he okay back there?" Adam said, nodding at the truck.

Phoebe had forgotten all about Evan, who, on cue, yanked the tarp down, a wide grin on his face.

It was disconcerting. They didn't smile much, the dead.

She and Adam exchanged a look of mild apprehension. She knew that Adam would not allow himself to show fear, and she was pretty good at being unflappable herself, but they were now in uncharted waters.

She felt Tommy's light touch on her arm.

"The music is . . . loud?" Tommy said.

"Very."

"We will . . . turn it down," he said. "It takes much . . . to make the . . . dead . . . feel."

"Must be hard of hearing, too. Do you guys live here?" Adam said above the renewed attack of an old Iron Maiden song. Phoebe poked him in the ribs. It took him a moment to realize why.

"Uh, so to speak. I mean."

Tommy smiled—it almost was a real smile. "Some of us do."

They followed him into the house. Beyond the foyer was a larger room where a number of figures were recognizable only as vague gloomy outlines blocking whatever dim light source there was.

"Kill!" Evan shouted. Phoebe's heartbeat tripped. "The music!"

For an instant, Phoebe's mind flashed to *The Return of Living Dead* and the scene where the punk chick takes off all of her clothes and starts dancing just before all the zombies come rushing out of their graves to claw her to death as they drag her down into the muddy soil.

The music stopped, and the only sound was a hollow thump as Tommy slapped the grinning Evan, Three Stooges style, in the back of the head.

"Welcome to the . . . Haunted House," Tommy said. "I'd like you to meet a few . . . people."

There were a dozen kids in the large room, which was empty except for two mismatched cabinet speakers resting on the floor and a short lamp with an amber lampshade on the fireplace mantel. Wires ran from the speakers, and a thick yellow extension cord ran into an adjacent room that had couches and chairs; there were a few more kids in there, but the room was in darkness, scarcely penetrated by the amber light.

Tommy said, "Zombies, this is Phoebe and Adam. Adam and . . . Phoebe, these are the . . . zombies."

Phoebe waved. Adam said, "Hey, zombies," but he was too far away for her to poke him again.

She recognized a few of them. Sylvia was there, as was the big kid Mal from their little adventure in the woods. He made his fingers twitch at them. Tayshawn came out of the dark room and said hello. Karen was wearing a long white dress that looked made of moonlight. She gave them an easy wave.

Tommy answered Tayshawn's unspoken question with a nod. "But softer. For our . . . guests."

Tayshawn disappeared, and a moment later a Slayer song filled the house, at a volume that was just a notch higher than Phoebe would have listened to on her iPod.

"Where do you get the power?" Adam asked, shouting into Tommy's ear.

"Generator," he replied. "Gas powered."

"How do you get the gas? You all have jobs?"

Tommy smiled. "We do . . . now. Some of us."

Phoebe looked around the room. A few of the kids *were* trying to dance, just as Tommy said. Evan's shoulders were giving a sort of Saint Vitus spasm; Mal, not quite as fast, was trying to bob his head along with the music, but was catching only every fourth or fifth beat. There was a girl with only one arm who was swaying slightly, her fingertips pressed against the wall as though to draw the music's vibrations into her lifeless body.

"'Angel of Death,' huh?" Adam said, picking up the title from the shrieking chorus. He wasn't much of a music guy, and Phoebe's three thousand attempts to change that character flaw had been met with complete resistance. He liked Kenny Chesney and maybe some classic rock. "And calling yourself zombies. You guys are big on irony, aren't you?"

She wondered if it was his size that made Adam confident enough to just start talking, to dive in and throw out one-liners that had all the marks of being insensitive. But that was Adam. She wondered if she were big or beautiful or the smartest kid in the school, would she possess that type of confidence.

"It is an ironic state that we are in, don't you think?"

This was from Karen, who had glided over to them. Like a ghost, Phoebe thought. Now who was being ironic?

"You have to admit, the whole idea of the dead coming back

to life is somewhat ironic. It is sort of the reverse of the . . . goth culture thing, wherein the living . . . romanticize things dead and of the dark."

Phoebe felt her cheeks flush and wondered if their crimson hue could be detected in the amber light. She couldn't tell if Karen was purposefully making fun of her or just pointing out reality as she saw it.

Karen was the only dead girl Phoebe knew that she could say without hesitation was beautiful. Colette, pretty in life, had lost more than a little of her luster in death; her dark eyes were now shrouded and her soft brunette curls looked brittle and mousy. Karen, though, was stunning. The dress she wore was spaghetti strapped and ended just below her knees; her bare shoulders were flawless, as was all of her skin, really. Her voice was free of the glottal hitch that the other dead kids exhibited, and contained all the appropriate inflection and nuance lacking among most of the dead. She was barefoot, and even her feet looked ethereal.

The differently biotic, Phoebe thought. Karen's eyes were white diamonds even in the murky light.

"I'd give up irony for reality any day," Karen said, her eyes seeming to bore deep into Phoebe's head.

Karen blinked. She leaned over and kissed Phoebe on the cheek and turned away. It happened so fast that Phoebe didn't have time to react. She watched Karen cross the room to Sylvia, who was standing motionless against a wall. She took Sylvia's hand and tugged her into the dark room. She realized that Karen's dress reminded her of the one Marilyn Monroe wore in that movie where she stood over the subway grate. *Gentlemen Prefer Blondes*? *Seven Year Itch*? Somehow the cool imprint of Karen's lips brought heat to Phoebe's cheek.

"What was that all about?" Adam said. Phoebe shook her head, words failing her.

"You would . . . think," Tommy said, "that Karen . . . would have it the . . . easiest . . . among us."

Phoebe nodded, waiting for him to continue.

"The reverse . . . is true," he said. "Ironically enough."

"She's amazing," Phoebe said.

"We have more . . . people . . . joining us every day."

"Yeah," Adam said. "I noticed that. There seem to be more zombies around than before. I had no idea so many kids had died around here."

Phoebe watched Tommy look up at him. "Most . . . did not die . . . around here."

"Oh, really? Where do they all come from?"

Tommy might have been smiling; it was difficult to tell in the light. "They come . . . from all around. And there are . . . reasons . . . to come."

Tayshawn cued up a Misfits song, "Dust to Dust," one of Phoebe's favorites, and the sudden shred of guitar cut through their conversation like a saw blade.

"Would . . . you . . . like to see . . . the rest of the house?"

"Okay," Phoebe said. "Adam, are you coming?"

"No thanks. Hey, Evan, you have any snacks here? Chips or anything?"

They all stared at him, and much to Phoebe's horror, Adam

made the corner of his mouth twitch up in a perfect parody of a differently biotic smile. Evan made a sound like the bleat of a small foreign car horn, the DB version of laughter. She wasn't sure what she wanted to kill Adam for more—the unsubtle way he cut her loose with Tommy, or the risks he was taking by offending their hosts.

But Tommy was smiling. "Let's go."

She followed him up a creaking staircase that ended in gloom.

"Uh, Tommy," she said, "you know I can't see in the dark like you guys."

"Right," he said, and offered his hand. It was cold and smooth.

She shivered, partly from his touch, and partly from the thought that in a few more steps she would be in total darkness, with only his hand to guide her.

"So," she said, sounding nervous even to herself, "you said that some of you . . . your friends stay here?"

"Yes," he said, his back now visible only as a vague grayish outline. "Some . . . parents . . . do not approve. Mal stays here. Sylvia. Careful. This is the last step."

"Not you?"

No," he said. "I . . . stay . . . with my mother. We live in a mobile home . . . at Oxoboxo Pines Mobile Home Park. Turn here. There is another flight of stairs."

The darkness at the top of the second set of stairs was complete. The music throbbed through the darkness, but they no longer had to shout to be heard.

"Really? With your mother?" She thought she was being led along a corridor that must have run parallel to the stairs. She was afraid that if she reached out with her free hand, there wouldn't be any walls. His hand, which seemed to be warming in hers, was like a tether that anchored her to a swiftly crumbling reality.

"Really. In here."

She heard him open a door, and pale light reached her eyes from two huge windows in the far wall. One of the windows was broken, and wind shrieked into the room as though wounded by the jagged glass shards clinging to the frame. It was very chilly in the room.

Tommy wasn't cold. He let go of her hand and walked toward the window.

"I love this view," he said.

Hugging herself against the cold, she joined him by the window. They were high enough so they could see far into the Oxoboxo woods. The clouds above were rolling gray cotton against the dark sky; somewhere behind one of the spooling clouds was the moon. There was a flash, and a forking bolt of lightning cut the sky.

"Wow," Phoebe said. She looked over at him, mainly to erase the mental image of torch-bearing peasants clustering at the foundation of the house. He was staring off into the distance with an intensity that the living could never hope to match.

"The lake is beyond those trees," he said. "On clear nights when the moon is out you can see it glittering. Like the stars, only here on earth."

"I'd like to see that." Pheobe's voice was wavering as the cold began to seep through her skin.

"You're cold," he said. He took her hand, and it almost felt as though his hand were warmer than hers.

She wished she could say something clever and witty like Adam would have, something like *Yep, did ya forget I was still alive?* or *All the dead boys say I'm frigid.* The lines came to her, but she found she couldn't speak them like she would have if she had been with just Adam or Margi.

Tommy led her outside. "I want to show you one other room." They went back down to the second floor and along the corridor. Phoebe's sense of disorientation was now complete; she knew the big windows upstairs faced the backyard of the house, but she thought they had taken a right turn at the foot of the landing, which would put them back in that direction. The music was a dull vibration from somewhere far away.

Tommy stopped.

"Phoebe," he said, his voice echoing in the room.

"Yes, Tommy?"

"Do you trust me?"

Uh-oh. "Why wouldn't I?"

"I need you to trust me."

"Okay," she said, "I trust you."

He let go of her hand.

"Good." His voice seemed to recede in the darkness. "Please lie down."

"Uh, Tommy, I don't know . . ."

"Please," he said. "It isn't like that. Trust me."

Phoebe could hear herself breathe in the silent darkness. *What the heck is this?*

"On the floor?"

"Please."

She couldn't see him. She wondered if Adam could hear her scream if it came to that. And what if her scream was the zombies' cue to ambush Adam, to attack him and rip him limb from limb while she was up in the darkness alone with Tommy?

"Please," he said. "I . . . I . . . I . . . am not . . . going . . . to . . . touch you . . . if that . . . is what . . . you are . . . afraid of."

He was hard to read, like all the differently biotic. Their facial expressions were minimal, their body language unreadable, and their voices flat and toneless. She couldn't see him, but Phoebe thought she detected a sadness in his words as wide and deep as the Oxoboxo.

"Okay, Tommy," she said, crouching down until her fingertips grazed the dusty floor, the movement of her body kicking up smells of old paint and mildew. "I trust you."

She lay down and smoothed out her long skirt over her legs. She crossed her legs at the ankles and folded her hands on her stomach. Her eyes were open, and an eternity of darkness swirled above her.

"Thank . . . you," he whispered.

Her lips were dry. She licked them, trembling.

"I will . . . return," he said. "I need . . . to get . . . a flashlight."

"What?" she said. "You're going to leave me here?"

"Trust . . . me," he said. She could feel as well as hear

his footsteps on the floorboards as he walked away.

Phoebe, Phoebe, Phoebe, she thought. What have you gotten yourself into now?

Patterns of purple began to pulse out of the darkness, strange amorphous shapes that radiated and spiraled toward her. She wished she'd paid more attention in biology, so that she'd have some rational explanation for the effect, some knowledge of rods or cones or corneal refraction or whatever it was that caused those violet shapes to flow toward her. The stillness of the room let her focus on the sounds from downstairs— Michale Graves, maybe—but the music grew fainter and fainter, as though invisible purple hands were lifting her up into the darkness, faster now, carrying her through the roof and into the sky, somewhere far beyond.

Tommy, where are you?

She sneezed, the scent of rotting wood filling her sinuses. Her folded hands were like blocks of ice on her stomach. She was cold all over, and it was like the darkness was drawing the heat from her body. Above the music she could hear her breathing and her heartbeat, but neither seemed normal to her; her heartbeat too slow, her breathing too fast. She closed her eyes when the purpling dark revealed what looked like faces and clutching hands, but when her eyes were closed, the faces were still there.

"T . . . Tommy?" she said, her voice a flat whisper.

She lay motionless—even her shivering stopped. She knew then that she never should have trusted him; that he was never coming back, that he had left her alone in the dark.

She wanted to rise, to lift herself off the cold wood floor but she could not breathe. The dust coated her lungs, and she wanted to move but was afraid. Because what if she couldn't move? What if she tried to move and her body would not obey her? What if she and her body were no longer one because the purpling dark had sucked her spirit out like liquid at the bottom of a glass?

Was this what they felt?

A light cut into the darkness beyond. She lifted her head from the floor, thinking she heard the tendons in her neck creak. And there was Tommy with a flashlight, standing in the doorway. She blinked as he trained the light in her direction, and the force of her exhalation made the dust whirl and spin.

"Thank you, Phoebe," he said.

She watched her breath, a mix of vapor and dust, flow from her. "Can I get up now?"

"Please. I want to show you . . . something."

He waved the light over to the wall behind her.

"Look," he said.

She looked.

The wall was covered with papers that had been taped, or in some cases, nailed onto the crumbling plaster. She got her legs under her and walked closer to the wall. She looked at the papers, some fluttering in the drafty air. Most were digital images printed to computer paper, but there were a few scattered photographs and a couple of slick Polaroids.

The blank stares of a hundred differently biotic kids looked out at her as though in accusation.

"Every one of them . . . felt . . . what you felt just now. The cold. The darkness. The . . . fear."

She could see the fear etched into the blank faces. A young-looking boy in a Boston Red Sox cap looked away from the camera, his expression like that of a beaten dog too scared to meet the eyes of his master. A girl whose face was horribly burned stared straight ahead, her one lidless eye a bottomless well of pain.

"Every one of them . . . died . . . and came back."

There was a boy with a shaved, scarred head who had taken off his shirt and put a large kitchen knife into his chest and was looking with a disturbing placid calm at whoever had snapped his picture. Another dead girl in a party dress stood beneath a poster of Cinderella Castle at Disney World, her face sallow and unsmiling.

"You . . . cannot . . . know . . . what . . . we . . . feel."

She turned away from the wall and the forlorn children upon it, hearing the same hurt quality somewhere in the monotone of his words. There were so many of them on the wall. Dozens. Maybe hundreds.

"Because . . . we . . . do not . . . know what . . . we feel."

She took a step toward him.

"I need to . . . help . . . us."

She hugged him, and although their embrace was not long, she began to feel warmer by the time they joined the kids moving to the heavy metal blaring on the first floor.

CHAPTER FIFTEEN

DAM ROLLED THE TRUCK into his driveway about an hour later. Phoebe thanked him and wished him a good night and hurried across the short stretch of grass that separated their houses. He watched her go, and she must have known he was watching, because she waved again as she worked her key into her front door.

He waved back, wishing that a vampire would swoop down at her from the roof of her house, or a pair of lurking thugs would leap from the bushes, because then he could spring into action. He could launch a flurry of kicks and open-hand strikes to her would-be attackers and beat them into submission, and when he was done she'd know. She'd know that she was protected, and she'd know that he would always be there for her. She'd know everything.

He slapped the hood of the truck in frustration.

There were only three other cars and the truck at the home

of the STD, which meant that Jimmy and Johnny were still out, causing chaos. Fix cars, drive cars, break cars. Sometimes Adam looked with jealousy at their lives, which seemed so uncomplicated to him.

Inside, the STD was awake and in front of the television, flipping back and forth between a baseball game and some sitcom, a line of empties on the floor on the side of his recliner.

The STD looked over at him and nodded. "Hey," he said.

"Hey," Adam replied. "Mom in bed?"

"Yeah," came the wheezing reply. The STD's work shirt was open to his navel, and a tuft of wiry black hair poked out at the V of his once-white undershirt. His arms were still stained with grease.

"She was pretty tired tonight. I think her boss was giving her crap again this week."

Adam nodded. His mom worked at a bank, and her boss was an arrogant, brusque little man who had reduced her to tears on several occasions.

"How was your date?"

Adam looked for signs of sarcasm, but saw none in the weathered face. The STD liked watching television with the lights off, and the blue illumination from the screen lent his face a pale, differently biotic quality.

"It was good," he said. "We went to a party."

"Oh yeah? Did you have any beer?"

"Naw."

Adam felt his stare. "Well, you can get one now if you want. Long as you bring me one."

"Okay, Joe. Thanks."

Adam went to the refrigerator and cracked a couple cans of beer, one for him, and one for Big Joe Garrity, the STD. Joe wasn't such a bad guy once he got into his third or fourth beer, which was usually an hour or so after dinner. Adam handed him the beer and lay down on the couch, balancing his can on his wide chest.

"You like this girl, don't you?" Joe asked him after taking a noisy sip.

"Yeah," Adam said. "Yeah, I do."

"This the cheerleader? The blonde?"

"Holly?" Adam said. The Sox were up three to two, but there was one more inning to play. "Naw. I quit seeing her this summer for the most part."

Joe gave a quiet belch and shifted in his seat, almost dropping his can. "Pretty girl," he said. "Not a whole lot of personality, though."

Pershonality, Adam thought. His father, Bill Layman, had been an alcoholic too, but his "pershonality" went the other way when he drank. While the STD grew more tolerable, Bill Layman grew demonic. Adam sipped from his can, wondering why his mom needed to go for guys that drank. He wondered about Phoebe.

The STD swore when the tying run reached first after a grounder bounced off the third baseman's glove.

"You're right," Adam said, after a time.

"So who's the new girlfriend? Is it the one from next door, finally?"

And the truth shall set you free, Adam thought. He took another sip.

"Yep."

The STD was silent for a moment. The next batter chopped the ball right to the second baseman, who ended the game with an effortless double play.

"She seems like a nice kid," Joe said.

"Yeah," Adam said.

Joe fell asleep somewhere in the ninth inning between the careful dissection of the pitch count and the in-depth analysis of the batting order change. Adam listened to his snores until he heard one of his stepbrothers pull into the driveway, at which point he gathered the empties and dumped them into the recycling bin after washing them. Johnny came in, smelling of beer and cigarettes, and thumped him on the shoulder.

"Hey, bro," he said, heading down the hall to his room.

"Hey." Adam drained the remainder of his can into the sink before following him down the hall to his own room.

Phoebe took the bus the next day, so Adam was alone with his thoughts for the drive. He tuned into a sports radio station, something he never got to do when Phoebe was in the truck with him, and within minutes he was reminded that the pleasant glow Joe had been sporting last night would be gone today because the Sox ended up losing in the ninth on a two-run homer. Bye, Joe. Thanks for stopping in. Hello, STD. Adam wondered if any other kids had their home life governed chiefly by the consumption of alcohol and the Sox's record.

He arrived at school early. Some of the teachers were just coming in, and none of the buses had arrived yet. He pulled into the student lot at the bottom of the hill and debated going inside, then decided against it. He went through his backpack and found his creased copy of *Wuthering Heights* and tossed it onto the seat next to him as though he were planning on reading it. The radio personality was discussing the relative importance of the Red Sox game to the cosmos, and he took out his history textbook because they were due for a quiz, and he realized that the only reason he was waiting in his car was so that he could watch Phoebe leave her bus and walk up the steps and into the school.

Dang, he thought. He shoved *Wuthering Heights* back into his pack, got the duffel with his gear out of the truck bed, and started the uphill trek to the school.

He was about halfway up when he watched a green station wagon roll next to the curb in the bus lane, and then he saw a familiar shock of pale orange hair appear over the roof of the car. Evan waved at the driver and watched as the car pulled away. Adam jogged up another half flight of steps so he could get a good look at the driver, who was a woman with hair a shade darker than Evan's.

His mom, Adam thought. Dead kids can have mothers.

"Hey, Evan!" he called. "Wait up!"

Evan turned like he expected the shout to be followed by a thrown rock. Adam called his name again, and then Evan waved a pale hand and waited for him outside the school.

"Hey," Adam said, his breathing even, thanks to the weeks of conditioning, "thanks for a good time last night."

He noticed that Evan had a scattering of light beige spots across the bridge of his nose and under his eyes, the ghosts of freckles. He was about half Adam's size, a skinny little guy in an oversized T-shirt and jeans. He stood there looking up at Adam as though waiting for a punch line.

"That was pretty cool, seeing where you guys hang out. I mean, listening to the music you guys listen to and all." Adam shook his head and whistled. "That sounds really stupid, huh?"

Evan give his weird lamb's bleat of a laugh. "I wish . . . I could still . . . whistle," he said. "I . . . try . . . and try . . . but I can't get it. I used to be a . . . great whistler."

"No kidding?" Adam said, not knowing what to say next, and feeling stupid for having said anything in the first place. A bus roared up along the road next to them as Evan tried to say something, but his words were gobbled up by the guttural engine.

"What?"

"I . . . said . . . that you and . . . Phoebe . . . were the first . . . living . . . kids we've had over," he said.

"Really? Wow, what an honor," Adam said. "So, do you . . . stay there?"

"I stay with my . . . family," he said. Another bus chugged up the hill, and Adam could see Margi's pink spikes through a window toward the back.

"Oh yeah? Was that your mom that dropped you off?"

Evan nodded, and Adam thought he could detect the slightest hint of a smile on his pale face.

"Cool," Adam said. "So hey, I was wondering . . . I've got a question for you. But don't take it the wrong way, okay? I don't mean to be insulting, so please don't be insulted, okay?"

Evan looked like he was trying to shrug, but one shoulder lifted considerably higher than the other.

"Shoot," he said.

"So what I was wondering," Adam said, conscious that behind him the buses had started to release their passengers. "What is it like . . . what is it like to be dead?"

Evan looked at him with his dull, unblinking blue eyes long enough for Adam to think that, despite his precautions, he'd insulted Evan after all, but then the smaller boy spoke.

"I don't know," he said. "What is it like . . . to be alive?"

His expression didn't change as he laughed again, the sound like that of someone heavy stepping on a dog's squeak toy.

Adam felt himself grinning.

He looked over at the buses just as Phoebe got off. He started to wave, but she wasn't looking at him, her face shrouded by a curtain of shiny black hair as Margi talked at her, her spangled arms stabbing the air, emphasizing whatever ludicrous point she was trying to make. Tommy was right behind them.

Phoebe laughed, her hair falling back over her shoulder and revealing her open mouth, her smooth pale skin. Adam smiled, but then Tommy managed to catch up with them, blocking his view.

Adam sighed. "Let's get to class, Evan," he said, hefting his duffel and slowing his pace so the smaller boy could keep up.

CHAPTER SIXTEEN

"*G*OOD AFTERNOON, EVERY-one," Angela said, her brisk stride carrying her into the middle of the room. As she passed Phoebe, she put a soft, warm hand on her shoulder.

She was followed by Alish and a trim young man who Phoebe recognized instantly as Skip Slydell, the author of many books and articles on the whole undead movement. "Today we have a special guest who you will recognize from having watched the CNN video last week. Please welcome Skip Slydell."

Skip waved. "Thank you, Angela and Mr. Hunter, for letting me come here today. And thanks especially to your students for putting up with me for the next hour or so."

Margi looked at Phoebe and rolled her eyes heavenward, pointing out that every time Principal Kim or Angela introduced a guest speaker to the class they did it with a sort of over-the-top elated gravitas, as though the coming of the guest speaker were both a joyous and serious occasion.

The first thing Slydell did was hand out business cards to all the kids. Phoebe watched Tayshawn grip his in two hands and bring it within inches of his nose, his eyes crossing.

SKIP SLYDELL ENTERPRISES, the card read, and featured a studio head-and-shoulders shot of Skip beaming over a pile of books and products. IN ASSOCIATION WITH THE HUNTER FOUNDATION. There was an 800 number on the bottom of the card.

"Let's get to it, shall we?" he said. "Ms. Hunter has told me that one of the main goals of this foundation that you are all working for and learning in is something I call the successful acclimation of differently biotic persons into society, as well as to acclimate society to a point where it is more fully accepting of differently biotic persons within it. Does that make sense? Any questions?"

He did not wait for either question to be answered. He walked as he talked, with his large, soft-looking hands waving and pointing to accentuate his statements. He took great care to make eye contact with every person, and would hold the contact a few beats longer when he focused on one of the differently biotic people. He spoke so quickly that Phoebe thought it was unlikely that most of the dead kids could follow. She might have had trouble following had she not made herself a coffee when she came in.

"Could you all turn your chairs over here? Would that be okay?" There were two long tables at the back of the room, each covered with a white cloth that hid whatever was stacked from view. He stood in front of them.

"The question then becomes, How can we make that acclimation happen? How *can* we make that acclimation happen? It isn't easy to do, what we are planning. Change the culture. Changing the culture is very, very difficult, even in this country. You and I"—and here he held Sylvia's blank gaze for a pause of nearly twenty seconds—"you and I have not chosen easy work for ourselves. Not at all. It isn't easy to transform culture."

He leaned back against the table, staggering a bit, as though the enormity of their shared task had overtaken him and left him breathless. Margi was making a low humming sound that brought a smile to Phoebe's lips, because it meant Margi had turned on her bullshit detector.

"What we are going to do is not easy. But it can be done. Even here in America. Elvis Presley did it. Martin Luther King did it. Jimi Hendrix. John F. Kennedy. Bill Gates. Michael Jordan. The two guys that created *South Park*."

The American community of saints, Phoebe thought.

"And we can do it, too. Do you follow me? The fact of the matter is that the heavy lifting, the really hard work, has already been done. You know why?" He smiled. "Because the undead are a fact of life. That's a funny phrase, isn't it? Almost an oxymoron. Say it with me: *the undead are a fact of life.*"

No one joined him in the chorus, but a few of the kids looked a little uncomfortable—undead wasn't a word typically used in polite society, especially not in a room full of undead kids.

"How did what I just said make you feel? Think about that for a minute. The undead are a fact of life. How do you feel? Karen, isn't it? Could you share your feelings on what I just said?"

Karen blinked. "It's true," she said, and blinked again. "You've presented a reality that not everyone has chosen . . . to accept."

"Wow," he said, grinning at her. "Wow. A reality that not everyone has chosen to accept. Wow. I'm writing that down."

He withdrew a notepad from a leather case and began to write. "Exceptional. Thank you for that. What about the terminology I used?" he asked. "How do you feel about that?"

"I'm . . . neutral. But it bothers me when certain people use that word," she said, "about me."

"But it didn't bother you when I said it?" he asked, tossing his notebook on the table.

She shook her head, her hair swinging like curtains of platinum caught in a breeze.

"Thank you. That means a lot, really."

"Not yet, anyhow," she said, returning his stare calmly. Evan gave his one-note bleat of a laugh.

"Fair enough," he said, laughing himself. He peeled back one of the tablecloths like a magician about to reveal a trick. "Angela told me that you kids . . . you undead kids . . . like to call yourselves zombies, too. Is that right? Anybody can answer."

"Yes," Evan said.

"Do the same rules apply? You guys can say zombie, but you might get mad if somebody—somebody living says it?"

"Depends," Tommy said.

"On what?" Skip asked, nodding at him with encouragement.

"Depends on how they say it."

"Okay," he said, turning to the other half of the room, where the living kids sat. "What about you all? Don't just sit there like zombies, especially when the zombies are giving me all the answers! What do you think?"

"About what?" Adam said, the irritation evident in his voice.

"About the word *zombie*! Do you ever call Thomas Williams a zombie?"

"No."

"Well, why the hell not?" he said, throwing his hands in the air. He'd really worked himself into a lather now.

"Because I respect Tommy. I wouldn't say or do something that possibly could hurt him."

Slydell nodded. "What about you, Williams? You care what Mr. Layman calls you? Would you get all pissed off if he called you a dead head or a zombie?"

Tommy shook his head.

"Why?"

"Because Adam . . . is my friend."

"Hallelujah! " Slydell yelled, staring up through the ceiling. "You see that? Do you see that, everyone? Layman here won't call his pal Tommy a zombie because he respects him. And ole Tom wouldn't care if Adam did because he considers him a friend. You see that? Do you understand where I'm going here?"

He walked in front of Zumbrowski with his hands on his hips. "Do you know what those two are doing, Kevin? Sylvia? Margi? Those two are transforming the culture, and that is what it is all about."

He picked up his mystery gear on the table and began unfolding what looked like a black T-shirt.

"How'd you get to be friends, guys? Was it the football?"

"Yes."

"Pretty much."

"So it took a radical act—that of a zombie putting on the pads and helmet—for that to happen, didn't it?"

"I guess so," Adam said.

"You guess so? You *guess*? You'd better know, son, because you and Tommy are on the bleeding edge of a new society. You guys are it. Transformation always requires radical action. Do you follow? *Transformation always requires radical action.* If Elvis Presley had not taken the radical action of singing a style of music traditionally sung by black people, we may never have had the transformation that rock and roll enacted on modern society. If Martin Luther King had not taken the radical action of organizing and speaking around the cause of civil rights, we may have never undergone the transformation from an oppressive state to one of freedom and equal opportunity for all. And that transformation is not yet complete. You kids are living—or unliving, as the case may be—proof of that."

"What radical action did Michael Jordan take?" Thornton asked.

Slydell smiled at him. "Wise guy, huh? No radical action. He was just radically better than everyone else. That alone transformed the game. And that's what we're all about. Transforming the game."

Phoebe wondered how he could just talk and talk like this without ever pausing for breath. She thought that it would be fun—and exhausting—to watch him and Margi have a conversation, if only Margi was in a better mood.

"Okay. A little more philosophy. Then I'm going to get into how you can help me. And when I say how you can help me, I'm really saying how you can help society. How you can help yourselves. Help me do that. Okay? Now—you two, Adam and Tommy. You're friends. Did you have any dead friends before Tommy, Adam?"

"Not really, no."

"How about you, Tomás? Any blood bags you would call friends?"

Tommy's gaze drifted toward Phoebe. "A few."

"A few. Well, okay. But in this case it took a radical action on your part to *transform* Adam. Without the radical action, the transformation would not have occurred. Adam would have no undead friends."

"Hold up," Adam said. "You can't assume—"

"Stay with me, Adam. We'll get to your thoughts in a

moment. Without the radical action, transformation would not have occurred. Was everyone as thrilled with this action as Adam was? Did everyone embrace Tommy Williams onto the football team and everything was just hunky-dory? No? No! As I recall, it was protest in the streets! If the newspapers were accurate, as we all know they so often are, there were signs, placards, chants! Thrown fruit!"

Phoebe looked over at Adam, sitting slightly apart from the group as he always was. His hands were folded and his elbows on the tops of his knees. He was staring at the floor.

"That's the second necessary ingredient of culture change, people. The second key to transformation. Conflict. Radical action coupled with radical response. Only then can we get true change. There was a reason that I used strong words with you, impolite words like 'zombie' and 'undead' and 'blood bag,' and the reason was not because I wanted to be offensive. I used those words because *right now* they are radical words, and I wanted to provoke a radical reaction in you. Some of you are cool with using 'zombie' to refer to yourselves. Some of you are not cool with using the term at all. All apologies to Angela, but I need your help in figuring out a term we can *all* be cool with, because 'differently biotic' is not going to cut it. Too cold, too many syllables. No panache. Frankly, it just ain't sexy enough. Now, *zombie* . . . I personally think that makes a statement. The first step toward transforming a culture is to give names and definitions to the transformative aspects of that culture. You are *zombies*, kids. And you need to use that term with pride, *regardless* of the reaction that it provokes."

Phoebe wondered if any of the other kids realized that Skip had given them about three "first steps" in his talk. But he was like a train racing to get back to the station before sunset; Colette had raised her hand at some point during the unifying-effects-of-team-sports speech, and Slydell had still not allowed her to speak.

He unfurled the T-shirt he was holding. It was basic black with the words DEAD . . . AND LOVING IT! in greenish lettering that probably glowed in the dark. The word *dead* was written in a creepy movie-poster font, and the rest was in emphatic capital letters.

"What do you think of this shirt?" Skip asked. "How does it make you feel?"

"I . . . think it is cool," Evan said, his mouth twitching.

"Good. It's yours," he said, throwing it in Evan's face. "What about this one?"

The shirt was gray with a white fist and the words ZOMBIE POWER! in the same creepy font as the first. The skin stretched tightly on the cartoon fist so that the knuckles were clearly visible. "I've got a few of those." He tossed one to Tayshawn, one to Sylvia, and one to Thornton.

"This one is a little risky," he said, "a little more radical. Let me know what you think."

The shirt was black with white no-nonsense lettering. It said OPEN GRAVES, OPEN MINDS above a stylized image of an open grave in a cemetery.

"I like that one," Phoebe said at the same time as Karen.

"Really?" Slydell said. "Cool. I've got two."

There were a few other items. Hats, wristbands. Temporary tattoos that would work even on the rubbery skin of the dead.

"Okay, kids," Skip said, "here's my point. Don't be afraid to be who you are. And don't be afraid to tell people who you are, either. Understand that these things I've given you have been designed to provoke a reaction in people, and that the reaction will not always be pleasant. You have to be brave. But being brave is the first step toward transforming the culture."

There it was again, Phoebe thought, another first step. She ran the soft cotton of her new shirt through her hands. It *was* a cool shirt. . . .

"Last thing," Slydell said, "and then I'm going to get out of your hair. As you know, when I started talking to you today, I said I was going to need your help to make a change, and I do. Like it or not, one of the quickest ways to evoke a culture change is to get the message into the hands of the young and the hip. I need a street team, in other words, to help me get this message out. Many of these products are going to be carried in Wild Thingz! stores and at select music outlets. We're putting together a music compilation as well, one that will have the Creeps and The Restless Souls and other bands that you are probably familiar with. I'm leaving you with some homework. What I want you to think on, and write some ideas down to discuss, is what other products—be they fashion, entertainment, whatever—you think we could put out that would help us get our message of radical transformation out there, and really start changing the world. So think on that, and we'll have some fun kicking it around when the delightful Ms. Angela invites me back here. I'll have some more swag for you to take, too. You can e-mail me at skippy@slydellco.com. I'd love to hear from you. I'm out of time, and I'm outta here. Thanks!"

Phoebe watched him leave the classroom. A few kids clapped, and without turning, he lifted his hand above his head as though in triumph. The lounge felt drained and empty now that it was no longer filled with his words.

"We've still got some time," Margi said, glancing at her cell phone and looking bored.

"Hey, Daffy," Adam said, "you didn't get any loot."

Margi shrugged. She was still the quietest one in the group; she spoke even less than Sylvia or Colette, and did so only when called on, a fact that boggled Phoebe's mind.

"Maybe she's unclear as to what exactly our message . . . of transformation is," Karen said. "I know I am."

Margi looked ticked off, like she thought Karen was making fun of her. But before Phoebe could intervene, Adam spoke.

"I think the message is that we can bring attention to the plight of the differently biotic by getting our friends to buy T-shirts."

Evan, who was wearing both the shirt and a black baseball cap that read, simply, DEAD, laughed his abrupt and disconcerting laugh. He looked even paler with his red hair encapsulated by the black hat.

"The way to social change in America is through conspicuous

consumption, hmm?" Karen said. "That zombie theme goes way back."

She paused, and then winked at Phoebe.

"Cool shirt, though."

CHAPTER SEVENTEEN

*P*HOEBE DIDN'T LIKE LYING to her parents, but sometimes it was a necessity. No matter how progressive they might consider themselves to be—and Phoebe had to admit they were pretty progressive—there was no way that they would allow her to spend time alone with a dead boy.

She was sitting in the cafeteria with Adam and Margi, both of whom were staring at her with a mixture of concern and anger.

"God," she said, "you two look so much like my parents right now it scares me."

"I hope not," Margi said. "I'd like to think you'd tell me and Lame Man the truth."

"Now that you have ensnared Daffy and me in your impenetrable web of lies," Adam said, "go over again what we're supposed to say?"

Phoebe sighed. "I went over to Margi's to listen to some new music," she began.

"Ah. The old standby."

"Right. We listened to some music, and then Adam called to see if we wanted to go to a movie."

"Yeah, that's likely," Adam said. "What movie? I don't even know what's out."

"Wait a minute. Why would we go out with Adam?"

Phoebe sighed again. "Because we need to get out of your house in case your parents talk to mine. "

"Why involve me in the first place?" Margi said. "Why didn't you just tell them you were going out with Adam?"

Phoebe shrugged. "I didn't think about it. You know how these stories kind of get away from you."

Margi made a disgusted noise and slapped the remains of her cheese sandwich down on the table.

Adam was shaking his head. "So basically, to cover your tall tales, I need to vacate my house for the evening, lest your dad peek out the window and see the STD's truck sitting in the driveway."

Phoebe shrunk in her seat. "You don't have plans, do you?"

"I was going to get a jump on my English homework. I was going to read *Wuthering Heights* and have a nice bubble bath."

They laughed. "Seriously though, I hope I can get the truck."

"So what am I supposed to do?" Margi said. "Go hide in the woods with your other zombie pals?"

"I was thinking that maybe you and Adam could go to a movie. That way you could tell me the plot when Adam gives me a ride home."

Margi blinked at her and threw her dessert, a wrapped Hostess snack cake, which bounced off Phoebe's chest.

Adam looked at Margi and then back at Phoebe. "You're paying," he told Phoebe.

Margi had a few more questions for Phoebe on the bus ride home.

"I can't believe you just assumed I'd lie for you," Margi said, her pink spiked bangs grazing the window as she made a point of not looking at Phoebe.

"Yes, you can. That's not what is bothering you."

"Oh really, Miss Telepathetic? What is bothering me, then?"

Phoebe closed one eye and touched Margi's temple. "I sense confusion . . . and anger . . . and worry."

"Of course I'm worried, dummy! He's a dead kid!"

"Shhhh!" Colette was sitting three seats in front of them, with Tommy across the aisle.

"Don't shush me, Phoebe. It's weird and you know it's weird. Look, I have goose bumps! Feel my arm."

Phoebe did. "Yep, those are goose bumps. Or a bad case of arm acne. Or as I call it, armcne."

At first, her stupid comment failed to generate the laugh she'd intended, but Margi could no longer choke it back and snorted, shaking her head.

Phoebe clapped her on the back. "Now will you please be

cool? He's just a friend and we're going to his mom's house, okay? His mom gets home at four."

"A lot can happen in an hour."

"Puh-lease. Like you would know." She poked Margi in the ribs and Margi giggled, which only made her more irritated.

"It's creepy."

"Have an open mind."

"Ick."

"Go home and put on your Zombie Power! T-shirt."

"I didn't get one of those. I got Some of My Best Friends Are Dead, and only because Angela made sure that I didn't go home empty-handed."

"That's lame."

"Very."

"I've been thinking of some good ones for next week: Life Is Just a State of Mind, He Who Dies With the Most Toys . . . Is Sitting Over There."

"Funny," Margi said without enthusiasm. "Phoebe."

"Yeah?"

"Be careful."

Margi's stop was early on the line. Phoebe stood to let her out.

The bus rolled to a stop at the foot of the Oxoboxo Pines Mobile Home Park. The coarse driveway sand crunched beneath Phoebe's boots as she walked beside Tommy, who hadn't spoken since they disembarked.

"Where does Colette live?" Phoebe asked, then caught herself. "Stay, I mean?"

Tommy smiled. His mouth seemed more pliable lately; instead of the slight twitch on one side, both corners of his mouth stretched upward.

"The Haunted House."

"Really? When her parents moved . . ."

"The laws . . . do not always protect . . . the dead. And sometimes they do. A parent is no longer legally . . . responsible . . . to take care of their . . . deceased children. Colette was abandoned. As were many of us."

Phoebe thought about Colette's parents, of a day trip they had taken to the beach the year before Colette died. Phoebe remembered being wedged in the backseat between Colette and her brother on the long ride to Misquamicut. Mrs. Beauvoir spent the day sunning herself while Peter tossed the Frisbee back and forth to her and Colette, who had no aptitude, even then, for the game. Mr. Beauvior slept in a lawn chair the whole afternoon. After Colette died, he took a job somewhere down south, and they moved, sans Colette.

"How does she get away with it, though?" she said. "I mean, if I tried to go live in an abandoned house somewhere, they would come and get me and put me in a reform school or something."

"You aren't dead."

They arrived at a mobile home with blue shutters and a well-tended yard. There was a plastic awning above a walkway that led to the front steps. A number of plants and flowers sat in hanging pots from the frame and sitting along the ground.

Tommy withdrew a key from his pocket, a process that was much more involved for him than it would be for a normal kid. Phoebe watched him, unsure if she should offer to help.

"We are . . . inconvenient. No one knows what . . . to do with us. We do not know what to do . . . with ourselves."

He unlocked the door and they entered the living room. There was a couch and a television, and plants were everywhere. There was a small round table with four seats in the corner near a beaded curtain that separated the room from the kitchen. A fat black cat trotted over to them and sniffed at Phoebe's boots. Phoebe bent to pet the cat, and it arched its back in appreciation.

"That's Gamera," Tommy said. "He hates dead people."

Gamera enjoyed having his neck scratched. Phoebe looked up at Tommy, who was smiling.

"There's a shelter in Winford that many . . . zombies . . . stay at. St. Jude's Mission. It is run . . . by a priest who is sympathetic . . . to our cause. Colette stays there sometimes and . . . Kevin. It is not a home. The Haunted House is better, for most."

Phoebe rose, smoothing some cat hair off her jeans. Gamera twisted himself around her boot. "Where do the other kids in the work study stay? Karen and the others?"

"Karen . . . is with her parents. Evan also. Tayshawn stays with his grandmother, but the situation is . . . different. Sylvia is . . . at the foundation."

"She *lives* there?" she asked. Tommy smiled. "You know what I mean. I thought you said she was staying at the Haunted House."

"We wanted her to stay at the Haunted House. But her need is . . . great. And the foundation is . . . well equipped."

"Huh."

"Yes," he said. "We have concerns as well."

"Who is this 'we' you keep referring to? Is it the royal 'we'? The papal 'we'?"

She thought his smile grew a bit wider. "I want to show you something," he said, and motioned for her to follow him through the kitchen to a closed door, which no doubt led to his bedroom.

"Um, could you tell me where the bathroom is?"

"Back that way. On . . . the right."

"Thanks."

She left her hands under the faucet for a couple minutes, the cool water making her hands tingle and the floral scent of the hand soap filling her nostrils. Margi's words echoed in her head, and she stayed behind the locked door longer than she needed to.

She walked back. Tommy's door was open and his complexion had taken on a bluish cast as he sat in front of a computer screen in the dark. The room itself was a male version of hers, with books and a stereo and posters, the differences being that the stereo was a lot cheaper and there were sports stars mixed in among the musicians on the walls. And the room was a lot neater.

"I wanted to show you this," Tommy said, and motioned to the screen.

Phoebe saw that Tommy was on a Web site called mysocalledundeath.com. The home page was decorated with comic book zombies shambling from graves, and menacing pink people, mostly blond and buxom. Some familiar heavy metal mascots were present as well.

"What is this?" she said, leaning over his shoulder. There was a subtle scent to him, one that she could not quite identify. Something outdoorsy. She resisted the urge to touch his shoulder.

"My blog."

"Your blog? No way."

"Way. I've got close to a thousand subscribers."

"Wow." She leaned in closer. When he typed she could see the muscles of his arms move underneath his shirt.

There were a few hot links on the home page: Archive, Deadline, MSCU Alumni, Links.

"I try to write . . . every night."

"Can I read some?"

He clicked on the Deadline link, and there was an entry for the day prior. She began to read.

Week three of the Hunter Foundation's necrohumanitarian experiment. The class was subjected to the crass but persuasive arguments of Mr. Steven "Skip" Slydell, with whom all of you are by now well familiar, thanks to his being a good year's worth of blog fodder. Skip's main thesis seems to be that the zombie community can achieve legitimacy through consumerism and sloganeering. He dispensed swag to the class; I myself am now the proud owner of a new **Zombie Power!** *T-shirt. There is something almost endearing in his shameless hucksterism, and the gear he showered us with does have a certain radical chic to it. You can't help but question his motives, which almost certainly are profit driven, but at the same time you can't help but be drawn into his circle of "positive transformation." If there is cheesy packaging around a universal truth, does that make the universal truth inside any less valid?*

In a perfect universe, we would not need the Skip Slydells of the world to sell us the messages that we should be creating ourselves. But the fact of the matter is, until we as a group are able to fully take advantage of the DIY ethic that built this country, we are at the mercy of the Slydells. Until we have a press, a voice, a piece of the media, we need to take what we can get. Until we can get hired and have some economic worth, we need to take what we can get. Many of us by now have been dead for three years, meaning that by human terms some of us are now eighteen and should have the legal right to vote, but of course our death certificates are, for all intents and purposes, a complete revocation of our rights and citizenship.

So I'll work with Skip Slydell as best as I possibly can. I'll do so knowing that I am selling myself and all of you out, but that such sellouts are necessary to really make change happen.

At the bottom, there was a flashing banner ad that read, *Support Proposition 77.*

"What is Proposition 77?"

"A proposal to have the federal government issue a rebirth certificate to anyone who comes back . . . from the dead. It's what would grant us some rights and . . . citizenship."

"So you could hang with the humans, huh?"

He looked up at her. "Poor word choice?"

"I'm cool with it, but you know how us blood bags are. Seriously though, Tommy. This is incredible. You are a really good writer."

"Wish I was a better . . . typist," he said, wiggling his stiff fingers.

Their eyes met, and Phoebe imagined that her pale skin did not look much different than his in the soft blue glow of the computer screen.

Phoebe heard the front door open, and she jumped as though caught doing something wrong. Gamera leaped off Tommy's lap and ran into the living room.

"I'm hoooome!" a high voice carried throughout the trailer. A blond woman in a nurse's uniform walked in and hung her keys on a hook on the wall.

"You must be Phoebe," she said, crossing the kitchen and taking a hold of Phoebe's arms. Phoebe could feel the warmth of her hands even through the thick frilly material of her blouse sleeves. "I've heard so much about you. Welcome."

Phoebe could barely bring herself to say hi as the woman hugged her.

"Phoebe," Tommy said, "my mother."

"Call me Faith," she said, her blue eyes shining at Phoebe to the point where she wondered if the woman was about to cry. Faith released Phoebe and threw an arm around her son's shoulders, stooping to give him a loud wet kiss on the cheek. "Hey, you," she said. "How's life?"

"You tell me. I was just . . . showing Phoebe the site."

"My son, the writer," she said. "Isn't it great?"

Phoebe nodded, still in shock. She hadn't really been able to picture Tommy's mother, and the tiny woman's vibrant cheer wasn't at all what she'd expected.

"Thomas Williams!" Faith said. "You didn't give the poor girl anything to eat or drink. Some of us still have to do that, you know!"

"Sorry, Ma," he said, as his mother walked two steps into the kitchen and withdrew a bag of cheese puffs and a glass from the cabinets.

"What do you like, Phoebe? I have Diet Pepsi, milk, orange juice. I could make coffee. You like coffee?"

"I like coffee."

"Good girl!" she said. Her smile made even Angela Hunter's seem lopsided, maybe because there was a sincerity that was absent in the other woman's.

"She likes you," Tommy whispered.

"What? I heard that, Tommy. Of course I like her. Why wouldn't I like her?"

Phoebe watched her rifling through the cabinets, no doubt in search of misplaced coffee, which she eventually found in the freezer. She realized that Faith was as nervous as she was, but the woman was also so happy, the emotion seemed to be coming off her in waves. Phoebe felt a stab of guilt deep within her.

"My parents don't know I'm here," she blurted.

Faith stopped her shuffling and looked at her, a coffee cup in her hand. Her face grew a bit more serious, but her smile didn't leave her eyes. Tommy forced a sigh of air through his nose.

"We'll talk about that, Phoebe," she said. Her voice was soft and warm. "We have time. Do you like sugar? Cream?"

Phoebe said that she did, and then she followed Tommy over to the round table and waited for her coffee.

"So," Adam said, looking over at his companion. Margi had been sitting with her arms folded across her chest and a stormy expression on her pale face from the moment he'd picked her up. She'd been glaring out the window without speaking as he drove laps around Oakvale Heights and the twisting roads that radiated around the development. "What do you want to do?"

"I can't believe she would do this to me," Margi said, her bracelets jangling as she uncrossed her arms and threw her hands skyward. Adam didn't mind that she'd ignored the question; he was just glad she was talking. "Can you believe she did this to me?"

"We could go to the Honeybee if you want," he said. "Get some milk shakes."

"She's irresponsible, is what she is. Irresponsible. To think that we would just cover for her so she could go on a date with a dead kid."

"Any movies you want to see?" Adam watched her out of the corner of his eye, amused at seeing Typhoon Margi start to blow. He knew that Margi had no problem at all lying to cover for a friend. In fact, it was usually Margi who would suggest it.

"And then to make you do it, too," she said, turning toward him as though suddenly aware that he was in the truck with her. "Bad enough to make me do it, but you—that's just icing on the cake. Talk about insult to injury." Her eyes were fiery and wild beneath her pink eye shadow.

He almost wanted to pursue that line of thought, but Margi wasn't always a reliable source of information, and the last thing he wanted, regarding Phoebe, was misinformation. So he let it go.

"I've got a Frisbee if you want to play Frisbee," he said. "Phoebe and I toss a Frisbee around sometime."

"Phoebe is the sensible one," she said. "She isn't supposed to do stuff like this."

She sniffed, and Adam realized with a growing sense of horror that she might be ready to burst out crying.

"Could we go to the lake?" she said. "I used to like going there."

Adam nodded and headed for the access road that would bring them to Oxoboxo Park, a short stretch of public beach kept sandy by the town.

"I learned how to swim there," Adam said. "The

Oakvale Rec used to give lessons."

"Me too," Margi said, reaching into her enormous black purse and pulling out a wadded lump of tissues. "I was in Colette's class. We were Guppies together."

And then she just let loose with deep sobbing cries. Adam gripped the wheel and pressed down on the accelerator.

Like everything in Oakvale, Oxoboxo Park was a short drive away. The entire town was made up of a lopsided hub around the lake and the woods that surrounded it, and the park was nestled in the southern corner where the Oxoboxo River joined the lake.

The parking area was roped off, so Adam parked beside the ropes and paced around in front of the truck while Margi cried a little longer. After a few minutes she must have realized that her makeup was a complete ruin and the only sensible thing to do would be to take off as much of it as she could. Adam watched her rubbing at her cheeks and eyes with the wadded tissue balls. He thought she needed some air, so he opened the door of the truck.

"Daffy," he said, "why don't you come out of there? We'll talk."

"Don't look at me," she said through her sobbing. "I'm horrible."

"No worse than usual," Adam replied, but her wailing indicated that humor was not the answer. He looked out over the Oxoboxo where it met the wide crescent of sand that the town had put in years ago and replenished every year since. There was a cold breeze rippling the water and making it lap gently on the shore. Beyond the crescent and far on the other side, the trees were thick, their branches full of red, yellow, and orange leaves that had begun to fade, as though they'd been bleached out by the grayish sky above.

"Come on, Daffy. I'm just kidding. You'll always be beautiful to me."

She gave a curt laugh, and Adam turned—partly because it was the polite thing to do, and partly because he was revolted as a big saliva bubble blew from her mouth.

"Yeah," she said, "I buy that. I wish I bought that."

"Daffy . . ."

"You and Phoebe should be dating," she said. "Then I wouldn't feel so bad."

"Sure," he said, with no witty rejoinder coming to mind.

"Take me home, please. I don't feel so good."

"Not yet," he said. "You wanted to come here, we're here. Let's talk."

She looked up at him, her eyes red from crying. Then she seemed to catch her breath and compose herself.

Adam held out his hand and motioned for her to come out. She gave her puffy face a final scrub and then took his hand, allowing him to lead her out of the truck.

"Well," she said, "I guess we learned that I'm an idiot. A total, total idiot."

"Nah," he said. "You're just upset. And you were just about to tell me what's upsetting you."

She let all the air out of her lungs in a great rush, and then she leaned back into the cab to rummage through her purse some more. "Phoebe. Colette. Zombies. Wow, it really turned cold today, didn't it?"

"Why don't you start with Phoebe," he said. He could feel a muscle along his jaw twitch, and was glad when Margi returned from her purse with a pack of gum. He accepted a piece, trading it for his heavy letter jacket.

"This smells good," she said, pulling the shoulders of the jacket in. "What cologne is that?"

"My natural musk," he said. "Phoebe?"

"I'm just worried about her," she said. "It's weird, her dating a dead kid. Having us cover for her. Don't you think it is weird?"

"It's weird," he agreed, folding the cinnamon gum up into his mouth and starting to chew.

"She's not talking about it, which is also weird. She isn't really telling me what she feels."

Me either, he thought, but didn't see any point in discussing that. "She probably doesn't know. Not everyone is struck by lightning when they think they have feelings for someone."

"I know, I know. I guess I just find the idea . . . creepy."

"Tommy is a good guy," he said, hoping she didn't notice the caution he felt in his voice.

"Sure," she said. "But he's dead. Where can it go?"

He didn't have an answer to that, so he started loping toward the water.

"Adam," she said, "can we leave now?"

He turned back to her with a wise comment on his lips, but he'd caught the tone of her voice, and he saw that she was shivering within the shelter of his coat.

She looked terrified.

"Daffy . . ."

"This is where she died," she said, her voice barely audible over the leaves rustling in the wind. "Not here, but over on the other side, where we used to hide out. The Weird Sisters, we were *so* spooky. Spoooooky! We had our own secret grotto deep in the woods. That was where she went under, right outside of the grotto."

"Who?" he said, knowing as soon as he said it. "Colette?"

She nodded, rubbing at her eyes, sending her bracelets clinking. "I thought maybe if I came here with you, you know, someone as big as you, I wouldn't be afraid. I know you'll think I'm making fun, but how could a girl be afraid if you were with her? I thought that maybe I could walk down to the water and put my big toe in and it would be all right again. I wouldn't be afraid."

"Margi, I wasn't even thinking when I mentioned the lessons. I'm not a very smart guy most of the time."

"But I still am. Afraid, I mean. I'm still afraid."

Adam looked back at the water and thought the whole surface of the lake had just darkened, like a giant mood ring.

"I haven't been back here since," she said.

"Margi," he said, "her drowning wasn't your fault. She blacked out, had a seizure or something. It wasn't anybody's fault."

"*That* part wasn't my fault," she said, so low he could barely understand her. Two tears rolled down her cheeks, leaving fresh grayish tracks on her skin.

"You could talk to her," Adam said.

"That's what Phoebe says too," she said. "But it's so hard, Adam. It's so hard to see her, to watch her walk or try to get up from her chair when class is over. And the way she looks at me . . ."

"Margi . . ."

"I thought the class might change something, Adam. I really did. I thought I'd have some major breakthrough or something, and just be okay with things. But I'm not. I'm not okay. The more time I spend with dead people, the more time I spend *thinking* about dead people, and I don't know how much more I can take. I start thinking about *being* a dead person. And now with Phoebe ditching us for zombies, I just don't know what to do."

"She's not ditching us," Adam said.

"I didn't let her in," Margi said. "She was calling and I didn't let her in."

"Who was calling, Margi?" he said. Was that some bizarre, Daffy-esque metaphor for what she was going through with Phoebe?

"I'd really like to go home now, Adam," she said. "Please."

Adam nodded. Her crying jag had left her looking disheveled and urchinlike in his jacket, which covered her like a tent.

"Sure, kid," he said, and climbed back into the truck.

Pulling out of the parking area, he realized that she hadn't looked at the Oxoboxo the entire time they'd been there, not even when the only view of the lake was in the rearview mirror.

CHAPTER EIGHTEEN

"*A*REN'T YOU COMING, PETE? We're going to be late."

A half dozen scathing retorts bubbled up through his subconscious, but Pete let them dissipate without comment.

"You go ahead," he said, watching from the foyer as Williams got on the bus. "Tell Coach I have diarrhea or something. I'll be out in a while."

"Really?" Stavis said. "You sick?"

Pete turned back to him and shook his head. The dead kid was moving pretty well for a dead kid, much better than the girl that he let on the bus before him.

"You want me to get the nurse, or something?"

"No, TC," Pete said through clenched teeth. "No, I don't want you to go to the nurse. What I want is for you to get out of here and go to practice and tell Coach that I'm sick. Tell him that I will be on the field as soon as I clear my colon."

"You want me to say *that*?" Stavis said. "I can't say that. He's gonna be pissed."

"TC, make something up. You're a creative guy."

"Yeah? You really think so?"

"Yeah, I really think so. Now go away."

Pete set his backpack down and took out the roster he'd ripped off the office wall. The blue sheet was creased and torn in places, one gummy strand of yellow masking tape still affixed at the remaining corner. There were four of them on that bus. Phoebe Kendall, Margi Vachon, Tommy Williams, and . . . some other dead chick. Either Sylvia Stelman or Colette Beauvoir, because the slutty-looking one was Karen DeSonne. One of the girls, either Sylvia or Colette, got picked up every day by a blue van that also took a zombie who must be Kevin Dumbrowski, because Evan Talbot was the redheaded freak who lived in Pete's neighborhood and Tayshawn Wade was the black zombie. Well, the gray zombie, anyhow.

That left only Adam Layman and Thornton Harrowwood, who were no doubt getting suited up to head out to practice with lunkhead Stavis.

Williams was a missed opportunity, Pete thought. The idea that he and Stavis had had the chance to put the hurt on him and failed to do so still rankled. And he'd tried. Every touch that Williams got, every time Williams lined up for a block or to cover, Pete hit him with everything he had. No matter what he and Stavis threw at him, Williams got up again like it was no big deal.

Pete had heard that the zombie was off the team. He was glad about it, sure, but it would have been much more satisfying had the zombie left with broken bones that had no hope of healing.

Big talk, Martinsburg.

That's what Coach had said to him, and the words still rang in his head like a shout in an empty gymnasium.

"Big talk, Martinsburg. I hear you yapping all the time about what a big deal you are, all these girls you've supposedly made. Big man."

Pete had been hanging around the locker room after their first post-zombie game. Most of the other players had already shuffled off to the bus, but Pete was holding forth with Stavis and Harris. He'd been feeling pretty good about himself; he'd gotten a sack, another interception, and made a few key backfield tackles. He'd only been burned on one play, really, but even giving that one up, they'd beat the far weaker Waterford team by three touchdowns.

Something he said must have set Konrathy off, because he'd ordered the rest of the kids off to the bus but told Pete to join him in the hall. Pete thought about it, the tone Coach had taken with him, and he felt the muscles jump along his arms. A week later and he was still angry.

"Yeah, you're a regular god to the rest of these dumbasses—morons like Stavis who don't know any better. But Layman doesn't buy your line of crap anymore, does he? And that dead kid, he never did buy it, either."

Pete was glad that Coach had ordered the rest of the team onto the bus so that they weren't around to watch him getting chewed on. He was also glad that they weren't there to hear how his voice cracked when he tried to answer. "Coach," he had said, "at least we ran him off the team."

Konrathy gave him a look like Pete was something to be scraped off his cleat. "You ran off nothing. He quit on his own terms. I had hoped that Stavis at least could get the job done, but he was a wash, too."

Pete was humiliated. He'd wanted to tell Coach that he'd been a coward for caving in to Kimchi in the first place, and that he'd been a coward again for not scrubbing Williams from the team. Konrathy had no right to fault him for not obliterating the zombie. At least he tried. What did Coach do, except make hand signals?

Pete walked under a huge handmade banner announcing the upcoming homecoming game against the Ballouville Wildcats, and the homecoming dance that followed.

"You're all talk, Martinsburg," Coach had said. "I've heard you crow about teaching those dead kids a lesson. All you've taught them so far is a lesson in how big a coward you are."

Damn, Pete thought, draining his energy drink in one swallow. He slammed the lid of the trunk of his car, and there she was, the zombie chick with the short skirt, slipping into the woods across the lot.

He sent the bottle bouncing off the hood of some loser's Impala.

Here's some new info for you, he thought, heading for the break in the trees.

He could feel his fury like a tight bubble within his chest as he entered the woods, tendrils of anger coursing through his veins. His fists were clenched and his mouth was dry. What right did this dead slut have walking around the woods in skimpy skirts and kneesocks while Julie lay still in her grave in some California cemetery? Why did she have a face like a porcelain doll, with pure white skin, while Julie was rotting somewhere beneath the earth?

Pete stifled a cough by pressing his fist to his lips. He wasn't sure what he was going to do; it was like a curtain of red fog had fallen across his vision, and it would not dissipate, no matter how many times he blinked. All he knew was that this zombie had no right to be wandering around these woods.

No right at all.

The path was wide enough to admit a small car or a pair of bicycles riding side by side, and it wound like an uncoiling snake after a sharp downward slope. Leaves crunched underfoot as he began walking. He thought about his last trip into these woods, when Williams had summoned his zombie friends from graves hidden within the forest. He stopped at the edge of the forest to watch her walk away.

He watched her plaid skirt twitch left and right. She was wearing headphones, the cord of which was plugged into something hidden within her small gray backpack. With her white kneesocks and patent leather, her boldness infuriated him. Where was she going? Off to some secret zombie lair in the woods, or some undead ritual on the shores of the Oxoboxo?

The dead girl was fast for a zombie. She cleared the slope and was a fair distance ahead on the curving path, just approaching a copse of thin birch trees whose branches leaned over and cut part of the path from view. The branches obscured her from the waist up, but Pete caught a glimpse of smooth white legs. He waited until she disappeared from his view before running. He figured that he would close the gap between them by the time he cleared the birches. There was no way that a zombie could outrun him; he was one of the fastest athletes in the whole school.

I'll catch her in no time, he thought as he began to sprint. Once beyond the birches, the path stretched out in front of him, long and straight.

The girl was gone.

Pete was beginning to tire of hide-and-seek. He peered around a thick clot of brush and then looked behind the remnants of a low stone wall. There she was, lying on the mildewed and mossy ground, leaves and crawling things twined in her hair, the flesh of her face rotting away, and one lidless eye fixing him with a cold empty gaze. He stumbled back because it wasn't the zombie lying there, it was Julie, Julie in the kneesocks, scuffed patent leathers, and a skirt too short for decency; it was Julie waiting for him behind trees and in dark corners.

Pete swore and rubbed his eyes, his rage morphing into another feeling entirely. Maybe if there weren't any zombies, he could leave Julie where she belonged, dead and buried. He cursed again, and when he turned, the dead girl—Karen—was fifteen feet away from him, standing beneath the shading veil of the birch branches, her hands clasped behind her back.

The dead girl stared at him through lowered eyes—eyes whose blankness creeped him out. They were like diamonds without the sparkle. She did not blink.

"You were following me," she said.

Pete nodded, feeling a muscle twitch in his jaw. He wondered if this freak had put the image of poor Julie in his head.

"Why," she said, "were you following me?"

He didn't answer. She didn't look frightened, but what little he knew about zombies suggested that they weren't the greatest at expressing themselves. He could charge her and knock her down before her cold dead lips could speak another word.

"Did you . . . want . . . to hurt me? Is that it?"

He nodded. He took one cautious step forward, as if she were a deer that was about to bolt, or a dog that was about to bite.

"Yeah," he said, his voice a low, soft whisper. "I do."

She lifted her head after a slow nod. "Like you tried to hurt Tommy."

She'd colored her lips a soft peach hue, and he thought he saw a ghost of a smile there. He couldn't tell if she was mocking him or flirting with him.

"Like I tried to hurt Tommy."

She made a sound like a sigh. "Will that make you feel . . . better?" she asked. "If you could . . . hurt me?"

"Oh yeah," he said, taking another step. There was a fallen branch on the side of the path, and he broke it over his knee. He was left with a sharp, jagged point of new wood at the end of a three foot section of branch. "I really think it would."

She nodded, her spooky diamond eyes never leaving his. "Then hurt me," she whispered.

He laughed and moved forward, holding the stake level with the point of the V formed by the collar of her white blouse.

"But use a rock," she said, nodding at the stone wall. "We aren't vampires."

Pete paused and considered the option.

"It's a start," he said, choking up on his grip.

Her peach lips parted as if she were about to reply, but then she nodded and undid the third button of her blouse.

"Go ahead," she told him.

She's really going to let me do it, he thought. The sick bitch.

He took his time, but was almost to her when he heard a noise behind him that raised the hair on his neck with its tone and volume—he imagined it was like the bellow of a large, prehistoric animal.

He turned and saw two figures at a distance on the path. One of them was the big black zombie, making the noise again—Pete realized he was shouting the dead girl's name. He was moving as fast as his dead legs could carry him, which wasn't very. His right leg seemed locked at the knee, and the left twitched out in a violent spasm with every step. The overall effect was like watching an old drunk trying to evade the police while at the same time having a heart attack.

The other one, though, Pete thought, the other one was scary.

He was moving just fine, an Asian-looking kid with long

black hair, black jeans, and a black leather jacket. He was almost running. And he was smiling, which was weird, because zombies rarely smiled, especially not with their teeth.

"Hurry," the dead girl said, and he whirled, intent on doing her right then, and not taking his time like he'd wanted to. But then he saw in her pale dead face that it wasn't her zombie pals she was warning.

"You're last," he said, tossing the stick away. He forced himself to walk, not run, back down the path toward the school parking lot.

"Is it just me," Thorny said, leaning back in his chair as he unwrapped a chocolate-chip granola bar, "or is this the longest shift of all time?"

"It's just you," Adam replied. He was staring at the four monitors that cycled real-time images from the dozen or so security cameras throughout the foundation. Periodically, monitor four would blink in the lab where Alish was explaining something or other to Kevin and Margi in their white lab coats emblazoned with the Hunter Foundation logo—a big gold HF on a black shield. Adam thought it looked like something you'd see on a yacht cap. Tommy sat next to him in the blue work shirt that both he and Thorny wore, the emblem sewn above the left pocket. Adam had been trying to figure out if Tommy blinked when the monitors flashed and switched cameras.

"No, seriously," Thorny said, putting his feet up on Duke Davidson's desk. "We've been here, what? Four hours?"

"Three."

"See what I mean?" Thorny said. "This is an eternity."

"The shifts go by a lot faster," Adam said, "when you aren't with me."

Tommy's smile was reflexive, but it only reached one side of his face. He got up and stretched, and Adam thought he could hear vertebrae snap and pop into place along his spine.

"You stretch?" Thorny spoke through a bite of crunchy granola. Maybe it was his chewing that Adam heard. "What does that do?"

"It . . . helps," Tommy said.

"How?" Thorny asked, and Adam turned toward him. "No, seriously. How can it help? You don't have to get the blood flowing, right? And . . ."

His question died on his lips as Duke Davidson walked in and slapped Thorny's feet off of his desk, almost sending him crashing to the floor. Adam thought that old Duke moved pretty quickly for a guy who looked like an older, less pleasant version of the differently biotic students in his class.

"Don't you three have something to do?" the man said, his words like the cracking of a whip.

"Um, we're watching the monitors," Thorny said. Duke looked at him, his bloodhound eyes causing Thorny to shrink back in his chair and swallow an unchewed hunk of granola bar.

Adam figured ole Duke for an ex-cop. Either that or an ex-con; he'd read somewhere that a lot of former prisoners of the state ended up in security. For such a tall, spider-limbed fellow, he thought that Duke carried himself with what Master

Griffin called "centered balance"—a way of movement that was economical and always enabled the prepared to act quickly to whatever came their way.

"Watching the monitors," Duke said, leaning forward. "Why don't you do a trash sweep?"

Thorny was about to answer that they'd already taken out the trash, but Adam cut him off before his insolence got them even more chores.

"Yes, sir," he said. "We'll get that done."

He led Tommy and Thorny out into the hallway.

"Let's go to the lab," he said.

"What?" Thorny said, quickening his step to catch up. "What did I do?"

Adam noticed that Tommy didn't have any trouble matching his own stride. "Nothing, Thorny. You didn't do anything."

"Except show a lack of . . . ambition," Tommy said.

Adam continued to find Tommy's sense of humor amusing; it was so quiet and wry. So *deadpan*, he thought, smiling to himself.

"What?" Thorny, clueless, asked.

"Forget it. Let's get going."

"I hate the lab."

"Why?" Tommy asked.

"They . . . *do* stuff there." He lowered his voice. Adam would have found Thorny's comment funny if he hadn't looked scared when he spoke. "Experiments."

"Well, this is a scientific facility. At least on paper," Adam said.

"Yeah, but there's more than that."

"What . . . do you mean?"

The smaller boy looked at each of his companions in turn, and then at the ceiling as though searching for hidden cameras or microphones. His voice dropped to a dry whisper.

"I heard Alish and Angela talking about Sylvia and Kevin, about taking 'samples' from them." He ran his hand through his thick mop of hair. "What *kind* of samples, I wonder?"

"Come on," Adam said, although in a sense it didn't surprise him. How else were they going to learn about the dead?

"No, really," Thorny said, "I heard them. He said he couldn't figure out why some of the zombies could walk and talk better than the others."

"He hasn't . . . stuck me . . . with any needles," Tommy said.

"It isn't your shift in the lab," Thorny said. He grew quiet as Margi turned into their hallway, coming toward them with a huge stack of papers.

"Yet," Thorny whispered.

"Hi, boys," Margi said. "I get to make copies."

"Lucky you," Adam said, thinking that she looked a little happier than the grainy Margi he'd watched on the monitor screens. He suspected it had more to do with her getting out of lab duty than it did with seeing them.

"That's a big . . . stack . . . you have there," Tommy said.

Margi's eyes narrowed at him, and she picked up her pace.

"Was that a joke?" Adam asked. "Was that you being funny?"

"What . . . did . . . I . . . say?"

"I don't get it," Thorny said.

But Tommy did, a moment later. Adam could almost see the realization creeping into his eyes. He thought that he'd witnessed the closest a zombie ever came to blushing, and it lightened his mood as they continued on their way.

But his mood darkened again when they reached the door of the lab and it was locked. It was the one room in the facility their key cards could not open.

CHAPTER NINETEEN

*P*HOEBE LIKED EVEN MELLOW music played loud, so she was wearing her headphones as she read Tommy's words on the screen. She was listening to a This Mortal Coil album, one she'd copied out of the vast collection that Colette's older brother had amassed before going off to war. When she heard the violins, it felt as though the bows were being drawn over the strings that attached her brain stem to her spine. She shuddered with the sensation, thinking of Tommy and Colette and everything she was feeling.

She tapped idly on the down arrow, scrolling through the page. The skin of her bare arms was a spectral white, smooth and luminous in the dark room.

Like Karen's, she thought.

We make deals with the devil every day, metaphorically. I know there are those who would say that some sort of deal with the

devil was made for our very existence here. But the deal
I made with one of the many devils in my life was a
literal one.

I have written extensively of my reasons for going out for
the football team here at Oakvale High. I would not have
achieved any of my goals had I not gotten a chance to actually
play, and the coach refused to put me in. He was being
pressured internally from the school administration, and also
getting flak from the media and the few political figures
sympathetic to our concerns. But my devil was stubborn, and
he refused to bend under the pressure. So by halftime I hadn't
played a minute of the game. And I would not have been able
to play the three minutes and thirty-three seconds of game time
I did, if not for what I said to him in the locker room during
halftime.

I wish I could tell you what I'm sure many of you would
like to hear—that I threatened him, that I frightened him with
the promise of an undead horde visiting him in the night. But I
didn't. I offered to quit.

Phoebe leaned forward and read the line a second time, but
it read the same. *I offered to quit.*

"What?" Coach said. He could barely stand to look at me.
"I will quit the team if you play me today. Put me in for a
series of plays."
His expression was like that of a distrustful dog being
offered a piece of meat.

"You'll quit?"

I nodded. "All of this goes away. The whole circus. And if anyone asks why I quit, your name won't come up."

He looked at me for a minute, his face full of hate. He didn't answer, and when he walked past me, he made sure that we did not touch.

He put me in, and I played. But real life is not like the movies. The team did not rally around the undead misfit, nor did my spectacular play inspire a sweeping change of attitude. The kid I tackled pretty much fell down because he was so scared of me—and I can't blame him.

Certain attempts to exploit us aside, some of Mr. Slydell's concepts ring true. Transformation is usually a result of radical action, and in today's world, a dead kid playing a team sport is a radical action. What Slydell leaves out is that much radical action leads to violent reaction, and that violence simmered around school the day of the game.

I was never afraid during the game. The protestors could have thrown hand grenades and nail bombs, and I would not have been afraid for myself. I'm already dead.

But I was afraid for my friends who have not experienced what I have. And I was afraid for the other living people who were there, the ones who have compassion mixed in with their fear. I would not want those people hurt just so that I could prove a point by playing football. That would certainly have happened if I'd stayed on the team; the violence simmering through the bleachers would have boiled over at some point, and people would have been hurt.

I know many of you will think that backing out was
wrong, that I had a chance to battle with the demon and I
blinked. I won't argue, but I will say that I did what I set out
to do, which was to plant a seed. I did not want to water that
seed with the blood of the living.

Phoebe leaned back and stretched. She rested her fingers lightly on the keyboard. There were a few replies posted already, the first of which was a short diatribe from AllDEAD, who called Tommy a coward and said that only through violence and death will the "blood bags" have an understanding of what it means to be dead in a world made for the living.

Phoebe licked her lips. AllDEAD missed the point; Tommy's decision made her admire him even more. She started to go through the process of acquiring a blogsite login so she could leave a post, stopping herself twice. She wanted to post her own experience of sitting in the stands watching Tommy and feeling as though she were seated in the eye of a hurricane, a hurricane blowing over the surface of the underworld. But in the end, she didn't do it.

She dreamed of Tommy that night. He was alone on the football field, in his gear but without a helmet, beneath a fat harvest moon. She was in the stands, clapping, but surrounded by angry people who were shouting and booing. A crowd of dead kids stood in the shadows of the Oxoboxo woods. Tommy was looking at her, walking toward her across the field, and then people began throwing food at him. Heads of lettuce, hot dogs, apples, bottles of soda. A tomato hit him just above his numbers. Phoebe stood as a few of them began shooting. She had an armful of poetry that fluttered around her like dead leaves as bullets tore into his uniform and passed through his body. He still kept walking. A thrown bottle with a flaming rag stuffed in the neck burst against him, sending flames racing up his side. Bullet holes stitched a line across his chest; he was closer now, and she saw black holes in his cheek, his neck, his thighs. The fire began to melt his skin. He took one step onto the bleachers, and she woke up.

The fourth week of Undead Studies class—Phoebe herself had begun referring to the class that way—began with Tommy relating some of the recent acts of violence that had been committed across the country on differently biotic persons. Phoebe had read most of the stories on Tommy's Web site, but hearing him tell the stories aloud lent them an even more harrowing quality.

"They ran down a girl . . . in Memphis," he said. "She was . . . thirteen. She . . . died . . . twice in two . . . weeks."

"Terrible," Angela said, shaking her head in sympathy. Phoebe looked around to gauge the reaction of her fellow students; the dead kids were impassive and the living ones seemed to have difficulty looking at anyone or anything except for the floor, as though they in some way had participated in the atrocities that Tommy was describing.

Phoebe felt it, too, the lurking sense of guilt that they were somehow responsible for the crimes.

"There was another report . . . of a white van . . . in

Massachusetts. And the murder . . . of a zombie."

White vans appeared in many of the reports on the blog. Tommy had a theory that many of the random acts of violence committed against his people weren't so random. Angela, Phoebe noticed, neither approved nor condemned the theory.

"Thank you, Tommy," Angela said, after he described how a zombie with two high-caliber rifle bullets in his head was found in his parents' backyard. "Why do you think these stories never reach the national news?" she asked the group.

"Racism," Thorny said. He'd been shaking like a wet greyhound since sitting down, having pounded two cans of soda from the fridge as soon as he reached the class. He'd told Phoebe and Adam that he was trying to OD on sugar to gain some weight.

"I mean, bioism. Is that a word? What I'm saying is that there are a lot of people out there who hate zombies, so the media isn't reporting everything like they should."

"Maybe," Margi said. She was in a mood today, and Phoebe knew that whenever her friend got that way she could say just about anything. "Or maybe all of these stories are just urban myths."

"What makes you say that, Margi?" Angela asked. Tayshawn, cursed, and Margi looked at him before responding.

"I . . . I just mean that it seems really weird that all these zomb . . . I mean all these DB people are being killed and no one would do anything about it."

"Why would anyone do anything about it?" Karen asked. "It isn't . . . illegal . . . to kill a zombie."

"I know. I know. I just can't believe that people would just watch someone get killed and not do anything about it."

"Would you?" Karen asked. "Do something about it?"

Margi's mouth opened and closed with a shocked abruptness. Her face went as pink as her hair.

"Of course we would," Phoebe said, covering for her as best she could. "It is just so strange that Tommy has to go hunting for these stories, though. Especially the white van. What do you think that is? Some sort of fanatical group?"

"The . . . government," Tayshawn said.

"Do you believe that, Tayshawn?" Angela asked.

He nodded.

"I . . . was . . . left," Colette said.

All heads, some more slowly than others, turned toward her, but Phoebe looked over at Margi. There was a small stuffed animal, a black cat, on a key ring attached to her bag, and she was squeezing it hard enough to make her knuckles white.

Angela, apparently less interested in government conspiracies than she was in Colette's feelings and experiences, nodded. "Left, how?"

Colette was a long time in answering. "Left . . . by . . . everyone."

Angela started to speak but then stopped when she realized Colette had more to say and needed no further urging, only the time to vocalize her thoughts. This was their fourth group session, and the slower of the zombies—Colette, Kevin, and Sylvia—never spoke until directly prompted by Angela—until now.

"My . . . parents . . . would not . . . let . . . me . . . in the . . . house. I . . . walked . . . from the . . . hospital . . . morgue . . . in . . . Winford. Seven . . . miles."

Phoebe stared at the floor. If she hung her head just so, her long dark hair might prevent others from seeing the tears in her eyes.

"I . . . knocked . . . on . . . the door. I . . . rang . . . the . . . bell. My . . . mother . . . was . . . screaming . . . for me . . . to . . . go . . . away. I . . . knocked . . . on the . . . window . . . and the . . . window . . . broke. Daddy . . . he . . ."

Phoebe heard herself sob, and she felt Margi shift away from her on the sofa.

"Daddy . . . came out . . . of the garage," she said, her staring eyes like portals into another world. "He had . . . a . . . shovel."

"Jesus Christ," Adam said.

"I . . . left. I . . . stayed . . . in the . . . woods. Three . . . days. I went . . . to . . . my friend's . . . house."

Margi jumped off the couch. "You were dead, Colette! What was I supposed to do? You were dead!"

"My . . . friend . . . would not . . . let me in." She looked at Phoebe. "None of . . . my friends . . . would let . . . me in."

"I was scared, Colette!" Margi said, her voice a thin shriek. "You were all . . . all . . . I was scared!"

Phoebe wanted to say something, but she couldn't move; her own guilt had paralyzed her. All she could do was cry, which she did, the makeup around her eyes running down her cheeks in thin black rivulets.

Colette turned toward Margi and then she stood up. Margi flinched and tripped over the couch, nearly falling down. She ran out of the room.

"This is probably a good time for a break," Adam said, but Angela shook her head. Phoebe found the strength to stand, fully intending to go find Margi. Colette called her name, and she froze in place.

"Stay."

Phoebe turned toward her. Colette was so impassive, so cold and slow. She was blank and expressionless, with none of the tics or inflections attempted by the more functional dead kids. Phoebe felt like Colette's black eyes were boring through her skull.

"Please."

Adam touched her arm as he walked by. "I'll go find Daffy," he said quietly. Phoebe sat.

"What happened then, Colette?" Angela asked.

Colette remained standing. "I . . . hid. In the . . . woods. And then . . . in the . . . lake. Tommy . . . found . . . me."

Tommy lifted his left shoulder—a shrug. "It is a . . . gift."

"What did you do when you found her?" Angela asked.

"I . . . talked to her. I brought her . . . home."

"Home? Your home?"

Tommy nodded.

"Your mother didn't mind?"

"My mother . . . helped."

Angela's eyebrows arched. "You've brought other differently biotics home to your mother?"

Tommy nodded again.

"Do they stay?"

"No room."

"Where do they go?

He gave the half shrug again.

Angela turned back to Colette. "Colette? Where did you go after spending time with Tommy?"

"I . . . left. Went . . . to . . . the . . . house."

"The house?"

"She spent time with me," Karen said. "And with Evan, too."

"You have a house where you stay?"

"Some of us," Tommy said, "stay together."

"Where?"

"It would not be a good thing for . . . everyone . . . to know."

"True," Angela said. "But certainly you can trust the people in this room?"

"Certainly," Tommy said, his mouth twitching. But he didn't say, and none of the other differently biotic kids chose to fill the gap of his silence.

"Very well," Angela replied. "Thank you for sharing your story, Colette. I'm sure that was a very painful experience for you. Sharing, I mean. We're about out of time for the day."

Phoebe felt like her heart was frozen in her chest. The students shuffled past her. She was still crying and couldn't seem to speak.

Colette sat next to her on the couch. Phoebe looked at her, her eyes stinging and her vision blurred from the makeup that she'd tried to wipe away. Colette's gaze was unreadable.

"Colette, I . . . I'm . . ."

Colette reached for her in the now-empty room.

Phoebe could hear the STD yelling when Adam picked up the phone.

"Yeah?"

"It's me."

"Hey."

"How's Margi?"

"Couldn't really tell. She wouldn't speak to me. We got permission to leave early, and from the shuttle I drove her home. She thanked me, that was about it," he sighed. "How are *you*?"

"Um . . ."

"Yeah, I figured. Frisbee?"

"Okay."

"Give me a half hour. I've got to do some crap for the STD first."

"Okay."

It got dark too early, so Phoebe suggested they go over to the football field, where they could play under the lights. She felt better the moment she was in Adam's truck, and then felt better again as he tossed the moon-yellow glowing disk to her, throwing it in a soft lazy spiral.

"Can't remember the last time I saw you in sneakers," he said, looking down at her black tennies. "Don't those boots you wear all the time kill your feet?"

She tossed the Frisbee back, wincing as she saw that it was going to drop about five yards short.

"No, they're really pretty comfortable. And I wore these just last week when we were out here."

"Oh," he said, running for the disk and snagging it the moment before it hit the turf. Adam could throw a Frisbee about two dozen different ways, and this time he threw it sidearm. Phoebe caught it on the angle behind her back.

"Sweet," he said. "I was worried you'd lose it after lying around all day drinking coffee and writing goth poetry."

"Oh, you heard about that?"

"Heard about what?" he said with mock innocence, and ran back so he could catch the disk she'd thrown high over his head.

"Never mind."

"Okay." He looped the next one with a quick over-the-forearm throw he snapped from his wrist. She tried the behind-the-back move, and it bounced off her side.

"Awww," he said. "So, what's the deal?"

Phoebe picked the Frisbee off the turf and sailed it over to him chest high, finding the range.

"Colette hugged me."

"Oh," he said, flipping it back to her in the same manner. "That's a good thing, right?"

"Uh-huh. I was crying like a baby."

"It's an emotional thing, her hugging you. A little scary, too."

She had to run for his next throw and caught it on her

fingertips. "Yeah. But look how scary everything was for her."

He nodded, easily flagging down her return throw. He moved with an effortless grace uncommon in kids his size. "You can't feel what other people are feeling. You can only try to imagine what other people are feeling."

"We let her down, Adam."

"You aren't talking about the lake, are you? That wasn't your fault."

The next one went right to her, and she admired the backspin he'd put on it. "No. Her drowning was no one's fault. I'm talking about her return."

"Oh."

"She came to our houses, Adam. And we turned her away."

He was a long time in answering. "Second chances," he said. "She hugged you."

"Yeah."

"Margi will come around."

They played for forty-five minutes, changing topics to give their thoughts about Margi and Colette some dwell time. They had a good laugh at Thornton, who'd worn a *Some of My Best Friends are Dead* T-shirt to school earlier in the week and had gotten a detention from his homeroom teacher, which Principal Kim revoked.

"What do you think of Tommy quitting the football team?" she asked.

"I'm disappointed. He was pretty good."

"Did you talk to him about it?"

"No. I figure he didn't want the protests and stuff getting out of hand."

She smiled. "When did you turn into such an insightful guy, Adam?"

He ignored her. "I like that sweatshirt. You should wear white more often. I didn't think you had anything that wasn't black."

"Not true. I have clothes that are gray, umber, and noir."

"My mistake." He laughed. "Let's get out of here."

The first thing that Phoebe did when she got home was check her e-mail, but Margi hadn't replied. Nor had she answered her cell phone.

"Dad, did Margi call?"

He looked up from his mystery novel. "No calls, I'm pleased to report."

But Phoebe wasn't pleased. She was worried.

CHAPTER TWENTY

NGELA SAT IN THE OFFICE with Phoebe and Karen as they worked what would be their last shift in the clerical pool. Next week Phoebe would go off to the wild world of facilities maintenance while Karen would get to do some real work in the lab. Phoebe was not happy about the change, having no desire to spend any time with Duke Davidson, who she found to be creepier than just about anyone she knew.

"I wanted to thank you girls for all the work that you did here," Angela said. "You've been a lot of help."

"It's what we're here for," Phoebe told her. "I just wish we could have found more positive comments for you."

Angela laughed. "Eventually. Eventually I think we'll see a begrudging acceptance of what we do. Society will just have to grow."

"What do you think it will take for society to do that,

Ms. Hunter?" Karen asked as she straightened a sheaf of papers.

Angela looked at her. "I wish I knew, exactly, Karen. I think it will be a combination of things. But chief among them will be a great deal of effort from people like you."

Karen looked up with the flat expression of the dead, something Phoebe noticed she could switch on and off at will, a mask for her.

"What do you mean?" she said.

"I'm sorry. I don't mean to make you feel pressured. But I think for the differently biotic—zombies—to ever get true acceptance, it will be because of people like you."

"Like me?"

"High-functioning zombies. You speak with few pauses. You move well. Your face is more expressive," she said. "When you want it to be."

Phoebe watched Karen for her reaction, but she maintained the empty gaze.

"High-functioning," Karen said.

"Please don't be insulted. But surely you are aware that you are different from most of the differently biotic students. You could almost . . ."

"Pass?"

"I was going to say, see the others looking up to you," she said. If Angela was insulted, she hid it well behind her smile. "The differently biotic community needs leaders. Art. Culture. People like you and Tommy could make a difference."

"Because the others . . . could look up to us."

"And because you can communicate well. You could be the public face of the differently biotic."

Karen did an approximation of a frown. "Oh my," she said.

"It's true, Karen," Phoebe said. "You're beautiful."

"What a sweetie you are, Phoebe," Karen said, allowing herself to smile. When Karen smiled, her face was almost magnetic in its beauty, but Phoebe found the rapid transition to such beauty from emptiness somewhat disconcerting.

"Well," she said, "it's true."

Angela nodded. "There's something within you and Tommy that some of the others haven't tapped into yet. A creativity . . . a spirit . . . I don't know what it is. But I know that neither of you show it enough. Especially Tommy."

"That isn't true," Phoebe said, but Karen spoke over her.

"I . . . appreciate what you are saying. But you are . . . assuming . . . that living people want us to act, walk, and talk like them. I don't think that is true."

Phoebe wrote www.mysocalledundeath.com on a piece of paper along with her site login ID and password.

"You don't think that makes it easier for people to listen to you?"

"For some. I think that for others it is harder. The more we act like them the more they are aware we aren't. It makes them paranoid."

"Really?"

"I think it would . . . absolutely blow peoples' minds if they couldn't . . . tell we were dead."

"Hm."

"Tommy is very creative," Phoebe said, interrupting.

"I'm sure that he is," Angela said. "He just doesn't let on that he is."

"That isn't true," Phoebe said. "He has his own Web site."

"A Web site?" Angela said.

Phoebe nodded. "And a blog. Dead kids from all over the country read what he writes. So I don't think you should just assume that people aren't creative or socially conscious just because they aren't blabbing about it in class."

"I'm sorry, Phoebe," Angela said. "You're right. I shouldn't make those sorts of assumptions."

"Then again, you make a really good point," Karen said. "I probably should do more to be socially conscious. I mean, it's clear that the younger dead do look up to me, in a certain sense—Colette and Sylvia, anyhow—and I should probably . . ."

"What is his Web site, Phoebe?" Angela said.

"www.my—"

"Who knows, maybe I could run for student body president or something. Get it? Student body? I can see the headline: 'Karen DeSonne buries the competition by a landslide.' Get it? Buries? Ha-ha."

Phoebe looked over at Karen, who was not only speaking faster than she'd ever heard a dead person speak, she was speaking faster than Margi, even.

"Phoebe?" Angela said. "The Web site?"

"mysocalledundeath.com."

She could have sworn that Karen sighed when she gave

the address, but of course the undead didn't breathe.

Angela smiled her ever-present Cheshire cat smile. Phoebe wondered if she'd just made a big mistake.

Adam watched Phoebe and Margi cross the cafeteria, and he saw Margi's hand shoot out in a blur of jangly silver bracelets to grip Phoebe's arm and steer her away from the table where Karen DeSonne sat, alone, her place setting surrounded by a ring of Tupperware.

Karen had spread out a cloth napkin, and on the napkin she'd set a squat Thermos bowl, like the kind a kid would take chicken soup or macaroni and cheese in, and a smaller round container, a bright red apple, and a cup of yogurt. She put out a plastic spoon and popped the lid off the little container. Adam peered over to see a carefully stacked pyramid of carrot sticks. Yet another tub contained sliced strawberries.

Margi steered Phoebe away from the dead girl's picnic, angling over to where Adam sat by himself, munching on the second of his roast beef sandwiches. He watched Phoebe shake free of Margi's grip before they both took seats across from him.

"Hi, Adam," Phoebe said, irritation evident in her voice. Adam nodded, not wanting to stop observing Karen, who sat and stared at the table she'd arranged with serious concentration.

"I can't take it," Margi whispered, slapping her own lunch bag on the table. "I just can't."

"Gee, she's all alone . . ." Phoebe started, but Margi was shaking her head.

"She has food, Phoebe. Food. She has food, and you know they don't eat. I can't take it anymore, it isn't right, it isn't natural . . ."

"Shhh," Phoebe said. "Keep it down, will you?"

Margi pushed her lunch, and an orange rolled out of the mouth of the wrinkled bag, onto the floor.

Adam looked at them for a moment, filling his mouth with another bite of sandwich so he wouldn't be expected to say anything. Phoebe looked at him, signaling that he should step in, as if they were Margi's parents. Margi was busy acting hysterical. Her hands were shaking, and Adam didn't think that this was her normal melodrama at play here. He swallowed.

"Hey, Daffy," he said. "Are you okay?"

Margi bent to the table, her voice dropping to a harsh whisper. "She has *food*, Adam. Soup . . . and . . . and . . . *milk* . . ."

Adam nodded. He reached across the table and placed his hand on hers. "I know. She's got a regular picnic over there. But she isn't eating any of it. See?"

He nodded over at the next table, but Margi would not look up.

"She probably just wants to be normal, Margi. She's probably just trying to act like any other kid in the cafeteria."

"But she can't, Adam! That's what I'm talking about. That's exactly what I'm talking about!"

Phoebe was looking at Margi as if she were the weird one. Adam shrugged.

"I'm quitting the class," Margi said, slipping her hand out from under Adam's, the cool silver bangles and rings passing under his fingertips like water. "I need to go to the nurse." She stood up and all but ran from the room.

"Gee!" Phoebe called after her. "I'll just bus your table for you, is that okay?"

"She's upset," Adam said. He didn't like to see Phoebe get sarcastic with her friend; it wasn't like her at all.

"And she won't tell me why," Phoebe said. "I could kill her."

"Then you could get her to sit with Karen."

She ignored the joke. "There's something she's not telling me, something about Colette. I got Margi to join the work study because I thought it would help her get over this thing, this fear or whatever it is, of Colette."

"It's hard," Adam said. Over at the next table, Karen was staring at her food like she was trying to levitate it from the table. Martinsburg, walking by carrying a tray, turned to his shadow, Stavis, and said something that made the larger boy laugh. "Death is scary."

"But it doesn't have to be," Phoebe said. "Especially not now."

That didn't make much sense to Adam, but he didn't say so. For a moment he watched Phoebe pull the crust off her cheese sandwich before trying to change his approach. "Are you sure that Margi joined to get over Colette? Are you sure she didn't join because of you?"

Phoebe looked up. "What do you mean?" She sounded angry.

"I don't know," he said. But he did. It was why he had joined, too.

From the corner of his vision he watched Stavis and Martinsburg sit down a few tables away, still looking over at Karen. They were leering at her.

"Hey, you want to go sit with her?" Adam asked.

Phoebe brightened. "Sure."

They picked up their things and walked over to Karen. She was perfectly still.

"Can we join you?" Phoebe asked, and Karen nodded slowly. Adam gave Stavis and Pete a meaningful look before sitting down. Pete blew him a kiss.

Karen looked up at them, a smile returning to her face as though someone had flipped a switch inside of her.

"Isn't it pretty?" she said. "The red strawberries, the way they glisten, the bright orange of the carrots. I like my navy blue napkin, too."

"It's very nice," Phoebe said.

"I'm so glad that I can still see colors, you know?" Karen said. "I mean, I wonder sometimes if they are muted, like some of the pigments in my eyes washed away when I died, but at least I can still tell that this is red and that is orange and the milk is white. I can't imagine going through life color-blind, can you? All the colors washed out of the world?"

"No, I can't," Phoebe said. Adam just nodded.

"My eyes used to be blue," she said.

"Now they are like diamonds," Phoebe told her. "They might be the prettiest eyes I've ever seen."

Karen lifted the little cup of strawberries to her nose. "I wish I could smell them," she said. "Sometimes I think I can, just a little. But then I . . . wonder . . . if maybe I'm . . . remembering what they smell like. Which is ironic . . . because they say that . . . smell . . . is most closely . . . linked . . . with memory."

"The soup smells good, too," Phoebe said.

Karen made a noise like laughter. "Soup! Yeah, remember soup? Gosh."

Adam couldn't smell the soup because Phoebe was sitting so close to him that they touched, and the scent of her shampoo filled his nostrils. He wished that he had a third sandwich, if only so he could give his hands and mouth something to do. He thought that Karen was freaking out in her own way, just like Margi. Was it possible for any girl, living or dead, to be sane for more than a few hours at a time?

"I can still . . . hear. And . . . feel." She smiled at them. "I . . . think."

He wanted to tell Phoebe to hug her or something, but then Karen started putting the lids back on her containers.

"Thank you for sitting with me," she said. "And thank you, Adam, for acting protective toward me. It's kind of funny, the idea of protecting a dead girl, isn't it?" She giggled, and the noise was much more authentic than the previous attempt.

"What . . . what do you mean?"

"Oh, I saw you. Those mean boys. I'm aware. Hyperaware, really. Might be because I can't . . . feel . . . as much."

She put her hand on his. Her fingers were cool and smooth.

"Don't let them hurt the others. They want to, you know. There's something there, something in him, the good-looking one. Something beyond fear."

"Who? Pete?"

She nodded. "Just don't let him hurt . . . the others."

"I'll try."

"I know you will," she said. "You always do."

She patted his hand twice.

"So, Phoebe," she said, "where is Tommy taking you on your date?"

Phoebe blushed all the way to her neck. Adam would have laughed if he hadn't had a sudden ache at the pit of his stomach, one that no quantity of roast beef sandwiches could fill.

Pete had almost worked out what sort of public spectacle he was going to make of the dead girl, but then Adam and Scarypants sat down and kind of killed the idea. Not that he was scared of Adam—he wasn't—but he didn't want the final showdown with Lame Man to be in the school cafeteria. Pete was as realistic as Adam was big, and he knew that he might not have what it took to beat the big oaf in a fair fight, so he would need to wait for an unfair fight.

Lunch was almost over when Adam walked over to the table.

"Can I talk to you for a minute, Pete?" he said. "Alone?"

Pete looked up, smiling. "We gonna fight?" he asked.

The Lame Man shook his head. "Only if you throw the first punch."

"Talk, huh?" Pete said. He smirked at Stavis and a few of the other hangers-on. "Let's go talk."

They went to a corner of the cafeteria, which was beginning to empty. Pete watched Scarypants and Zombina leaving, and he made sure that Adam saw him doing it.

"Pete," Adam said, "this has got to stop."

"What?" Pete said, still watching them as they disappeared into the hallway outside.

"This campaign of hate that's going on. Threatening people."

"Threatening people?"

"Tommy. Karen. Thornton told me that you said you and Stavis were going to stomp his ass some day."

"Not threats," Pete said, smiling. "Promises."

The smile widened when he saw his words get through the armor Adam wrapped around himself.

"Pete . . . we were friends."

"*Were*," Pete said. "Like you said. You picked your team."

"All because Coach told you to rough up a kid and I wouldn't go along?"

"Not a kid. That's what you don't seem to get. Not a kid. A zombie. A dirty, rotting, bug-infested zombie. That's who you picked over me."

"I don't get it. Why all this hate?"

Pete licked his lips, and he was close, he really was, to telling Adam all about Julie. But he'd never told anyone. No one except his father knew anything about her.

Pete shrugged. "Civic duty."

"He knocked the wind out of you. So what. And so we had a big fight in the woods. Let it end there. I'm willing to walk away from it now, if you are."

Pete laughed. "Adam, I've got a list in my pocket. It's all the people in your freakin' Zombie Love class. I take that list everywhere I go. And you've got to know, everyone on it, every one of you, is going to get hurt."

"You . . ." Adam was so angry he couldn't even speak, which was good for Pete. He was sick of listening to Adam anyway.

The bell rang. Pete turned and joined Stavis, who was watching from the doors.

CHAPTER TWENTY-ONE

*A*WKWARD, PHOEBE THOUGHT.

She was sitting in the passenger seat of Faith's PT Cruiser. Tommy sat in the backseat, no more talkative than a piece of luggage. Faith was driving them to the mall, where they were going to see a movie.

The evening grew more awkward before it got better.

"Do your parents know where you are tonight?" Faith asked.

"Um," Phoebe said, "they know I'm going to the mall to see a movie."

Faith glanced at her, but the brief look fell on Phoebe's conscience like the proverbial ton of bricks. "And do they know how you are getting there? Or who you are going with?"

"Um," Phoebe said.

Faith nodded. "I love my son, Phoebe," she said, "but this will be the last time I'll cover for you. You need to let your parents know what you are doing. This isn't fair to them."

Tommy made a noise in the backseat like he was trying to clear his throat. It was a horrible noise, one that Phoebe never wanted to hear again.

"You're right," she said. "I'll tell them."

Faith reached across the seat and patted Phoebe's hand, her touch warm on Phoebe's skin.

"I know you will, honey," she said. "You're a brave girl. There aren't many girls your age who would befriend a living dead boy."

Phoebe returned her smile, but she didn't feel very brave. Tommy was brave. Karen was brave. Adam was brave because he risked getting kicked off the football team for Tommy.

"Mom," came a dry, froglike voice from the back, "I'm not living dead. I'm a zombie."

"Oh you," she said. "You know I don't like that word."

"Zzzzzzzombie," he replied.

Phoebe turned and caught him smiling while his mother laughed.

"I'll pick you up at ten," Faith said, and then she drove away, leaving them at the big neon mouth of the Winford Mall. Phoebe felt even less brave standing there on the sidewalk with Tommy. A woman walked by them, clutching her plastic bag close to her. "Winford Mall" was written in a bold cursive script in pink neon above the doors. Phoebe looked at the letters and frowned.

"We could go," Tommy said, "if you want." He reached for the cell phone on his belt.

Phoebe shook her head, wiping the damp palms of her hands on the sides of her black jeans. She then held her hand out to Tommy.

"No," she said, "we've got a movie to see."

He looked at her for a long moment, the neon making bright streaks of pink and orange on the flat glossy surface of his eyes.

He took her hand and they went into the mall.

There were strange looks directed their way the moment they entered. A kid in a Patriots jersey turned to his friend and said, loud enough for them to hear, "Hey, check it out! *Dawn of the Dead!*"

His quick-witted buddy chimed in with, "Yeah, but he hasn't eaten her yet."

They shared a raucous laugh, and Phoebe flushed, but she grasped Tommy's hand more tightly as he tried to step away, his fists clenched.

"Don't," she whispered. They walked on.

Dawn of the Dead notwithstanding, Phoebe knew that actual dead people rarely entered the malls. One didn't see the differently biotic hanging out at the bowling alley or shooting the breeze outside Starbucks. They had no need to go to a restaurant, and apart from Tommy Williams, very few had been seen participating in or observing sporting events. Zombies, for the most part, were homebodies—the few of them who were allowed to stay at home.

They walked down the hall, past a chain restaurant and a jewelry store into an open atrium, where they could look over a chest-high railing onto the level below. A cluster of small, frail birch trees grew from a hole recessed into the white tile floor. The crown of the birch tree was about even with the edge of the railing, the thin branches sporting small, dark leaves. As they approached the rail, a small brown bird flew from somewhere in the rafters and alighted on a nearby branch.

"A sparrow," Phoebe said. "Poor thing."

"I know . . . how she feels." Beyond Tommy's shoulder, Phoebe saw an older woman standing outside Pretty Nails, frowning at them. Tommy turned just as the woman gestured.

"Did she just throw the evil eye at us?" he asked.

"I think so," Phoebe said. "Or something worse."

Phoebe looked around her. Was she just imagining it, or was everyone staring at them?

Maybe it was all in her head.

Either way, it was a long walk to the theater on the other end of the mall.

They walked past a Wild Thingz! store on the way to the theater, and Phoebe pointed at a small display in the front window that had the *Zombie Power!* and the *Some of My Best Friends are Dead* T-shirts, along with a couple of caps, bandannas, and armbands bearing similar Slydellco. slogans. There were also a few bottles and tubes arranged as part of the display. Phoebe started laughing when she realized what they were.

"Oh my God," she said. "Zombie hygiene products!" There were shampoos, skin balm, and two different toothpastes.

Her favorite was a body spray that had a large silver Z on a cylindrical black bottle. The fine print read: *For the active undead male.*

"Maybe I should get some," Tommy said, smiling. "I'm pretty . . . active."

"I'm sorry," Phoebe said, still laughing. "I don't know why I think it's so funny."

They went in among the racks of T-shirts and goth gear, Phoebe's mood improving as M.T. Graves's voice wailed from the store speakers. They asked the clerk if they could have a sample of Z. The clerk did a double take at them. She could have been Margi's stunt double except her spikes were purple and she had a wide silver ring through her nose to go along with the bangles and circlets of leather on her arm.

"Oh, wow," she said, smiling. "A real live zombie! Wow, I've been hoping one of you guys would come in, yeah." She explained they didn't have samples but Tommy was free to "take a whiff" from the display bottle in the window. He took her up on the offer and asked Phoebe what she thought.

She inhaled the air around him. The scent was mostly spicy but with a strong hint of something citrusy. Lime, maybe.

"I love that stuff," Purple-Margi said. "I bought my boyfriend a bottle. Jason wears it all the time."

"Thank you," Tommy said, turning to Phoebe. "How does it smell?"

"I like it," she said. He bought a bottle.

The clerk's friendliness toward them lifted some of Phoebe's paranoia, as did the idea of undead hygiene products. But the more she thought about it, the more it creeped her out.

Okay, so the dead didn't sweat anymore, and obviously they weren't rotting or there would be some real problems. Maybe odor-causing bacteria couldn't live off their skin, or something.

"Mom said I had to take you to a . . . chick flick," he said, and she realized that they were at the theater.

"Mmmm. *Strays and Surfboards* or *Mr. Mayhem*," Phoebe said. "*Strays* it is."

Tommy paid for the tickets and bought her a tub of popcorn and a soda. Faith had warned Phoebe in the car that he was going to be paying for the whole thing and not to cause a scene because "you could be causing enough of a scene already." The freckled kid manning the popcorn station looked like he was swallowing a frog when Phoebe turned and asked Tommy if he enjoyed liquid butter substitute on his popcorn.

"I used to love liquid . . . butter substitute," he said. Phoebe laughed. Tommy didn't seem to mind when she forgot about him being dead.

There weren't any dead characters in the movie, a light romantic comedy about a woman dogcatcher who kept impounding the adorably incorrigible chocolate Lab puppy of a guy who designed surfboards.

Phoebe thought the movie was boring, and the idea of sitting in the dark next to Tommy and eating popcorn began to strike her as patently absurd. If you had your life to live over again, Phoebe Kendall, she thought—you'd probably spend it watching the madcap antics of Ruffles the dog and patiently await the release of *Strays and Surfboards II*.

The movie's obligatory bedroom scene brought memories

of lying on the dusty floor of the Haunted House in pitch-black darkness, for some odd reason. Phoebe was thankful they played the scene for laughs; Ruffles leaped up on the bed during the festivities, and surfer boy smashed a lamp trying to evict the loveable scamp.

Phoebe glanced at Tommy during the scene. He stared ahead, unblinking, as the dead were prone to do, and she wondered what either of them was doing there.

They went back into the too-bright light of the mall around nine o'clock. The few people who had been in the theater stumbled blearily into the foyer, lurching not unlike the more traditional zombies of movie history.

"Did you like . . . the movie?" Tommy asked.

"The dog was cute," Phoebe said.

He murmured agreement, a long sustained sound. "Me . . . neither."

"Tommy," she said, "is this like football for you?"

Tommy cocked his head to the side, just like Ruffles had when he saw the dogcatcher lying on his spot of the surfer's bed in that awful movie.

"What . . . do you mean?"

"I mean, being with me. You joined the football team so you could prove a point, not because you had any great love for the game. Is that what being with me is like?"

They walked past a clothing store. There were fewer people in the mall at this hour and, it seemed, less attention coming their way. Maybe night people were just more accepting of the differently biotic.

"Who said," he replied after a moment, "that I don't like football?"

He was joking, surely. Or was he? It was hard to read the humor of differently biotic people, much like it was hard to read real meaning in e-mails sent late at night. He was about to say more but then saw something in the next store and nodded in that direction.

Phoebe followed the line of his vision toward the bookstore, where Margi was reading a book from a stack set on a display table near the front. She saw them at the same time they saw her.

"Hey guys," she said, putting the book down and trying as best she could to be casual—which was one thing that Margi never was. Normal for her would have been to chatter nonstop.

Phoebe looked at the title that Margi had been leafing through. *And the Graves Give Up Their Dead*, by Reverend Nathan Mathers.

"Mathers?" she said. "Good reading, Margi?" She scanned the back cover copy and began to read it aloud: "'In this thought-provoking and controversial book from one of the nation's preeminent experts on the living impaired phenomenon, Reverend Nathan Mathers draws equally from ancient theological texts and today's headlines. Mathers offers a solid argument that the existence of the living impaired is a warning sign of the coming Apocalypse, and he outlines what Christians must do to prepare themselves for the event.'"

"Well, I'm sold," Tommy said, but Phoebe was waiting for Margi to say something.

She didn't, for a while. Instead she flicked her pink spikes out of her eyes and avoided eye contact with Phoebe. "I think there's a lot of fear," she said.

"This is . . . progress," Tommy said, looking over the rest of the wares on the display table. "Look, there's a few of . . . Slydell's books. '*The Dead Have . . . No Life,*'" he read. "'*What Parents Need . . . to Know About Their Undead . . . Youth.*' My mom . . . has that one."

"You aren't really quitting the class, are you, Margi?" Phoebe asked her.

Margi looked away. Phoebe was more nervous asking her that question than she was walking hand in hand with a zombie.

"I need to, Phoebe," Margi whispered, so that Tommy couldn't hear. Not that he would have; he was already turning pages in a book some lawyer had written: *Civil Law and the Dead.* "I can't take this."

"*This?*" Phoebe said, bordering on shrill. "Margi, I . . ."

"I gotta go," Margi said. She mumbled something about having to meet her mom. Phoebe didn't try to stop her.

"Tommy?" she said.

"Hm?" he said, taking his nose out of the book to respond. "Did Margi . . . leave?"

"Yeah," she said, and Tommy put the book down.

He looked at her for a moment. "Mom said I should get you . . . a milk shake. Mom says . . . you like . . . milk shakes."

"I love milk shakes," she said, wishing that he were easier to read.

They went to the Honeybee Dairy, one of the last

non-chain storefronts in the mall. Honeybee Dairy was just about Phoebe's favorite restaurant; she'd spent many a time having burgers and shakes with Adam and Margi at the original one in Oakvale.

Colette, too. Colette used to go with them.

They sat down at the long counter on shiny silver bucket stools that were cushioned with red vinyl. They chose the counter because it was empty. A few of the booths had customers: a quartet of rowdy teens, a young couple Phoebe recognized from the movie theater, a trio of blue-haired ladies. All eyes seemed to follow them as they sat down.

"I wish I could help you . . . with Margi," Tommy said. "I can . . . understand . . . what she is feeling."

"Can you?" Phoebe said, but what she thought was, Can Colette?

He said that he could. "I've heard it from people . . . on my Web site. The dead . . . lived once . . . but the living . . . have not yet died."

"You speak of the dead as though they are all the same," she said. "Is it really that way? You're still different people, right?"

"But bound . . . by common experience."

"Really? Did all of you see . . . experience, whatever . . . the same thing when you died?"

He started to answer, but then stopped. Phoebe thought that maybe this common experience wasn't really so common. How could it be when Karen could practically run a marathon and win a beauty pageant, and Sylvia needed a ten-minute head start to make it up a flight of stairs?

A kid not much older than them with a Honeybee T-shirt and a paper hat on his head came over to take their order. Phoebe ordered a maple-walnut shake. She empathized with the kid, who turned beet red and stammered when he turned to Tommy.

"And . . . and for . . . you? Sir?"

Tommy's mouth ticked upward in the lopsided grin Phoebe still had not quite grown accustomed to and shook his head. The boy turned and moved swiftly to get Phoebe's milk shake.

"At least he's trying," Phoebe said. She was angrier than she realized; she thought Tommy's smirk had a hint of condescension in it. "Most of the people here would just as soon pour the shake over our heads."

Tommy nodded, the smile disappearing. "Do you think it would . . . help . . . Margi if she read . . . my blog? It might help her . . . to see . . . that we're just . . . kids . . . too."

A wadded napkin from the rowdy quartet hit Tommy in the back, but he either did not or pretended not to notice.

"It might. It might, actually." She signaled to Mr. Stammer. "Could I get that to go?"

Tommy shook his head. "You have a right to sit here . . . with me." There was strength in his voice, the same implacable strength she felt in him when she held his hand or touched his shoulder.

"I don't want to cause trouble, Tommy. Not tonight."

He looked over at the table just as a second napkin bounced

against his shoulder. There were muffled giggles from the quartet that soon died off under the weight of his stare.

"You know," he said, "I have been thinking of the . . . blog . . . as a way to give hope . . . to the dead. But maybe its real value would be to bring . . . understanding . . . to the living."

Stammer brought the milk shake in a waxed paper cup. Phoebe was a little disappointed; part of the whole Honeybee experience was sipping the shake from a wide-mouth glass, the cold metal cup with a refill beside it.

She started to stand, but Tommy gripped her arm.

"I have one question," he said, "before we go."

His eyes betrayed nothing.

"How do you get," he said, "the walnuts up the straw?"

She laughed, and he smiled—a real smile, devoid of smirk. He dropped three singles on the table and they went outside to wait for his mother.

"No torches?" Faith said as they got into the vehicle. "No tar and feathering?"

"You sound . . . disappointed," Tommy answered.

"I can't believe you guys can joke about that," Phoebe said. "It happens."

"That's why we joke," he said. "It is a way of saying . . . thanks."

"Is that maple I smell?" Faith said.

Phoebe apologized and offered Faith a sip. "I'm sorry; we should have gotten you something."

"Can't," Faith said, waving brightly colored nails. "I'm on Weight Watchers."

Faith dropped Phoebe off up the road a bit from her house, on the far side of the Layman's. The STD's truck was parked in the drive, and Phoebe hoped that neither of her parents had spotted Adam, her alibi for the evening.

"Phoebe," Tommy said, climbing out of the car, ostensibly to move to the front seat. Phoebe noticed that Faith was doing her best to appear interested in the bushes outside the window on her side of the car.

"I had a great time, Tommy," she said, her words coming out in a clipped blur. "Thanks so much."

"Phoebe," he repeated before she could turn. Her heart was beating like she'd just had a triple shot of cappuccino.

What would she do if he leaned forward to kiss her?

He remained a respectful step away.

"I . . . just . . . wanted you . . . to . . . know," he said, "I . . . wanted . . . to be out . . . with you . . . because . . . I wanted to be out with you."

She smiled, and then held out her hand.

"Thank you, Tommy," she said. "Me too."

He took her hand. His skin was cool to the touch, so much so that she wrapped his hand in both of hers.

"Don't answer now," he said, "but would you go to the homecoming dance with me?"

He cut off her response by lifting his free hand to his mouth, pressing his index finger against his lips in a gesture of silence.

"Don't answer yet," he said. "For now. . . . I just want to think that you might."

When she let go and began walking to her house, her heart was still tripping in cappuccino overdrive from excitement, fear, or both. She wasn't quite sure.

CHAPTER TWENTY-TWO

OMMY'S VOICE WAS COLD and steady as he read the article. Adam watched him from across the room, and he could tell that Tommy was extremely angry.

"'The assailants used shotguns and a flamethrower at Dickinson House, a privately funded shelter for living impaired persons just north of Springfield, Massachusetts. Seven living impaired people and two employees died in the fire. A third employee by the name of Amos Burke is quoted as saying that the assailants were "two men in dark uniforms and glasses that escaped in a white van." Burke also said that "two of the differently biotic persons residing at Dickinson house managed to avoid destruction, but judging from the burns that they suffered, they probably did not want to. I swear the zombies were screaming," Burke said. "But I couldn't tell if they were happy or in pain." Burke was at the shelter to work off some court-appointed community service time after being caught trying to rob a liquor store in Northampton.'"

Tommy set the newspaper down in his lap. The class was quiet for a few moments.

"Thank you for sharing that, Tommy," Angela told him. "I'm sure it was not easy to read."

"I can't believe it," Phoebe said. "Why hasn't this made any news on television? My parents watch CNN for two hours every night, practically, and I hadn't heard anything about this."

Karen shook her head, and Adam watched the platinum waves flow from side to side. "This happens all the time. Zombies are getting . . . murdered . . . all over the country, and it . . . rarely . . . makes the news."

"That's just crazy," Thorny said. "I can't even believe that could happen in America."

Adam wondered if Thorny was really that gullible, or just trying to act like he was. He was also wondering, in light of his recent conversation with Pete Martinsburg, where Sylvia was. He somehow doubted that her social calendar was keeping her away from class.

"What do the rest of you think?" Angela asked. "Do you think this is really happening?"

"Something . . . is happening," Evan said. "How would this . . . make the . . . news?"

"It's why it *didn't* make the news that . . . interests me," Karen said. "*The Winford . . . Bulletin* is a small paper. Why did it run the story and *The Hartford . . . Courant* did not?"

"You ask me what I . . . think," Tommy said. "I think that someone is . . . killing zombies."

"Really?" Angela asked.

Tommy nodded. "This has been happening since . . . Dallas Jones. It has happened for years. But now it seems more . . . systematic. And notice how the writer felt the need to . . . discredit the witness."

Adam leaned forward. "Why isn't this story reported more widely? Nine people died."

"Two people died," Karen said, her voice a soft whisper. "Seven people died again."

"What . . ." Everyone turned toward Colette, who was sitting with Kevin Zumbrowski at the back of the room. "Is . . . being . . . done . . . for . . . the two . . . that . . . survived?"

"We were contacted," Angela said. "And are hoping that they will be sent here so we can help them."

"They were burned . . . severely . . . over eighty percent . . . of their bodies," Tommy said. Adam noticed that anger made his speech more hitched than usual.

"Can you guys really feel pain?" Thornton asked.

"We can feel pain," Tommy and Karen said, as Tayshawn and Evan said, "Yes."

Angela addressed Tommy when she spoke. "Really?"

Phoebe thought that her question was genuine. Angela's ever-present expression of warmth and empathy had given way to one of curiosity, as though a deep-seated assumption had been challenged.

"We do not feel . . . much," Tommy responded, "unless the . . . stimulus . . . is intense."

Angela nodded.

"I was . . . shot . . . with an arrow . . . once," Tommy said. "It hurt."

Now it was Phoebe's turn to be surprised. She hadn't seen anything about that in his blog.

"You feel more," Karen said, "the more you . . . come back."

Angela turned her smile on Adam. "We're hoping that we can help those poor children just like we are doing for Sylvia," she said. "Dickinson House had a wonderful reputation for working with the differently biotic, but I'm sure that suffering this recent trauma has really set them back."

Adam wanted to ask just what exactly it was that the foundation planned to do for them.

"What?" Angela asked, and he realized that he had been staring at her.

"Adam," Angela said, "did you have something you wanted to add?" Her voice took on a slightly challenging tone.

He cleared his throat. "Um, you mentioned Sylvia?"

Angela nodded. "Yes. Sylvia is not in class today because she is participating in some tests that we hope will lead to higher functionality for her." She looked toward the back of the room, where Colette and Kevin were sitting. "If things work out well, it should lead to a higher degree of functionality for all differently biotic kids."

"Hey, that's great," Adam said.

"We think so. But regarding the crimes that Tommy just told us about . . ."

Adam nodded, thankful that Pete had yet to make good on his promise. But the thought of Pete gave him an idea.

"Yeah," he said. "What I want to know is, what if there really were some kind of group out there hunting down dead kids? How would they go about it?"

"What do you mean?"

"Dead kids . . . dead kids aren't citizens anymore," he said. "They don't have rights, right?"

"Adam, you know that the Hunter Foundation is committed to the rights—"

"Yeah, I know," he said. "That isn't what I'm talking about. I mean, your social security card expires when you do, right? So no one is really keeping records on dead kids, are they?"

"I read somewhere that there may be as many as three thousand differently biotic people in the United States," Thorny said.

"Yeah, I did last week's homework too," Adam replied. "And there are two dead kids in Canada now; great. But those are statistics, not records."

"He's right," Phoebe said. "I read something that said the documentation on the living impaired is very poor because so many of our laws were put into question all at once. There was a bill calling for the mandatory registration . . ."

"The Undead Citizens Act," Angela said. "One of the first of many fear-inspired bills to be shot down in Congress. Senator Mallory from Idaho introduced it by comparing differently biotic people to illegal immigrants."

"Many . . . parents . . . do not want anyone to know . . . their child . . . has died," Evan said. "My parents . . . kept my death . . . out of the paper."

"No health care, ha-ha," Karen said. "I can't even get a library card."

"You're making a joke," Angela said, "but this really is a serious issue. You can't legally leave the country. You can't vote or drive."

"They want . . . to draft . . . us . . . though," Tayshawn said.

"That's true. There's legislation that calls for the mandatory conscription of all differently biotic persons within three weeks of their traditional death."

"How can they do that?" Phoebe asked. "Some of them are only thirteen years old and we're thinking of sending them into war? That doesn't make any sense."

"It makes great sense," Tommy said, "if one wants to get rid . . . of us."

"I'm not sure the government wants to wait around for their shadow organization to take us all out," Karen said. "I guess it would . . . be quicker to have us all registered and shipped to the Middle East."

Adam looked at her. "Why do you think it is a government organization?"

"Who else would have the funding or the need? If the undead rights movement succeeds, if Proposition 77 passes, it will mean that the government will be spending a considerable amount of tax dollars to . . . deal . . . with building the infrastructure. It is probably more . . . cost effective . . . to buy some black suits and flamethrowers."

"Do you feel that you can help in any way? Or is the situation completely beyond control?" Angela asked.

Tommy spoke first. "I think . . . we need to continue . . . to remind people . . . we are here. We need to challenge the perceptions . . . of the living."

"We need to get us some guns," Tayshawn said.

Adam wondered if he was the only one to notice the sudden lack of pauses in Tayshawn's speech.

"Let's take a break," Angela suggested.

When class was dismissed and they started heading down the long gray corridor and out to the portico, where the foundation van—the *blue* foundation van, Phoebe noted—awaited them, she decided she would cast a spell to break up the cloud of disillusionment.

"Hey, Tommy." Phoebe bumped into him with her shoulder.

He looked at her.

"Yes," she said.

It took him a moment to figure out what she meant, but once he had it, he gave her a wide smile, and she leaned into him with her shoulder again before skipping ahead of him down the hall.

CHAPTER TWENTY-THREE

PHOEBE BROKE HER BIG NEWS at the dinner table, which even she would admit, in retrospect, had not been the wisest thing to do.

"I'm going to go to homecoming this year," she said. "I'm going to go with Tommy Williams."

Her mother was beaming, but only because she didn't see her husband's reaction. He'd just lifted a spoonful of his wife's French onion soup—one of his favorites—to his lips, and was about to slurp it down. Then he lowered the spoon.

"Tommy Williams?" he said. "Isn't that the dead kid?"

Her mom gasped.

"They're called differently biotic now, Dad," Phoebe said, unable to keep from raising her voice.

"I don't care what they are called, you aren't going to any dance with a dead kid."

"What?"

"Honey," Mom said, "is this true? You want to go to a dance with a differently biotic boy?"

"What does it matter what . . . what *biotic* he is?"

"For God's sake, Phoebe, being friends is fine; a little weird, maybe, but fine," her father said. "But going out on a *date*? What is that? Why can't you go out with the Ramirez kid or someone? Or Adam?"

"Because Tommy asked me!"

"Really, Phoebe?" her mom said again. "A differently biotic boy?"

"I knew that something was up when you asked me to take you to the football game," her father said.

"Nothing is *up*. Tommy is just a . . ."

"But I figured I'd go along with it . . ."

". . . a friend, we're friends . . ."

". . . because I hoped that you were finally developing some normal, healthy interests."

"Normal, healthy interests?" she said, her voice shrill even to her own ears.

"Yeah," her dad said, glowering. "Like in boys! *Living* boys!"

Phoebe looked at her dad, slapped the table, and got up.

"You just sit right down, young lady," he said. Instead she got up and stomped off to her room.

She shut her door—barely managing to keep from slamming it, because that was what they would expect her to do. She turned her stereo on full blast and fell onto her bed.

Her mom came in a while later.

"Hi, Phee," she said, knocking on the door as she opened it.

"Hi," Phoebe said, trying not to sniffle. Her mom sat down next to her on the bed and smoothed out her bedspread.

"Your dad doesn't mean to be a bully," she said. "It just happens sometimes."

"I know," Phoebe said, starting to cry again. "It's a lot to take in. But we really are just friends."

"That's good, dear."

They were quiet a moment, and Phoebe closed her eyes and let her mother run her fingernails through her hair.

"My hair was never this black, or as shiny. You know that Dad just wants the best for you. We both do."

"I know, Mom."

"So you know why we would be concerned by you going to a dance with a . . . with a differently biotic. Is that the term?"

"I guess so," Phoebe said. "But really, it's just a dance." She sat up and tried to read her mother's expression.

"Phoebe," her mom began, "high school is a very special time. A very special time, but a very short time. You get a few good years, the last really protected years of your life. Pretty soon you'll be off to college, and then to a career, and who knows what."

Phoebe thought about Colette and the others, and she wondered how much of anyone's time really was protected. But she remained silent and let her mother build up to whatever point she was trying to make.

"Phoebe, can you imagine going through the scrapbook twenty years from now, and looking back on what is supposed to be the best time of your life? Can you imagine sifting through prom pictures and yearbooks, and there you are, standing with a dead boy in a tuxedo? Is that really what you want?"

Phoebe's eyes welled up again. She felt as though she'd been slapped. Almost as if she were *watching* the exchange between her and her mother, and she knew that deep down, this would be the moment she remembered—her parents reaction to one of the first things that really mattered to her.

"Do you understand what I'm saying, Phoebe?" her mom said. "Is that what you really want for a memory?"

Phoebe closed her eyes and waited a long moment before opening them.

"Mom," she said, "I understand what you are saying."

"I knew you would, honey."

Phoebe breathed deeply. "But I think you need some understanding, too. The best times of your life that you are talking about—Tommy and the other kids don't get to have those times, do you see? Those times were taken from them. What will they have for memories? Getting rocks thrown at them by school kids? Spending prom night hiding out because they were afraid somebody might drag them into a field and set them on fire?"

"So this is an act of charity?"

"No. No, it is an act of *friendship*. I keep trying to tell you and Dad that, but you aren't listening."

"Phoebe," her dad said from the doorway. "It isn't just that. Do you remember the crowd from the football game? What do you think they'll do if they catch wind that a living impaired kid is taking a real live girl to a school dance? Then it won't be just him that is getting pelted with rocks. It'll be you."

"Dad . . ."

"Listen to me for a minute, Phoebe. Do you know what it would do to your mother and me if something happened to you? You saw those people. They were nuts. Do you know what it would do to us if you got hurt?"

Phoebe sat up on her bed. At once her tears seemed to dry up.

"I *could* get hurt," she said.

Her dad folded his arms and leaned against her doorway.

"I could get hurt a thousand ways. They could throw rocks. The bus could crash. Someone could dump a bucket of pig's blood over my head, and I could make the school explode with my telepathetic powers."

"Phoebe . . . "

"Wait, Dad. Wait. What if I did get hurt? What if I was killed; what if I died?"

"Don't get hysterical, Phoebe."

"I'm just asking the question. What if I died? I don't think Colette's parents figured they would have to think that one through, either."

Her parents looked uncomfortable.

"Well?" Phoebe said. "Would you want me to come back?"

"Of course we would," they said as one.

Phoebe hadn't been sure of the answer, but now that she had it she was glad she'd asked.

"Tommy's mom wanted him to come back, too. And he did, and that's the way the world is now. We can pretend, but we can't really hide it. And you can pretend that you can protect me so every decision I'm going to make in life is going to be free from consequence, but you can't. Every action has consequences. I could go to the dance, and the worst that could happen is that Tommy could feel normal for a little while. Maybe I'll even have fun. Or maybe I'll get yelled at and shunned and have to sneak out the back. But you know what? I'd rather live with the consequences of my choice than live with the consequences of fear. *Your* fear."

Her dad sighed. "Nice speech."

Phoebe's eyes narrowed.

"No, I'm serious," her dad said. "That's probably the speech I should have given you instead of acting like an idiot."

"Dad."

"You're a responsible kid, Pheebs. You're okay. We've always been able to trust you not to do anything stupid. Maybe I wish you had different tastes in clothes and music, but it hasn't seemed to hurt you." He paused to run a hand through his thick, dark hair. "Do you think you'll be putting other kids in danger, though?"

"We'll be quiet about it, Dad," she said. "No one else needs to know until we get there. If there's trouble, I'll leave. I'll even call you if you want."

"This . . . boy, he can't drive, can he?"

"He's renting a limousine."

"Uh-huh."

She knew he was smart enough to sense another story lurking beneath her reply, but he was also smart enough to decide they'd had enough combat for one night.

"Can we think about it?" he said.

She smiled. "You will anyway."

He hugged her. She felt brittle, as though the wrong word from either of her parents could shatter her into a million pieces. Her parents seemed to sense what she was feeling as they got up to leave the room.

"We saved you some soup," her mother said.

"I'm not hungry," Phoebe said, trying to inject her words with enough perkiness that they would believe her. "Is it okay if I give Adam a call?"

The dead kid was singing, Pete thought. Unbelievable.

Pete was crouching behind a shed with Stavis and Morgan Harris at the edge of the dead kid's property, and the dead kid was singing as he worked, his high voice flat and inflectionless as he belted out the words.

"'Wouldn't it be . . . nice . . . if we could wake up,'" he sang, pausing to run a pale hand through his red hair. Pete laughed, watching him move the Weedwacker around the front gutter, just at the edge of where a ring of tulips lay wilted and browning, snuffed out by the early October chill.

"Can you believe this freakin' kid?" Pete said, watching him swing the whirring cord into one of the tulips, kicking up a confetti of shriveled petals. He didn't bother to whisper, even though Stavis and Morgan both looked like they wished they were somewhere else.

Pete hefted a heavy maul, its blade dull from years of hacking cordwood and years of disuse.

It had taken the dead kid twelve pulls to get the Weedwacker started, and it was almost painful to watch his jerky undead limbs trying to coax the machine to life.

Ha-ha, Pete thought.

Pete had been planning this one for weeks. He'd noticed that the Talbots' cars weren't in the driveway when he got home from practice on two consecutive Thursdays, and the pattern held true today, the third Thursday. He'd watched the dead kid doing yard work on those other days as well; first it was picking up sticks that had blown down, or raking leaves, but the kid always ended with the Weedwacker. He loved that thing. Pete wondered if he could feel the machine vibrating through his dead fingertips.

The Talbots lived at the end of a cul-de-sac in Oakvale Heights, the nicer of the two main housing developments in Oakvale. The woods behind their house had trails that eventually led to the lake, and Pete imagined a nest of filthy zombies somewhere in the dark heart of the woods out there. He dreamed about them, and when he awoke, he fantasized about setting the whole forest on fire.

A noise like laughter escaped the dead kid's throat as he missed one of the high notes by a mile and passed the Weedwacker along the base of an oak tree.

Pete ran toward him, lifting the heavy maul over his head.

Adam reached out to catch the spinning disk.

"You told them at *dinner*?" he said. "Phoebe, that is just classic."

"I know," she said. "Impeccable timing, as usual."

She was wearing a heavy black hoodie, which was big enough to fit Adam, with drooping sleeves that hung down to her extended fingertips. Adam had told her she looked like the Ghost of Christmas Yet to Come.

"What did they do? Did they freak?"

"What do you think?" she replied as the Frisbee bounced off her knuckles. "Made Dad practically cough soup through his nose. French onion soup, no less."

"Now there's an image. Your mom's?"

"Yep."

"That's a shame," he said. "Your mom makes good soup."

He watched her retrieve the disk off the turf. She was sucking her knuckle, which had split open when the Frisbee hit her hand.

"Yes, she does."

"So where does that leave you? They going to let you go?"

She nodded, whipping the disk at him with her special backspin toss. He nabbed it without incident.

"Yeah. I got a big speech about how they were concerned and blahdey-blah, and I thought Mom understood, but I think she's actually worried I'll want to put prom pictures of me and a dead kid on the mantel. Plus, I think she implied she was worried I was a lesbian."

"Ouch," he said, tossing it back. "Are you?"

"Yep, that's me," she said.

He put the next one high over her head just so he could see her run, the long sleeves of her hoodie grazing the Astro

Turf as she sprinted across the field.

"They had some good points, though," she said, her breathing labored. "I hadn't even thought that maybe some people would get all crazy about me going with him."

"Segregation redux," he said. "They're right; I'd keep it quiet if I were you."

"Did you just say *redux*?"

"I've been studying up," he said. "I heard chicks were into big vocabularies, and I don't have a date for the dance yet."

"What about Whatsername?"

"What about her?" he said. "So, are you ever going to tell me if you are serious about the dead kid, or what?"

"Please," she replied, snagging one of his loopy hook throws, "don't go down that road again. I'll let you know as soon as I do, okay?"

"Okay."

"We're friends," she said. "I really admire him. He's working hard to help other differently biotic people, you know?"

Adam did. When Tommy spoke in the DB studies class he transformed into this sort of undead charismatic leader. And the students, living and not living, hung on his every word. It was hard not to admire him.

"You think I'm a freak, don't you?" Phoebe asked.

"Naw," he said, wondering how much his answer meant to her. The Frisbee bounced off his palm, a rare miss. "Truth is, if I had any real guts, I'd be asking Karen."

He couldn't see her expression in the shadow of her hood, but he hoped it made her happy and relieved.

"She's pretty hot," he said.

Phoebe laughed and offered to buy them some milk shakes at the Honeybee Dairy, which seemed oddly perfect on such a chilly night. They passed a pair of police cars speeding the other way toward the Heights, lights flashing and sirens blasting—a sight that was rare in their quiet town.

Adam figured it probably didn't mean anything good, but for the moment he was just glad that he could be with Phoebe and pretend that their time together was something more than it really was.

CHAPTER TWENTY-FOUR

*P*HOEBE HAD TIME FOR INTRO-
spection on the bus ride to
school the next morning. With
Adam taking the truck, Margi wedged all the way in the backseat of the bus with her eyes closed and her headphones on, and
Tommy sitting with Colette instead of her, she was alone.

She put on her own headphones and cued up an older
album by the Gathering, wondering why Tommy seemed to be
ignoring her. Was he regretting inviting her to homecoming?

There were other kids on the bus, but they tended to avoid
Margi and her as much as they avoided their differently biotic
classmates. Pockets of students toward the back, freshmen for
the most part, were hacking around and cracking zombie jokes.

"What do you call a zombie in a hot tub?" she heard
one say.

Phoebe watched a paper airplane sail toward the front of
the bus, banking past the seat where Tommy and Colette sat.

Tommy turned around, his normally blank expression trans-formed into a mask of hate. Phoebe sat up in her seat, and the hecklers fell silent, remaining that way until the bus rolled up to the curb outside Oakvale High. No one moved from their seats until Colette and Tommy exited the bus.

She watched them walking toward the school. Tommy was very close to Colette, hovering almost, as they made their way up the steps. She saw him knock the smirks off more than a few kids with his glare.

She hurried off the bus and into the school, trying to catch up. She saw that he'd taken Colette by the arm, and she fol-lowed him down the hall as he escorted her to her homeroom. Phoebe knew that Colette's lower degree of functionality meant she'd been placed in remedial classes, even though when she was alive, Colette had been at the top of her classes. But Colette's parents had abandoned her, and Phoebe guessed that no one at St. Jude's Mission really knew how sharp Colette was, or had been.

Phoebe willed herself to turn invisible as Tommy reentered the hall after seeing Colette into her room. She hid behind a bank of lockers and waited for him to walk past. He didn't even notice her as he continued down the hall, and she saw that his hands were balled into fists.

She followed him, an easy thing to do, as other students took great pains to avoid close contact with the zombie. He went to his locker, and it sprung open after three steady turns of his wrist. Her poem was the only ornamentation.

She hugged her books to her as she approached him.

"Tommy?" she said. He didn't turn and went about with-drawing his books from his backpack and stacking them in a neat pile on the top shelf of the locker.

"Tommy, are you mad at me?" she said.

He turned toward her, his expression unreadable.

"I'm confused by the way you're acting, Tommy. Did I do something wrong?"

He stopped to look at her but did not answer.

"What is it, Tommy? Is it about the dance?"

His features seemed to soften.

"They . . . murdered . . . Evan," he said. He slammed his locker shut with a force that echoed throughout the hallways.

She didn't understand at first, but when what he was say-ing registered, a cold ripple passed through her body.

"Oh, Tommy," she said, and she laid her hand against his cheek, ignoring the snickers of students passing by, making rude comments about the goth girl and her dead boyfriend.

The only thing she could think about at that moment was Tommy, and right then she didn't care who knew.

The casket was closed at Evan Talbot's second funeral. Phoebe stood with Adam, Tommy, and Karen, and stared at the black box in the moments before it was lowered into the earth. She was leaning against Adam, clutching his arm and trying to draw strength from him, the tears running freely down her face.

She half expected the lid to slowly open and for Evan to call for help, his high, sardonic voice echoing in the satin-lined prison. She imagined him popping right out of the coffin the way he had popped out from under the tarp that rainy night they had all gone to hang out at the Haunted House, his orange hair askew and clownish above his grinning face.

But these things did not happen.

She looked over at the Talbots as they clung together at the front of the small crowd that had gathered to pay their respects. Angela and her father, both in well-tailored clothing of the purest black, stood beside them, Alish leaning heavily on his mahogany cane. He was wearing a long, trailing, gray scarf that protected his scrawny neck against the chill wind.

Phoebe tried to imagine the pain that the Talbots were feeling. To lose their only child, *again*—how could they bear it? Right then, Mrs. Talbot looked over her shoulder at where Phoebe stood with her friends. She turned back and slouched against her husband, who held her tight and tried to stop her from shaking. He was not successful.

"The mysteries of death have grown deeper in recent years," the priest said. Father Fitzpatrick was a young, solid-built man who Phoebe had learned was responsible for the St. Jude's Mission. She watched him look each member of the cortege in the eyes before gazing heavenward.

"No one, save the Lord, knows why Evan Talbot was taken from his parents . . . not once but twice."

Phoebe heard herself sob, from a distance. It was as if she had floated out of her body and was now staring down onto the tops of the heads of the mourners and the lacquered surface of the coffin. She saw Principal Kim standing near the back in a reserved gray suit, dabbing at her eyes with some wadded tissue. Father Fitzpatrick resumed his eulogy.

"But I would like to think that Evan Talbot helped to play some small part in God's divine purpose, the purpose that He, in his boundless wisdom and endless love, has set for each and every one of us. I would like to think that He would not wish us to dwell on the fact of this boy's second death, but instead reflect upon his second life, which his parents—perhaps touched by that wisdom and that love—chose to take as the gift that it was.

"We can debate whether or not Evan was truly alive after returning to us. Contrary to the opinions of many, I think that is actually a spiritual question and not one for the scientists."

He paused. Phoebe thought she could see her own reflection in the glossy finish of the coffin, and she thought of Margi, who had broken down in hysterics by her locker when Phoebe suggested that they attend the funeral together. Reverend Mathers would be quick to agree with Father Fitzpatrick on the idea of the undead being a spiritual question; although, unlike Fitzpatrick, he would be unlikely to find anything positive to say regarding that question. There were plenty of religious leaders within the Catholic Church who would agree with Mathers as well; in performing the funerary right, Fitzpatrick was risking criticism and perhaps even censure.

Fitzpatrick slapped a knobby fist into his palm, and the sound of the slap brought Phoebe back into her body.

"One thing cannot be denied. Evan Talbot chose to take his own return as a blessing. Evan Talbot used his second—call it chance, call it life, call it what you will—to try to bring the world a little understanding. He used his return to try to educate those of us who cannot understand what he and those like him are going through. And he tried to be a positive example to those of us who understood all too well. He did this through his humor. His joy. His happy-go-lucky personality.

"Buoyed by the selfless love of his family and friends, especially that of his parents, Evan tried to make a difference," he said, punctuating each word with another press of his fist into his palm. "And by making a difference, I am certain that Evan Talbot fulfilled God's purpose for him here on earth."

Phoebe looked at her friends through her tears, searching for some sign that they could believe as Fitzpatrick did. She was having trouble imagining a God that would require such a purpose—dying, rising, and dying again—from a fourteen-year-old boy. Karen and Tommy were like statues, Karen's eyes shrouded behind a gauzy black veil. Tommy's tearless eyes stared blankly ahead at nothing at all, it seemed. Did he also wonder what it was like to be in there in darkness, the smell of wood and satin and *rot* filling his nostrils?

Or did he not have to wonder because all he had to do was *remember*?

Adam just looked angry, and he would turn occasionally, as though taking in the rows of headstones spreading out across Winford Cemetery.

"Let us pray," Father Fitzpatrick said.

Phoebe turned her head and saw a single tear trickle out from beneath the hem of Karen's veil.

For a second time, Phoebe felt as if she were leaving her own body. This time her knees buckled, and she fainted dead away.

Adam took her to school the next day, and when she climbed into the truck she tucked her long black skirt under her, thinking that she would never be short of clothing that was appropriate to wear to a funeral. She laughed, a bitter sound that echoed in the stale air of the cab.

"Are you okay?" he asked. When she didn't reply, he turned on the radio. She turned it off.

"No, I'm not," she whispered. "I'm terrified."

Adam nodded.

"It's weird," she said. "All these things you don't think of until you have to. What it all means."

"I was scared when you fainted," Adam said.

She laughed again, and this time without the harshness. "I didn't even fall, thanks to you. You could toss me over the goalposts if you wanted to, couldn't you?"

"Yes," he said. "I'm pretty damn powerful."

He let his words hang a moment, hoping they would make her laugh. They didn't. He wasn't just scared when she fainted. Lately the idea of Phoebe being hurt—it filled him with a vague ache, a frustration that no number of push-ups or reps on the exercise racks were going to take away.

He sighed. "But I get scared, too. I thought you might like to know."

"You're a good friend, Adam," she said. "Even if you

refuse to be seen talking to me at school."

He chucked her shoulder—lightly, so as not to launch her bodily through the car door. *You're a good friend, Adam*—that was the line that made him want to cry, nearly as much as Evan's funeral had.

"The best. And it isn't you I avoid; it's Daffy."

Phoebe looked away.

"Aw, hell," he said. "And I was doing so well, too. Open mouth, insert size fourteen foot."

"I'm really worried about her. She can't deal with any of this—Evan, Colette, Tommy—I don't know what to do or to say to her. There aren't any scripts written for this sort of thing."

"I hear you."

She slapped the dashboard, a decidedly un-Phoebelike move.

"Who could have killed him?" she asked. "The description in the newspaper was awful, just awful. What kind of monster would do that? Never mind what sort of monster would write that article. They wouldn't have written it that way if he hadn't been a zombie. They didn't even run an obituary."

"I know," Adam said. The steering wheel squeaked with the force of his grip as his hands tensed.

"I think I know exactly who killed Evan," he said.

As she looked at him, realization dawned in her face, and Adam wished he hadn't said anything at all.

Phoebe set her tray down and slid onto the seat next to Margi, who was picking at a cluster of green grapes. They were in the far corner of the cafeteria and facing the wall, which was painted an industrial gray.

"Nice view," Phoebe said. Margi ate a grape.

"Can we talk, Margi?"

Margi shrugged.

"Look, I know that Colette upset you," she began, not really knowing where to start, but Margi was already shaking her head.

"It wasn't what she said. It's what I did."

"What you did?" Phoebe said. "What *we* did. I turned her away, too."

Margi sniffed. "She was right, what she said."

Phoebe nodded, putting her arm around her friend's shoulders.

"When people die, you always are going to wonder what they went through, you know? You wonder what they were thinking. If they think that you let them down."

"And now I know," Margi said. "But I knew it all along."

"Margi, this is different. You get a second chance. You can talk about it with her, if you want."

"Yeah," Margi replied with little enthusiasm.

"She doesn't blame you for her death," Phoebe said. "Or me, or anyone. She's just upset with how we reacted to her return. But she'll forgive us, I know she will. She'll see that no friend could ever understand something like that."

"Yeah."

"Yeah, really? As in, 'You are so wise and correct, Phoebe,

as usual'? 'I'm so glad that you love me and I love you and we're great, forever friends'?"

"Yeah," Margi said, wiping her eyes. "All of that."

"We haven't talked for like two weeks," Phoebe said, and gave her a sisterly squeeze. "I miss you, Margi."

"Me too," she answered. "You went to the funeral?"

"I did. With Adam."

"I'm sorry I didn't go with you guys. It's so horrible, what happened to Evan. I can't even believe it. He seemed like a nice kid."

"It was sad. His parents looked . . . they just looked lost, you know?"

Margi nodded. "I'm sorry I dropped out of the class, too. I'm so good at doing stupid things."

"I bet you could talk to Angela or Principal Kim. I bet . . ."

"I'm not so good at undoing stupid things. Angela called my parents after I dropped out, and they figured that the class probably wasn't doing my mental health any good—my already fragile mental health. You know how they are, Phoebe. They never got the whole goth thing and the music and all, and my sister Caitlyn is such a girlie girl, with the Barbies and the pink dresses and everything." She was quiet for a moment. "I guess I've been spending too much of my time staring at the walls in my room, and my parents got worried. They want to send me to therapy and everything."

"Again?"

"Again. It worked so well the last time; look how well I'm adjusting."

Margi picked out a grape and popped it into her mouth. Phoebe took two.

"How is everyone?" Margi said after a time. "I mean, Tommy and the others. How are they dealing with Evan's death?"

"Today will be hard," Phoebe said. "A few of us are working a shift at the foundation tonight, and tomorrow is the first class after he was . . . he was killed."

"I wonder what they are thinking. The zombie kids, I mean."

"Tommy and Karen didn't talk about it much."

"They wouldn't." She gave a little laugh. "Did you see what she was wearing today? Another little plaid skirt, a white blouse, and kneesocks. And I swear to God she's got patent leather shoes on, doing the Catholic schoolgirl routine again."

Phoebe laughed with her. "She's crazy. It's like dying has given her a license to act however she pleases, to do whatever she wants. Death seems to have frightened some of the kids, but I think it's freed her in some way."

"She had another apple, Phoebe. I swear to God. She was eating it. What is up with that?"

"You're kidding."

"No, I'm serious. Where does the food *go*? I mean, I thought their bodies didn't like, *work* or anything anymore. I thought the scientists figured it was a mold spore or something living in their brains, and that . . ."

"A mold spore? Where did you hear that? *The Enquirer*?"

"No, seriously, I heard that . . ."

A shadow fell across them, and Pete Martinsburg slapped the table with an open palm. They both jumped.

He placed a wrinkled and torn piece of paper onto the table, smoothing it out, taking great care not to damage it. He leaned over and stared at each of them in turn. Phoebe drew her black sweater tighter around her shoulders.

"Hello, dead girls," he said, taking a black Sharpie out of the pocket of his jeans.

"Leave us alone, moron," Margi said, all traces of the unsure, fragile girl gone.

He laughed. "Just wanted to express my condolences."

He took the cap off the Sharpie and drew a single black line on the page about halfway down. He held the paper up to his eyes and nodded with smug satisfaction, the black line visible through the thin paper. It was then that Phoebe realized that what he was holding was the acceptance list for the undead studies class.

"You're completely heartless, aren't you?" she whispered.

He shrugged, capping his pen. He folded the list back into a tight square and put it away, leaving his hand over his shirt pocket.

"Still beating," he said. "Unlike most of your friends."

Phoebe, her eyes filling with tears of rage, tried to stand, but he shoved her back on the bench, his hands lingering on her for a moment.

"No, don't get up," he said. "I'll see you soon enough."

Adam must have seen them from across the cafeteria, because he was rushing toward them through the milling students. Pete aimed an obscene gesture his way and slipped into the crowd.

"Are you all right?" Adam said. "Did he hurt you?"

"No," Phoebe said, but she didn't mean it.

CHAPTER TWENTY-FIVE

*A*DAM DRUMMED HIS FINGERS on the steering wheel. He fiddled with the climate controls, unable to find a balance of warmth and fresh air. He checked his rearview mirror for the thirty-seventh time.

"Adam, is something wrong?" Phoebe asked.

Adam didn't look at her. Even the sound of her voice was now like a sugar rush, and he had taken it for granted for years.

"Oh, I don't know," he said. "What could be wrong?"

"I know," she said. "I still can't believe it."

She thought he was talking about Evan. But the real "wrong" of the day was that the girl that he might actually be in love with had unresolved feelings for a zombie, a zombie who he was bringing her to be with.

"So we're going to the Haunted House, huh?" he said. "We're just picking him up?"

"That's the plan," she said. She tagged him on the arm. "Hey, I almost forgot. Do you have a date for homecoming yet?"

He swallowed hard. "Yeah."

Phoebe slapped him again. "Karen? Did you ask Karen? You didn't ask Margi, did you? I mean, she would have told me, I think."

Adam shook his head. "No, and no."

"Oh," Phoebe said, all enthusiasm draining away from her voice. "Whatsername?"

Adam nodded.

"Oh."

He wheeled into the dirt turnaround at Tommy's trailer park. Tommy was standing on the little patio in jeans and a chambray shirt. Adam thought that he looked like a well-dressed scarecrow.

"There's your boy," he said, but Phoebe had already rolled down the window to wave. Tommy waved back.

Adam watched Phoebe climb out of the truck and sort of half skip to the zombie. He thought she was going to hug him, or worse, give him a kiss, but she pulled up short. Adam swallowed and closed his eyes tightly, but when he opened them, Phoebe and Tommy were still there, together. There was space between them, but Adam thought it was less space than usual.

"Did you see the white van?" Tommy asked. He was looking at Adam when he said it.

"White van?"

Tommy nodded, and Adam thought he seemed excited

about the van sighting. "About ten minutes ago. A white . . . van turned around . . . in the park."

"Must have missed it," Adam said. "I wasn't really looking for one, to be honest with you."

Adam watched Phoebe touch the zombie on the arm. "You think . . . you think it might be one of *those* white vans?"

"I . . . don't know."

"I don't think we passed one, man," Adam said. "I don't think we passed many cars at all."

"Oh God," Phoebe said. "You don't think they know about the Web site, do you?"

Adam turned away. In a trailer a few doors down, an old woman wearing curlers and a green house frock was pouring cat food into a silver dish from a very large bag.

"Only a matter of time," Tommy said. "I think there is . . . a white van . . . waiting to pick a lot of us up."

Maybe. The old woman looked up and saw Adam, and waved. No white vans in her world. Either that or she was half blind and had no idea she was living next to a zombie. He waved back.

"Adam," Tommy said, "if we see a white van . . . please . . . do not go . . . to the Haunted House."

"You got it, captain," Adam said.

Tommy moved pretty quickly when he wanted to. He reached the truck first, opened the door for Phoebe, and helped her to get inside. Adam tried not to grit his teeth as he put the truck in gear.

* * *

There was a slim boy with long black hair standing on the porch when they arrived at the Haunted House. He was wearing a black leather coat with thin, rusted silver chains dangling from the pockets, and there were patches bearing the names and logos of various punk and metal bands stitched into the leather. The patches looked dirty, the jacket worn to a gray smoothness at the shoulders and elbows. He seemed to be studying his scuffed black combat boots, and his hair hung down in a dark curtain, obscuring his face.

"That is . . . Takayuki," Tommy said, climbing out of the truck. "Try not . . . to let him frighten you."

Adam returned Phoebe's confused glance with a shrug. They got out of the truck.

Adam watched her catch up to Tommy and call a perky hello to the boy on the porch. The kid didn't move, apparently too interested in the dull gloss of his boots. But his head snapped up like a cobra's the moment Phoebe set foot on the porch steps. Phoebe gasped, and Adam saw why.

The boy was missing a large section of his right cheek. There was a thin band of flesh on the right side of his mouth and then a glaring absence of skin that revealed his teeth all the way to the back molars. At first glance it looked as if he were smiling, but it was clear from the way the dead boy's black eyes regarded them that he was not.

"It is a mistake," the dead boy—Takayuki—said, the missing cheek giving his speech a strange lisping quality, "bringing the beating hearts here."

Tommy stepped in front of Phoebe. "They are . . . my

friends," he said. "Keep your . . . insults . . . to yourself."

"We cannot have . . . friends among the breathers," Takayuki said, and Adam could see his grayish tongue through the hole in his cheek. "How many reminders do you need?"

Karen stepped out of the Haunted House and onto the porch. "Phoebe, Adam!" she said, half skipping past Takayuki. "'Scuse, me, Tak. Good to see you!"

She made a great show of hugging Phoebe. Adam wasn't the best at reading undead body language, but it was clear from the subtle shift in Tak's shoulders that Karen's actions—or Karen herself—had an effect on him.

"Tak makes a heck of a greeter, doesn't he?" she said. "Don't you, Takky? We should pick you up an application from Wal-Mart."

Tak returned to staring at his boots.

"Come on in," Karen said, taking Phoebe's arm and waving at Adam. "Everyone is dying to see you."

Adam watched them go in, and he watched a look pass between Tommy and Tak. He drew closer and saw that the dead boy was skeletal beneath the heavy leather jacket. Both the jacket and his black T-shirt had random holes in them, and there was an unpleasant smell in the air around Takayuki. The other zombies did not have a smell that Adam had noticed, except Tommy and Karen, who wore colognes or used shampoos. It wasn't rot or decay that Adam smelled, but more of an unknown chemical.

He made a point of bumping the dead boy with his shoulder as he walked by.

"Oops, I'm sorry," Adam said. "Smiley."

"Smiley" fixed him with a baleful glare. His left arm shot out with a speed akin to Master Griffin's, and the dead boy's fist opened as though he were welcoming Adam inside the door.

And then he really did smile. The effect was horrific, as muscles high on his cheekbone strained to lift the ragged remnants of skin still hanging on to his face.

Now why did I go and do that? Adam thought, sidling in through the doorway, keeping one eye on the swift zombie. Like I don't already have enough enemies for life.

He turned toward the main room of the Haunted House in time to see Phoebe hug Colette.

Good for you, he thought, glad that Pheeble wasn't frozen with fear after her encounter on the porch with Smiley. Colette sort of smiled back, and Phoebe brushed some lank gray-brown hair out of the dead girl's eyes. Tayshawn was there, as was Kevin, the big dude Mal, and the girl with one arm. There were some new faces (none as striking as Tak's), about thirteen or so dead kids overall.

But no Evan, he thought. The atmosphere of the house seemed changed without the little guy, the court jester of the undead community. Adam thought back to the boy riding around in the bed of his truck, rain pattering on the heavy tarp. Differently biotic kids always had a sullen vibe, but they seemed even more so with Evan gone.

"Let's get . . . started," Tommy said. "Thank you . . . everyone for being here. I wanted to talk to . . . all . . . of you . . . about what happened . . . to Evan."

Takayuki glided into the house like a shadow. Adam could hear leather—or his skin—creak as he folded his arms across his chest. He wasn't sure, but he thought he saw that Tak was missing a patch of skin on the back of his hand.

"Evan was . . . murdered," Tommy said. "There is no other way . . . to say it. I do not know if it was a . . . random . . . act, like so many acts of violence against us . . . are, or if it was . . . part of a . . . larger plan."

Adam saw Phoebe looking at him, and he cleared his throat.

"I know who killed Evan," he said, a cold shiver passing through him as the eyes of the dead turned his way. "It was Pete Martinsburg."

"You know . . . this?" Tommy asked. "You have proof?"

"I know it in my heart."

"He told me he did it," Phoebe said, her voice barely above a whisper.

Takayuki laughed. "You trust these . . . breathers, your great . . . friends, and they kept this from you?"

"I didn't keep it from him—" Phoebe began, but Tommy lifted his hand, cutting her off.

"What will we do about this," Tak said, "fearless . . . leader?"

Tommy turned toward him.

"We will . . . tell . . . the police," he said, and Adam thought that some of the quiet confidence had bled out of his voice. "We will . . . post . . ."

Smiley made a spitting gesture, although he produced no

spit. "The police will do nothing. Words . . . will do nothing. How long must we wait . . . for breathers . . . like him . . ." He pointed at Adam, who noticed Tak's long, black nails, which Adam assumed were painted, because none of the other dead kids had nails like that. . . . "to come and . . . exterminate . . . us?"

Tommy shook his head. "Your way . . . will get . . . us . . . exterminated . . . much faster."

Takayuki favored Tommy with his hideous smile. "Certain types of . . . death . . . are preferable to others. Write your words. Maybe someone is . . . paying attention. For those who prefer . . . action . . . come with me."

Tayshawn was one of those who preferred action, Adam noticed. About five of the zombies shuffled toward Takayuki.

Karen was walking toward him as well. Adam watched her place her hand on Tak's arm. He looked at it as though it had the ability to cause him physical pain.

"Tak," she said.

"No, Karen," he said. "Enjoy your . . . prom committee. Keep . . . pretending."

Adam watched her recoil as though she'd been slapped. He thought she would have started crying, if she could. Tak led his band out of the Haunted House.

They were silent for some moments, and Adam looked out the window to the backyard as the zombies trudged around the corner of the house toward the Oxoboxo woods. Adam noticed that Karen was watching them through the window as well.

"I . . . apologize . . . for Tak," Tommy said to the room,

although his words were directed mainly at Phoebe. "We react to . . . the mixed blessing . . . of our return . . . differently."

"Sure," Adam said, seeing how uncomfortable Phoebe felt. "No matter how it goes down, it has to be a traumatic experience for you. For each of you."

Dead heads nodded in agreement.

"Yes. Yes," Tommy said. "My point earlier . . . was that there are those . . . who do not want us here. And now that there are . . . many . . . of us . . . there may be more . . . Evan Talbots. We must be very . . . careful . . . in coming and going . . . from this house, and from any of the other . . . places . . . we gather. I have seen . . . a white van . . . in Oakvale. I do not wish to . . . panic . . . you, but the events that the media . . . does not want the world to know about . . . are very real. We must take care."

He waited for the message to sink in before continuing.

"We have talked about the . . . homecoming dance . . . at Oakvale High. We will be having an after party . . . here . . . for all of you. Karen has a few . . . words . . . to say."

Karen turned away from the window. "Yes. Thanks, Tommy. I've spoken to . . . the people at St. Jude's Mission, and they have dresses . . . and suits for any of you who do not have . . . the means . . . of getting them."

So that was what the crack about the prom committee was all about, Adam thought, noticing how off-kilter Karen's speech was. Most people wouldn't be able to tell that Karen was differently biotic at all from the way she spoke, but Smiley's actions clearly had had an effect on her.

"We are going to decorate," she continued. "Our DJ just left with the other Lost Boys, but I'm sure we can . . . convince them . . . to attend. If not, we'll . . . make due. And despite some votes to the . . . contrary . . . we are going to invite some trad friends."

Trad, for traditionally biotic. Adam winked at her, and he thought it reignited the glint in her sparkling eyes.

"I'll bring the soda and potato chips," he said. Karen and Tommy smiled, but the joke fell flat with the rest of the group, including Phoebe, who looked mortified.

Adam felt a stab of regret, and realized that he really would miss Evan and his crazy sense of humor.

"I'm going to go home . . . through the woods," Tommy said. "Karen and I . . . have some things to do."

Adam turned away from the instant disappointment he saw on Phoebe's face.

"Really, Tommy?" she said. "It's such a long walk, and it's getting late. Why don't you come back with us?"

"Thank you, no," he said. "Late means nothing to us. We don't . . . tire. We don't sleep."

"Useful for cramming," Adam said. "Pain-free all-nighters."

"Yes."

"Is Smiley going to be trouble?" Adam asked. Phoebe hit him hard on the arm.

Tommy blinked. "Eventually," he said.

Adam figured as much. "Well, thanks for the invite. See you tomorrow."

"Good night."

Adam turned away so he wouldn't have to see them kiss, if that's what they were going to do. He heard Phoebe say good night, and then she was beside him walking out to the truck. He could feel her irritation with him radiating like heat from the sun.

"What?" he said once they were inside the cab, noticing as she pulled her door shut with extra vigor.

"Do you have to be so rude?"

"Was I rude?" he said, spinning the truck around before heading down the long winding path.

"Potato chips and soda? *Smiley?* God, Adam, did you have to say that? How do you think that makes them feel?"

"Hopefully it makes them laugh. I think they have a sense of humor just like any other teenage kids."

"Smiley? Why don't you just call the girl with one arm—"

"Don't say it," he said. "Don't even say it, because that is totally different and you know it."

"How is it different?"

He knew he should just shut up, because with each word he said he could feel her slipping away from him. No more Frisbee, no more riding around town and going to Honeybee Dairy, no more Emily Brontë jokes, and no more hanging out and talking about anything and everything.

No more Phoebe.

He knew he should shut up, but he couldn't. "Well, she wasn't insulting you and scaring you, for starters."

"Oh, so you were protecting me?"

"Sticking up for you," he said. "And for trad people and

breathers everywhere. I should have beat the hell out of him, is what I should have done."

She snorted. "Yeah, that's a great idea. Just beat the hell out of everyone who's a little different than you."

"Since when did this become about differences? This is about one kid acting like an ass."

"Just one?" she fired back. "Don't think you need to protect me, Adam Layman. Tommy was doing just fine talking to him and sticking up for me."

"Whatever," Adam said. "Just like he did such a great job protecting you out in the woods."

"Hah!" she said. "Like you did any better!"

Well, there it was. Only her presence and maybe some restraint molded by Master Griffin kept him from pounding his fist bloody on the dashboard.

He pulled into his driveway ten silent, fuming minutes later, and Phoebe's slam of the truck door was like the lid of a coffin slamming into place, trapping him.

Maybe then she'd pay more attention, he thought.

She didn't wish him good night. He watched her storm across the thin stretch of lawn separating their yards. They'd known each other all these years and never had a fight—not even an argument. Some teasing, some debates, an insult here or there, but never a fight.

That was then. Everything was different now.

Everything.

CHAPTER TWENTY-SIX

ARGI LOOKED AT PHOEBE uncertainly, as if maybe Phoebe wouldn't want Margi sitting next to her on the bus. She sort of shuffled and stood there like a kid in time-out.

Not another one, Phoebe thought. She made a face and pulled Margi into the seat with her.

"Hey, watch it," Margi said. "I bruise easily."

"Well, toughen up," Phoebe said. She sniffed.

"Ohmigod, you're crying! Look at you! You look terrible!"

Margi began rummaging in her enormous black purse for tissues that were no doubt wadded up into tight balls and smelled faintly of patchouli. Phoebe laughed and felt two big tears roll down her cheeks.

Margi leaned in close to her. "What happened?" she said. "Did that dead kid try something? I knew something was up there, I just—"

Phoebe hugged Margi and told her to shut up. She felt Margi kiss her on the top of her head and hug her back. Then Margi actually shut up.

Phoebe knew her eyes were all red, and she hadn't bothered to put any eyeliner or makeup on this morning, even though she needed it after crying for what seemed like half the night. She'd even cried on her algebra homework, for God's sake.

"Will you come back to the DB studies class, please, Margi?" she said.

"You should drop out, Pheebs. After what he tried, you shouldn't have to sit in class with him."

"It wasn't him," Phoebe said. "It was Adam."

"Adam? Adam got fresh with you?" Margi said, leaning back. "My God, I was right! I knew he had a thing for you! He . . ."

Margi handed her a tissue, and Phoebe gently untangled herself from her friend's embrace and rubbed at her eyes. "No, you goof. Adam didn't try anything. We had a fight, that's all."

"Oh," Margi said, looking disappointed. She gave Phoebe a sly smile. "Well, that makes more sense. You wouldn't be crying if Adam tried something."

"Margi!"

"Adam's hot, Pheebs! Admit it, girl. That body is like some kind of happy experiment. It's like he was manufactured in a nympho scientist's secret laboratory."

"A nympho scientist?"

"Lots more of us girls are going into the hard sciences," Margi said. "I saw it on the news."

Her delivery cracked them both up.

"You're just trying to cheer me up," Phoebe said after getting herself together.

"True," Margi said, brushing Phoebe's hair back from her tear-stained face. "Did it work?"

"Always," Phoebe said. "Please come back to the class."

Margi patted her arm. "My parents are going to ask Principal Kim if I can get back in. I tricked my therapist into thinking it was good for me, which just shows how much a waste of money those headshrinkers are, because two weeks ago I had him convinced the class was making me suicidal."

"You're too much, Margi."

"I know," she said, sitting up straight. "So why the hell don't I have a date to homecoming?"

"Maybe because you're too much?"

"Could be. Norm Lathrop asked me, actually."

"Norm's nice."

"Norm's a dork," she said. "But he's a nice kid. He made a mix CD for me."

"Uh-oh."

"I know. It's a sure sign of infatuation. He actually picked some songs I'd like, some Switchblade Symphony and some . . ."

She stopped as the bus rolled to a halt to pick up another passenger. Colette. She swayed from side to side as she made her way down the row of seats, as if the floor of the bus were pitching on an unsteady sea. Phoebe waved. Colette stopped at the seat before theirs and looked at them, her dark eyes like a starless night.

"Hi . . . Phoebe," she said. There was a long pause as she tried to form her next words. "Hi . . . Margi."

Margi took a deep breath, which made Phoebe wonder if she were about to hyperventilate.

"Hi, Colette," Margi said. Her grip bit Phoebe's arm like a bear trap. "I'm really, really sorry I've been such a bitch to you," she said. "I promise I'll try to stop."

The old, living Colette seemed to rise up like a ghost through the dead flesh of her face for a brief moment, and a shadow of the pretty, happy girl they'd spent countless hours with looked at them and smiled.

"It's . . . okay," Colette said. She sat down heavily on the seat in front of them.

Phoebe felt like crying all over again, but from happiness. Margi turned to her and shrugged as if what she'd done was not the monumental event it was.

"Shut up, Phoebe," she said, releasing the death grip on her friend's arm.

"Margi, I . . . I don't know what to say. Thank you."

Margi squeezed her hand.

They were quiet a few moments, and then Colette's head rose like a balloon over the bus seat, and Phoebe winced as Margi latched on to her arm again. It *was* a bit disconcerting: Colette's staring, emotionless face.

"Hey . . . Margi," Colette said, "would . . . you . . . like . . . to . . . go . . . to . . . a . . . party?"

The grip relaxed, and Margi rubbed Phoebe's arm as though to erase whatever pain she might have inflicted.

"I'd love to," she said.

School was a blur, but Phoebe always found the days they headed over to the foundation to be like that. They got to leave an hour early, which helped, but there was something about the sheer anticipation of heading over to the DB studies class. Anything could happen there, unlike her other classes, which even after only six weeks seemed like a dull and predictable routine.

And then there was lunch, which usually was the fastest time of the day but seemed eternal due to Adam's hulking presence a few tables away. He sat with Whatsername, which gave Phoebe feelings of guilt that she didn't quite understand.

"Have you talked to him yet?" Margi asked as she scraped the final remnants of a chocolate pudding cup with a plastic spoon.

"Talk to who?" Karen said. Phoebe had insisted that they sit with Karen, and Margi had not protested too much, for a change.

"Adam. He and Pheebs got in a fight," Margi said, licking her spoon.

"Oh," Karen said as Phoebe hit Margi. Karen hadn't brought a lunch today, and Phoebe thought she seemed a bit more like her nonchalant self.

"It wasn't a fight," Phoebe explained. "Just an argument. People argue."

Karen nodded, and reached over to pat Phoebe on the arm with her long, cool fingers. Her nails were painted a fiery red. "Don't waste your time fighting," she said. "Life is too short. Trust me."

"Speaking of that," Margi said, getting the last of the pudding off the spoon, "why do you guys think you came back, anyhow? There are so many theories. Something in the water, something in the inoculations American babies get—"

"Mold spore," Karen said. "Don't forget the mold spore theory."

"Yeah, right!" Margi said, pointing at Phoebe with her spoon. "I told you so!"

"There's even crazier ideas out there," Phoebe said. "Alien abductions . . ."

"Signs of the Apocalypse," Karen said.

"Too much junk food."

"Fallout from Chernobyl."

"The power of prayer."

"First-person shooter games."

Phoebe and Karen looked at Margi, who held up her spangled arms in a defensive posture.

"Hey, I don't write the news, I just report it."

"What is a first-person shooter game?" Phoebe asked.

"You, know, one of those computer games where you go around blasting things."

"Usually zombies," Karen said. "Never played one in life or death. Might explain . . . Evan and Tayshawn, though. And Tak. But that's it."

"Who is Tak?" Margi asked. Karen pretended not to hear her.

"Uh, Karen," Phoebe asked, "as a . . . a differently biotic person, why *do* you think you came back?"

Karen smiled and leaned back in her chair, stretching. She had on a black bra beneath her near-sheer white blouse.

"Well," she said, "speaking as a differently biotic person, I think the cause for my return, and the return of differently biotic persons everywhere, is simple. There is only one answer."

"Which is?" Margi asked, and Phoebe nudged her with her elbow.

"Magic," Karen said, and winked.

"Come on."

"I'm serious, Margi," she said, and Phoebe could not penetrate her expression to determine whether or not she really was serious. "It's magic."

"Well, that's enlightening," Margi said.

"Sorry. You asked."

"Karen," Margi asked, "would it be okay if I asked you a personal question?"

"Aha," Karen said, leaning forward and over the table so that her face was about six inches away from Margi's. "Whenever someone living wants to ask a personal question of the dead, it is either, How did you die? or What was it like when you were dead?"

Phoebe felt herself flush with embarrassment, and even her brash friend looked a little sheepish. "I was going to start with the first one, yeah."

Karen nodded and leaned back again. "You aren't the only ones with telepathetic powers, you know."

"I'm sorry if I hurt your feelings."

"Oh, honey," Karen said, grazing Margi's face with a light caress of her fingertips. Margi, Phoebe noticed, managed to keep from flinching. "Some people say we don't have feelings . . . to hurt. I know that you are trying to understand, not hurt, so don't you worry."

"Okay."

"And I'm going to answer your question. The first one. But just the one, and then this interview is over, okay?"

Phoebe and Margi both nodded, and then all expression left Karen's face. The light that seemed at times to twinkle in her diamond eyes went out. The transformation was so sudden and unexpected that Phoebe was shocked.

"I took . . . pills. A bottle . . . full . . . of them. And I . . . drifted away," she said, her voice growing more and more faint, as though she were drifting away right in front of them. "I killed . . . myself."

"Oh no," Margi whispered. Phoebe reached out to Karen and held her arm, as though trying to tether her to this earth. Karen turned her expressionless gaze on Phoebe and the light slowly began to return to her eyes.

"So now you know," she said. Karen lifted Phoebe's hand to her mouth and kissed it as she stood up from the table. "Don't tell anyone. See you in Undead Studies."

"Oh my God," Margi said as Karen walked away, "I can't believe it."

Phoebe looked down at the peach-colored imprint of Karen's lips on the back of her hand.

"Can you believe it, Pheeb? Karen would be the last person I would expect to commit suicide. And I thought that suicides didn't come back."

Phoebe couldn't take her eyes off the kiss, like a tattoo on her pale skin.

"Hey, Gee," she said, "did you hear her say telepathetic? I've never used that word with Karen."

"She said telepathic," Margi replied.

Phoebe shook her head. "No, I'm pretty sure she said tele*pathetic*. Our word."

"Well, I don't think I've ever had a real conversation with her before," Margi said, "so she didn't hear it from me."

"I know," Phoebe said, resisting a strange desire to bring the back of her hand to her own mouth. "That's what I mean."

For some reason, the fact that Karen had used one of her and Margi's code words seemed more mysterious to Phoebe than the revelation of her suicide. Karen was just plain different—truly more differently biotic—than other people, zombie or otherwise. She contemplated this until the announcement to meet the Hunter Foundation van called her from her sixth period class.

She could see that Adam was already in the bus, making a point of sitting in the back, pretending to be engrossed in a paperback novel. *Wuthering Heights*, Phoebe thought. The three dead Oakvale High students—Karen, Tommy, and Colette—were also on the bus.

Colette, she thought. Karen must have heard the word from Colette. She was happy she had solved the mystery, but sad that she no longer had anything to distract her from her feud with Adam.

"Rotten egg," Thorny said, beelining past her and ascending the steps with two energetic hops. Phoebe sighed and climbed aboard, taking the seat next to Tommy near the front. All the other students but Adam were within a few seats of each other, a fact not lost on the ever-aware Thornton Harrowwood.

"Hey, Adam," he called as the bus doors closed and the driver pulled away from the curb, "what are you, antisocial?"

Phoebe turned back, but Adam didn't even look up from his novel.

"Something like that," he said.

"Is something wrong?" Tommy asked her.

"No," she said, turning back toward him. "Nothing much."

Phoebe avoided his gaze, which was penetrating even on days when she had nothing to hide.

At DB class, Kevin and Angela were the only two people in the room when they arrived. Sylvia apparently had not finished her mysterious "augmentation," Margi had yet to be readmitted into the class, and Evan would not be returning. Phoebe went to get coffee before sitting down, and Karen followed her over to the counter.

"Hey, where's Tayshawn?" Thorny asked.

Phoebe looked over her shoulder as she made herself a blond coffee and saw that Angela seemed to be having difficulty turning up the wattage on her smile.

"St. Jude's told me that Tayshawn has not been back to the shelter in a few days. They do not know where he is, and he has not checked in at the foundation."

Phoebe sipped her coffee and then realized that Karen was staring at her.

"Could you make me one of those?" she said, pointing to her Styrofoam cup.

"Take mine," Phoebe said. "It's a little too sweet."

"Oh, that's just you," Karen said, taking the cup in both hands as though drawing from its warmth, and then she took a delicate sip.

"So he's what, missing?" Thorny asked. "You don't know where he is?"

"I'm afraid not," Phoebe heard Angela respond.

"Jeez," Thorny said, "people are dropping out like flies."

Phoebe had her coffee ready in time to see Adam hit Thorny in the back of the head with his open palm.

"What?" Thorny said.

"Have a little respect."

"What? What do you mean?"

Phoebe felt bad for him, watching as the realization crept

over him. She sat on the sofa between Colette and Tommy.

"Oh. Oh, yeah," Thorny said.

Angela ran her tongue over pursed lips. "Well," she said, "the first thing that I would like to talk about today is the loss of one of our classmates. I must say that I was surprised when Principal Kim informed me that none of you signed up for counseling. I would think that Evan's death has left you confused and hurting, and you should know that the private counseling available to you will help you with those feelings."

"We had mandatory counseling," Adam said.

"Which should have been a start," Angela replied, sounding annoyed.

Phoebe looked around the room. Inappropriate or not, Thorny was right: they were dropping like flies. No one said anything until Tommy cleared his throat with an odd wheeze.

"You should know that Tayshawn . . . is fine," he said, "but he will not be . . . returning . . . to class."

"You've seen him. You know where he is?" Angela asked.

"Yes."

"Can you tell me where?"

"No."

"Can I ask why?" she replied. "You know we are only concerned for him, the same way we're concerned for all of you."

Tommy nodded. "I know. But he has a right . . . to his privacy."

Angela was about to respond when Thorny interrupted her.

"Can I ask a question? I'm not trying to be funny, either. But how do we know he won't be back?"

"Tayshawn?"

"No, not Tayshawn," he said. "Evan."

Adam's hand rose above the back of his chair and tagged Thorny on the head again, a gesture Phoebe thought extremely hypocritical after all of the insensitive comments he'd made at the Haunted House.

"Ow, quit it," Thorny said, slapping back at the larger boy as Angela asked Adam to keep his hands to himself. "I'm serious. How do you guys know that Evan isn't going to come back again? He did once. Is there any chance it could happen again?"

Tommy answered.

"We can be . . . destroyed," he said. "Whatever it is that . . . brings us back . . . we need our . . . brains . . . to survive."

"Oh."

"Evan's brain was . . . was . . . stopped," he said, "with no hope of . . . starting it again."

"Oh jeez. I'm sorry about that. I'm sorry I asked."

Phoebe closed her eyes. It was almost too horrible to contemplate.

"What about other internal organs?" Adam asked. "Do you need a heart?"

Karen slurped her coffee. Angela looked annoyed with her.

"There are different theories on that, Adam," she said. "Some differently biotic persons seem to not have any problem existing without organs that you and I need to survive. In most of the case studies those organs no longer appear to have any real function, and in fact are incapable of function. It is hard to tell, of course, because there isn't a big enough pool of people to study."

"Study me," Karen said.

"Most?" Phoebe said, before Angela could respond.

"Excuse me?"

"You said *most*. In most case studies the organs do not appear to have any function."

"Well," Angela said, leaning back in her seat, "it is unfortunate that Alish isn't here to comment, because he is far more familiar with the work than I am. But there have been a few cases where differently biotic people seem to have, or have developed, some organ uses. There was a girl who had a functioning pancreas, I recall."

"I wonder if my bladder works?" Karen said, taking another sip of coffee.

Phoebe noticed that Angela was all but ignoring Karen— she was that unnerved by her coffee break.

"And . . . there was another case of a boy whose heart began to beat again. He had started to manufacture blood cells."

"How do these guys move their muscles without blood?" Adam asked. "Is that what the augmentation process does? Regenerate blood and organs?"

"No, the augmentation process isn't geared specifically at regenerating organs," she said. "It is more about surgically enhancing a differently biotic person to have a higher level of functionality."

"I think my taste buds are coming back," Karen said. "I can taste the sugar." She crinkled up the empty cup, and a thin beige trickle ran along her hand. "What is involved in the augmentation process?" she asked, her clear retinas fixing on Angela as she sucked the coffee off of her skin.

"It has . . . something to do with reestablishing neural pathways. I'm not very clear on the science; you would need to talk to Alish," Angela said, and she set her clipboard on the carpet near her feet. "Let's take a break, shall we? Ten minutes?"

"We just started," Thorny said.

Angela's exit from the room was sudden and swift. Phoebe could hear the echo of her heels on the glossy burnished tiles far down the corridor.

"What was that all about?" Thorny asked. "What's eating her?"

"I wonder if I could be augmented," Karen said.

Phoebe lifted her own cup and realized the peach imprint of Karen's lips was still on her skin, fading like the afterimage on a television screen.

"I should . . . go . . . first," Colette said. Kevin, as motionless as a mannequin on the futon next to Karen, nodded

"I'm not sure that . . . the science is there . . . yet," Tommy said.

"Oh, you think?" Karen said. "I wonder if they will let us see Sylvia?"

Tommy shook his head. "I asked," he told her. "So did . . . Tayshawn."

"Maybe they've got a white van parked around back, too,"

Adam said. Phoebe threw mental daggers at his back as he got up from his seat to get a soda.

They heard Angela's heels tap a staccato beat up the hall.

"Hey, Thorny," Karen said, her diamond eyes twinkling. "Before she gets back, do you want to go to a party after home-coming?"

CHAPTER TWENTY-SEVEN

*P*ETE SAW JULIE OVER BY the dead kid, waiting for him with her books clutched against her chest while the zombie was taking his books out of his locker, one at a time. Leaning against the wall with her ankles crossed, she looked over at Pete and blew him a kiss. Pete cursed and took a step back.

"Makes you sick, doesn't it?" Stavis said in his ear. "Me too."

Pete jerked his head as though reacting to a mosquito. It wasn't Julie after all; of course it wasn't Julie, because she was dead and under the ground miles away. This was Little Miss Scarypants, and the rapturous look on her face as she waited disgusted him almost as much as the mirage of his dead girl-friend.

Williams said something to Scarypants, and she gave a flirty little laugh, her eyes lowered in a falsely coy manner. Yeah, I've got your number, Scarypants, Pete thought.

"You'd think it would be illegal, a boy like him and a girl like her."

"Why do you even talk, Stavis?" Pete said, turning toward him as Williams closed his locker. Pete noticed that he brushed against Phoebe as they sauntered down the hall.

Pete'd been watching for patterns, just as he had watched the Talbot household for patterns. Eventually they would begin to emerge. Sixth period seemed to be their one rendezvous period throughout the week; they'd meet at his locker before algebra, they'd sit through the class, and then they'd walk to his locker and down the hall to separate classes. The information wasn't useful, yet.

Stavis looked hurt, as much as a gargantuan doughboy could. "Pete, I just meant—"

"Forget it," Pete said. "Let's go to class."

Pete shared most of his classes with Stavis; he was a lot smarter, but Stavis tried harder; the end result being that they were in classes a shade tougher than remedial. They were headed to English, a class they shared with a few other underachievers. Pete knew he could get out of the classes if he tried, but what was the point? He'd never be up there with the braniacs like Scarypants and her friend Pinky McKnockers, and he'd have a cushy job waiting for him after college in his dad's company anyhow. No point in overachieving.

Pete looked up at Stavis's round pasty face, which was knitted with concentration. He made a mental note to try and go easier on Stavis; with Harris backing out of the plan, Stavis was really the last person Pete could count on.

"So is he the one?" Stavis asked, his voice a stage whisper.

"Yeah," Pete answered. "Either him or corpse bride there."

"He's the one that punked us in the woods, right?"

"That was him," Pete said, too irritated to even berate Stavis properly.

He still had his list; he carried it around in his wallet. After taking out Dead Red from the neighborhood, Williams seemed the obvious next choice. The slutty zombie could go last; no one was likely to miss her. Pete figured that he'd put the hurt on living kids a lot better if he took out all their dead buddies first. He could—and did—slap around that puny Harrowwood kid whenever he felt like it, either in practice or outside the locker room. Pete smiled, thinking about the block he'd dropped on purpose against Ballouville so that their big tackle could paste a good one on the kid. He'd sat out the rest of the half.

There was a wide cardboard sign above the corridor archway proclaiming the date and time of the homecoming dance. Pete thought that Oakvale should have waited a week and had it on Halloween, seeing as how a bunch of the students had built-in costumes.

"We still going to do it at the dance?" Stavis asked.

"No, I've got a better plan now."

"Really? What is it?"

"I heard about a party," he said, "and we're going to crash."

That was the one good thing about having a little punk like Harrowwood in the locker room, a guy who had to use his mouth to make up for his shortcomings. Thorny had started running his mouth about this "sweet party" he was going to after homecoming, and how not that many people were invited, and blah and blah. Adam had shot Thorny a look, but it was too late.

Pete had caught up to Harrowwood in the parking lot and had the full story in two slaps. "What party?" *Slap.* "I don't know about any party." *Slap.*

"The zombies are having a big party 'cause most of them can't go to the homecoming. Heck, most of them don't even go to school. . . ."

"Where?" Pete had asked, but that was the one question Thornton couldn't answer.

"They won't tell me," the runt had said. "I'm supposed to follow Layman over there. He's been a couple times."

"If I find out you are lying to me, Thorny," Pete threatened, "I swear you'll be partying with them permanently."

"I'm not." The fear in the kid's eyes told Pete what he'd needed to know. "I swear it."

Stavis's nasally voice brought him back to the present. "A party? What kind of party?"

"A zombie party," Pete said, imagining a whole house full of worm burgers, and then imagining the house on fire.

"No way."

"Way," he said, seeing flames rising, smoke curling up under the moonlit sky. He was smiling as they arrived at their class.

He'd planned on being a little earlier to class than the rest of the pack, which was easy to do, because the nosebleeds weren't too interested in punctuality. There was only one other student in the class, and she looked up at the board as the teacher passed an eraser over the grayish surface, her stare more vacant than school on a Saturday.

"Ugh," Stavis said.

Pete laughed and winked at him. He gripped him by one bulbous shoulder.

"Talk to you later, man," Pete said, and went over to sit next to the girl.

"Hey, kid," he said, smiling, "I hear there's a big party going on after the dance."

Colette swiveled her head toward him with all the alacrity of a slowly oscillating fan, and it took her a while to bend her mouth into a smile, but Pete suddenly felt like he had all the time in the world.

Phoebe jumped as a cat screeched like its tail was being stepped on. Gargoyle leaped off of her bed and started barking at the four corners of the earth.

The unearthly sound was her computer's way of letting her know that Margi had just signed on to the Internet. The name Pinkytheghost appeared next to an avatar of a pink Casper-esque phantom that fluttered like a sheet on a clothesline along with Margi's first message of the night.

I got my dress 2day. U have yrs?

Phoebe shushed Gargoyle. His bobbed tail stuck straight up, and his low growl was more endearing than threatening.

Phoebe typed back *Yep*.

U promised we would both wear black. Is yr dress black?

Phoebe sighed, because Margi typed like she talked: fast and incessant. Phoebe had been reading the latest installment of mysocalledundeath.com and was trying to decide how she felt about it. Because, unlike a good many of the differently biotic topics it contained, this one was deeply personal to her. The title of the blog, which Tommy had posted earlier that day, was Homecoming.

Nope, she typed.

Promise-breaker, came Pinkytheghost's reply. And then, *Me neither*.

Phoebe smiled, hoping that if she ignored Margi for a few minutes her friend would get wrapped up in some other Internet diversion.

So what are U doin? Pinky/Margi asked. So much for her theory.

Phoebe scrolled down the blog entry and read what Tommy had written.

*I'm going to the homecoming dance at my school. I have a
real live date. And when I say real live date, I mean an actual
living, breathing, traditionally biotic girl.*

Phoebe frowned and turned down the Bronx Casket Company album she'd been listening to on her MP3 player, on the odd chance that one of her parents crept into her room. She didn't want them to read the screen.

R U there? Pinky/Margi typed.

Phoebe typed back *No*. Never mind her parents; she didn't want Margi to read this blog. Or Adam, or Karen, or anyone else. She had a vision of Tommy whisking her around at the party, showing her off to all his dead friends and saying, "Hey, everybody, this is my traditionally biotic girlfriend," and then forgetting her name.

Don't be a b****, Margi typed. *Is my special fluffy boy there?*

Phoebe looked over at Margi's special fluffy boy, who had resettled at the edge of her bed.

Gar says hi, she typed.

She turned back to the blog.

> *The dance will not be our first date. We have gone to a movie at the mall. She has been to my house and has met my mother, who likes her a lot. I like her a lot, too.*

That's what you get for writing poetry, Phoebe thought, her pulse racing from more than the music. She wanted to call Tommy up—Tommy or Faith—and ask him to pull what he had written. What if the hordes of protestors her father had warned her about were reading this? What about the faceless white van patrol; what if they were monitoring his posts? She wasn't comfortable with this at all; in some ways it was like a kid climbing up on a table in the middle of lunch to declare his love for a girl he barely knew. Uncool. Definitely uncool.

XOXOXO special fluffy boy, Margi sent.

Phoebe made a noise of exasperation that caused the special fluffy boy to lift his head from his special fluffy pillow.

She looked over and assured him everything was all right.

"I just wish our friend would shut up," she said under her breath. Gargoyle returned to his reclining position, looking disappointed.

What can it mean for a differently biotic boy—a zombie—to "like" a traditionally biotic girl? And what would it mean if the living girl "liked" him as well? Would society crumble? Would nations fall into the sea? Would the heavens open up? Would the falcon no longer be able to hear the falconer?

Phoebe rubbed her eyes. This was a little esoteric for Tommy, whose typical writing was quite literal except during the times he was speculating on the anti-zombie conspiracy he saw stretching across the country.

What R U listening to? Margi sent. When Phoebe rushed a response of BCC back, Margi's response was swift even though she upped the point size of the font and colored it red.

No way! Me 2! Telepathetic!

Yeah, Phoebe thought, unable to get too excited.

I don't know what will happen. I don't know if anything will happen. I don't know if a mob of traditionally biotic people with minds less open than my date's will drag me bodily from the gymnasium and put me to the torch. All I know is that I want to go to the dance with her, and actually dance. I know this because I know that when I am with her, there are times,

*even if they are brief, when I no longer feel like a zombie. There
are times when, for an instant, I forget that I've died and I no
longer breathe and my heart no longer pumps blood throughout
my body.*

*I forget these things when I'm with her. I think that if
I could dance with her, just once, I might feel like I was alive
again.*

She could feel tears building up, but she blinked them away
and forced the air in and out of her lungs in a steady rhythm.

No pressure, Phoebe, she thought, and an escapee from her
tear ducts plopped onto the space bar of her keyboard. She
laughed and wiped at her eyes.

There were a few posts under the Comments section of the
day's blog. The first was a single word from a poster by the handle of BRNSAMEDI666, who wrote a single word, all caps:
SELLOUT!

Why should traditionally biotic people have all the fun,
Phoebe thought, recalling the naked anger on Smiley's—
on Takayuki's—face as she and Adam entered the Haunted
House.

On cue, another post from PinkytheGhost arrived.

R U & Lame Man still fighting? ☹

Phoebe frowned, signed off, and put her computer into idle
mode before sitting on her bed next to Gar, who rolled over in
anticipation of a belly rub. It seemed easier than trying to
respond to Margi's question.

* * *

"You're late," Pete said, letting Stavis into his room through the garage. He had the whole basement floor of the house—a raised ranch—to himself, while Moms and the Wimp occupied the top two floors. There were three usable rooms in the basement: his bedroom, his exercise room, and his recreation room, which had a thirty-six-inch plasma television, another gift from dear old Dad. Stavis walked to the short refrigerator in the corner and popped open a can of beer. He didn't ask for permission.

Pete lifted the rifle he'd stashed behind the couch and pointed it at Stavis's head as he turned around.

Stavis swore and stumbled back against the fridge, spilling a good quarter can of beer on himself and the floor.

"Easy, stupid," Pete said, lowering the rifle sight. "You spilled all over yourself."

"You scared the shit out of me, Pete!"

"Take it easy," Pete said. "Enjoy your beer."

Pete watched him take a long pull off the beer, and he tried to keep from laughing. Stavis's normally beady eyes were as round as hockey pucks.

"Throw me one of those," he said, hoping to distract Stavis before he wet himself.

"Where the hell did you get that thing?" TC asked, carefully handing Pete an unopened can as though he were afraid a sudden movement would get him plugged. "Is it your step-dad's?"

"Hell, no," Pete said after taking a long drink. "The Wimp doesn't believe in guns. Thinks they should be criminalized, that sort of thing."

"What is it? Where'd you get it?"

"It's just a .22. There's a guy up the street who uses it to shoot the raccoons that come up through the woods to raid his garbage."

"Did he sell it to you or something?" Stavis asked.

Pete smiled at him. "He doesn't know it's gone."

TC downed the last of his beer. "Wow," he said, and Pete told him to help himself to another one.

"It's just me and you this time," Pete said. "Harris is wussing out."

Stavis slumped onto the sofa. He pushed the Xbox to the side of the coffee table and set his drink down.

"That last one was pretty gross," Stavis said, and Pete watched him rub a beefy hand over his close-cropped hair. "Who'd have known those zombies had so much gunk left inside of them? It was like you whacked a rotten watermelon or somethin'."

"Or something," Pete said. Stavis looked flushed, and beads of sweat had popped out on his forehead. "You're with me on this, right?"

"Oh, absolutely, Pete," he said, and belched loud enough to shake the dust off the plasma screen. "You know it."

"I need to know, TC," he said, "because I'm going to take another one of them down. Williams. He's got it coming."

"I know, man, I know. I'm with you."

"They aren't people, TC. You know that, right?"

"Who knows what they are," TC said.

"No one, that's who. I saw on the news that they think

some kind of parasite crawls into their brains and controls their bodies after death."

"It might be hairy," Pete said, drawing on his beer. "They've got this house where they all hang out, over on the other side of the lake."

"Like ants," Stavis said, belching again.

"Yeah, like ants. They'll all be there, too, so I need to know you got my back. If Scarypants or anyone else tries to get in the way, you have to take them out for me."

Pete got jumpy just thinking about it. Williams was like some kind of unofficial leader of the dead kids, sort of like Pete himself was the unofficial leader of most of the school. If Williams went down, it should be pretty easy to get rid of the others, and in getting rid of the others, maybe he'd be able to get rid of Julie, too. She just wouldn't leave his head. It was as if she'd walked out of his dreams and into his waking life. He'd seen her twice since the incident in the hallway.

"I got your back, man," Stavis said, and leaned over to clink his can against Pete's.

Loser. "That's good, man. You know I appreciate it."

Pete looked at Stavis and sipped his beer and considered telling him all about Julie: how he met her, what they did, how she died. He thought about telling Stavis these things, and then Stavis belched loud enough to peel paint off the walls.

Pete sighed, all impulses to relieve himself of his innermost secrets gone. "Cool. We still riding together? I'll pick you up around seven thirty."

"Seven thirty," TC agreed.

Pete grinned. "You still going with Sharon, right?" he said. "You know she's a pig."

"Oink, oink," TC said, and Pete laughed as TC launched into an increasingly obscene imitation of snuffling sounds.

"And you know we aren't going to have time for any of that stuff, right? We've got to dump the girls and get over to this zombie house before their party is over, you got it?"

"Aw," TC said, disappointment clouding his sweaty face.

Pete waved it away. "Don't worry about it. I'll get you a makeup call. Maybe a real girl, one of my friends from Norwich."

"Awright!" TC said, leaning over yet again for the can-clinking thing. Pete obliged.

TC crushed his can, his thick, stubby fingers wadding it up like a tissue. "Hey, you steal bullets, too?"

"Naw." Pete chuckled. "I got a box at Wal-Mart."

"Wal-Mart," Stavis said. "That's freakin' classic."

"Yeah," Pete said, reaching for the remote. He'd bought a whole box, but he planned on using only one.

CHAPTER TWENTY-EIGHT

*P*HOEBE, IN HER HEART OF
hearts, wanted to wear black.
She and Margi had sworn they
would never attend any of the ridiculous dances and socials that
the school sponsored throughout the year. But on the other
hand, they both harbored a secret desire to at least be *asked* by
someone to go. They'd made a half-hearted pact that if they
ever went, it would be in dresses of flowing black taffeta, complete with veils; Weird Sisters to the end.

Phoebe turned in front of the mirror hanging from her
closet door, admiring the way the sleek fabric—a silky, almost
shiny white—cut in and hugged her middle and fell along her
hips.

She turned back to face herself, pleased that she'd gone
with the white dress in the end. Black looked great on her, but
something about going on a date with a dead kid while wearing
a dress appropriate for a funeral just didn't feel right. She

didn't need the attendant barrage of comments from her parents, either. The worst comment she'd had to endure thus far was one from her dad about the neckline of the dress, which of course was lower that he would have liked. Phoebe was thankful that he kept whatever Bride of Frankenstein jokes, which were surely buzzing around his skull like angry hornets, to himself.

Phoebe scanned herself from head to toe before settling on a staring contest with her reflection. Her skin was pale but not sickly; it was not as free from blemish or as even in tone as Karen's, but it didn't have the bluish cast that hers did in certain light, either. Phoebe was slim, and although her figure, again, was not as stunning as Karen's, it was at the very least attractive. Chasing after the Frisbee in the school yard had helped shape some dangerous curves, she thought, and her arms and legs had some nice definition that they would have lacked had she spent every free hour writing goth poetry.

She looked deep within her eyes, which were a warm greenish-hazel color. She liked to think that they were flecked with gold, and if the candles in her room flickered just so, they were.

She was pretty, she realized. Maybe even very pretty.

The thought made her breath catch in her throat. When she broke contact with the pretty young girl in the mirror, she reached for the fuzzy purple notebook and pen that she kept at all times on her nightstand, opened to the first blank page, and began to write.

"The limousine left when the driver realized that my son was differently biotic," Faith told them, a hint of apology in her voice. "It looks like the kids will be in the PT Cruiser tonight."

Phoebe overheard her talking in the kitchen as she came down the stairs. Her parents stood off to the side of the kitchen, uneasily talking to Faith and her undead son, who looked uncomfortable looming in the doorway in his blue suit jacket and tie. Faith saw her enter, and her face lit up.

"Phoebe, you look beautiful, honey!" she said. "Just beautiful!"

"Thank you," she murmured in reply. She was wearing enough makeup to mask the color that rose to her cheeks, but there was nothing she could do to ward off the spots of blush that she could practically feel rising along her throat. The plunging neckline was a Pyrrhic victory at best, it seemed.

"Isn't she beautiful, Tommy?" Faith said, but Tommy just stared.

Phoebe blushed, but she stared back. The suit fit him wonderfully, seeming to accentuate the quiet strength that she found so attractive in the way it fell across his broad shoulders. The corner of his mouth twitched up in a smile.

From the corner of her eye, Phoebe saw her father open his mouth, and she steeled herself for soul-crushing embarrassment.

"I'll drive," he said, looking surprised at his own offer. "That is, if the kids don't mind."

Phoebe, taken aback by his sudden generosity, shook her head. He smiled back at her.

"We're being rude," he said. "Can we get you a drink? Mrs. Williams? Some coffee?"

"Coffee would be great," she said, smiling and extending her hand, first to Phoebe's dad and then to her mother. "I'm Faith. I don't think you've met my son, Tommy."

"I haven't," her father said. "Watched him play a little football, though."

Tommy stepped forward and shook his hand. "Mr. Kendall," he said, and Phoebe watched their exchange with growing fascination. She realized that her father had most likely never touched a differently biotic person prior to this moment. Even her mother allowed him to take her hand.

"Tommy," her dad said. "Faith, why don't you come in for a while?"

The obligatory photo shoot was awkward, and Phoebe could see her mom's hands trembling as she snapped a few digital pictures. Very few pictures, Phoebe noted. But Faith snapped away with her camera until Tommy finally suggested that it was time for them to be going.

Her dad invited Faith along for the ride, but she remained behind to talk with Phoebe's mother over coffee and some of those biscotti that Phoebe couldn't stand but Margi loved. Rather, the biscotti that Margi loved to feed Gargoyle, who orbited the kitchen table with a greedy look on his furry face. Phoebe kissed her mother and hugged Faith. Faith winked at her when Phoebe turned and waved from the door.

Phoebe and Tommy slid into the expansive backseat of her

father's car, and laughed politely at his lame chauffeur jokes. Phoebe wondered if maybe in some ways she'd lucked out by going with a differently biotic boy instead of a living one, because she knew that if it was a living boy, her dad would have grilled him relentlessly, developing a sudden interest in the boy's lineage, his address, his father's place of employment, what he liked to do in his spare time. With Tommy, there was a wall of mystery that her dad was too polite to breach.

"Phoebe tells me that you quit the football team," he said. "That is a shame. It looked like you knew what you were doing out there."

"Thank you, sir."

"Mr. Kendall is fine."

"Thank you, Mr. Kendall," Tommy said, and aimed a slow wink at Phoebe, making her smile.

"It couldn't have been easy for you, putting that uniform on. Knowing that you were going to have . . . some resistance."

"I wanted . . . to play. That made it a lot easier."

"You did well," Mr. Kendall said. "Very well."

Phoebe wished that he would drive a little faster so that they could get to the dance before he said something stupid.

"Why did you quit, then?" her dad said.

Too late, Phoebe thought.

"The world . . . wasn't ready for one of . . . us . . . to play a school sport. At least I showed . . . that it could be done."

"I think it is damn shame, and a miscarriage of justice. It must be very frustrating for you."

348

"Being a . . . zombie . . . can often be frustrating," Tommy told him.

"Is that what you call yourselves? Zombies?"

"Oh, look," Phoebe said. "Is that a deer up ahead in the Palmers' field?"

Her father ignored her. "It just seems a pretty, I don't know, negative thing to call yourself. Zombie. Zombies were never the good guys in the movies, from what I remember, so I doubt the term will win you any points politically, you know what I mean?"

Phoebe squeezed her eyes shut. Drive faster, she thought, trying to send a telepathetic message to her dad. But as usual, he appeared to be immune.

"No burning crosses," Mr. Kendall said, "and I don't see any rotten fruit. I guess that's a good thing."

"Thanks for the ride, Dad," Phoebe said, scrambling to get out. There were rows of cars in the loop where the buses picked up and deposited the Oakvale High students every weekday. There were small clusters of students chatting, boys in new sport jackets and ties, their shoes buffed and polished to a high reflective glow. She stepped onto the curb.

"Have fun, kids," her dad said, accepting a quick peck on the cheek from Phoebe. "I almost forgot, how are you going to get to the party later?"

Phoebe felt her heart sink, and hoped that the feeling didn't show on her face. She'd forgotten all about the party, and with the limousine service unwilling to transport zombie cargo, they were left without a ride. One detail she'd failed to mention when discussing the party with her parents was that it was a differently biotic party.

Phoebe opened her mouth to answer when Tommy interrupted her.

"I called Adam Layman, Mr. Kendall," he said. "He'll give us a lift to and from the party. I hope that is okay."

"Adam, huh?" her dad said. "Be sort of cramped in that truck of his."

"We'll manage, Mr. Kendall. I can always go in the back."

"Don't wreck your suit," her dad said. "Okay then, kids. Have fun."

"Bye, Dad," Phoebe replied, hoping he couldn't see how relieved she was. Adam was perhaps the only boy on earth that her father entrusted her with, probably because he would do random acts of pure goodness like shovel their driveway when Mr. Kendall was away on business, and he'd accept no payment for his deeds other than a movie with Phoebe and maybe a bowl of Mrs. Kendall's French onion soup. Adam was her father's favorite for son-in-law—despite the obviously platonic nature of his and Phoebe's relationship—an idea only sidelined by the fact that the STD would one day become the other grandfather to their children.

"Be home by midnight, okay?" he said. "I don't want you turning into a pumpkin."

"Yes, Dad,"

"Good night, Mr. Kendall," Tommy said. "I'm glad I finally met you."

Her father shook his hand again, and Phoebe noticed that the move was a natural one, free from the hitch of trepidation he'd had the first time they touched. Progress was progress.

"Me too, Tommy. Have fun."

They watched him drive away, and Tommy, smiling, offered his arm.

"Mom was right," he said. "You're beautiful."

She took his arm. "You look nice too, Tommy," she said. They walked toward the school. "Are we really getting a ride from Adam?"

"Yes," he said. "Is that okay?"

"It's fine," she said. "But it might be a little chilly in the cab. Adam and I aren't speaking right now."

"Adam mentioned that," he said. "Actually, he said . . . that you weren't speaking to him."

She looked away. Just the thought of Adam made her sad, and she didn't want to be sad, not tonight. She wished that she could have showed him her dress before Tommy had come over. He would have said something nice, and he would have just stood there, looking at her. She could always count on Adam to be uncomplicated in the way he appreciated her.

Stop, she thought. She squeezed Tommy's arm; it was like stone beneath her fingertips.

The clusters of students loitering around outside the dance turned toward them, but with no more scrutiny than they had for any of the other arriving couples. Phoebe told herself that they were more interested in finding fault with her dress than they were in criticizing her date. They walked into the school unmolested, Tommy's stride less tentative and awkward than many of the flustered boys ambling around in their starched shirts, pulling at their constricting ties.

Tommy handed their tickets to a chaperone at the gym door. The darkened gymnasium was done up in paper streamers and balloons, and there were a number of multicolored spotlights casting a glow over the students as they danced on a low platform that had been brought in for the occasion. Freckles of light appeared on Phoebe's arms, reflected by the large mirror ball above the dance floor. Warm, cologne-scented air washed over them.

Phoebe had never attended a school dance before. She thought it all looked beautiful.

They saw Mrs. Rodriguez talking with Principal Kim by a loose throng of parents and teachers standing guard near the punch bowl. The principal saw them and walked over, excusing herself from a waving Mrs. Rodriguez. Phoebe said hello.

"Karen and Kevin are already here, Tommy," Principal Kim said. "Are you expecting any of your other friends tonight?"

"I expect Adam . . . and Thorny . . . to be here," he replied. "If they were able to raise . . . the money . . . to rent dates."

Her smile was wry and reserved. "I'm sorry," she said, "I meant—"

"You meant any of my dead friends," he said. Phoebe gripped his arm.

Principal Kim nodded. "Tommy, we discussed this. You know I do not mind any of the students coming to the dance.

You know I am only trying my best to ensure your safety and the safety of everyone at Oakvale High."

"I know. I saw all of the . . . police cars . . . in the lot."

"We always have the police present at a dance."

"State Troopers?"

The principal's smile didn't waver. Phoebe had the sense that Tommy was being petulant, a sense that was confirmed when he looked away from her.

"None of the . . . others . . . are coming."

"Thank you, Tommy," Principal Kim said. "And just to remind you of some of the finer points of our discussion, seeing as you seem to have forgotten them: if the media or any protestors arrive, we will promptly escort you, your date, and the other differently biotic children out of the gymnasium and then out of the school."

Tommy nodded.

Principal Kim smiled at them with genuine warmth. "Good. Now go have some fun."

"What was that all about?" Phoebe asked as the principal drifted away from earshot. Tommy untangled his arm from her, his hand brushing hers as it fell.

"When they . . . counseled us . . . after Evan was murdered," he said, referring to the mandatory sessions that each participant in the Undead Studies class had had with the principal, the school psychiatrist, and a pair of lawyers, "she asked what we . . . what I would do. I told her I would live . . . my life and continue my work. I told her you and I were going to homecoming. I told her you and I . . . would dance."

Phoebe let his words sink in for a moment. "But she was afraid there would be a protest?"

"Or worse. I agreed . . . that we would leave at the first sign . . . of trouble."

Phoebe sighed. "So I guess I could turn into a pumpkin after all."

"What?"

"Never mind."

Phoebe caught sight of Karen over his shoulder. She was at the perimeter of the dance floor, dancing with a fluid grace that most of the living students would envy. She was wearing a clingy blue dress that had a wide yellow belt cinched at her waist and a hemline that ended just above her knees. When she spun, which she did often, the hem rose to an almost indecent level and showed off her stunning smooth legs. Kevin was standing in front of her in a sacklike black suit with a horrible brown knit tie, his arms lifting and falling with every seventh or eighth beat. His left arm seemed more motile than the right.

"Oh, look," Phoebe said. "How cute!" But Tommy was already moving toward them.

"Hi, kids," Karen said, a swarm of silver lights crossing her face as a strobe glanced off the mirror ball above. "Phoebe, you are absolutely stunning. And what a handsome date you have." Her eyes seemed more crystalline, and they glittered like stars in the flashing dance hall lights.

"Thanks, Karen," Phoebe said. "You might actually be the most beautiful girl I've ever seen."

Karen laughed, caressing Phoebe's arm with a hand that glided in time with the music. "You're sweet. I'm just trying to bring my date, Kevin here, back to life." Her hand left Phoebe's skin, which tingled where the dead girl had touched her. Karen did a lazy wave that took in the rest of the dancers.

"And the rest of these boys," she said. "I'm trying to knock dead."

"Well," Tommy said, "you are drop dead . . . gorgeous."

"Funny," Karen said, batting her eyelashes, "You aren't so bad yourself."

Phoebe's experience in such matters was rather limited, but it felt as though they were flirting right in front of her.

"Killer," Kevin said. They all laughed.

Karen grabbed Phoebe's hand. "Dance with me." And Phoebe did.

Margi arrived twenty minutes or so later, her dress mostly pink with black accents—black ribbons in the front and back, a wide black belt, and black shoes. She had a puffy black flower pinned in the pinkish nest of her hair.

The dress was snug in an attractive way, and if Phoebe's dad had found *her* neckline risqué, he would never have let Margi leave his house with what she was wearing. Phoebe thought she looked great. So did Norm, judging by the way he stood wiping sweat off his forehead with the back of his bony hand.

"Norm's car wouldn't start in my driveway," she said. "Dad had to jump-start it." Norm Lathrop looked gawky and nervous lurking behind her; he was swimming in his suit. His eyes were wide behind the thick lenses of his glasses.

Phoebe opened her mouth to reply, but Margi was quick and sharp.

"No jokes, please!" she said. "I have the rest of my life to look forward to those!"

Phoebe laughed and hugged her.

"Norm," Margi said, "these are some of my friends I was telling you about. You know Phoebe. Tommy, Karen, and Kevin. They're all dead."

Phoebe was shocked, but Kevin waved and Karen blew a quick kiss, unfazed by Margi's bluntness. Neither had stopped dancing.

Norm waved back, and was drawn out in the front only by Tommy's offered hand, which he shook like it was a snake he was trying to kill.

"Careful, Norm," Tommy said. "We break . . . easily."

"Oh God, I'm so sorry!" Norm said, dropping Tommy's hand like it had bitten him. Margi patted him on the shoulder.

"They're kidders, Norm," she said. "Take it easy."

A popular club hit came on, and Margi began to sway, her hips brushing against Phoebe and then poor Norm, who looked like he was about to melt into a puddle at her feet.

"Remember what I told you, Normie. When you are with me, you have to be prepared to dance."

Norm tried his best, and managed to work himself through their loose circle to practice his moves next to Kevin, probably because he figured he couldn't possibly look inept next to him. Phoebe smiled at the thought, because he was wrong.

A half hour later, Phoebe was breathless and sweaty while her zombie companions looked about as unruffled and energetic as they ever did. Which wasn't very, in Kevin's case, but Karen and Tommy were doing just fine.

She excused herself and went over to find a chair with the wallflowers. The DJ cued up a popular rap tune with an aggressive BPM count, one that made Phoebe glad she'd taken the moment to sit a spell. She found a seat and watched Tommy and Karen share a joke, their bodies moving almost but not quite in time with the rhythm—just like most of the living students. Kevin, a huge smile on his round face, was trying his best, even though he was occasionally jostled by Norm, whose dancing was becoming more and more daring, or more and more spastic, depending on how one chose to look at it. Margi waved at Phoebe and then laughed at something Karen said as Karen executed a sinuous move that Phoebe thought really might be able to bring the dead to life.

Phoebe wasn't sure if she was happy or sad in that moment, so she decided she felt a bit of both. At least they'd been there nearly an hour and no one had poured pig's blood on them.

She looked around the room for Adam, surprised that she hadn't yet spotted his massive form looming over the rest of the puny student bodies. No sign of Whatsername, either. Adam was too good a guy to waste his time with a gum-snapping bimbo like her.

Speaking of wasted time, she wished she hadn't blown up at him. It wasn't fair. Besides, it had been barely a week since her snit fit, and she already missed him. It didn't seem right to be here at a dance and not at least see him and share a joke together.

"Hey, Phoebe," a low voice said, cutting through the bass beats and her thoughts. It was Harris Morgan, Martinsburg's crony, the one whose nose she'd bloodied in the forest. He stepped toward her.

"Hey," he repeated.

"Leave me alone," she said. She tried to rise, but he stepped in front of her chair, meaning she'd have to brush against him if she wanted to stand up. The chair was flush against the wall, so she wasn't going anywhere.

"It isn't like that," he said.

"What's it like, then?" If she called for Tommy, would he hear her over the sound of Karen's laughter? Maybe he'd be too caught up in the bass beat that seemed to give him and his friends a quicker step. Or maybe he'd be watching Karen too intently, intoxicated by the subtle scent of lavender that Phoebe smelled wafting from Karen's hair when she spun.

"I'm just trying to talk to you," he said, "to warn you."

"Go away."

"I think Pete and TC are up to something," he said.

"Really? Are they rolling freshman for soda money in the little boys' room?" Her tone was belittling, but she was certain that Martinsburg—and probably this jerk in front of her—had been responsible for the retermination of Evan Talbot.

She decided she wouldn't call for Tommy, no matter what happened. If Harris tried anything, she'd stand up and shove him as hard as she could.

Morgan shook his head and held up his hands. "No. No, I think they're planning something serious. Something that is going to hurt people. You and your friends."

"What do you care?" She rose, brushing him back with her body. She'd dropped him once, she'd do it again, pretty dress or not. And then she'd leave and let all the zombies and living zombies have all the fun they wanted.

Morgan shook his head. "I'm just telling you, is all." He turned away.

"Hey," she said, and he stopped. "Is he here? Pete and the big one? Are they here at the dance?"

"They're coming," he said.

They stared at each other a moment longer, until Harris looked away and drifted back into the stream of students milling around the edges of the dance floor.

Phoebe remained standing, and she didn't really notice that the flashing lights had been lowered and turned to blue as the first slow song was spun by the DJ.

"Phoebe," a voice called. It was Tommy, looking awkward for the first time that night as he shouldered his way through the kids, many of whom were escaping the dance floor while others were just setting foot on it.

"Will you . . . dance with me?"

Phoebe smiled and took his hand.

"Gross," Holly said. Adam saw what she was commenting on: Tommy Williams leading Phoebe out onto the dance floor so that they could slow dance to an old Journey song.

His reaction was far different, but he kept it to himself.

"What's with your friend, anyway?" Holly said. Adam thought that if she was angling for an invite to dance, she had a funny way of going about it. He didn't bother to answer. He watched Thorny pull his giggling date out onto the dance floor. Haley Rourke was a junior and nearly a foot taller than Thorny. She was the star forward of the Lady Badgers basketball team, and Adam thought they were a great match, personality-wise. She was very athletic but shy, and Thorny did his best to be athletic and was one of the least shy people he knew.

Thorny had tried to pal around with Adam, but Holly was making it difficult because she didn't approve of either Thorny or his date. She'd much rather be hanging around people like Tori Stewart and Pete Martinsburg, who'd breezed into the dance about five minutes ago.

Adam watched Phoebe loop her hands around Williams's shoulders as the dead boy placed his hands on her hips. He wanted to look away, but found he couldn't take his eyes off her.

She looks happy, Adam thought.

"Why would she want to dance with a dead kid, anyway?" Holly was perfectly capable of carrying on a conversation with herself, Adam knew. "I'm surprised they even let dead kids in here, it's so gross. That one kid dances like a bug that has been stepped on. And the girl . . ."

"Hey, Holly," Adam said.

Holly looked up at him. "Yes, Adam?"

There was an expectancy in her eyes that he felt bad about, but not enough to change his mind.

"Do you think you could get a ride home from Tori or someone else?" he asked. "I'm not feeling so great, and I think I'm going to take off."

He didn't wait for her answer; he just turned and left her standing there in her pretty yellow dress, her mouth open but for once not producing any sound.

"Okay," Pete said, "we've made our appearance. Let's get out of here."

TC nudged him in the ribs. "Hey, what about the zombie?"

TC pointed right at Williams, who was spinning slowly with Scarypants. Piggy Sharon and Tori were giggling behind him, and Pete found himself really regretting giving them the bottle of schnapps for the ride.

"You want to go mess with him?" TC asked, his voice carrying over the music.

"Not now," Pete said. "Soon."

It wasn't just Williams. Dancing next to them was the slutty dead girl and the other zombie kid on his list. Pete thought he moved like a twitching bug.

"'Kay, girls," he said, turning back to Tori because Sharon was a little sloppy, "TC and I have to go do that little trip I told you about. We'll see you later at Denny's party."

Tori pouted up at him, stumbling a little as she presented herself to be kissed. Pete obliged, tasting the peppermint alcohol on her lips. TC and Sharon locked up like a pair of wrestling octopi. Pete wondered if they had killed the whole bottle.

"Whereya guys going?" Tori asked.

"Special mission," he replied.

"Got a prank to pull," TC said, squeezing Sharon to him with one heavy arm. "We're gonna get—"

"More booze," Pete said, and gave TC a look intended to sober him in a hurry. TC shut his mouth and let go of Sharon.

Pete kissed Tori a second time. "We'll see you later."

As they were leaving, Pete saw Adam across the floor, walking toward them. Adam saw them and drew up short.

Pete smiled and pointed his finger like a handgun at Layman, who looked as if someone had just kicked him in the gut. Pete winked and dropped the thumb hammer, mock shooting Adam in the head. Then he led TC out the door.

362

CHAPTER TWENTY-NINE

*T*HE PLAN WAS TO MEET ADAM outside at ten, but Phoebe hadn't seen him all night. Whatsername was there, clustered in the corner with two other cheerleading harpies. Phoebe wondered what the deal was.

"What are we going to do if Adam didn't come?" she asked Tommy, who danced next to her in a loose circle with Karen, Kevin, Margi, and Norm.

"He came," he said. "I saw him talking with his date earlier."

"I haven't seen him all night," she said. "He's sort of hard to miss." But she missed him a lot, actually. All night she had been wishing that he was there, dancing with them. She couldn't even imagine him dancing, but she wanted to see it.

"Norm has . . . a car," Tommy said. "So does Thorny. Or his date, I forget which."

"I'm going to see if Adam is outside," she said. "I'll be back."

Oakvale had a strict no-reentry policy aimed at foiling parking lot shenanigans of various stripes, but Principal Kim was a sucker for kids as well behaved and academically achieving as Phoebe was, so she was able to get an exception after only five minutes of wrangling. She hurried out the door. There was a girl sitting on the stone steps. She was crying under the wary eyes of a pair of cops standing watch at the curb. There were a few cars parked in the loop, one of them being the STD's truck. She could see Adam slouched in his seat, staring off into the night sky. The sight of him sitting there by himself, so solid and dependable, erased all of her anger at him.

Phoebe ran over to the truck as fast as she could in her heels. She called his name.

He rolled down the window and turned his Van Halen CD down.

"Hey, Pheeble," he said without enthusiasm.

"What's going on?" she said.

"Lost my date," he said.

"Really?"

"Really. I like that dress. It looks like moonlight. Ghostly. Maybe even spectral. Shimmery."

Phoebe smiled. "Flatterer. Thanks."

They looked at each other in silence for a moment, and Phoebe thought it was strange, this distance between them. She'd almost forgotten what a judgmental jerk she had been.

"Listen, Adam . . ." she began.

"I'm sorry, Phoebe," he said; and she had never noticed how like a little boy's his face could become. Adam was so big, so quietly confident and mature, she'd always thought of him as being much older than she was, but there was something in his eyes, something hurt and vulnerable, that she'd never seen before.

"No, Adam," she said, "I was really . . ."

He shook his head. "Don't even. And don't worry about it. You'd better get your dead pals soon, though, because these cops have tried to roust me a few times."

She laughed; it was like his strong arms had just lifted a big weight from her back. "*Roust?* They actually tried to roust you?"

"Roust," he answered. "What I said."

"You know, you have a pretty good vocabulary for someone who can't get through *Wuthering Heights.*"

He lifted the battered paperback off the seat. "I just now finished it," he told her. "I'm a changed man."

"Well, good for you."

"Absolutely. And hey, I was just kidding about the rousting. Stay longer if you want. You looked like you were having fun."

Something about his comment seemed off-kilter, but she couldn't identify what it was. He'd seen her, but she hadn't seen him?

"Yeah, I am," she said. "The dead kids are, too. You should see Kevin dance."

"I did. He's a better dancer than I am."

"I doubt it. Especially after karate and *Wuthering Heights.* Grace and romantic prose? You'll be the terror of girlhood everywhere if you get on the dance floor."

"Yeah."

Something was bothering him. He was acting like he had that night he'd asked her to play Frisbee, when he didn't want to share whatever it was that was weighing on him. But she knew him well enough to realize that no amount of prodding would pry loose whatever it was; he'd share it in his own good time—if ever.

"Okay," she said, and knocked on the door of the truck twice. "I'll go do some rousting and get this party started."

"Great. See you in a few."

"See you."

She was halfway up the steps when her friends came out en masse from the building. Kevin's shoulders were still rolling and twitching as though permanently infused with rhythm. Tommy jogged ahead to her.

"Margi said that Norm would like to take us," he said. "Margi . . . said that he is more socially . . . inept . . . than most zombies, even."

The last bit he did in a fair approximation of Margi's signature machine-gun delivery.

"God love her," Phoebe said, looking over to see Margi and Karen goofing on something poor Norm had said. "But Adam's right over there."

"Oh, I'll go with Adam!" Karen called, waving at him as he sat in the now-warming truck. "I'll see you all at the Haunted House. Maybe."

Kevin didn't seem to mind; he looked like he was trying to perfect the undead version of the Robot, which was very strange to watch without any music playing, so Phoebe followed Tommy and the others out to Norm's car.

Phoebe looked back once, to see Karen practically bouncing into Adam's truck.

That will be good for him, she thought, but really she wasn't sure. She wasn't sure what she thought about it at all.

Norm was a much more cautious—and less-skilled—driver than Adam, and he might have had some additional nervousness about having a pair of zombies in the backseat; but it wasn't often he got invited to parties, so he managed to get them there in one piece. They arrived just as Adam and Karen were heading up the porch steps.

Phoebe was the first one out, and she saw Mal, his huge figure filling the doorway, waving his absurd four-fingered wave.

"How . . . was . . . the . . . dance?" she heard him say.

"Great," Karen said, grabbing Adam's hand and pulling him along. "No one threw rocks or bottles or even insults. I think Kevin might have . . . stepped on a girl's toe, but that was as violent as it got."

Inside, the dead were dancing to a loud club mix that blared throughout the house. Phoebe had never seen so many zombies in one place before There had to be at least two dozen of them, just in the foyer and the front room, all swaying and jerking beneath an array of decorations and lighting.

"You like it?" Karen said, detaching herself from Adam for the moment. "I got my parents to buy the lights. And look at the little disco ball. Isn't that just the . . . cutest?"

"You did a great job, Karen," Phoebe said. She caught sight of Colette dancing in the corner by herself. She reminded Phoebe of the blissed-out hippie girls from the Woodstock movie her dad had made her watch a few years ago. Karen hadn't waited for her answer, though. She'd whisked Adam to the center of Club Dead and was spinning around him, the hem of her short skirt rising in a provocative floret of silky material. To Phoebe's surprise, Adam started moving his arms and feet.

"Oh man," Norm said. He was as pale as any of the dead people in the room.

"Breathe deeply," Tommy said. "I'll introduce you . . . around."

Tommy introduced them to a few of the people lingering in the foyer, most of whom were expressionless and seemingly blasé about the introductions. The music was incessant but the strobe light flashed in intermittent waves, making the dancers look even more halting and bizarre. The scene threw Phoebe's perceptions off. She said hello and shook a cold hand or two, but it seemed as though some of the zombies were less than happy to meet her. Conversely, she thought Tommy was a little too happy to be showing her off.

It could be the lights and the music, she thought.

Someone grabbed Tommy's shoulder from behind.

"Tayshawn!" Phoebe said. "How are you?"

He didn't answer her and spoke directly to Tommy.

"Takayuki . . . wants to talk . . . to you," he said. "More . . . are arriving . . . daily."

Phoebe watched Tommy go from festive to serious in a heartbeat. "Where is he?" he asked. "Upstairs?"

Tayshawn nodded, and Tommy turned back to her. "I'll be right back," he said.

She watched them go up the dark staircase, where she pictured Takayuki hanging upside down and hidden in an empty closet somewhere.

Brr, she thought, and went back to watching the dancers, squinting whenever the too-bright strobe flashed. Pretty much everyone was moving, but she couldn't tell if any of them were having fun, because most of the zombies wore no expression as they twisted and shook. The exception was Colette, whose smile looked more and more natural each time Phoebe saw her. She was chatting in the corner with Margi and Norm.

Thorny arrived with his date just as Tayshawn came back down the stairs, alone.

"Tayshawn!" he called, raising his arm for a high five. "How are you, man?"

Tayshawn left him hanging, making his way with purpose through the dance floor to the other room, where the stereo equipment awaited him.

"Dang," Phoebe heard Thorny say, and then he caught sight of her. "Hey, Phoebe. Do you know Haley Rourke?" he said, leading Haley deeper into the room. Phoebe thought she looked terrified; Phoebe said hello, but the tall girl was frozen in place.

"Thorny," Phoebe said into his ear, "did you tell her that there would be mostly differently biotic people here?"

"Huh?" he said, swinging his arms to the new tune that began to blare through the speakers. "You think I should have?"

Phoebe started to reply when she saw Tommy and Takayuki coming back down the stairs. Tak kept walking out the front door.

"Is everything okay?" Phoebe asked him.

"Yes," Tommy said. "We have had . . . new arrivals. Some for . . . the party. Others . . . to stay."

"That's good, right? The more, the merrier?" She wanted to ask about Takayuki, but didn't.

"Yes," he said. "But it might get us . . . noticed."

"Isn't that what you want? To be noticed?"

"What do you mean?"

"The blog," she said. "Playing football and all that. Aren't you just trying to get people to notice your cause?"

She wanted to add *dating a trad girl*, but she didn't need to. The sentiment was obvious; it seemed to hang unspoken between them during every conversation.

He took his time answering. "It is . . . important," he said, "for . . . people to understand our situation. What we go through."

"Won't this help?"

"It could. But not everyone sees . . . the same opportunities that I do."

"Tak?"

"Yes. And Tak . . . is not alone."

An old power ballad began, and many of the couples,

zombie and otherwise, began to break off into pairs. Phoebe watched as a pair of zombies, the boy in a suit jacket two sizes too big for him, moved toward each other into an awkward, spidery embrace. Norm was crouching so that his head rested on Margi's shoulder, some of her hair spikes poking behind the frames of his glasses and into his closed eyes. Haley Rourke was clinging to the much shorter Thorny as though he were the last free rock in a stormy sea.

She looked back to Tommy, who was scanning the room, watching his people reach for each other in the muted light beneath the glittering mirror ball above them. His invitation to dance seemed to her an afterthought.

"Actually, Tommy," she said, "could we go somewhere and talk a little more?"

"This house . . . is full of zombies," he said, managing to affect a disgusted expression. It made her smile.

"Yes, it is."

"A walk in the woods? Like when we met?"

"Like when we met," she said. "I'd like that. It's a little chilly, though."

He gave her his jacket, which carried a subtle scent that she had a hard time placing at first but then recognized as Z, the cologne they'd laughed over at the mall—the "scent for the active undead male."

She followed him out the back door and into the woods.

Adam gently guided his dance partner around so he could peek out the living room window and watch Tommy and Phoebe enter the Oxoboxo woods. Karen's grip on him was tight.

He held his breath as they disappeared into the tree line, their bodies swallowed up by the darkness. He wondered if that's what it felt like to be dead.

I hope you know what you are doing, Pheeble, he thought. No wait. I hope you have no idea what you are doing. I hope you . . .

"She doesn't know, does she?" Karen said, breaking his train of thought.

"What?"

Karen's diamond eyes glittered like the stars.

"Phoebe," she said. "She doesn't know how you feel about her, does she?"

"No," he replied. "How do you?"

"Telepathetic," she said, shrugging. Beneath his rough hands, her body felt airy and fragile, her bones like those of a bird. She pressed her face against his chest.

"Actually, it is a combination of things. Your body language. The way you look at her when you are with her, the way you look at her when she doesn't know you are looking. The way you look when you aren't with her. The way your overly serious face softens when you are speaking to her. That sort of thing."

"Ah. My overly serious face. It betrays me every time."

"Sorry. I meant to say your overly cute and serious face."

"Okay," he said. "That helps."

"Adam, look," she said, fixing him with her cut-diamond

eyes. "Take it from me. Don't wait around to die for love."

"Great advice. What exactly does it mean?"

"It means you should find the right time and tell her how you feel."

"The right time for her? Or for me?"

Again he felt the subtle shift of a delicate skeletal structure beneath his hands.

"Just the right time."

He looked out the window, where shadows seemed to move among the trees.

"What about Tommy?"

"Tommy is Tommy," was her quick reply. "And your feelings aren't really Tommy's concern, are they?"

He thought there was an edge in her voice. "What about your feelings? Do you have feelings for Tommy?"

She laughed and squeezed him again. "I've got feelings for a lot of people. Dead people, trad people, whatever. . . ."

He laughed and smoothed her silvery hair.

"You're a special girl, Karen." And without thinking, he brushed her hair behind her ear with his fingertips and bent low so that he could kiss her cheek. It was an act of pure impulse, one that he was scarcely aware of doing until the cool smoothness of her skin against his warm lips reminded him of who he was, and what she was.

"Oh," she said. "Oh, thank you, Adam."

The glittering stars in her eyes were going nova, like they weren't merely reflecting light but, instead, projecting it.

"No," he said, hugging and then releasing her. "Thank *you.*"

The song changed into something more frenetic, and he pressed through the dead with deliberation toward the back door.

CHAPTER THIRTY

*P*ETE COULDN'T BELIEVE HIS
good luck. Even with TC half in
the bag and reeking of pepper-
mint, they'd managed to find the place—a short hike through
the woods after stashing the car in one of his old make-out
turnoffs. The roads around the Oxoboxo were full of these
bootlegger turns, and he knew each one.

They'd just arrived when Adam's battered truck and the
second car with Scarypants and Williams arrived. For fun he'd
sighted along the barrel and aimed at the big zombie on the
porch. At his head, specifically, which sat on his wide shoulders
like a lump of melted candle wax.

Pop, Pete thought, and then aimed at Karen and Adam in
turn as they went up the stairs. Then TC almost gave them
away with a loud sneeze.

"Shut up, you idiot," Pete had said through clenched
teeth.

"What?" TC said, grinning. "The music is wicked loud, and they can't hear too well anyhow."

Pete wanted to crack him with the rifle butt, right in his grinning moon face. He turned back, and Tommy was halfway up the steps, at the center of a loose knot of people. Scarypants was with him, and their usual crowd. Also some dweeb who Pete vaguely recalled roughing up on a few occasions.

Pete aimed at Tommy. While other kids had been day-dreaming about all the wholesome fun they'd have at the big school dance, Pete had spent the week shooting cans and assorted woodland critters behind his house. He even put a round into the Talbot's chimney, just for fun. His finger was loose around the trigger.

Head shot, he thought, squinting.

"Why didn't you shoot 'im?" TC asked as they watched Williams enter the house.

Pete was sweating; he felt damp at the armpits and on his neck. He and TC had shucked their semiformal wear and put on dark sweats and sneakers for their mission.

"I didn't have a clear shot, stupid," he said, leaning back against a tree.

"So what do we do now?" TC asked.

"We wait."

"But I've got to piss," TC said, whining.

"So go piss! Just be friggin' quiet about it!"

TC lumbered off to relieve himself, moving with all the grace of a moose.

He returned and they waited, watching that little runt

Harrowwood and his freakishly tall date arrive, and then they saw some way-too-happy metalhead dude leave and walk into the woods in the opposite direction. Pete thought he looked familiar.

"Was that a zombie?" TC asked.

"Couldn't tell," Pete answered. "Probably."

"Look!" TC jumped up and pointed.

"What?"

"They just left! They went out the back door!"

"Who? Williams?" Pete said, picking the rifle off the ground and rising.

"Yeah, and the goth chick! They walked off into the woods."

"Okay," Pete said, "there must be a path back there. We'll move along the tree line until we find it. When we catch up to them, you grab Julie, and I'll bust a cap on dead boy."

"You got it, Pete," TC said, but Pete was already moving, glancing at the house every few steps just in case any more zombie lovers decided to take a moonlight stroll.

"Hey," Pete heard TC say as they circled, "who's Julie?"

A muscle in Pete's jaw twitched, but he didn't answer.

The moon wasn't helping much, its reflected light casting only a murky gloom through the bare trees, but Phoebe didn't want to ask Tommy for his hand. She didn't know what signals she wanted to send him. She was already wearing his Z-scented jacket, and that was signal enough, even though all it really signaled was that she was cold.

"The woods aren't made for heels," she said, pausing to slide her shoes off.

"They are unkind to nylons, as well," he said.

She agreed, but thought twice about taking those off.

He was faintly luminous in the poor light.

"Did I ever tell you how I died?" he asked.

She shook her head, not sure if he could see.

"It was a car accident. My father was driving. A drunk driver ran a red light and . . . plowed into us. He survived, but he killed my father." He made a noise that was either a humorless laugh or a sigh; Phoebe couldn't tell in the darkness. "Me too."

"I'm sorry," Phoebe said.

"Dad was killed instantly. I took a little longer. One of my ribs had broken and punctured my lung, so I ended up . . . drowning in my own blood."

"Oh, Tommy," she said, "that's horrible."

"No picnic," he said.

She felt his hand slide over hers, and he led her to a stone bench alongside the path. She let him guide her.

"It happened at night, at an . . . intersection in front of a big church. I could see the steeple through the shattered windshield. We'd spun around a couple times and ended up in line with that steeple. I looked up at the steeple and . . . prayed that my dad was still alive. I remember praying for that because I knew I was a goner and I didn't want my mom to be all alone."

Phoebe, mixed signals or not, squeezed his cold hand. Tommy had never seemed so vulnerable before.

"The first thing I thought when I . . . came back," he said, "was that God got it wrong. I was thinking, no, God, not me. My father. You were supposed to save my father."

"Faith must have been happy that you came back," Phoebe said.

"She's . . . well-named," Tommy said. "Dallas Jones was . . . famous . . . by then, and she says she knew I would . . . come back."

"Faith has faith," Phoebe said. "What about you?"

"Coming back," he said, turning to face her, "explains . . . certain things. And it makes others . . . more of a mystery. I'll try to tell . . . you . . . someday."

Phoebe felt herself growing warm. She turned away and looked off into the dark woods, but her grip on his hand tightened.

"Why do you think that . . . zombies . . . like you and Karen are so different from the others?" Phoebe said. "I mean, why are you able to run and play football, and Karen can dance and drink coffee, and poor Sylvia has trouble walking? Your death was as violent as anybody's."

"I thought it was obvious," he said.

"I guess I'm slow, then," she said. "What?"

"Love."

"Love?" She wished that she could see more of his face than his faintly glowing eyes.

"Love. I live with my mom, who loves me. Karen has her parents and her sister. Evan's parents loved him . . . unconditionally. That's the whole and only difference between us and kids like Colette. Her parents skipped town when she came back."

"Yes," Phoebe said, at once amazed and embarrassed that she'd never really made the connection. "Sylvia? Tayshawn?"

"Sylvia was at St. Jude's, along with Colette and Kevin, and now she's at the foundation getting augmented. They are taken care of at St. Jude's, but I wouldn't call it love. Tayshawn stayed with his grandmother in Norwich . . . for a while. But it didn't work out."

Phoebe's pulse was racing through her as she struggled for a response. She wanted to say something to Tommy, something that would make things better for him, but the only response she could come up with was one she was not ready to give.

She thought that Tommy might have sensed it, too.

"I . . . I just . . . thought," he began. "I thought that . . . if . . . I . . . could get a girl . . . a real girl . . . to love . . . me . . . to kiss . . . me . . . I'd come back . . . even more."

And there it was again, Phoebe thought, turning back toward him. "A girl," he said. Not "Phoebe." *A girl.*

"Tommy . . ."

"I know," he said. "Believe me . . . I . . . know . . . what I'm asking."

He turned and looked at her with his strange eyes, and she thought that she could see all the pain and hurt deep within them. All the pain and hurt of someone whose life had been taken too soon. Before he could experience any of the things that young men experience.

"I just thought," he said, leaning closer to her, "if I . . . could . . . kiss . . . you . . ."

She opened her mouth to answer, but then there was a crash

in the woods behind them, and she felt herself being lifted from the bench by strong, unyielding arms.

She had been about to kiss him, Pete thought. That cheating bitch Julie had been ready to give herself over to that maggot-infested corpse.

"How could you, Julie?" he said, his voice just above a whisper as he stepped to the edge of the path a few feet away. He'd sent Stavis around back of them, hoping that if they heard him stumbling they'd run right toward where Pete was creeping up. But Williams and Julie had been so into their little pillow talk that they hadn't even heard Stavis until it was too late.

"Pete," she said, her voice shrill and scared as she wriggled in Stavis's grip. Pete watched her try to kick him in the shins or higher up, but Stavis put a knee into her backside.

Pete lifted the rifle and sighted down the barrel, focusing on the center of the zombie's forehead. The zombie just stood there, looking at him with his empty eyes.

"Pete, please," she said. "We—"

"Quiet," Pete told her.

"Pete, please, this is—"

"I said shut up!" he screamed, and he shifted his aim from the zombie's face to hers. Her eyes grew wide, and she stopped struggling.

"Hey, Pete," Stavis said, "the zombie . . . I think the zombie—"

"You too, Timothy Cole," Pete said. He only used Stavis's real name when he wanted instant obedience. "Put her down and shut the hell up. Step over there so you don't get messy."

Stavis hurried to comply, tripping over fallen branches.

Pete watched her look over at her undead lover, the final insult. He was tired of them mocking him in his dreams, mocking him in his waking life. She was probably already infected with the zombie disease. And if he let her go, she'd probably infect even more people.

The barrel of the rifle quivered, but he forced it to remain steady. She looked back at him, and her eyes were wide with fear.

Head shot, he thought. Only way to take out the undead.

"I loved you," he whispered. Then he pulled the trigger.

Adam paced along the dead grass in the backyard, trying to decide if this was the right time, and exactly what he should say.

Hey, Pheeble, he thought. Before you go and kiss this dead guy over there, you ought to know something. You mean more to me than Frisbee and lame jokes about the size of my vocabulary. You mean more to me than a thousand Whatsernames ever could, even if I did ignore you in the hallways for most of our school years together. And Pheeble, if I need to, I'll listen to groups like the Restless Dead and Zombicide and the Drumming Mummies or whatever, and I'll wear black and burn incense if I have to. I'll go have my tarot cards read and I'll pay attention to Daffy like she was an incredibly interesting and insightful savant instead of just some chattering goof. I can do it, Pheeble . . . Phoebe—

He heard a crash somewhere in the woods down the path, and then he heard Phoebe shriek.

He ran down the path, calling her name. At first he thought maybe Tommy did something he shouldn't have, but then he saw Phoebe standing with Tommy, and he saw Pete Martinsburg standing at the edge of the path, training a rifle on them.

On Phoebe.

He ran, calling her name. He ran as fast as his legs could carry him.

He heard Master Griffin's calming voice in his head.

Focus, he said. *What will you do with your power?*

Adam reached Phoebe just as Pete pulled the trigger.

When it was over, and Phoebe was once again surrounded by people who loved her, she would remember his moment of hesitation. It might have been that his undead limbs just did not have the reaction time that was required to come to her aid, but when she looked over at him, Tommy Williams, leader of the zombie underground, had hesitated.

Pete Martinsburg hesitated only as long as it took to pull the trigger.

Adam didn't hesitate at all, and that was why he fell.

CHAPTER THIRTY-ONE

*T*HE RIFLE SHOT SPLIT THE silence of the woods. Pete saw someone step in front of Julie, and he watched that someone fold in half as if he had been leveled by a squad of invisible tacklers.

Adam. He'd shot Adam Layman.

"Jesus Christ, Pete!" Stavis yelled, looking at Pete, his fat face a mask of shock and fear. He took off into the woods.

Scarypants screamed Adam's name and dropped to his side.

Pete aimed at her another moment before throwing the rifle into the brush, and then he also started running. He ran without thinking, tripping and almost breaking his ankle on a low stump. He ran until he found what appeared to be one of the many paths that twisted through the Oxoboxo woods like drunken snakes. Breathing heavily, he slowed his pace to a loose trot, his racing mind, trying to figure out which direction he'd left the car. He had no idea where he was.

"Leaving . . . the party," a voice said from behind him, "so soon?"

He turned; it was the guy who had left the house earlier, and then Pete realized where he'd seen him before. It was the zombie from that day when he'd let the slutty zombie go. The happy guy, the metalhead. Pete saw the glint of chains that hung from his leather.

"Screw . . . yourself," Pete said. The other only smiled as he approached.

Pete turned and tripped over a rock in the path. He rolled onto his back, and the zombie leaned over him, burning the image of his ruined face into Pete's brain.

"Did you think I would . . . kill you?" the zombie asked him, his voice a reptilian rasp and his dark hair hanging down like the tendrils of a jellyfish. "Death is . . . not for you. Death is . . . a gift."

Pete saw then that he wasn't smiling, even though he could see all his teeth. That's when Pete screamed.

Phoebe fell to her knees in the dirt beside Adam's body, tearing the hem of her pretty white dress as she did. Adam had gone over as if leveled by an invisible tackler. It looked like the wind had been knocked out of him, and his big body seemed to deflate as he'd hit the ground.

"Adam?" she said. "Oh my God. Adam, are you all right?"

She had her hands on him now, feeling his arms and shoulders for a sign of injury, and when her fingers touched his chest, she watched a roseate bloom appear and spread in the center of his clean white shirt.

She screamed. "Adam? Adam can you hear me?" Tommy was kneeling next to her, his hand on Adam's shoulder as he started to shake. Adam's mouth opened and closed and his eyes rolled up in his head. He coughed, and a thin trickle of blood appeared at the corner of his mouth. Phoebe pressed her shaking hands against the stain spreading on his shirt and asked God to help her hold Adam's life inside him until help arrived.

"He's going . . . into shock," Tommy said.

She could feel his life ebbing through her fingers.

"No, Adam!" she said, "Don't go! Please, God; don't go, Adam!"

Then his eyes focused and he looked right at her and opened his mouth to speak. He was trying to say something but he was choking, and she was telling him, "Shh, help will be here soon."

He smiled at her, but then she saw the light leave his eyes. His large frame gave a massive convulsive shudder, and then he died.

She held her breath. Adam was motionless.

"Don't go," she heard herself cry, but it was like she was outside herself, like she had left her body behind the moment Adam left his. She looked down at herself, slumped over Adam, her body convulsing with sobs. Tommy knelt beside her, his face cast in shadow.

She looked around her, but Adam—his spirit—was nowhere to be seen.

Then Tommy touched her arm, and she was back inside her body. The stain was still spreading on Adam's white shirt, and she could still feel his life ebbing through her hands.

She heard voices coming up the path, but it was too late. Adam was gone.

The dead gathered around Phoebe. Karen and Colette and Mal and Tayshawn and the ones she didn't know—the burned girl and the girl with the missing arm—they stood in a loose circle around where she and Tommy knelt beside Adam's lifeless body. She thought it was like a funeral, in reverse. The mourners were all dead, and she, the sole living person, was about to be lowered into the earth.

She looked up at them as they stood as still and silent as the trees, and she wanted to scream at them to help her, to use whatever strange powers they had to bring Adam back.

She saw Margi standing among the dead, her hands shaking as she punched numbers into her cell phone.

"How can you just stand there?" Phoebe said, looking at Colette, looking at Mal. She tried to lift Adam up by getting his arm around her neck, but he was too heavy. "Why aren't you helping me? Karen, please!"

She heard Margi talking into her phone, and she tugged at Adam's arm with newfound hope, remembering how many policemen were a short drive away, outside the homecoming dance. The Oakvale fire department always responded to emergencies with immediate attention. She pleaded again, looking up as Takayuki drifted in among his fellow dead.

"Please!" she said, stumbling as Tommy tried to help her lift Adam's body to a sitting position. "Please help me!"

"They're coming," Margi said through her tears.

Karen walked forward and knelt down, putting a cool hand on Phoebe's shoulder. Her diamond eyes twinkled like far-off stars as she placed her other hand flat against the center of the red stain spreading on Adam's shirt.

"There has to be something you can do, Karen," Phoebe begged. "You can, can't you? Can't you help him?"

Karen blinked, snuffing out the stars for a moment, and shook her head.

"I'm sorry, Phoebe," she said. "I'm so, so sorry."

Phoebe's mind cycled through a range of responses. Rage was the first; she wanted to hit Karen, to slap her face, to call her a liar, then she wanted to throw her arms around her and cling to her until the police came and Adam's body was taken away.

"I . . . have him," Tommy said, and Phoebe let Tommy bear his weight gently back to the earth.

"No," she said. There had to be some hope. The police were coming, they could bring him back.

Not knowing what else to do, she hugged Adam's body to her, trying to keep him warm.

Adam opened his eyes.

He thought he felt rain on his cheeks, but when his vision cleared and became acute, even in the gloom, he saw that Phoebe was leaning over him and crying.

He watched her as she caught her breath.

"Adam?"

He laughed, and he made some lame joke about what a hero

he was. Two trips into the woods to rescue her, and he had been knocked flat on his ass for both. Phoebe smiled, but she only seemed to cry harder. He realized that he must be a little dizzy from having the wind knocked out of him, because what he tried to say and what came out were two totally different things.

She shushed him and put her finger against his lips. Funny how much warmer her finger was than Karen's cheek. He tried to make another joke, but he still hadn't gotten his wind back, so all he could produce were short gasping sounds. No big deal. He'd had the wind knocked out of him plenty of times on the field. Just sit back and relax.

He didn't like seeing Pheeble cry, though. He raised his right hand with the idea of brushing away her tears, but— funny thing—it was the left that moved. He watched his hand as it sort of twitched and then lay still on his chest.

His wet chest.

His *really* wet chest. He tried to lift his hand out of the wetness, but his hand wouldn't obey. Phoebe lifted her hands from him in a gesture that she no doubt meant to be reassuring, but as her hands were covered with blood—his blood—she didn't quite get the effect she wanted.

Pete, he thought. The freaking idiot.

Phoebe was still sobbing, and Adam was aware of other people around him. Tommy and Karen were at his side. Daffy was on her cell phone, apparently unable to stop talking even for a few minutes.

He saw that Daffy was crying too. Karen, maybe. Karen Starry-Eyes, that would be his new nickname for her. Her eyes winked like penlights even in the darkness of the Oxoboxo woods. Of course she couldn't really cry, even though Phoebe insisted she'd seen a tear roll down her face at Evan's funeral.

Poor Evan, Adam thought. He'd really liked that kid.

Adam knew then why they were all crying. He opened his mouth to tell them they didn't have to.

"I'm okay," he said. Or tried to, because that wasn't what anyone heard.

"Shhh," Phoebe said, and she actually leaned forward and hugged him to her. He thought he'd be thrilled if he weren't numb all over.

"Don't try to talk," she whispered, her lips close to his ear.

He tried anyhow, before she could say what he knew she would say next, but the noise he made just sounded like a long choking wheeze.

"You're dead, Adam," she whispered.

He tried to turn, but the flesh was both unwilling and weak.

He heard the catch in her throat as she tried to get the words out. "Pete killed you."

The realization hit him with a force almost equal to that of the bullet. His first thought was to protest, to tell her that she was wrong, but he knew in his heart, the heart that was no longer beating, that she was right.

"I love you, Phoebe," he said as she cried, but the only sounds that came out of his body were strange, strangled noises, nothing like human speech at all.

* * *

Phoebe stayed with him until the police came. Her pretty white dress was neither white nor pretty any longer; the hem was tattered and dirty, and it was covered with Adam's blood. He'd taken the bullet high in the chest because Pete had been aiming at her head. The thought should have terrified her, but all she could think about was Adam and how different everything was going to be between them.

Seeing him lying there, his eyes unblinking as he tried in vain to form words she could understand, she could only think about how bad she'd felt in the few days they hadn't been speaking. She was crying and she couldn't stop crying, and although it was absurd, she knew that some of her tears were for those few lost days. She wished that she could rewind to the last time they'd been together at the Haunted House, and she wished that she could take back the things she'd said. She wished he had let her finish her apology.

Most of the zombies dispersed into the woods, melting into the forest like phantoms the moment the flashing lights of the cruiser began to cut through the darkness. Phoebe watched them disappear, thinking back to the night when some of them had seemed to form out of the very darkness and woods to rescue them.

Tommy and Karen stayed until the police came, as did all of the traditionally biotic kids. Colette stood with Margi, and they held on to each other after Margi finished making the calls on her cell phone. Haley said she knew some first aid and CPR, but everyone there knew it was useless; Adam was gone and then he wasn't.

Phoebe wasn't sure, but she didn't think many differently biotic people came back as fast as he had. He'd only been gone a few minutes. The longest minutes of her life, but maybe that was something to be hopeful about. Maybe his rapid return from the shores of death meant that he would gain control of his voice and body faster than some of the others. Maybe.

Tommy tried to console her, but she didn't want to be consoled. Margi and Karen both tried to talk to her, but she didn't want to talk, either.

Adam had run into the woods to save her. Not once but twice. Seeing him lying there, looking up at her trying to speak, she knew that it was her turn to enter the woods for him. She took a deep breath and dried her eyes on the bloodied sleeve of her dress, the dress he'd said looked like moonlight.

Even when the ambulance arrived sometime later and the paramedics gently pried her arms from Adam, who twitched and coughed unintelligible sounds as they lifted him onto the stretcher, Phoebe could only think of this one thing:

Bringing him back. Bringing him back as far as she possibly could.

Acknowledgments

I'd like to thank the following people for their help in bringing *Generation Dead* into print:

For their invaluable advice, assistance, and guidance: Al Zuckerman, for *everything*; Alessandra Balzer, with whom I shared a wonderful "telepathetic" link throughout the editorial process; F. Paul Wilson, Rick Koster, Elizabeth and Tom Monteleone, and all of the instructors and students at Borderlands Boot Camp; my first reader, Rosina Williams; Robin Rue, Matthew Dow Smith, Tom Tessier, Scott Bradfield, and Doug Clegg.

For their love and support throughout: my parents, Elaine and Jeff Waters; my brother Mark Waters and family; the entire Pepin lineage; Linda Waters, Sandra and Ted McHugh, John Fedeli, Mark Vanase, Dan Whelan, the staff at P.G.'s for the office space; all my friends at SM; Thor, and Bonny.

And just for being: Kim, Kayleigh, and Cormac.